Melissa!

Love
Kerry

Copyright ©2006
Poe Ballantine

Library of Congress
Cataloging-in-Publication Data

Hawthorne Books
& Literary Arts

Ballantine, Poe, 1955–
Decline of the Lawrence Welk empire :
A novel / by Poe Ballantine. — 1st ed.
p. cm.

SUMMARY : College dropout Edgar
Donahoe hooks up with a friend
on a Caribbean island, where his
misadventures include being
stalked by a murderous island native
and getting caught in a hurricane.

ISBN 0-9766311-1-3

1. Interpersonal relations – Fiction.
2. Alcoholism – Fiction.
3. Caribbean area– Fiction.
I. Title.

PZ7.B19925Dec 2006

[Fic] – DC22

2004025278

9   1410 NW Kearney St.
8   Suite 909
7   Portland, OR 97209
6   hawthornebooks.com
5   *Form* :
4   Pinch, Portland, OR
3
2   *Editorial Services* :
1   Ben George

Printed in China
through Print Vision

Set in Paperback.

First Edition

For Mrs. Ramsey, wherever you are.

DECLINE OF THE LAWRENCE WELK EMPIRE

A NOVEL

POE BALLANTINE

HAWTHORNE BOOKS & LITERARY ARTS
Portland, Oregon | MMVI

DECLINE OF THE LAWRENCE WELK EMPIRE

— To begin then with things simple, the Perfessor said, I propose this question to the enlightened company which I behold before me: What is human life?

— Human life is a myth, Mr. Shawnessy said.

— Amen, the Perfessor said.

— To be most human is to be most mythical.

— This is wisdom, said the Perfessor.

— A myth is a story that is always true for all men everywhere.

— An oracle speaks, the Perfessor said. But are there any new myths? I doubt it. In their wisdom, the Hebrews and the Greeks have furnished us with all our myths. Will there ever be another mythical race?

— Yes, Mr. Shawnessy said. The Americans are a mythical race. We are making a new myth, the American myth.

— What is this American myth?

— It's the story of the hero who regains Paradise.

ROSS LOCKRIDGE, *Raintree County*

1.

IT SEEMS THAT ALL I DO IN THIS CITY IS DRIVE. UP THE coast. Down the coast. I drive to Clairemont Mesa. I drive to Linda Vista, Hillcrest, and Old Town. Here's your large pepperoni, sir. Here's your mushroom and sausage. Two hundred miles a night. And San Diego is getting crowded. And America is going to hell. And you can't get to the beach anymore. And the disco era has sneaked in on us under the guise of a legitimate rhythm and blues revival. And my friends are all busy, getting married and making money and going off to college. And I'm twenty years old, going nowhere but down the face of a four-foot wave or to deliver a number two with onions and two grape Fantas to 2525 Cherokee Ave.

So when my parents suggest that I enroll in school, not community college but a real state university, and they're going to pay, it seems like an answer. It seems like salvation. It's like Linda Lovelace discovering her clitoris. All the pictures I had of myself as another of those leathery old straggle-headed, milky-eyed forty-year-old beachcombers shuffling bewildered (hey dude!) down the boardwalk, wondering what happened to his youth, suddenly and thankfully shimmer away. Oh, how can purpose be so vigorously restored!

Born again, grateful for a second chance, I settle on Humboldt State University, a nestled-in-the-redwoods academy of science famous for its marijuana and burly women, the last hippie outpost of California. It seems perfect to me: cheap, far away, no

frats or sororities, not far from the ocean, and entrance requirements just above the Wyoming Community College for Ceramic
Arts. Decadent, hypocritical, polluting America has become
increasingly odious to me, but there's nothing I can do to change
her, so I will retreat to live in her woods with hairy, uncompetitive people who have disabled social lives and drink dark beer and
smoke dope. I think I may be a lawyer. I despise lawyers of course,
there's the trouble with the whole plan. But I'm good at words,
and most people secretly admire lawyers. Most people want their
children to become lawyers. Most people who hate lawyers will
hire one the instant they're in the slightest trouble. And I'd like to
be one of those guys who sues corporations that pollute rivers
and crack up oil tankers. There are good lawyers, just as there are
good witches. Rare, yes, but why can't I be one?

School is fun! It's really just an excuse to goof off. They don't
offer law at HSU, however, so I am pre-law. I like the sound of
this. Everyone else seems to too. What's your major? Pre-law. What
is pre-law, anyway? It's anything you want. You just get your BA
in something and then apply to law school. In my case I've listed
my major officially as psychology. I'm a screwed-up, immature,
frightened, hypocritical, underweight kid, and here's some cheap
help. It's also a breezy major. I've got classes like Existential
Psychology and The Psychology of Creativity, descriptions too
choice for a boy with a golden shovel. But I'm also honestly interested in "how people tick."

Okay, I'm a little old for the dorms, but my parents are footing the bill and I've been slow out of the gate all my life. I didn't
learn to ride a bicycle till I was ten. I didn't quit wetting the bed
until I was in fourth or fifth grade. And I'm not going to mess
up this opportunity. It won't be like community college, where
I took every opportunity to duck Political Science or Art Composi-
tion and smoke a doobie in the bushes. If I bear down I should
be able to finish my degree in three years, after which I will immediately ensconce myself in some woodsy law enclave with low
requirements and more hairy, uncompetitive potheads, and pass

the state bar by the time I'm twenty-six. My parents will be able to send Christmas cards with cheerful form letters again. Forthwith I will begin suing corrupt industrial giants. I'll have some money to spend too and maybe finally I can meet a girl who respects me.

Larry, my dormitory roommate, is a kid from Grass Valley who doesn't smoke or drink. It's unfortunate I don't spend more time with him. What a steady influence he would be on me. Not that I don't try. It's just that we have little in common. He turns the insides of my eyelids to cotton. His girlfriend is even more boring. How can people be this dreary, and why is it that they never smoke or drink? They don't even play cards. So it isn't long before I've discovered the Tooley brothers, Andy and Brian, down the hall. A couple of more relaxed and amiably redheaded D–average students you won't meet. On their door like a big welcome sign is a red triangular warning– *Approach with Caution: Party Zone*. Inside these refreshingly depraved chambers, Thin Lizzy, Kiss, and Roxy Music boom on the stereo. Pretty special ed. majors with bloodshot eyes drift in and out. In the middle of the cluttered, swamp-smelling floor, like a chalice in a legend, stands a three-foot acrylic bong, smoke lifting in a luscious, perennial magic curl from the mouthpiece.

The rest of the semester is a fog, and my grades start to slide a bit, but I've never had more fun or felt more simpatico with a group of lads, especially the Tooley brothers and Karlo, an industrial arts major with a nose like Cyrano de Bergerac, and the bespectacled Tee Willie Cunningham, a big Who fan who actually plans on getting good grades and going to med school, though how he can sit in a murky room for hours drinking whiskey and beer and listening to loud music and expect to become a medical professional is another of the great conundrums of our age. Give him credit. He is usually the first to leave. He mumbles the word "study," and stumbles out the door. I'm always the last to leave. Sometimes I'm surprised by the sun. Often I miss those preposterously early classes, but psychology is not an exhaustive science. Even the professors seem resigned to the flexibility of a good line of horseshit. As long as you keep using terms such as *cognitive* and *affect*, everyone seems happy. Actually, I'm amazed at how much psychology seems to be helping me. I never knew there were so many screwed-up, anxious, immature people in the world. I am buoyed with the security of knowledge that I am not alone.

What really amazes me, however, is how quickly even a thousand miles from home, wearing no swimming trunks or suntan lotion, I've fallen in with the same kind of people as always, pot-smoking, card-playing, music-loving, late-night party hounds. Are they really friends or just props for the lonesome ceremony of self-annihilation? But you know, they say that 80 percent of all males in their teens and early twenties are alcoholics. And I love these guys.

The parties come one after the next like the waves on Waimea Bay. One Saturday night Karlo, Tee Willie, the Tooley Brothers, and I have swallowed some magic mushrooms down in the Tooley room. T-Rex is roaring on the box, Tee Willie is ranting about God, Karlo de Bergerac is endeavoring to titillate a special ed. major—when there's a knock on the door. Knocks are never good. Usually it means a Living Group Advisor and a sinsemilla shakedown. Brian Tooley answers cautiously, peeking out, then begins waving at me urgently across the room.

"What is it?" I say, hopping down from the windowsill, where I have been contemplating anagrams of the abracadabra.

"It's Mountain," he says, his wide eyes crystalline, his lips wandering over his face as if he's about to spray root beer from his nostrils. "He wants to talk to you."

I step out into the hall. Many say that Sullivan Moses, or "Mountain" as he is generally known, right tackle for the H S U football team (one of the worst college teams in the country), looks like Sylvester Stallone. This evening, however, poor Mountain resembles someone kicked between the legs. Pale and bent with hands pressed to his thighs, his great bulk heaving, the big man seems to be struggling for air. How much of this attitude is attributable to my own warped perception is difficult to assess. "What's going on?" I demand, closing the door behind me.

He waves me down to the bathroom.

I didn't like Mountain when I first met him, straddled backward in his chair, grinning big-eared under his ball cap with a puddle of snuff in his lip. I mistook him for a cocksure and shallow athlete. I learned over the next few weeks that he was the opposite—humble, courteous, wry, and uncomfortable around people. I was also shocked to learn that in addition to being very bright, a math major, a chess player, and an admirer of the classics, he was a practicing Catholic.

"I was with Julie up on third," he says now, his eyes rolling up in his head. He pauses to press his lips together. "And she uses this contraceptive foam and I think, I think it went up my spout."

It's disheartening to see such a heroic figure so easily beguiled, but despite strong guilt signals from the Vatican, usually Mountain is to be found in the company of a woman, enthralled as a dog and oblivious to all other pleasure. These cycles usually last about three weeks, after which he will make a brief appearance at one of our poker games or parties and then find himself a new girl to dote on. I've pegged him for a mother complex.

Poor chap. I nod, wishing I had not taken the mushrooms. I don't know why he's sought me. He must know that I've worked in a few hospitals, that I have a passably good knowledge of anatomy and physiology, but this still shouldn't qualify me. I'm simultaneously flattered and terrified that he would come to me for help.

"I think you'll be all right, Mountain," I say, squatting slightly to try and see up into his rolling blue eyes.

"It's a spermicide, man," he whispers gruffly, revealing the large gap between his front teeth. His nose, I note, is of significant proportion, more Roman than French, I would say, and crimped-up near the bridge. "It's gonna scorch my filberts."

I picture the sperm-killing foam marching in corrosive ranks into his testicles, blinding the young tadpoles, scalding the delicate tubules, and rendering him permanently neuter. I can't really deal with this right now.

"But it's designed for *sex*," I say, siding feebly, as a good lawyer would, with the manufacturer. "I've never heard of anyone having trouble with a contraceptive foam."

"Yeah," he rasps, bending over to cup his knees. "You're probably right."

"Look, they have to test this stuff," I add, my doubt accumulating, even if I did work in five hospitals. "It'll pass, I'm pretty sure. Just give it time."

"Okay," he says, gritting his teeth.

I slap him on his broad back. "Party down at Tooleys' if you're up for it later."

He nods a thank you, licks his lips, and limps away.

About five minutes later another knock sounds on the Tooley door. Mountain is white as soap, doubled over and trembling in agony. I slip out into the hall again. I'm *flying* on these damn mushrooms, rainbows and grins evaporating in paint-thinner whirlpools off my oblong head.

"Bad?" I say.

"Bad."

I whirl around, clear a path back through the revelers, and yank the phone off the hook. "Turn off that stereo!" I cry. "Where's the phone book? I have to call the hospital!" Everyone stares at me dumbfounded. I manage to dial correctly. It's almost midnight. I try not to enunciate too loudly into the mouthpiece: "Student has retracted spermicide into the urethra. He's in a great deal of pain."

The voice on the other end says: *Bring him in as soon as you can.*

Brian Tooley rounds up Larry, my roommate, who doesn't smoke or drink, and Karlo, Larry, and I race Mountain the seven miles to St. Joseph's Hospital in Eureka. Mountain thrashes back and forth on the front seat. It's the roughest seven miles I've ever known.

We all sit in the hospital waiting room nervously leafing through *Vogue* and *Sports Illustrated* (identical magazines on drugs: senseless, smeary, and stinking of cologne). Karlo wonders aloud if they'll have to amputate. Larry shakes his head the while, expressing distaste for the libertines. After twenty minutes or so a chagrined Mountain finally comes lumbering out, biceps bulging against his shirtsleeves, the color returned to his face.

"What happened, man? Are you all right?"

"They just had to flush my radiator," he says with a relieved grin. "I'm going to be all right."

From this point on, especially since he's temporarily lost some of his zest for the carnal delights (and didn't the Pope warn him?), Mountain is my devoted companion. He makes sure I have cigarettes, checks on me at least once a day, and advises me on homework problems. After a futile night of trying to woo a freshman from Fresno or Ukiah into my bunk, I find that Mountain is usually up, door open, reading Winston Churchill or studying a chart from one of his lost-treasure fables. Despite possessing a sturdy analytical mind, he ventures up into the hills now and again with pickax and pan, and one among many of his alchemical hypotheses is a method by which gold flakes from the ocean can be cheaply extracted. It doesn't bother him that every last gold story ends up with the finder cursed or dead. I suppose that makes him a hobbyist. At any rate, he waves warmly and invites me in. He has beer in his dorm fridge and reefer to smoke. If he doesn't have any of his own stash, he goes door-to-door, alms for the poor. Fellow students don't seem to mind when Big Mountain wakes them.

And now he's a regular at our evening gatherings as well. One night my roommate Larry has gone back home to Grass Valley, and because our dorm room is so orderly and clean, we decide to have a drinking contest there. About three in the morning Mountain is declared the winner, after which Karlo pulls my pants down to my ankles and I fall over and collapse the Styrofoam cooler, flooding the room with ice water that makes the carpet stink for weeks. Larry is not pleased when he returns. I also overhear the Living Group Advisers the next day plotting against me. Apparently I am a bad influence on the younger students. Perhaps, I mutter to my compatriots, there will be a tribunal in which hemlock is involved. Good thing the semester is almost over.

2.

MOUNTAIN IS A SAN DIEGO BOY—CLAIREMONT HIGH IS
his alma mater—and I'm able to get him a summer job at the
Del Mar racetrack, where I've worked the last two summers. It's
just a seven-week season, perfect for an academic interlude
and a few extra bucks. Mountain and I toodle around in an electric
cart and fill concession stands with hot dogs, relish, buns, candy
bars, and the like, before the admission gates open at twelve.
I usually drive so Moses can salute bystanders and say, "Smoke
'em if you got 'em," or "*Manga la puerta*," a phrase he believes is
Italian for "Eat the door." It's a six-hour shift, and except for getting up early, it's easy work. We've rented a small studio apartment in the barrio of Solana Beach, just down the street from the
Blue Bird Mexican Restaurant, one of five Mexican restaurants
on our street, about two miles from the track.

Throughout the day Mountain emits rarely explained chort-
les, snickers, and squeaks, his eyes crinkling and moist with
mirth, as if talented mice have assembled privately in his brain to
do special reenactments of Rogers and Hammerstein. Rarely,
like most of my friends, can I predict what he will say. Sincere one
moment, devil-may-care the next, he pronounces the anthem of
his youth in a side-mouthed Hollywood gangster voice: "Get
maaaxed, go on a *triiiip*, one WAY!" Midsentence he'll strike one
of a myriad of madcap action-photo poses: a cross-eyed racecar
driver, a gay tap dancer, an inbred tobacco heir, a hapless prize-
fighter, Maria the flirtatious tortilla maker. He possesses a merry

and absurd sweetness, a politeness bordering on sheepishness that, combined with a body mass that can block out the sun, endears him to most everyone. Except for the constant flux of women, towels on the bathroom floor, and an occasional nose-bleed, Mountain is the perfect, but always delightful, roommate, spontaneous and easygoing as you please.

We eat hamburger and beans, party every night (one WAY!), and lose our money on the horses. None of the neighborhood bars ever asks us for our IDs ("Why do you think they call it a *bar*rio?" says Mountain), and we both know a couple of other places where I can drink. Mountain drinks anywhere he wants. Despite his sorry excuse for a mustache, he looks twenty-eight, and even though he's got a first-rate fake ID, he rarely has to show it. Everyone seems eager to accommodate the big man. America is all about the Big Man. One more point about Mountain Moses: despite his guilt, sensitivity, deeply marred Catholicism, and courteousness, he's got a sadistic side. He loves to fight when he gets a little booze in him, and he's very clever at stirring up trouble. For a while there, because of his size, I thought he was the type who innocently attracts violence, but more than once now, like that time with the Huns in Ocean Beach, when he was almost arrested for using a guy's face to clear a row of trophies off a shelf, I've seen him throw an elbow, sit in the wrong chair, or deliberately spill someone's drink just to get the ball rolling. If he likes you he's inclined to call you "Johnny." But if he calls you "Burt," get ready to swallow some teeth.

When Mountain's women appear, I have to disappear. I could stay if I liked, but the apartment is small, and he gets the strangest territorial jackass mating stupor in his eyes. For friendship *and* health reasons, I don't want to get on the wrong side of Mountain Moses. I don't ever want to be "Burt." And given the choice, I'd rather not watch him melt into a lump of helpless jujubes. Maybe this is one of the reasons the women never stay long—he's too easy, too lovey-dovey, *too* sweet. So I don't mind taking a stroll while he gets the fructose out of his system. I'll wander up to the Blue Bird for a margarita, borrow Mountain's car and drive down to the beach to whump on a few waves, or if the horses are running I might fool around with a few bets since I can park and get in with my employee card for free.

On the evening of my twenty-first birthday, Mountain is off with one of his girlfriends. I couldn't expect him to remember that today was my twenty-first. We haven't been friends that long. Anyway, a twenty-first birthday isn't that big a deal. Halfheartedly waiting for the phone to ring, I study his altar, a short bookcase at the head of his bed containing photographs including several mousy-looking girls I don't know, his knockout sister, and his then-very-young mother and father; a baseball signed by LA Dodger Maury Wills; two Rolling Stones ticket stubs; a glass doorknob; several treasure maps; some kind of weird washing machine spring; and his five "traveling classics": *Zen and the Art of Motorcycle Maintenance*, *The Brothers Karamazov*, *In Watermelon Sugar*, *The Principia Mathematica*, and *Smither's Definitive Guide to Lost and Hidden Treasure*.

I don't know why I got all dressed up. Most of my friends don't even know where I live. I wonder for a minute if I should call and tell them. It's getting late. I'm certainly not going to go out by myself to celebrate my twenty-first. What could be sadder than that? Sitting on a park bench with an inflatable doll?

I switch on Mountain's little black-and-white TV. A pretty face introduces her potbellied guests, who are proud to be unemployed. They brag of their affairs. America mocks her heroes, embraces her slobs. I switch over to the news: GM is on strike. There's another oil embargo, long lines at the gas stations. A serial killer named Johnny Jumpup or something like that has popped up and if I'm not mistaken the journalists are *thrilled*.

I hate the 1970s. It's the pimp rococo decade, dull-eyed complacency, endless consumption, and softheaded children in clown clothing finding an excuse to give each other gonorrhea in the park. The previous generation represented ideals such as love, equality, landing on the moon, and civil rights. My generation represents teen pregnancy, disco music, Sun Myung Moon,

escalating crime rates, big gas-guzzling cars with wheel covers
and chrome that falls off and doors that don't close and all the
people who make them out on strike and scratching their venereal
sores. America is dying and no one cares.

I stick my head into the fridge. Along with many cartons of
leftover Chinese food, I find a half-gallon carton of Tropicana,
sniff cautiously, and sip. Carton in hand, I stare out the window.
I wonder how many serial killers, glorified extortionists, and
environmental criminals they have in India. But what's this, headlights in the driveway? My heart soars. It's Mountain Moses.

Mountain strolls in showing that big gap between his two
front teeth. He's dressed in tie and suit jacket and slacks. Everyone at school says he looks like Silly Stallone, but with those big
chimp ears, that twinkle in his blue eyes, that bent honker, those
pin-striped pleated slacks, and that faint excuse for a mustache,
tonight he looks like a dead ringer for Clark Gable. Mountain, I've
decided all at once, is the best friend I could ever have.

"Well, looka who's here," I say, turning off the television.

"Where is everyone?" he says, looking about with a tug at
the sleeves of his jacket.

"You're looking at them," I say. "Where were you, at a cos-
tume party? You look like the maître d' on *Leave It to Beaver*."

He glances at his wing tips, then holds out his arms, hands
backward, as if he's about to leap from a thirty-meter board.
"Had to go to her parents' house for dinner. Croquettes. No beaver.
Begged off dessert to make it for your birthday."

I smile and swirl my carton of Tropicana. "What did you
get me?"

"I'm going to get you *drunk*," he says in a John Wayne voice,
hooking his finger at the air.

"How did you *know*?"

"Enough of this gay banter," he says, glancing at his watch.
"We've only got six hours."

Mountain drives his father's El Camino. His father and
mother are divorced. He doesn't talk much about his mom. Father,

I gather, is the uncommunicative intellectual type who spends his evenings with vodka on the rocks under the reading lamp.

We argue about what place to go. Mountain likes crummy working-class bars where he can find fights. I like more-upscale places with the possibility of women. Mountain doesn't go for bar women. He finds his girlfriends in grocery stores, dormitories, at beaches or ball games, anywhere he can exhibit his dimples, apple cheeks, and charming, gosh-golly befuddlement in good, clean, and wholesome light. Come to think of it, I have never seen him with a girl when he was drunk. We compromise by hitting alternate bars.

"No fights too early, Mountain," I warn him at bar number one, a cement hole in Mission Beach called Murph's, where a sprinkle of semibikers have gathered like moose around the mossy pool table. Mountain and I really stick out here, me in a floral pirate blouse, green cuffed bell-bottoms so tight you can see the breath mints in my pockets, platform shoes, glistening hair coiled artificially, eyes bloodshot from the vanity of hard contact lenses, a draping of gold at the neck—and Mountain arrayed like a senile father in a sixties sitcom. "All right? I don't want to get blood all over this new shirt."

"You're not fighting," he grumbles.

"Yes, but the guy will fall on me after you punch him," I return. "Do you remember the last time? That shirt cost me twenty bucks." I point a finger. My hands are so long they alarm me sometimes. "You see that donkey-headed guy down there by the dartboard?"

Mountain glowers down the way past a medium-hot blonde staring at him, who looks as if she'd enjoy a physical contest with Mountain, or failing that, between her boyfriend and this stranger who pleases her eye. "I see him," he intones, his ears pricking. "Looks like a *Burt* to me."

"He's not staring at you."

Mountain rolls his shoulders and cracks a malevolent grin. "Yes, he is."

"No, he has a walleye. *Strabismus*, it's a muscular disorder."

"Maybe I can knock it back into place for him."

"You don't want to pick fights with the handicapped."

"I don't like people named *Burt*," he says.

At Murph's, even if it's a biker haven, my incredible string begins. From here on out, regardless of the tavern we select, I am served for my free birthday drink a flaming asshole. I try not to take it personally. Don't ask me what's in a flaming asshole (floor wax?). All I know is that I present my ID and I am served this syrupy concoction on fire. Mountain thinks it's funny, but he has one with me since we are brothers. You have to drink them quickly to keep from burning your face off. Even tossed back with expert quickness, these little pots of fire still crackle off the bottoms of your mustache hairs.

"Why don't they call them Phantom of the Operas?" Mountain wonders aloud, licking his lips as if to feel if they are still there.

"They should serve them with extinguishers," I agree.

Bar two on Seventieth Street is a bona fide disco with the mirror ball spinning over an acre of dance floor. I hate discos as much as the next guy, but where else are you going to find so many gorgeous chicks? I stand at the headland of the bay of dandies, admiring the tide. Mountain is bored, however, even if he knows how to dance—there isn't the vaguest prospect of a fight—so we finish our drinks and head east down El Cajon Boulevard to a backwater part of town, littered and forgotten, as if a glacier pushed through a trailer park and came to rest here.

Mountain parks along the curb in front of a small closed grocery with salamis hanging in the window. Next door is a neon dive called The Mambo Lounge. The place has obviously been here for at least two wars, though this is the first I've noticed it. I follow Mountain through a gray curtain drenched in smoke and perfume, past a cigarette machine and into a purulent, velvet darkness, petite coin-sized tables arranged around a dance floor that looks like a bottomless pit. Mountain swivels his head as if he expects to recognize someone.

"Where are we?" I say. "Morocco, 1953?"

"About right," he says, pointing toward an open table by the dance floor. An expiring couple draped over one another follows the wheezy inflections of a Tony Bennett song. The waitress, about forty, in black Danish S & M lace, sidles up with her tray. "See your IDs, boys?"

Mountain mutters, "How old do you gotta be to drink here, fifty?"

"Only twenty-one," she drawls, dropping the cards on the table. "What'll you boys have?"

"It's my birthday," I announce.

"Oh oh," she says, and here come the liquid mini bonfires.

"The place looks like a convalescent hospital," I remark. "What time does the bingo start?"

Mountain rolls his big shoulders and plucks at the knot on his tie. He's still looking around as if he expects to recognize someone. The drinks arrive. Mountain lifts his glass. "To the great state of ecstasy."

We toss them back, eyes clenched against the inferno.

I brush at my lapel. "Is my shirt on fire?"

"Siss-KWAH!" Mountain says to the waitress, who is staring at him with less-than-professional curiosity. "Two more, dear." He seems suddenly content here. I don't know why. The patrons are too old to fight.

The moment the waitress is out of earshot Mountain cocks his jaw and belches. He's a gifted belcher, able to articulate phrases such as "Buick Riviera" or "George Washington Carver." Through eructation this evening, with a few drinks under his belt, he's ambitious and tries: "The Origin of Consciousness in The Breakdown of the Bicameral Mind."

I congratulate him, even if he did run out of gas on the last syllable.

He drops his head in modesty and begins an impression of Paul "Bear" Bryant, the legendary Alabama football coach, which consists of little but the word "Alabama" mumbled over and over.

Then he cries suddenly, grimacing in pain, clutching an imaginary wheel. "Action photo!"

"What is it?"

"Kamikaze pilot spill hot coffee in lap."

"Here's one," I say, left hand behind my head, right arm extended. "Shot putter with loose toupee."

"Forgot my chute," he says, arms flailing.

"Watch out for those Girl Scouts!"

"Marilyn Monroe!" he says, lifting the tails of his jacket and clapping his eyelids.

"Forgot to shave your legs!"

"So, big fella," he says, shoving at imaginary goldilocks with the heel of his hand. "What's new in the development of thought and the analysis of ideas?"

My coaster is stuck to my arm and I finally manage to shake it free. "Why is there no practical philosophical application to the problem of happiness?"

"What's the problem?"

"Happiness."

"Life is sad," he says, his gaze swinging over my shoulder as someone enters the door. "Have another drink."

"Would that I had one."

He fiddles with his cuff links. "Where is that dame?"

"Probably reloading the balls in the bingo machine," I say, fluffing the curls on my perm. "So what are your plans after you get your degree, Mountain?"

"Don't like to think about it," he says, pushing his empty shot glass to the edge of the table with an index finger. "Cal Tech, eventually. Not really ready for the grindstone yet."

"How about travel?"

"Sure," he says, lips sealed, eyes rolling up. "Don't know where I'd go, though. Maybe Arizona, New Mexico. Spanish hid a lot of gold out there."

"I'd like to get out of America," I say, watching a pillar of red light behind the bar holding in its electromagnetic prison tight coils and marbles of tobacco smoke.

"What's wrong with America?" he says, his forehead ridging.

"I've never fit well here," I say.

"Why not?" He seems offended.

"People come here for one thing," I say, hammering my shot glass down for emphasis. "To be rich. And they'll do anything to get it—lie, cheat, kill, steal, poison a river. You ever been to Canada?"

"Nope. Had real maple syrup once."

"It's clean there. The people are nice. You know why?"

"Maple syrup?"

"Because nobody goes there to get *rich*."

He tongues his bottom lip, then scratches his big chin. "Rich ain't all that terrible of an idea."

"A dream about money is a dream about shit."

"Who said that?"

"Sigmund Freud."

"Don't tell me you wanna live in *Canada*."

"I was thinking more like the coast of India, or maybe Africa, someplace with decent surf and no crowded freeways."

He crooks an index finger and scratches the part in his hair. "How about an island?"

"Yeah," I say. "That'd be good too."

"With nekkid girls," he says.

"And parakeets."

"And buried treasure." His eyes suddenly light. "Let's go."

"It wouldn't be bad."

"An island," he says, tapping his nose. "Yeah. Jesus, *pirate* gold. Hey, where's Inga?"

"Here she comes. See the woman behind the flames?"

The drinks are placed flickering in front of us. Mountain says—the blue lambency of blazing liqueurs playing on his eyes—that on our uninhabited island not far from Tahiti we will probably need a generator, a compressor, milking goats, and two topless house servants who speak no English. I add some laying hens and a still, and install a sunken Spanish caravel full of gold doubloons in the cove nearby to please his treasure-hunting instincts.

"We should leave now," Mountain says, tossing back his pot of fire.

As I raise my asshole to my lips, a consumptive-looking rake in a black evening dress and tattered stole is limping toward me, her hands so thin they appear to be bone, her face lizard-white, her cheeks collapsed. If I believed in zombies I would get up and run. I'm terrified for a moment and when she leans down suddenly into my face, the flaming asshole barbecues my nose.

"Hello, Mom," says Mountain.

"Hi, Sullie," she says in the charred, cement-mixer voice of the inveterate smoker. I've forgotten until now that his real name is Sullivan. "Where you been, baby?"

With sangfroid slowness he lights a cigarette. He smokes leaned back with the cigarette between his second and third fingers, covering the lower half of his face with his hand, as I imagine French aristocrats or Charles Boyer would do. "I'm going to college now, Ma," he says.

"College?" she says, stifling a yawn. "Well, that's nice. Who's your friend?" She tips her skeleton head at me and her eyes are dancing now.

I toss off my extinguished drink, the tip of my nose thoroughly scorched. "I'm Edgar," I falter.

Mishearing me, she unwittingly assigns me a new nickname. "Deadwood!" she cries, flipping back her stole in a blast of bug spray and cedar oil, moths flapping all around her head.

"I'm a friend of Mountain's through college," I explain, feeling for a blister. "Sit down, please, Mrs. Moses."

"What kind of name is that, Deadwood? Are you a camp counselor?"

"It's not really my—oh, never mind," I say, wondering as she creaks into a chair, her eyes a frosted and moribund vacancy, how she could be related to the vital and venerable man sitting across from me. Her teeth are caked with lipstick and her hair is a whorl of mad licks, as if coiffed by the tongue of a cat.

"What are you boys doing *here*?" she asks, laying her chin on the back of an emaciated hand. "You like older women?"

"Ah, just drivin' around, Ma," says Mountain, slitty-eyed and finding sudden interest in the plumes of smoke rising from his cigarette.

"It's my birthday," I explain, gulping the last bit of residual syrup from my shot glass.

"No!" she says, regarding me with wonder. "We must dance."

"No, Mrs. Moses," I reply firmly, afraid she was going to say something like that. "Thank you, but I don't dance."

"Of course you do." She swats the air.

"No, really I don't."

"No, we must." She totters to her feet and extends a hand. "It's your birthday."

"I don't dance," I repeat.

"Come."

It's plain I won't win. You can't argue with the dead. The pickled hag that is somehow Mountain's mother leads me to the black hole of a dance floor and we stride through the dingy, necrotic vapor with all the geezers nodding off into their diluted Smirnoffs. We don't dance as much as we simply prop each other up. I have no concept of where to put my feet. I can feel her nipples and her hipbones jutting through her dress. She moans in my ear, "How old are you, honey, sixteen?"

"Forty-three," I reply, my hand on her very palpable spine.

She cackles hotly into my ear.

Mountain watches us wistfully, hand in his hair.

"New York, New York" is finally over. You know I used to *like* that song. They must have played the long version. Mrs. Moses throws an arm around my waist and drags me back to her son. My plan if she asks me to dance again is to feign an epileptic seizure.

"I want you to meet Mel," she wheezes, wiping a snake of hair from her eyes.

"We gotta go, Ma," says Mountain.

"You can meet Mel, first," she gurgles. "He's right over here."

Mel is poised on a stool at the bar, drumming his knee with three fingers. He's a skinny guy about fifty with a barrel chest, big horn-rims, and a haircut like a Muppet. Everyone smiles and nods around except Mountain. Mrs. Moses is doing that blurry thing with her teeth and wagging her skull around airily, as if she is having the time of her life. "Mel is a contractor," she says.

"So this is your *son*," booms Mel cheerfully. "You're a strapping one, aren't you?" He's trying to touch Mountain, slap his shoulder or grip his hand, but Mountain keeps his distance. "This your son too?"

Mrs. Moses tips her head in pride. "No, this is Deadwood, Mountain's good friend from college."

"Deadwood," says Mel, pleased. "You must be a poker player."

"We're gonna go, Ma," says Mountain.

"Don't run off so *soon*. Stay for a drink."

Mel is already signaling the bartender.

Mountain turns and, without another word, walks off. "Nice to meet you, Mel," I call. "You too, Mrs. Moses."

She waves as if from the prow of a ship, the *SS DEATH*, I think.

I catch up with Mountain and we break from that mummy rag of a curtain, cigarette smoke dangling from our clothes. Fresh air never felt so good. My nose still feels like it's on fire.

"Thought she'd be here," he says, and then adds with a sigh, "well, at least she's still alive."

"Forget it, man," I say.

"Oh, I forgot it a long time ago," he says, shoving hands down into his pockets. "Well, come on Deadwood, let's go finish your birthday party."

3.

AFTER FLAMING ASSHOLE NUMBER FIVE, WE'RE AT TINA'S in La Mesa, a yuppie joint with chrome bar stools, and the women are looking *good*. They smell like Dunkin' Donuts and have that Ingrid Bergman aura of gauze all around them. I love women as much as Mountain, but I am much less discriminating. I will sleep with them all, single mothers, anorexics, divorcées, toll-booth operators, and overweight chicks who like Kenny Loggins.

By asshole number seven I'm ready for the Red Coat Inn, a popular nightclub attached to a bowling alley. Good bands play there, even the Cascades, one of the few San Diego bands to actually have a *Billboard Top 100* hit. Remember "Rhythm of the Rain," with all the dingle-bells? Tonight on stage is a solid April Wine impersonation. Mountain grabs a booth and I head for the bar. The place is packed with stunning, fluffy-headed disco nymphs and I'm rearin' to go. But first I've gotta pee. A shock passes through me as I catch my reflection in the mirror. I've got a good eye for fashion, but this poor red-nosed fop in the mirror looks like a male hooker. He looks like the sort of Binaca-blasting Beau Brummel I loathe. I'm shaken. At all times I seem to be two conflicting entities, one who despises, and the other the very thing I despise. I wash my long hands in the sink, plump up the curls in my hair, and decide that I don't look that bad. Besides, if I dressed any other way, women would pay no attention to me. I don't have Mountain's visceral John Wayne appeal.

On the way back, a button-nosed blonde in a silver cocktail

dress smiles at me. She's dancing with a sperm whale in a green Bee Gee suit. I bet I could steal her. I wish I could dance but even drunk I have no more familiarity with the rite than a chimp operating a Ferris wheel. I'm dance-handicapped. I have Dancing Deficit Disorder. I'll have to try and talk to her later. I wedge to the bar, lay down my ID, and order up two flaming assholes. No point in changing drinks this late in the game.

As I negotiate the blazing shots back across the crowded floor, I am jostled and then knocked completely down. The liquor hits the floor and two puddles of cool, liquid blue flames burst up and ripple across the parquet in front of my eyes. I try to rise but a wave of humanity bangs me back from the other side. The floor has tilted, it seems. Legs are buckling all around, wavering like seaweed in a giant aquarium filled with whatever they put in those flaming assholes. I've never seen a place erupt so quickly. I imagine crazed bowlers have entered and are pitching sixteen-pounders at the crowd. Several other people go down around me, including the blonde in the silver cocktail dress. For a moment I don't mind anomie. What more intimate way to meet women? Then I see fists spinning above heads and I close my eyes against a spray of flying glass. The guitarist of the April Wine Impersonators is pleading over the mike for order, which only seems to fuel the rampage.

As I peer out from under a booth, the melee parts just long enough for me to spy a man dressed in a lime green leisure suit smash a pitcher of beer over another man's velour beret. Mountain is just off to the left laying out a hairy-looking cretin with beaver teeth. His face becomes strangely tranquil and uncomplicated, that orgiastic cruelty illuminating his eyes as he sets to his task. I'd lay eight-to-one he was the cause of the insurrection. Oh, but he is a maestro with those fists, that right hand like a wrecking ball. And don't we all love to do things we're good at? What am I good at, I wonder? Well, I can play Scrabble fairly well, and I can cook a mean Hamburger Helper. I'm a good surfer. I love music. I'm a marvelous bullshit artist, so good in fact that most people are convinced I'm always telling the truth, which takes all the fun out of it.

The cops will be here any minute or the bowling alley will burn down, so I decide to ease out into the free-for-all and coax Mountain from the premises. The going is not easy. A bar stool flies through the air. Three women, arms locked, are doing the can-can on a fat guy who seems to be enjoying himself. Here comes a slim, young debaucher swinging across the room on one of the light fixtures. The whole spectacle is like the closing sequence in *Blazing Saddles* with walls coming down and the dancers flailing with the cowboys. The guitarist is down in the fray now, hammering someone with his Les Paul.

I make distinct progress toward Mountain but then the hordes crush all around again and I'm flung against the plywood skirt of the bandstand next to a very nice pair of legs wrapped at the juncture with blue panties. I would like to enjoy these legs, but someone kicks me in the head. I am aware I have drunk too many assholes. I wonder if I will be trampled and killed or wake up tomorrow in a hospital with a permanent boot print on my face. I hear someone shout, "Cops!" and I see their blue menace and steel. Now Mountain is pulling me up by my shirt and dragging me till I get my feet. "Come on, Deadwood," he growls cheerfully. Then the bang of the emergency exit doors and an exhilarating rush of cold air.

We beat for the car. It's hard to run in platform shoes. I vow that this is the end of my disco days and living in a culture where to attract women you must dress like one. Mountain's car is parked down by the Cinerama. The streaks of madly spinning red lights flash across our backs as we jump into his El Camino. Mountain turns the key and takes off without looking back. We jump out of the driveway down by the Mayfair, swing through a green light, and head west on University Avenue. I glance over my shoulder to see more police cars pouring into the lot.

"What happened?" I say, touching my jaw.

"Guy swung at me," he says, still out of breath. "Said I was staring at his girl. I had to knock him out."

"You know, one *time*, Mountain, I'd like to go out drinking with you and have a quiet night."

He shrugs as if to say, *Birds gotta fly, fish gotta swim.* "You all right?" he says, taking a right on Fifty-Fourth Street.

"Yeah, just a little kick in the head," I say. "And a burnt nose."

"How'd that happen?"

"Some asshole."

"Where you wanna go next?"

"How about Madagascar?"

"Is that the new one in PB?"

"No, that's an island in the Indian Ocean just off the African coast."

Mountain turns to stare at me. The spinning lights of a cop car zip past.

"I'm serious, man. Why not?" I ask. "What have you got here that's worth staying for?"

He checks his mirror. "We'll be back in school in two weeks," he says.

"I wish I'd brought a change of shoes," I grumble, rubbing my ankles. "These heels are killing me."

"To hell with those assholes," he says. "Let's go get us some *margaritas*."

4.

NEVER HAS A SUMMER PASSED WITH SUCH AGREEABLE speed, and now even school is something to look forward to. My second semester at Humboldt, or Ho-Hum State, as Mountain likes to call it, picks up right where I left it. All the lads are back. Though Karlo, Tee Willie, and the Tooley boys haven't changed much, I've cast aside my sissy pirate blouses and platform shoes, sheared off my salon-curled hair, sold my jewelry, and flushed my contacts down the toilet (tired of bloodshot eyes and crawling around on the floor looking for a lost lens). The era of the hetero woman-man is over. Mick, you can wipe off your bloody lipstick. With my short hair and new plastic-framed glasses, it takes a few moments for my old comrades to recognize me. Also, I've decided to ease back on the festivities a bit since I'm going to need at least a B average to gain entrance into a decent law school.

But the parties never stop coming, and it seems a waste to let them pass without me. One night, only a few weeks after school starts, there's a poker game down in the Tooley room. We've bought a half gallon of Safeway gin, which some are mixing with orange juice, others dry vermouth and green olives on tooth-picks. Mountain and I are in the second category, swilling freely and making Gaelic jokes.

"Shut your piehole, Edgar Donahoe," says Andy. "The bet's to you."

"I'm not anti-Gaelic," I mutter, dashing off my ninth martini. "Just because I've never been to a Gaelic bar."

Mountain fans his cards in his meaty hands, shakes his head, and says in a perfect New England accent: "I say aftuh we shoot the Demo-crats, we send all the Gaelics back to San Fran-cis-co."

I throw away my cards. "In the words of a famous Cartesian, 'I quit, therefore I fold.'"

Brian loads the long bong, packing in that sticky, pine-smelling sinsemilla that costs forty dollars for a quarter ounce but is *worth* it, people, let me tell you.

There's another kid named Andy, a bedazzled freshman just grateful to be in our sophomoric presence, sitting at the end of our makeshift table and obediently losing his money. "Tell you what," I say. "Let's all be mountain ranges. I'll be the Himalayas." I point to Karlo. "You be the Pyrenees. Tee Willie, you're the Sangre de Cristos. And you two … " I indicate Andy and Andy. "You guys be the Andes."

Oh whore whore *whore*. My compatriots laugh so hard some of the chips fall off the table. I find this a good time to mix another Safeway martini. Am I not hilarious when I'm swacked?

"What about me?" says Mountain, pouting. "I want to be Mount Sinai."

"You're drunk, Moses."

"Hot puppies."

"Deal the cards, doughface!" shouts Karlo. "And fix me a bong."

"Seven stud."

"What's wild?"

"Ask not for whom the bong tolls," says Brian, handing the bong across to Karlo. "The bong tolls for thee."

My perception starts to get hazy at this point, but I know the sun's not up yet, and I'm winning money at poker even if I'm drunk as a giraffe. Tee Willie has slipped out. It must be very late because all the lights in the dormitory across the way are off. I raise the window and with one of those orange highway cones that make perfect megaphones, I begin shouting at the darkened windows. "Wake up you dope-smoking sheep diddlers!" I call to them. "Rise and shine you hairy-legged fairy queens!"

Mountain grabs the megaphone: "Eat Jesus!" he cries. "Not war!"

Karlo and the Tooley boys are in stitches. The other Andy, the doe-eyed freshman, suggests meekly that maybe it's too late for this. Mountain and I are still under the impression that we're being hilarious, which is one of the many downsides of alcohol.

Mountain bellows in his great baritone: "Is that tapioca in your beards, men, or are you just glad I came!"

As we continue to shout clever insults the lights in the windows across the way flicker on, angry faces appear below raised blinds, and a Living Group Advisor, fists balled, is marching in his slippers across the lawn. It's Clyde. I recognize Clyde. I pissed him off two weeks ago. I don't like Clyde much. He's an undeveloped suburbanite like me, except he gets a free room and oodles of arbitrary power simply for sucking up to the authorities. I step out into the hall to meet him. When he sees it's me, he begins to swear, "Goddamn it. You again, Donahoe?"

Mountain swings out of the room behind me. "Put 'em up, Burt," he says, curling his fists in a nineteenth-century bare-knuckle pose. "I'll pulverize ya."

"I'll *expel* you, Moses," Clyde bellows. "Donahoe, you might as well start packing your bags now."

By now most of the students on my wing are awake, peering blearily out their doors.

In the morning, I'm brought with Mountain, the Tooley brothers, and Karlo before a tribunal called the Citizens Action Review Board, a sort of kangaroo court composed of four LGAs, including Clyde, and led by Deirdre, a hefty nymphomaniac with one contiguous eyebrow, who doesn't like me because I'm always after her girls, even if I never have much success with them. I would've tried Deirdre but I hate waiting in lines. "What do you have to say for yourselves?" she says, wriggling snootily in the fumes of her short-lived reign of importance.

"We're sorry," says Andy, who always does the talking. Both the redheads are bowed.

"It won't happen again," adds Karlo, who is only months away from graduation and cannot risk antagonizing the academy.

Mountain is extravagantly silent and giving off his usual aura of danger and private amusement.

Deirdre, apparently satisfied with the kowtowing of my comrades, and not yet willing to undertake the task of grilling the likable right tackle of our illustrious football team, now turns to me. "What do you have to say for yourself, Edgar Donahoe?"

I'm not in the mood to give in to this self-important panel of ass-smoochers with their knickers in a knot. Students are all they are, my own people. I'm not normally the rebellious type. Maybe the truth is that I can see I have no future in psychology or law and I am looking for a dramatic way out. Maybe I'm still drunk.

But I say calmly, "Expel me if you like."

"What?"

Mountain chuckles softly.

"Without truth and beauty, civilization dies," I say, lifting my head.

"What does that have to do with being drunk at three in the morning and shouting out the windows?"

"America is *dead*," I reply. "It doesn't matter anymore."

"You've been warned three times already."

I shrug. "Give me the hemlock."

"You won't apologize?"

"No," I say. "Your smug little gang of four sticks in my craw."

"Very well," says Deirdre with a dry lift of that firm and expert upper lip. "We'll convene and inform you tomorrow morning of your status with the university."

But I don't give them the pleasure of their convention. The next day at ten a.m. I drop all my classes in a heroic farewell. I feel like Bolivar liberating the Venezuelans. Some professors urge me to stay, but I've suddenly seen the light and the error of my ways and the notion of freedom is ringing in my head like a phone

call from the gods. Do you really think I'm going to be a *lawyer*?
I'm too old to be living in the dormitories anyway.

Mountain sticks his big-eared head in my door as I zip up
my only suitcase. "What are you gonna do, Johnny?" he says.

I turn about. All night I didn't sleep, my mind teeming. "I'm
leaving the continent," I tell him.

"Where you going? The island?"

"If I can."

Mountain, cool-eyed, nods. "How are you going to get there?"

"Hitchhike."

"I'll come with you," he says.

"Let's go," I say, my heart swelling.

"I can't, man," he groans. "My dad's paying for everything.
I'm a year away from graduating."

"Well, wish me luck then."

"Come on down to my room, man."

"I've got to be going. I'm no longer a student here."

"I just want to play you a song. I'll give you a ride down to
the highway."

Mountain's room is furnished in milk crates, cinder blocks,
and probably seven hundred record albums. "Well, Deadwood,"
he says, extending a hand. "Don't know if I'll ever see you again,
but it's been a barn burner."

"Yes, it has," I reply, shaking his hand, my stomach falling.

He turns his face away suddenly and clears his throat.
"What do you want to hear for your last song at Ho-Hum State?"

I believe he thinks I will choose something rousing and
defiant, Ramones or AC/DC, but instead I pick a sad song, "Time
Waits for No One," by the Stones. "Do you remember when they
sang 'Time Is on My Side'?" I ask him. "Well, it didn't last long,
did it?"

"Do you really believe America is dead?" he asks.

"Are you kidding? Have you seen the social pathology index
lately? The Goths are standing at the gate, man."

He shrugs. "Still seems like it wouldn't hurt to get your degree."

"You'll regret not coming with me," I say, snapping my finger at the air. "Because it's all coming down, Johnny. You'll see."

He drops his head. "I'll drive you down to the highway."

"I'll get my suitcase."

As he stops along the edge of the highway, he seems amazed that I'm actually going to go through with it, especially since it's October and cold, and I only have a hundred and fifty dollars that my father gave me for college expenses (beer) for the month.

"You sure?" he says, standing at his open door. "It's *raining*, man. It isn't too late to go back."

"Adios, Mountain. Thanks for everything."

"Good luck, man." He pumps my hand—for a moment I think he may shed a tear—then he turns all at once and climbs stiffly back into his car.

The highway is nearly empty and the passing traffic makes a lonesome ringing sound. I stick out my thumb. The rain increases. People don't pick up hitchhikers the way they used to, not with serial killers, social parasitism at an all-time high, and cloudy-headed malcontents like bad hangovers from the sixties terrorizing society simply because their parents are rich. Nevertheless, I imagine I will end up in Wales or Asia, in an opium den or the bed of a glamorous, diamond-studded harlot who will teach me the secrets of the Orient. I can still see the university on its safe little knoll, peeking up through the mist of the mighty redwoods. I think of going back. All I'd have to do is say I'm sorry.

A bashed-up red Pinto pulls over. The window rolls down. A fat blond guy wearing a jade earring leans over. "Where you headed?" he says, wiggling a can of Coca-Cola at me.

"East," I say.

"I'll give you a ride to Elko," he says, with a wink.

"Elko?" I say.

"Nevada. I'm going to visit my sister there."

The rain beats on my head. I climb into the car. In a Pinto

you sit nearly on the ground. Behind you is a gas tank that will explode into flames with the slightest impact. Talk about a flaming asshole. My benefactor smiles at me like an angler who has caught himself a nice trout. The floor below me is a landfill of Coca-Cola cans. I wonder if those people who apologized to the Citizens Action Review Board are smarter than I am. Undoubtedly they are. Jesus Christ, and I almost had a B average.

5.

OUT ON HIGHWAY 80 JUST OUTSIDE ELKO, NEVADA, A '73 Oldsmobile pulls over. The window slides down. I crouch to peer in. Two ruddy young men in white shirts are smiling at me. "Where you going?" they say.

"East," I say.

"How far east?"

"Africa, maybe," I say.

They continue to smile, like a couple of fresh lobotomies. Weirdos are out here by the thousands. Cold, heavy drops of rain begin to slap the pavement and the back of my neck. "We can take you as far as Salt Lake City," says the smiler on the passenger side, who has snake nostrils and two front teeth extracted from a Goofy mask.

"Okay," I say, climbing in clumsily out of the rain. The driver stares at me from his rearview mirror. The passenger turns to grin with those root stump teeth, arm laid up along the seat.

People think hitchhiking across the country is romantic and fun. It isn't. It's terrifying and cold. It makes you miserable in your guts. It makes you want to go back home and be satisfied with a Jell-O life. The freaks are all on your wavelength, and they all want something from you. Like the first ride I caught from Arcata with that spooky Coca-Cola addict with the jade earring, who wanted to get a motel when it started to get dark. And he kept asking me about my girlfriend and my sex life. Having studied psychology, I know how perverts behave. I told him to drop me off at the next stop, said I needed to keep going, but he laughed, as if he felt sorry for me or by the mercy of demons was giving me a Get-Out-of-Sodomy-Free Card, and took me straight on through to Elko, where his sister supposedly lived, though he went around the block twice after he dropped me off, and later I bought a bag of Planters' Peanuts and a cream soda and spent the night in the bushes at the China Ranch Park.

I wish Mountain had come with me. I think back to that first semester when he and Karlo returned from a shooting expedition, and as the rifles were being put away in Mountain's room, Mountain's gun discharged accidentally. The bullet whizzed past Karlo's ear, nearly killing him. Mountain cried. The sight of him blubbering like a child welded his soul to mine. I find I'm already missing him. And if he were here now these two buffoons wouldn't even think about trying anything funny.

Since I first put up my thumb—and especially now as I settle into the backseat and the two weirdos continue to stare— I've been thinking of a friend of mine from the old neighborhood, Troy Katchpole, who got raped by a one-armed truck driver at the age of sixteen while hitchhiking through Tennessee. Before I set out on this trip I always thought privately that Troy could've avoided his fate with the depraved amputee. He should not have checked into a motel room with a guy he didn't know, and even then he should've been wary and at the first sign of queer behavior made some excuse about getting ice and scrammed. But now, out here stark alone, trying to stay out of the rain, the darkness coming, I have a sudden rush of complete empathy and understanding for Troy. Because hitchhiking is the ultimate self-solicitation. The minute your thumb goes up you're meat on the side of the road. You're like a hooker standing under a streetlight. The whole *point* is to get picked up by a stranger. And once you're in someone's car, you're in *their* possession.

But these scrubbed young men are weird in a different way. They are the Chumley Brothers, Elder and Elder Chumley, Mormon Elders, that is to say, and considering the possibilities, a good spin of the hitchhiking wheel. And since I am a captive audience, the Chumleys waste no time getting to doctrine, the sacred history of the Americas inscribed on golden tablets (lost, of course), the Angel Meroni (rhymes with balone-eye), American Indians as one of the Ten Lost Tribes of Israel, and John the Baptist in Upstate New York in 1829. Once a radical, murdered by the cowardice of orthodoxy, Jesus is now a shameless tool of conformity, the centerpiece to the greatest sales pitch on earth.

Yes, Christ, second person of the Trinity and foundation of world order and intelligibility, came to LA in the early sixties but was mistaken for a folk singer. I marvel laconically in this grandmother-scented Olds with its immaculately dark carpet, and nod along as if I have never heard more hallowed verse. The fact is, I have simply stopped wasting my breath on overzealous religious types who know more about God than I do. Most zealots in my experience are either hiding something or running a scam. All rejoinders sink in the tar pits of their dogmatic forebrains. They aren't happy unless they're arguing. They only pretend that they have ears. If they picked up God Himself along the side of the road they'd probably still argue with Him.

And it's nice that they really don't care about me, where I'm going or why, how I've come to this execrable state, begging rides in October in the rain. They don't even see me really. They blab on for hundreds of miles as the windshield wipers thump at the steady autumn rain and I wonder if they really think I am suddenly going to convert, join the choir, and find myself some nice wives and settle down. Not that I wouldn't love a blast of virtue and old-time religion—believe me—I would, but if I were God I would not want people moaning at me or constantly bitching or rattling trinkets. I would appreciate an occasional acknowledgment, yes, a thank you or a plateful of cookies (no, wait a minute, that's Santa), but I'm God, the Creator. I'm absorbed in the full spectrum. Sin, conflict, suffering, and rigged dog races all fit into the scheme. If you have faith in Me, let Me do My work. Don't hump My leg. Don't nag Me about the weather and your bursitis. Stop all your gimme gimme. And don't make up fiddle-faddle about golden tablets (lost, of course) while killing and ostracizing other groups because their fiddle-faddle about golden tablets is not compatible with yours.

No, I think the Westerners for the most part have it wrong. God is flexible and multifarious. He's an oak tree, a guillotine, *and* a bottle of Greek olives. Simultaneously He exists and does not. He's a roaring, all-loving, cross-eyed, horny-browed drama-turge who'll drop a kid down a well or reveal the secret of the benzene ring through a dream. And I'm headed *east*, brothers and sisters. I'm getting myself *oriented*. I'm transubstantiating the threshold, passing by the great gamble of sacrifice through the majestic membrane of mysticism, whose tenets grow so vague as you continue east that even the shamans lie fuddled in their huts and suck listlessly on their hookahs.

6.

I'M ON THE SIDE OF THE ROAD IN SALT LAKE CITY, IT'S *snowing* and I don't own a decent jacket. I'm a California boy, barefoot and shirtless eight months of the year. I spent the entirety of my youth upon the ocean. I don't even own a hat. I wish I knew how to fold this Book of Mormon into a hat. What am I going to do with this book? I've been taught that you don't throw books away or make them into hats, not even *Love Story*. I read everything in my dad's library when I was a kid, Irwin Shaw, Updike, Ayn Rand, Huxley, McCluhan, Thomas Wolfe, a four-volume compendium of the world's great thinkers, and yes, *Love Story*. I even read the Bible, one of the bloodiest, horniest, and simultaneously most boring books of all time. But my father taught me that all books are sacred. Looking back, trying to remember the "good times," all I can think of is books. I realize now that I should've just stayed in school and become a librarian or maybe switched my major from psych to English Lit, graduated, and opened up a used bookstore.

But it's too late for that, isn't it? There is no turning back. I made sure of that. The past is a bridge of cinders. Here in the tenuous present I stand on the highway again, shivering, waiting for a ride, and thumb through the pages of the Mormon Bible. The King James Bible, wicked and carnal as it may be, feels true, especially the parts where Christ speaks, but this Mormon doctrine seems a stretch.

Jesus, but I am far from home. And it's cold. And I keep

thinking of Troy Katchpole, who confessed his story to me late one night while half-drunk at a keg party. At first I thought he was making it up or getting intimate with me in some weird way, but then his face turned gray and he had to stop talking. I felt like I might have been the first one he'd confided in. He told me much about that night. Except for the missing arm, however, he never described the driver, and so over the years I've come to imagine him as a gaunt Merle Haggard just out of federal prison, a black cowboy hat on his head, shifting gears with his prosthesis and turning an occasional beam of approval on my sixteen-year-old friend. He must've been strong to overpower Troy, a football player and a wrestler. Or maybe he was charming or fatherly or seemed harmless with only the one arm. I imagine the motel room, the wall heater, the two beds, the mirror above the dresser, the humiliating image in that mirror. Maybe he got Troy while he was asleep. I wonder if he threatened him, perhaps with a knife or a gun. I wonder if the old pervert insisted on kissing. I can't decide what happened the following day, if the creep brought him breakfast or a box of chocolates or promised to write or left him bleeding on the mattress.

The snow is so dry in Utah you can brush it from your clothes like confetti. It should not be blowing like this early in October, and I know soon it will let up and the sun will break. I have enough money to get a motel room if necessary, but I'd prefer to save it for something more urgent.

Up ahead a black semi shimmers out of the snow. The driver —I can't see him through the windshield—is grabbing gears, downshifting fast, as if he's suddenly changed his mind. Soon there is a hiss of brakes, and then the black body of the truck slides right up next to me. Quaint. How quaint. The passenger door swings open. It's ridiculous to be superstitious, worse yet to refuse a ride in the middle of a snowstorm. I swallow a dry lump of dread, climb the steps, and swing myself up into the cab.

Uncannily the driver looks like a gaunt Merle Haggard just out of prison. He wears a scrappy beard over inflamed, pimply cheeks and a black cowboy hat angles down across his brow. This would be the *first* time I've ever been clairvoyant, though I note with relief that he has two good hands. "Convoy," the C.W. McCall hit from a few years back, is playing softly on the radio.

"Haddy," says Merle, staring at me with black expressionless eyes.

"Howdy," I say, pulling the door closed after me. "Thanks for picking me up."

"Thought you were a girl," he says.

I nod and adjust myself in the seat, which is hard as a board. "Must be hard to see in all this snow," I offer.

He digs around for a gear and we ease back out on the road. "Where you headed?" he says.

"East."

"Any place in particular east?"

"Far east as you're going," I say.

"Ain't going far east," he says. "I'm going to Cheyenne."

"Perfect," I say, staring straight ahead, almost wishing I had converted to Mormonism.

He fishes for gears and we gradually pick up speed. A VW 411 puttering in front of us looks as if it may be crushed under our wheels but Merle swerves out and passes it with a loathsome glance down. His CB begins to crackle. "Snake eyes, this is Jawl Boy, I'm still trollin', any luck yourself, come on back."

Merle ignores the chatter, finds another gear. Tom T. Hall is singing about how cold it is in Des Moines and I'm glad I'm not going to Des Moines, but it may be colder here, I tell Merle, who only offers me that dazzling black-eyed glare and I shut up.

I figure Cheyenne must be four hundred miles, and I'll be happy to have this leg of the trip behind me. Fifty miles pass amid the whirling, ghostlike snowflakes. I take a stab at the silence. "What are you hauling?"

"Oranges," he says, snapping the brim of his black Stetson.

"You coming from California?" (Why is my voice so high?).

"Yup. Haul steel out, bring oranges back. Goddamn fifty-five mile an hour."

I hate to think of California. Really, I never dreamed I'd leave. Not like this anyway.

We travel in stilted elevator silence for another fifty miles, the snow fluttering earnestly by, both of us looking down on the cars we pass. As we crawl up into Wyoming, I keep thinking of Mountain and wishing he'd decided to come. And for the thousandth time I wonder why Troy didn't fight the one-armed man.

Just before Green River, Wyoming, the snow starts tumbling out of the sky as if someone has slit the belly of a feather mattress with a knife. The truck splits the torrent before us, but I can see nothing ahead for more than a few feet and the snow is building on the road. We pass a dozen cars that have slid off into the ditch.

"Keeps snowing like this," Merle says, "we'll have to pull off."

My eyes are wide open now. I sit up straight and light another cigarette. To think that I could be in a warm dorm room now listening to records and eating a logger burger and studying my hokeypokey psychology and waiting for some girl to wiggle by. Did I leave that life of leisure *voluntarily*?

"I need to keep going," I say. "If you want, you can let me off at the next stop."

"Next stop is a motel," he says, gritting his teeth and shifting down as another car in front of us slides off the road. "Down here about three miles. We'll get us some beers and wait out the storm."

7.

IT'S SNOWING IN COLORADO SPRINGS WHEN PEGGY AND
Elaine, two cowgirls on the rodeo circuit from Cheyenne, drop
me off on Kiowa Avenue. My muscular, green-eyed companions
have been enticing, even frustratingly attractive company. I'm
afraid I have laid it on a bit thick, which I will do, especially with
women in pointed boots and tight jeans, but it's earned me curb-
side service and possible lodging at an unbeatable rate. Peggy
and Elaine's girlfriend, Gloria, or whatever her name is, has moved
away to Gunnison suddenly. She ran off with a bull rider, apparently. Still two weeks left on the rent. Peggy and Elaine insisted I
take the apartment since I've only got sixty-eight bucks and the
weather will only get worse as I head east. I was vaguely hoping
they might want to get a motel room together for a week or so
(there's one just up the street for eleven dollars a night), but they
have to be in Pueblo by three and to be honest I'm probably not
their type, the rodeo type, primitively dim with a ledge for a forehead and the ability to rassle an innocent animal to the dirt in 4.7
seconds, though I am obviously a recklessly charming world traveler and *bon vivant*.

It's cold outside, the curtain of winter has crashed early
upon Colorado, where I was born so long ago but of which I have
no memory. Neither do I have a heavy jacket. Clapping my
shoulders, I run up the dark stairs and find the key under the mat,
where Peggy said it would be. It fits. I push inside to the smell
of coal tar, horse urine, and burnt macaroons. Crude crayon horse

drawings and posters of men in various rodeo poses are tacked up all over the dark yellow walls, against which sit ancient garage-sale furniture packed in so tightly there's barely room to walk. Through the tiny kitchen I find a bedroom, even a bed—but the bathroom seems not to exist until I discover it out the kitchen door and across the community hall. Even if I have to share a bathroom, I still can't believe my luck. A free room! A bed! I run back down the stairs and give them the thumbs up. They smile at me from their idling, powder red Ford pickup.

"Do you want to come up for a beer or something?" I shout.

The flakes are floating down now big as butterflies. "Better get going before the roads get bad," Peggy shouts.

"Well, thanks again!" I yell. God, why didn't I ever learn how to rope a calf?

"Send us a postcard from Africa!"

I watch them pull away and disappear through a shivering curtain of giant, wobbling snowflakes.

Back up the musty stairwell I go. Eighty-five bucks a month and furnished. Even if the landlord decides he doesn't want to keep me (and why wouldn't he?), I'll still have a place to camp for a night or two. I can't believe I ended up in Colorado Springs. I know nothing about the place. Never been here, not consciously at least. I realize I've predicted the imminent demise of America, but it seems it will hold out for a few months at least, especially here toward the middle. When spring comes I'll head out again. My plan will be a little firmer then and I'll have worked up a stake.

I set my suitcase on the thin gray carpet, light a cigarette, and turn up the thermostat. The heat kicks on. I'm pleased. The refrigerator is empty except for a box of baking soda, a shriveled black onion, a cube of desiccated cream cheese, and a horsefly, heels up. I peek into the bedroom. No sheets or blankets, but the heat works, so I can sleep in extra clothes. Tomorrow I'll visit the Goodwill and also pick up a few items at the grocery store. I hope Gloria or whatever her name is doesn't change her mind or have a fight with the bull rider in their small trailer in Gunnison and decide to come back. Of course, maybe that would work out, especially if she crawls into bed with me and decides to stay. I close my eyes and smile.

I'm so tired I could fall asleep right here in this threadbare recliner, but I want to watch the snow flutter across the window for a while. It's a wonderful sensation being warm and free in a new place, where no one but two green-eyed cowgirls can find me, and no tattlers prowling the hallways or silly psychology classes in the morning. I wonder about fate, and then I think of God and the Chumleys, who gave me a ride from Elko and bought me two hamburgers cooked just the way I like them, crisp, almost burnt, with cheese and raw onions and a cup of hot coffee. And then the truck driver, Merle, whose real name was Curly. Curly had just divorced and was depressed. We played cribbage all night and drank canned Olympia and he talked despondently about his ex-wife and being alone. I told him about Mountain and how the divorce had ruined his mother. Divorce ruins everyone. The only winners in divorce are the lawyers, and all they get for their trouble is money, and a dream about money is a dream about shit. He liked all that. The next morning he took me on in through the snow to Cheyenne. I wish I'd thought to get his address. Curly was a good man. I'd never been so scared in all my life for nothing. No, I've had a lucky trip, almost as if someone were watching over me.

8.

IN THE MORNING I FILE AT UNEMPLOYMENT, WHERE I'M
sent five miles away to the magnificent five-star Broadmoor
Hotel, nestled in the foothills against the snow capped mountains.
I've never heard of this place. It's gorgeous, with a golf course
and a ski run and five restaurants. The personnel director glancing
over my application asks me if I'd prefer to be a kitchen runner
or work with the air-conditioning and heating team. I vote kitchen
job because it sounds warmer, plus probably a meal. What are the
odds of getting a job on your first try and then at a *five-star hotel*?
And the next morning I'm running trays of food up and down the
stairs, and I'm right about the free meal, schnitzel, peas and pearl
onions, and new potatoes in parsley and cream.

From work that afternoon I hitchhike straight to the King
Soopers on Uintah, then I stop at the liquor store. It's dark by the
time I get home, and I'm exhausted but I have a job, beer, beans
and franks, a roof over my head. And I love this little apartment.
When I open the screen door the creak of the hinge seems to
announce: "Here he is."

With my first paycheck I have a chat with Mr. Mondragon,
my surprised landlord (he didn't know Gloria had run off to
Gunnison with a bull rider) and manage to keep my one-bedroom
apartment, though I have to dish up another fifty for security.
Mondragon is pleased I'm employed at the Broadmoor. "Classy
joint," he says. "They pay pretty good, huh?"

"Not that well, no."

"How long you planning to stay?"

"Oh, I'll be leaving in the spring," I say.

"You don't like Colorado Springs?"

"I like it fine," I say. "But I'm a traveler."

He gives a savvy nod.

In the meantime, the weather has improved. And Colorado Springs—an undiscovered dulcimer village tucked into those lavender-smudged Rocky Mountains that have inspired so many poets such as John Denver—is quite tolerable. The job is a dead end, suitable for high school dropouts and teenagers with drug problems, but after only two weeks of my running food up and down the stairs from the main kitchen, a Tavern cook leaves and Chef Bruneaux, the Tavern chef, asks me if I'd like to take the cook's place. I'm elated. Plus there's a quarter-an-hour raise. I've always wanted to know how to cook.

And I seem to have a flair. I like the butter and the heat, the burns and sharp knives, the lunacy of the onslaught of waiters and waitresses during the rush, the shouting and desperation, the heavy, starched uniform and the puffy French hat. Except for the hat, cooking, I imagine, must be like war. Since most of the food is prepared upstairs and we merely spoon it back out of a steam table, omelets are the hardest detail to master. I'm a lunch cook, yes, but we make dozens of omelets daily, caviar and sour cream, Monterey jack and mushroom, Denver, bacon, avocado, shallot and crab omelets. It takes me about a week flipping scorched and runny eggs everywhere but back into the pan before I get good. At the right temperature the whipped egg and milk mixture foams up the pan sides like cake batter. Ferran, the executive chef, a waddling old French autocrat, looms over us. Rumor has it that any cook who even vaguely browns an omelet and dares to serve it will be dismissed. We've got these hot-handled steel French pans that you have to rub out with salt and half the time the eggs stick anyway, so I buy one of the first non-stick pans of the day, a T-Fal, and all the other cooks look upon me with reproach (see envy), but watch me flip that omelet without a snag or an oath every time.

Ferran grumbles, but he can't argue with a first-rate, cake-high, daisy yellow omelet. I'm more proud of my ability to make fabulous omelets than any A I ever got on a psychology exam.

Soon I'm transferred to dinner cook. Twenty-five cents more an hour and not so many omelets, but about as many tickets. The Tavern is the busiest of the five restaurants at the grand old Broadmoor. Our dining room (with the original Toulouse-Lautrecs hanging from the walls and Frank Fanelli and his Orchestra churning out the dance numbers live on stage) holds at least two hundred guests, and sometimes we turn the room over three times. Famous people come here too. A waiter will rush lisping into the kitchen, "Peggy Fleming is out there!" Not that I'm excited about celebrities, especially ice-skaters. As a matter of fact, I never leave the kitchen to look out over the glittering sea of wealthy diners. I don't admire the rich, who merely subjugate others for their comfort and amusement. I hold them responsible for the plight of America and the wastrel example they set for the rest of us. America is a corrupt and dissolving civilization whose pride has always been reserved for the wealthy and the famous, the so-called winners. I prefer the culture of poverty, from which all good things—humility, honesty, the words of Christ and Lincoln, rock music, and French onion soup—have evolved.

Dinner cook suits me. I can sleep late, stay up late, read books, lounge in front of the radio, make entries in my journal, sit in one of twenty pieces of furniture, and blow smoke rings at the ceiling. I've gotten into the habit of checking out three or four books a week from the library down the street. The gummy and lightweight ball of gossamer that passes for my brain has at long last, without the constant assault of recreational drugs, begun to awaken and reform. Late at night my noisy neighbors have all drifted off to sleep. When I was a friendless, asthmatic boy I used to sit in bed and read all night, my only pure satisfaction in life.

The only bad part about cooking the afternoon shift is hitch-hiking home in the dark. More than once I've had to walk. And coming to work I've been late a couple of times too. And now in

December it's getting cold. The winter snows have begun in earnest. I've tried to avoid it, but at last, reluctantly, I enter a car lot. I don't like cars. They're obscene contraptions, fossil-fuel furnaces. But I'm not going to hitchhike or walk anymore through the blizzards of midnight. I find a Fiat that I like. It's only a thousand bucks. It's a small car. It won't pollute too much.

The salesman is a ruddy man in a down jacket and green slacks who smells vigorously of cinnamon gum. He strolls over. "Nice car, huh?"

"Can I drive it?"

He positions his hands as if his thumbs are hooked into suspenders. "Key's in the ignition," he says.

This is my kind of car, I think, whipping it around the block. I've always seen myself, if I had to see myself in a car, in a European sports car. They're French, aren't they, Fiats?

In the salesman's office he creaks back in his chair, thumbs now hooked in the invisible suspenders of his Arrow sports shirt, and begins to amiably shake his head. "Can't sell you the Fiat," he says.

"Why not?"

"You got no credit. You been working only two months."

"What am I going to do?" I say, feeling tears well. "I need a car."

"Tell you what," he says, crossing his feet up on the desk and cradling the back of his head in his hands. "I'll sell you the Vega."

"The V E G A?" I look outside. A few flakes zigzag past the glass. I already saw the Vega. It's a Kaamback, a station wagon, and outside of a crumpled fender and a cracked windshield it isn't in bad shape, but I know that Vegas are terrible cars. The cocaine addicts who assemble them in Detroit put rocks in the wheel covers because they only make nine times an hour more than I do. "But I don't want the Vega," I say.

"Sorry," he says. "We'll finance you for the Vega but not the Fiat."

"How much is the Vega?"

"Thousand dollars."

"Same price as the Fiat," I say. "I don't get it."

"We'll extend you the credit," he says, "but you'll have to take the Vega."

I decide to take the Vega. I know after working only ten weeks with a job that pays only fifty cents over minimum that I'll be lucky to find anyone who will finance me. Anyway, I'm leaving soon. It won't matter. I sign on the dotted line and drive my Vega off the lot. It isn't so bad. Nice radio. Automatic transmission. Plaid vinyl seats. Two blocks out the driveway it dies. I stomp back to the lot. The flummoxed salesman has it towed back to the garage. "It's a gas-sending unit," he explains half an hour later, with a slap on my back. "You shouldn't have any more trouble with it."

"Right," I grumble, and I drive it away again, knowing I'll be back, knowing I've been screwed. They sold me the Vega because I was the only fool on earth who would buy it. A man with any backbone would've fought for the Fiat.

9.

THIS IS THE STRANGE PART ABOUT COLORADO SPRINGS:
I have made no friends yet. Usually I'm automatically social.
I come from that generation that uses drugs or "the party" as a
form of instant tribal cement. We are all brothers, pass that joint,
what was your name again? But I'm hesitant now. I'm suspicious
of my patterns, my lethargy, whimsy, and hypocrisy, my fear and
refusal to mature. If I make friends it will be the Tooley boys
all over again and I'll be running away shortly with no money to
a place I don't really want to go. I'll stop reading and thinking. I'll
lose sight of my goals, chief among them to master my consciousness. First I must read all the great books and acquaint myself
with their ideas. Second I must accumulate practical experience.
Third I must continue to travel and to pay attention to all that
goes on around me. Fourth I must take risks and not be afraid of
death, for consciousness, the very brain waves of the Creator,
even if lost for a moment in the pursuit of its promotion, will only
be restored to me again.

No, it is better to be alone. No more drugs or excessive drink.
I want to be an adult, intellectually complete, comfortable with
myself, with reliable friends who'll come to my birthday party.
Whatever associations I make from now on will be based upon word
and honor. It will take a while, I realize, to do all this: I have lost—
no, *wasted*—so much time.

More and more I think of my good friend, Mountain. My
parents (who are without explanation not angry about my running

away from school, because they apparently think this is some natural adventurous phase in the sequence that will somehow lead to success) reported that Mountain called looking for my whereabouts, and said they'd given him my address and work number. He has not written to me, however. I keep hoping to see him at my door. I'd write to him if I had his address, and if I wasn't saving money, I'd get a phone, just so I could talk with him.

When spring arrives I seem to have gathered little momentum to leave the country. I have over four hundred dollars in the bank, and my feelings about America haven't changed, but I wonder if four hundred is enough. Also I'm learning a trade. I've learned how to sharpen knives and make a roux, how to broil lobster tails and flambé. I don't know if I'll ever *enjoy* cooking professionally, but at least it's honest work. What does a lawyer do when he gets home, pull the wings off flies? When I get home I can cook anything I like. If I could pluck up the heart to ask a girl out on a date, I'd make her a nice meal. I don't know what's wrong with me. With my advance in sobriety, I seem to have retreated in confidence. Maybe I never *had* confidence. Maybe it was only the bogus bravado of *alcohol*.

And now the tourist season has begun. Summer and immeasurably busy nights are upon us. Tonight I am standing over a giant iron skillet, grease popping and burning my wrists as I flick stiff, glassy-eyed trout back and forth, waiting for that last trace of pink to leave the spine. The tourists never tire of rainbow trout meuniére, which is not trout in its own dung, but simply fried trout with brown butter and lemon. Chef Bruneaux regards me strangely as he informs me that I have a telephone call. No one ever calls me. He must think of me as a pitiful and inept loner. I wish I could explain it to him. Would he care if I were reading the complete works of Aristotle? Would he share with me his insights on Augustinian reflections on time and form? I wipe my hands down my apron and stride across the kitchen to answer the phone.

"Deadwood?" Mountain bellows, his voice wavering and crackling, as if he's calling me from a walkie-talkie.

"Mountain?" I shout back over the clank of dishes and bawling of waiters, my heart trilling. "Where *are* you?"

It sounds like he says Paris, but I can't make it out exactly.

"Where?" I shout, desperately jamming a finger in my ear.

Blythe, a waitress who is always slugging me in the shoulder, passes and threatens me with her pig knuckle of a fist. I would slug her back if I did not hope to sleep with her. Fortunately this is mistaken for chivalry. This is perhaps the essential microcosm of chivalry.

"You didn't get my *card*?" he says amid the tangle of crackle and fuzz.

"No!"

"Goddamn it. Hey, you were [*garbled*]." A whistling drowns his next few words. "[*Static*] out, man," he says. "I gotta [*place?*]. You'll love it."

I gesture at a passing waiter to let me use his pen. "Give me your address."

"Yeah, it's—"

The connection is lost.

10.

TWO NIGHTS LATER, RETURNING HOME FROM WORK, still forlorn over the mysterious whereabouts of Mountain Moses and wondering how I might be able to contact his father, I find a mangled postcard waiting for me in the mailbox. My breath stops in my chest. On the front of the card is a picture of a gorgeous tropical island with the seductively lovely name of Poisson Rouge. "Lose Your Cares on Poisson Rouge Isle," reads the legend across the bottom of the card. On the back are five words in careful, small print block letters: "I found your Paradise, Johnny." I flip the card hungrily over and over for more. No return address. No explanation of where the island is or how I might find it.

I am overcome by the fear that I will never have the courage of my convictions, and this blended with disenchantment and the prospect of a lifetime of line cooking melts quickly to resolve. This is the ticket out, the dawn, the door, the kind hunter opening the trap. I may only have one chance. The body's euphoria rises and begins to kindle and knock like good premium grade in the engine of a General Motors subcompact. I calculate my net worth: deposit back on my apartment, eight hundred blue book for dented, oil-burning, not-quite-paid-off Vega with 98,000 miles and cracked windshield, plus four hundred in my savings account equals ... not much.

My hands tremble as I read the summary from an encyclopedia from the Colorado Springs Library and learn that Mountain's Poisson Rouge is an island dependency of the USA.

USA? Why haven't I heard of it then? At a pay phone I call a travel agent, who gives me the eager pitch. Dollar the currency of the realm. No passport, smallpox vaccination, or visa required. Hit the bull's-eye and win a free teddy for your girl. "You'll love it there," he says. "They got white beaches and blue seas warm as swimming pools. Pretty black girls. They still bottle rum in an ancient stone distillery on the east side. You heard of the Mariner's Trove?"

"I'm not really looking for a tourist spot."

"Nobody knows about it yet. Only 3,700 people live there. Can't reach it by plane. You only got one hotel on the west side, and two thirds of the island is National Park. Can't touch it. Pretty rustic. Plenty of room if you want to roam."

"I'll call you back as soon as I sell my car," I say.

"We'll be here," he says.

Poisson Rouge has such a silky feeling on the tongue, like dahlia petals or the flesh of a tropical fruit. I will find myself a pretty black girl, settle into a hut on a beach, and write a novel, *Portrait of the Artist as a Young Mango*. Of all the beasts of the earth, Mountain is the only one who understands. Mountain knows. I must find him. I want to call him, tell him not to leave. I need to move fast, before he decides to mistakenly return to the plagued and merciless shores of the USA.

11.

NOBODY SEEMS TO WANT A VEGA, ESPECIALLY ONE THAT so bigheartedly burns oil and (why didn't I examine it more closely upon purchase?) has obviously been in a wreck. The few who come to look at it offer me peanuts for it, junker prices. That isn't enough to buy my TICKET, I want to explain. Look, they say, the windshield's cracked. It looks like somebody *rolled* the thing. I'll have to get new tires for it. How much oil does it burn? (Only about a quart every time I fill it up, I concede.) But eventually a man who knows very little about cars offers me four hundred (I'm asking six) and I sign it over to him before he can change his mind, cracked windshield, crumpled hood, Gumby doll still folded obscenely in the glove box, and a half-case of Quaker State thrown in for good measure.

I should be giddy at the prospect of my lifelong adult dream of escape from America coming true and the chance to recon-struct and master my consciousness in the garden where my inno-cence was lost, not to mention meeting up with Mountain again, but instead, from the moment my plane lifts from the tarmac of Stapleton Airport, I am unable to quell this whirligig of dull panic suspended just above my diaphragm. I feel as if I am making some grave and irreversible error. It isn't that I've spent all my money on a pipe dream or the possibility that the island may be a bust or that I continue to take risks without reward as if some firm, cata-strophic pattern beyond my ken is in place. It's something about that damn island, an unshakable foreboding, an instinct that foul play awaits. If something goes awry, I won't have the money to bail out. If I'd picked the place myself, made plans, saved more money, it would be different. The lurking premonition of doom blossoms into full-lipped certitude as the nose of the plane breaks through its first membrane of clouds. Ridiculous, I think, trying to shake it off. The inevitable traveling-alone-to-a-strange-new-place jitters. Too late to turn back anyway. I've got $232.32.

In the round decorative mirrors adhered to the hat of the old woman sitting next to me I catch several greenish, wincing reflections of myself.

"First time flying?" she says.

"No," I say.

"If you're going to be sick," she says, jingling her mirrors, "they have the bags in the pouches in front of you."

"Thank you," I say, smoothing the wrinkles on my shirt. "I'm not sick. Just a bit nervous."

She studies me with a mixture of pity and concern. "Where are you going?"

"Poisson Rouge."

"What is that?"

"It's a tropical island in the Caribbean."

"Oh really?" she says, revolving her mirrors. "Are you on vacation?"

"No, I have a home there, a wife. I'm a geologist."

Her eyebrows levitate above the frames of her glasses. "You seem young to be a geologist."

"I got my GED when I was sixteen," I say, beginning to leaf through the seat pocket before me, looking for that airsickness bag. Instead I find a *Rocky Mountain News* folded back to a page-three article about a girl who killed her boyfriend in Florida and disappeared. Now they're looking for two other missing boyfriends. I study the grainy photo of the murderess. She looks like a man. Her name is Janie Flame. In green ballpoint ink in a distinctly feminine hand, someone has written, "Go Janie Go." This is exactly the sort of thing I'm leaving, the formal rules of selfishness, ritualized enmity between the sexes, a society that turns its monsters into pop stars. I return the article. The old woman stares at me. I realize I should not have told her I was nervous if I was returning *home*. I need to stop misrepresenting myself so liberally. It's time to stop being ashamed of what I am. I'm ashamed of myself for being rude, for compounding the problem. Thankfully the stewardess is almost upon us with her cocktail wagon.

12.

I FLY FOR TWO DAYS IN A DARK GREEN FUNK. GOODBYE, Atlanta. Good riddance, Miami. The stewardesses driving their little cocktail wagons seem like old friends, my only allies against the New World Order. And then the continent is suddenly gone and I am in the airport in San Juan, Puerto Rico, amid that faint diarrhea-and-leather smell, the urchins on me like flies, the chaos, the poverty, the humidity, the rust, the whirling vectors of tropical disease, beriberi and elephantiasis, and my stomach roiling and pitching. It feels like a bile sac. My skin is a dry rash of puckered follicles. I think I might get hives. Through the looking glass, new language, no one knows how to wait in line.

At baggage claim one of my suitcases comes down the chute in an unzipped pile, my underwear strewn across the conveyor belt behind it. Humiliated, I scramble after my belongings. An airport employee in a blue blazer with gold epaulets who speaks crisp Caribbean English taps me on the shoulder and suggests I try the casinos. I glare at him. What kind of twit does he take me for? Doesn't he know what Freud said: "A dream about money is a dream about *shit*"? This is not spring break or carnival. I am not some bumpkin in his Bermudas in search of mai tais and a suntan. This is not a *game*. This is not a vacation. He's lucky I don't produce my French knife. It's ten inches of razor blade. Is it here? Yes, thank goodness it wasn't stolen. I zip up my bag and dash to catch the next flight. Soon this will be all over, I tell myself. Soon I will stop running and start living. I really hate this trip.

The thought of rejoining Mountain and the stewardesses blithely navigating their cocktail wagons are my only comfort.

Soon, however, there are no more stewardesses. Only angry, jabbering pilots with shredded cigars crammed into their faces. They leave the cockpit doors open, make no announcements, and swig vengefully from metal flasks. The sea grows bluer and then impossibly blue. I deboard my last plane and ride in a cab through a disturbing forest. The definition of civilization blurs.

It is late afternoon when the four o'clock ferry bumps against the dock of Poisson Rouge, a mist-wrapped volcano cooling in a crème de menthe sea. It is very much the picture postcard that Mountain sent me, though larger than my encyclopedia study led me to believe. This is my new home. I envision myself in loincloth with a machete, a fire on the beach, the riddles of life unraveling, the clear and benevolent eyes of God smiling down. The sun is setting. The waves skim up the silver sand to crisp against my ankles. A pot of clams and wild potatoes steams upon the fire.

Now at once there is a tumult, people scraping baggage and slapping on hats. Four yammering men jump over the rails with ropes. I stand to disembark. My legs and stomach begin to throb from dread. Normally I enjoy traveling. It's the arriving part that doesn't agree with me. I shuffle trancelike down the dock, a bag in each hand, Mountain's weathered postcard in my back pocket. No one pays me any mind. The sun on my skin is kingly and indolent as oil. The air is as heavy as the warm towel the barber lays over your face before he brings out the razor.

Before my eyes can assemble a complete picture of the world I am about to enter, black clouds suddenly form out of nowhere and cover the sun. I know that it will not rain. According to the several detailed pieces I read about this island, outside of the monsoon season several months away, this is a comparatively dry landmass, with even cacti flourishing in the more arid spots. My forecast complete, the sky rips open and the rains smashes down. Everyone dashes for cover. I huddle cold against a crude, three-color mural of an angry African face painted on the stucco wall of Meng's Sail and Scuba Rental, the rain clanking and plonking off the shelf of corrugated roof above my head.

All my fellow passengers are picked up by friends or the hotel shuttle, or whisked away by cabs. Before long I am the last remaining member of the ferry crowd. Now I will find Mountain. Though I have no idea where he might be, he should be easy to find. Broad-shouldered and tall, with that jaunty honker and those jolly blue eyes, he will stand out like Charlemagne among these mostly shorter black natives. There are only 3,700 inhabitants on the whole island, and three thousand of them live in this enchanting bay town. The minute I ask someone he will say, Oh yes, Mountain Moses. He lives over on such and such.

As quickly as the rain came it is gone. The sun lazily reclaims the sky. I heft my bags and stroll into the shady, still-damp plaza to rest on one of the wooden benches next to a stone drinking fountain whose sluggish jet tastes of sow bugs and moss. Under the cool mahogany trees I am grateful for a chance to collect my thoughts and catalog the town square: the scuba rental place, a small customs booth, an info booth, a duty-free shop, a post office, a gift shop, and hallelujah: a bar called Harry's. If the drinks are cheap at Harry's, I think the odds of finding Mountain there are very good. And no sense in leaving the matter in suspense. I leave my bags on the bench and saunter over.

Harry's is early Tijuana, stucco and corrugated iron roof, but when you step inside it is more the flavor of an English pub, with long tables full of blond yachting youths and native men slapping down domino tiles with malicious grins. The bar itself faces a long, bamboo-framed, green-tinted window that overlooks the bay. There is no sign of Mountain, inside or out. I resist perching for a quick drink or three, although I realize the calming effect of the alcohol may be invaluable. I ask the barman if he knows of a Mountain Moses. He lifts his chin at me as if I have recited something enthusiastically from *101 Dalmatians*. "Don't know 'im," he says.

"Thank you," I say. "I'll be back."

I return to my baggage. I feel briskly the fool and definitively alien, my stomach shriveled to the size of a pea. This is perfectly inane, not at all what I planned, a tourist trap in the middle of the Barbarian Sea. The rent on a single apartment up on that hill probably exceeds what I would pay for twelve beachfront apartments in Solana Beach. But Mountain, I suspect, has found something better, cheaper anyway. He will have answers. I feel compelled to speak with him this moment.

Down by the waterfront at the edge of the plaza I spy a pay phone on a pole. The bay is packed with sailboats, a shrimper, a trawler, a few yachts, a small freighter, one pleasure cruiser plowing its way toward the dots of land west. The clouds hang like prison towers in the sky. I look all around the pay phone. No book. I think of calling information. The glyphs in the front of the phone are indecipherable. In any case, the telephone is rarely a solution to a problem, only a connection to more problems, which in turn only create more problems. I resign the possibility with relief. Mountain, I know, would not have a phone anyway.

13.

FOR ANOTHER HOUR I SIT INERTLY BEMUSED IN THE lengthening shade of the mahogany trees. People are beginning to stare at me: a man gets off the ferry and sits in the plaza with his bags in the rain like a lunatic or a bum. He is either lost or unloved. Got the wrong island. Maybe he is looking for Mountain Moses, who writes prank postcards from San Diego, California. I rise finally and begin to ask around. I feel like a homeless person begging for quarters. Do you know where Mountain Moses lives? He is a big man, a black-haired, big-eared, toothy man, nose like Kilimanjaro and mad blue eyes. He's a chuckling, enigmatic, brawling, bashful, chess-playing man who talks about the ratio of the ordinate to the abscissa of the endpoint of an arc of a unit and dreams of finding gold. No, I don't know which side of the island he lives on. You must know him. I ask the man in customs, the sleepy misanthropic woman in the tourist info booth, a taxicab driver. From the looks I get, I might be asking the where-abouts of Nanook the Eskimo.

It begins to occur to me that I must have the wrong island. People would *know* Mountain. Unless they were keeping a secret. Unless he were in hiding. Or in trouble. Jailed. Perhaps he has left the island already? No, it's likely he was never here in the first place. He found the postcard in a San Diego coffee shop, smudged the postmark, and shot it off for a practical joke. No, again, not Mountain's style. Bar fighting and girl-obsession problems aside, he is a noble soul. The fact is, he would not be expecting me.

Because of the aborted phone call he would have no idea I was coming.

It rains on me several more times. Besides being wet, I am hungry and tired. The time is past for action. I see a taxi and run toward it, waving my arms. The driver is friendly, with stiff-fingered Joe Cocker hands that fly about as he speaks. I ask him about Mountain. He shakes his head and speaks in his wonderful, fast-talking, backward-accented Caribbean lilt. I lean down and strain to sort it out, plucking out recognizable syllables and trying to jigsaw them together. I think he might be deliberately trying to confuse me, as I did often with strangers as a child.

I gather that he has never heard of Mountain.

"Can you recommend a place to stay for a night or two?" I ask.

Amid more of the songlike gibberish, I am grateful to recognize the word *Rockefeller.*

"How much is that?" I say.

"Two hundred dollah a night." He laughs. His eyes shine.

"That's all the money I've *got,*" I tell him.

Turning almost completely around in his seat, he utters a few remarks that I accept as sympathetic. I nod at him glassy-eyed, hoping an affirmative will cover it. We are brothers after all, sons of Adam, sons of commerce. I resist explaining to him that I plan eventually to return to the wilderness to be at one with nature. He drops the taxi in gear and starts away.

"I hoped to find my friend," I tell him despondently, looking down into the checkered green lawn of the Queen's Park Cricket Grounds.

"Come on, Bob," he says with an encouraging nod, pointing up through the windshield, where the road tilts up past a run-down Esso station and disappears into a hole in the jungle. "Dot de Cross-Eye-Lan Row. Every ting cheapah up dis way."

The road is rougher than it looks, or the shocks in the cab have been removed. He drives as if he is getting up speed for a double suicide. I notice there is no meter. A rabbit's foot dangles from the rearview mirror. Like every motor-vehicle operator on the island, he drives on what I consider to be the wrong side of the road. According to the Colorado Springs *Encyclopedia*, this island was originally claimed by the French, then lost to the British, who installed their culture before selling it to the Dutch, who in turn resigned it to the U S A when the abolition of slavery made the operation of sugar plantations untenable. We pass the Esso station. A liter of gas is $1.29, making it nigh on $4 a gallon. Just before the road vanishes into the jungle, he jerks the wheel and swings off onto a cluttered path, dodging an oxidized refrigerator and a tabby kitten, then stopping all at once in front of a red-roofed two-story house with a gray coral stone exterior and white bougainvillea crawling up the side.

"Maul-veen," he says, in explanation. "She lib aroun' de bock dare. Telluh Alvin back loud." He smiles at me.

I prolong the pantomime of understanding and pay him a dollar over the fare. I want these people to know that I am a Democrat, a civil rights enthusiast, that I voted for the only black kid in our neighborhood for school president, that I am an undying admirer of Martin Luther King, and that the definition of the White Man's Burden is taking complete responsibility for everything that happened to the black man since the Portuguese landed on the Gold Coast in 1649. If *ever* I use the word "nigger" it is only when I'm quoting Richard Pryor or Mark Twain.

I drag my bags off the seat and slam the door. It rains. Alvin waves out the window, swings his crate of a taxi around, and clatters away.

Around the side of the gray coral stone house a garden has failed, or rather, a larger garden has prevailed. The walkway is overgrown with giant ferns and elephant grass waist high. Two skinny chickens dash out in front of me before whirling back into the thicket. A red-throated lizard flicks his tail and skitters away. I find the front door, on the porch of which sit three clay pots with pink, white, and black anthoriums, a Boone's Farm wine bottle, a dissolving cannonball, a ship's anchor, and an arrangement of speckled cowries and conches. Inscribed in the wooden lifesaver tied with white-painted nautical rope to the door are the words: GLADYS HOOKS' BLUE HAVEN INN.

"My Blue Haven," I mutter, preparing to knock, when a wiry little oil derrick of a mosquito squats on my forearm and promptly begins to drill. I splatter her. Another touches down, then a third. They land fearlessly, without hesitation, without even strategic approach, as if each is infinitely confident in its inexhaustible membership. I smack them as they come, prepared to take on the entire army.

In the middle of slapping myself silly, a dour old woman with crimped, tumbling gray-blue hair opens the door.

"Hi," I say, now nearly concealed in a tornado of ravenous mosquitoes. "I heard you have rooms available."

"Dot right, young mon." She looks me up and down, nostrils flaring, as if I am meat and selling myself by the pound. The mosquitoes do not disturb her. She has no lilting, beautiful, backward-accented words for me. I suppose that the average tourist does not make it this far. You have to tell the cab driver your entire life savings isn't enough for a single night at the big hotel.

"Ten dollah," she says, and I pay her.

"Numbuh tree," she says, giving me a key and a jerk of the head to indicate the general direction of number three. The door closes.

I look about, slap my arms, then hurry down the hill about three hundred feet to the cluster of metal-roofed huts her head-jerk indicated. The key fits in the door of number three. I push inside. The room has a bed and dresser and desk, its own bathroom. For ten dollah, very nice. The floor is cool, bare cement. The windows are tightly screened, like a good prison or insane asylum should be. The multitudinous bloodsuckers hump and hover against the tight screens, singing me high-pitched, tropical love ditties. Here is one group, at least, who are happy to see me. I run the faucet in the bathroom. There are no chips of wrapped perfumed soap, no taut sanitary ribbon across the toilet bowl. I light a cigarette and lean in the doorway. The smoke hangs like wet blue plaster in the air. I write my name inside it, *Edgar Donahoe*, and then return as the letters linger to add a question mark.

The mattress is firm but I am too tired and anxious to nap. If time is money then life is shorter than I thought. Ten bucks a night even if I don't eat, I'm out of cash in twenty days. And if I can't find Mountain I'll need an alternate plan quick. Too bad I don't have one. I wash my face and change my shirt and walk back down into town, where up close I see my first two Rastafarians, crabby black hippies playing reggae songs about Bob-eel-on on their boom boxes. Across the way is the fastidiously manicured cricket field called the Queen's Park Cricket Grounds. A game has just ended. I catch myself disapproving of cricket, thinking that baseball is proof of evolution, and then decide to quit being a snob and learn the game, when I notice a crazy, almost naked, and extremely bowlegged man no taller than a barrel of pickles, with a machete on his hip, arguing with a taller man in blue-and-white cricket silks with a Bible clamped under his arm. I cannot make out what is being said, but the conflict appears to be over religion and has risen to such a pitch I think the men will come to blows. I move closer, my betting instincts whetted. I would definitely wager on the crazy one with the knife. But the Bible carrier is ultracalm in his cool cricket silks.

"Do you know what *amen* mean?" he is saying.

"I'm not out of dat," spits the savage one.

The cricket-dressed Christian says: "It mean 'so let it be.'"

The bandy-legged one winces at this. He seems to be made of mud. His eyes are red as a bull's. The muscles on his right arm flex as if he is about to free his blade and lay his adversary out like a ring bologna. He growls a gutteral reply.

"Ode it now, Chollie Legion," someone calls with an almost affectionate snicker from out of the crowd.

"Dot right. Yer too close to de church."

Civilized Man keeps his chest thrust out, his chin high, like the posture of virile courage I have seen in history books depicting

British redcoats being shot down like ducks in a gallery. The man believes his faith will triumph. How quaint he would be in America. And how probably dead in the gutter.

Nevertheless, the bowlegged one finally climbs down off his toes in a disappointing shudder of sneezes and barks, and struts away, looking very much like an offended bulldog, his machete wagging mightily, a ripple of relieved laughter and head-shaking in his wake. The Rastafarians, not deigning to acknowledge the contest, move imperiously down the road among the pink and flowery tourists. "You ah fouling up de I-lawn," warns the reggae song ringing from their box.

I rest for a minute in the plaza, wondering which side was right. Though I admire Christianity in principle and on a number of occasions have tried to practice it, I have not trusted it fully since my first encounter with a televangelist at the age of five. I have known some real Christians, but most of them are frauds and hypocrites, spreading the gospel among the heathen while sinning opulently behind the duck blind of their pious conceit. Perhaps the bowlegged one wields the truth or is merely punished for being different or disfigured. I know that things are not always as they seem—no, let me clarify: things are often the *opposite* of what they originally seem.

It is evening, magical in beauty. The sun has tangled itself in the sails of the boats out in the bay. I buy a johnnycake and a semicool Old Milwaukee from the woman in the portable booth above the plaza and sit at a sticky picnic table equipped with a giant bottle of hot sauce. The johnnycakes, only 80¢, are simply fried, unleavened flour. Mosquitoes descend. I pour hot sauce all over my johnnycake. The hot sauce gives me the hiccups. A sign across the street cheerfully announces the construction of a Chase Manhattan Bank. The Rockefellers are sewing up the island. San Diego is already the sixth borough of New York City. The Caribbean will soon be the seventh. I get the feeling that the bowlegged one is fighting on the right side, a pagan, a naturalist, a purist, an environmentalist, a Rousseau, a Thoreau. Perhaps I have found an ally.

I ask the woman standing in her hot little booth about Mountain. You can hear the grease in the vat crickle and crack as the smoke pours up between the frying baskets. The sweat drips down her forehead. She shakes her head, popping out a fat bottom lip. My question not only fails to yield even scanty results, but seems to produce within my listener genuine melancholia. Perhaps Mountain has a role in the construction of that bank building across the street. I hiccup and tell myself everything will be O K. The best journeys always start out rough. Soon I will find my trail down into that gentle meadow. When Columbus came to these isles for "the riches of the Orient" half a millennium ago, he missed his mark by more than six thousand miles, yet he returned three more times before finally dying here. I will find Mountain eventually, and he will fix everything. This is a gut-felt certitude I cannot explain. It rains on me. I finish my Old Milwaukee and trudge back up the road to Gladys Hooks' Blue Haven Inn.

14.

IN THE MIDDLE OF THE NIGHT I WAKE UP SEIZED BY
asthma. I have not had an attack like this since I was a child.
It feels as if an octopus has mistaken me for a mollusk. I have no
medication. I walk outside in the dark and try to recover my
breath on the front steps. The air is so thick and wet you have to
be a fish to get the oxygen out of it. The insects scream and the
frogs, like half-witted sidekicks, cheer *gar–rup gar–rup*. I glance
to the jungle and understand that the cause of the attack is fear.

In the morning I crush my package of cigarettes into a ball
and drop them with a satisfying plunk into the metal trash can.
I am a natural man now with no use for dirty habits. I wander down
through town again, feeling more futile and alien than ever. The
sense of not belonging here is now overpowering. Around noon, I
return to the bar called Harry's, hoping to find Mountain. I take a
stool next to a jewel-decked woman in a sailor suit and sneakers,
who ignores me, and order a bottle of beer. A red-legged, potbellied man in a pith helmet down at the end is bragging about a
thirty-pound wahoo. Through the tinted window all the sails
of the boats in the bay are pink. A television is snowing green up
in the corner next to the stuffed remains of an enraged-looking
fish in the form of a spiked balloon. An unruly blue parrot
squawks from the top of the door, through which everyone on the
island appears to pass except Mountain. There are ships' em-
blems and cricket plaques all over the walls. I study a framed verse
from my father's era:

I'M NOT DRUNK.

Starkle, Starkle little Twink,
Who the hell you are I think
I'm not as drunk as some
Thinkle peep I am
Besides I've only had ten martonis
And anyway I've got all day
Sober to Sunday up in.
I fool so feelsh, I don't know
Who's me yet
But the drunker I sit here
The longer I get.

I nurse two more frosty bottles of Red Stripe than I can
afford, glancing at the door every forty-five seconds, certain that
Mountain will appear. No one speaks to me or asks me of my
whereabouts or intentions. Not a soul yet except for Alvin in his
taxicab has endeavored to make me feel welcome. I'm certain
it's my mood, combined with my class, and I know I am giving off
these I-don't-belong rays. Finally I tear myself away to go sit in
the plaza again under the mahogany trees, where I know Mountain
has just passed after picking up supplies and has returned for
the month to his tepee on the remotest part of the island. I congratulate myself because I've quit smoking for good, but then
I feel depressed because I have $178 and I am an imbecile. I watch
the ferry dock and unload its glazed cargo. The white people who
live here are the least friendly of all the residents and I make it a
point not to be numbered among them.

Two unmarked roads intersect the middle of town. I have
time to kill but I don't want to take the road that will return me
to Gladys Hooks' before it disappears into the forbidden forest, the
Road Less Traveled for a Jolly Good Reason. Eventually I'll have
to take this road, I know, which will one day soon lead to loin-
cloths, roasted wild piglets, and sweet, barbarous freedom. But
for now I follow the crowd up the safe tourist route lined with

shops, restaurants, a nightclub, a bakery, and a vulgarity called
Saul Schwartz's Rent-a-Thing, silver-and-green tinsel and
colored plastic banners flapping from twine strung between light
posts. "Things" are all-terrain convertible Volkswagens, squarish
and military-looking, manufactured in Brazil. A man wearing
a Saul Schwartz Rent-A-Thing T-shirt with a palm tree on it sits
across the street on the shady deck of a fancy, driftwood Swiss-
Family-Robinson-theme restaurant sipping on a Heineken.
I think it must be Saul himself, for who else would wear such an
obnoxious shirt? I have no great admiration for Rent-a-Car men,
but sitting on the patio of a driftwood club carelessly watching
the sailboats and sipping a Heineken seems exactly the right thing
to be doing. Two jovial young native men in flip-flops nod at me.
"Ah right," they say, with a bob of the head as they pass. The
natives say "ah right," coming or going, hello, good-bye, how ya
doin', thank you, or I'm just fine. It's a bigger word than *Aloha*.
"Ah right," I answer back. And then all the way up the hill I am saying, "Ah right" and feeling a little less out of place.

Nearly two miles up the road (ah right ah right) is the Rockefeller Plantation, off limits to the poor unless you are entering
uniformed through the back door. I am amazed that they have the
nerve to call this resort a "plantation." It must be staffed 90
percent by blacks, ex–slaves still working the Plantation. I turn on
my heel and trudge back toward home. Where is paradise?
I wonder: the fruit trees, the beach huts, the self-sufficiency, the
smiling, carefree natives, the rejection of four-slice toasters
and Best Western values? No wonder Mountain doesn't live in
town. He is in a cave on the beach, seminomadic, fishing and
eating red bananas and studying his treasure maps. I tell myself
with darkening, deepening doubt that I will find him and he will
reveal to me all the answers.

Ah right, one more night at Gladys Hooks, though Malveen
seems less pleased about taking my money than the night before.
The more I study her the more she looks, with her billowy, kooky
blue hair and those nostrils flared in indignant Southern pride,

like an elderly Bette Davis. She reminds me of all the people I have known in the States who worked a lifetime to accumulate money only to discover that they wasted their lives accumulating money. She actually has the audacity to doubt my ability to pay another night. Just because I'm *poor*, I'd like to tell her, doesn't mean I'm cheap or irresponsible. And I hope you enjoyed pushing Joan Crawford down the stairs.

In the late afternoon, merely killing time between rainstorms, I stroll down to the market below the Catholic church, where a large woman in a gigantic pajama dress stands behind a low counter waving a souvenir bamboo fan under her chin. A dust-clogged electric fan burrs ineffectually in the corner. The floor is crinkled gray linoleum. Many of the items on the shelves are drearily familiar: Campbell's soup, Dinty Moore stew, oval tins of Spanish sardines in tomato sauce, boxes of powdered milk, tampons, insecticide, clothespins. Except for rum, the prices are astronomical. Four dollars for a can of soup. A week-old N Y *Times* is $3. But who needs news? And I can make a fire with kindling, and soup with garden carrots and onions and the fish I caught in my own net this morning.

Off to the left, past a few wicker panels of straw hats, is a dirt-floor room with limp vegetables sitting in cardboard boxes on wooden shelves. Each overripe tomato has its own personal solar system of fruit flies. The heads of lettuce are flat and limp as if dropped from tall buildings. You can tie the carrots in a knot with the celery and make a new vegetable, carrolry.

"Where do you get the vegetables?" I ask the woman in the gigantic pajama dress.

"De ship comb every Winz-day," she replies and I chalk up a reluctant point for the industrial complex, even in decline. The soil here cannot be unsuitable for garden vegetables, I think. After all, it was fairly recently a series of plantations. Volcanic earth is notoriously rich, yes? I should have some fruit, something with vitamin A, but the vegetables are about as appetizing as something tipped out of a dumpster. The room has a heavy, wearisome air, dusty, concentrated, third-world sunshine, perpetuity, the veil of mystery lifted too many times. I understand suddenly why no one writes great opera in the tropics. There are three kinds of beer for sale: Old Mil, Bud, and Heineken. I buy a pack of Buds, not realizing that the Heinekens are the same price. Pajama Woman has no ice for sale.

I drink the beers warm in my room until I can laugh at my predicament. The gallinippers bumble and hump against the screens, homesick for my platelets. The rain switches off and on, thrumming the metal roof. The Rastafarians pass with their box booming: *Ommy Ommy go-een bock to Bob-ee-lon*. After the fourth beer I become nostalgic. Five and six make me think of a small-breasted scientologist I once knew in the biblical sense in the brief time I was in junior college studying art history. I wonder where she is now, married I hope, clear, smoking a bit less. I wonder if she'd like to come visit me here. I bet we could make a go of it. Great sense of humor that girl, tremendous thigh muscles too.

I fall asleep for two hours and wake up hot and cross as a crab in a pot of boiling lemons. A stroll into town makes the situation seem thoroughly hopeless. The tiny bay community looks like a broken-down carnival that should've moved on ten years ago. A mangy dog snaps up an abandoned johnnycake out of the gutter and quickly begins to sneeze from the hot sauce. A sultry young blonde smiles as she leans against a post waiting for some-one, but she doesn't seem to notice me. A pickup truck full of smelly, piebald goats passes. It's been a long time since I've felt like sitting down and crying. Fear dissolves to disgust. I sleep poorly that night but the asthma does not return.

15.

ON THE THIRD DAY OF THIS HERCULEAN LABOR TRYING to find Mountain Moses, I decide to leave the island. Outside of my Tarzan vision the only remaining beauty of the trip was my imagining of the expression on Mountain's face when I would knock on his door. But Mountain is not here. True, I could go off on my own, sleep in the jungle and live off mangoes and clams and hunt wild goats in my loincloth—I know I could—but I'm just not ready yet. I need a little transition time. Unless there's been a plane crash or a serious prescription problem, a man cannot simply leave the city, walk straight off into the trees, strip off his clothes, and return to his ancestors.

In the meantime, I must face facts. The only job would be as a cook in that classist resort a mile and a half away, and I'm not going to work there. I'm not going to simply transplant my urban life against a pretty postcard. Time to cut my losses. If I have to return to civilization temporarily it will be the next island over, Ravissant, a crime-riddled tourist trap with a twenty four-hour disco station. It won't be paradise, but then I won't have to torture myself with pristine vistas and the rent will be cheaper. I can get a job, save money, and then regroup. My feeling is that there is a better, more-primitive island somewhere close by.

So I pack my bags, return the key to the implacable Malveen Hooks (where is Gladys, anyway?), and with fresh trepidation percolating in my stomach stroll down to the dirt-floor market and buy a package of cigarettes. I smoke one, feel better, then smoke another and regret it. You take a drug and when it wears off nothing has changed except you feel a little worse. I mope in the plaza, lighting cigarettes and waiting for the four o'clock ferry. A black man on a rusty bicycle does a rickety rum-drunk tour around the plaza, the backs of his tennis shoes cut away like bedroom slippers. The sailboats out there and the magnificent color of the sea and the big scudding clouds look like a calendar photo pinned to an outhouse wall.

I stare straight ahead, sand-blind with inner loathing, trying to imagine a future that isn't a hole. Why does every decision I make fall flat on its face? Why does every dream I undertake dissolve like a sugar cube in the rain? To come this far and risk so much for NOTHING. I'd like to tear my money into little bits. I'd like to fall over off the bench and throw a fit. If I wasn't out in public I would punch myself in the nose. Idly my misted eyeballs follow a tall, wide-shouldered, long-haired man down by the pay phone. He wears a red-and-white checkered shirt that seems familiar. It appears that one of the sleeves is ripped. Though the figure seems too curly-headed and thin, I am struck with an irrational, heart-bouncing thought: Is this Mountain Moses at last?

Could it *be*? The ferry is coasting into harbor. If I don't catch this one, I stay another day, sprinkle another thirty dollars into the void. I fling my cigarette aside and stride across the plaza. My heart begins to bang against my rib cage. Everything about this figure outside his ranginess (look at the bone on the elbows there) is uncannily like Mountain. I reach up, defying good manners (my eyes and mind ravished in *idée fixe*), and put my hand on one of the great shoulders. The figure turns.

Mountain's placid blue eyes bug out of his head. "My God!" he bellows.

"Mountain!" I squeak, with the relief of a child reunited after being lost for hours in the mall.

Mountain thrusts out his hand. "Hot puppies!" he crows, showing me the great gap between his front teeth. "Deadwood Donahoe. How'd you find me?"

"I was just in the neighborhood," I peep, clenching his big hand and swallowing back a rack of insane hiccups, "and I thought I'd drop in."

"Goddamn it, if I had my pistols with me I'd shoot them in the air," he booms, whacking me across the shoulder. "How did you *get* here?"

"By land and by sea," I say, blinking deliriously. "Took me three days."

Those cheerful blue eyes, the great crooked nose poised above that split in his grin—it's the most welcome sight I've had in years. He wears a scrappy beard now and his hair, uncut for months, falls in every direction, the big ears like rubber flaps sticking out from the sides of his head. "You come to visit or you come to *stay*?"

"I don't know," I answer with genuine confusion. "What about you?"

"You kidding?" He pounds me on the back again. "Check the signpost up ahead. You just entered PARADISE, man. How did you *find* me anyway? These goddamn phones. I tried to call you back."

"I just guessed," I reply modestly. "I finally got your card. Actually, I was about to get on the ferry and leave."

"Leave?" He jerks his thumb at the pay phone. "I was just trying to get an oil pump from Ravissant. The phone is still out."

A dark-haired girl lingers a few feet away, watching the sailboats in the bay. She turns, arms crossed, as if she is cold. It is eighty degrees out at least and windless. She is wearing blue Bermuda shorts and a dark blue polo shirt. She seems ambivalent about my appearance, the degree of risk I've taken, the distance I've traveled, and the stupid luck of an oil pump. She is late twenties, I guess. She has a plain, troubled face and one dimly rust-stained front tooth. Her ears stick out slightly from a mass of black hair cut in the style of Huckleberry Finn. A mole above her upper lip reminds me of a chocolate chip. I dread the thought of her being Mountain's girlfriend. I won't be able to stay with them if

she is. She seems a bit old for Mountain anyway, but then again
he likes his women in all colors and brands, as long as they aren't
barflies like his mom. "This here's Kate," he says, and my heart
sinks as I see that familiar look of obedient devotion suddenly
drain his expression. "Kate, this is Deadwood Donahoe, old school
chum of mine."

"Hi," she says, with a vague and distracted nod.

"How do you do?" I say, bowing my head.

"He quit school a week before I did," Mountain adds, looking
down upon me as if I taught him everything he knows.

"You quit too?" I say.

"Yeah, Refried Clyde went and broke his nose on my fist a
few nights after you left." Mountain studies his hand for a moment
as if he were shocked by its behavior. "How long you been here
anyway?"

"Three days."

"Three DAYS? Where'd you stay?"

"Up at Gladys Hooks'. Numbuh Tree."

Kate suppresses a yawn.

Mountain chuckles. "Where's your stuff?"

I point back toward the plaza.

"We live over on the other side of the island with all the redlegs and the horseshoe crabs," he says, clapping his fingertips
like pincers. "We'll pick up a bottle of nose paint. Scotch all right,
Johnny?"

"Scotch is great there, Johnny."

"Kate, honey, you got any money?"

Kate doesn't have any money, only a glance for the bay, like
a mental patient trying to recall a card game she played with
her uncle next to the radiator once in Pennsylvania. Mountain,
bristling with self-amusement, cracks a dumb grin. "Well, who
needs money when you're funny?"

"I've got some money," I say.

At the duty-free shop we buy a bottle of Johnny Walker Red
for four bucks. Then we climb into a decrepit little blue Toyota

and clatter away up the hill until we disappear like a clunky Russian satellite into the forbidden hole in the jungle, the threshold that legend says will lead us to the good life on the other side of the isle.

16.

THE TOYOTA IS A WRECK, SUSPENSION SHOT, DRIVER'S-
side window gone, springs sticking up through decomposing seats.
The radio is missing. The vinyl on the dash is changing to moss.
The vents pour up a plastic-smelling heat. The quivering hood,
lashed shut with a coat hanger, threatens to spring loose and
smash the windshield into our teeth at any minute. A rust-framed
hole in the floorboard permits me to observe the road spinning
away underneath my feet. Whenever Mountain shifts gears it
sounds like coins jingling in a wooden box. But I am happy. I don't
care if Mountain has a crappy car or a petulant girlfriend or that
they're flat broke because a) it won't last, and b) I didn't come to
call socially. I stare out the window with a glow in my chest and a
love for the splendor of nature as we wind through tunnels of purple that break into occasional staggering sweeps of turquoise sea.

The waves running up every beach I've seen on Poisson
Rouge have been the kind of miniscule events you see at the edges
of swimming pools when someone does a cannonball off the
diving board. But I knew before coming here that there wouldn't
be much decent surf, which is fine with me since my goal is not
to be a sun-ruined beach bum with a beer belly and a busted grin
but a man who can handle himself in all circles, who can build a
fire or a house, who can defend himself, who can recite Keats and
Christ and kill a wildcat with a single arrow, in other words a man.
My woeful boyhood and long suburban vacation have both unrav-
eled to their merciful end.

I can't hear much over the whine and miss of the engine and the rattle of the corroding frame. Kate seems lost back there among the scattered, swirling blue shadows. A parrot flies across the road and streaks the windshield. The difficulty of conversation is compounded by the lavish reticence of Kate. I don't really care. I am like one rescued from certain death, laconic in the helicopter ride home. Gazing out the window, I wonder how I will return to nature. It shouldn't be hard. I think of lean-tos, mud huts, tepees, tree houses. In the day I'll sleep on the warm sand. Eventually I'll learn how to trap lobsters and fish. All I'll need initially is fire, a roof, and a few basic tools.

A pair of tourists sails past us on the right, waving from a green Volkswagen Thing.

"Saul Schwartz strikes again!" I shout.

"You know Saul?" says Mountain, turning with one raised eyebrow. Hard to get used to this clean-cut Catholic kid with long hair and a beard on his big jaws, but I suppose it's standard equipment for the island dweller.

"I saw his place!" I yell in the direction of his ear.

"I work for him!" he shouts, glancing back and forth eagerly between the road and me.

"At the car lot?"

"No! He's doing some salvaging on the south side."

"Salvaging?"

"Why do you think I *came* here, man?" he says, thumping a fist up against the tattered roof liner. "More wrecked ships and buried treasure here than anywhere in the Caribbean."

The tourists disappear around a corner. I want to see them again but they are gone. Where do they come from? I wonder. Where are they going? Do they love each other? Are they afraid to die? How do they feel about driving on the wrong side of the road?

"How long you been here, Mountain?"

"Almost six months," he says, fingering back a handful of curls.

"How'd you find the place?"

"Friend of my dad told me about it," he shouts off the back of his hand. "Said I'd better get out here before everyone else does."

Behold a sea of blue hydrangea, elephant grass, and shadows as deep as those on any planet, orange hulks peeking out. Vague evidence of a sign, a fence, a booth, all concealed now in humps and hills of guana tail and yellow spaghetti vine. A white van sits in the middle of the yard, paneled with mildew, tires gone, blue Bengal clockvines snaking through the broken windows.

"They call it the Valley of Miracles," he says, dodging a pothole.

"Looks more like a junkyard," I say, noting the scattered tires.

"That's how valuable car parts are around here. Beats hell out of paying three hundred for an oil pump."

I reflect on the topography as the road switches back and forth, sunlight intermittently striking through the canopy in long, eerie cathedral floods. Islands generally fall into two categories: accretions of coral and volcanoes. Coral islands are typically flat. Volcanoes climb out of the sea. Poisson Rouge is impressively steep and thus falls into category two. Supposedly its cauldron is extinct, but that's what they said about Martinique, which blew up like a pumpkin with a firecracker in it in 1902, killing forty thousand, the only survivor a bearded murderer scheduled to be guillotined the next day (he was released). Earthquakes are common as well, since a volcanic archipelago describes a fault line, a bubbling, molten seam in the earth's floor. Most people who come to visit paradise don't think about this. Mountain swerves between the potholes. I can't see most of them, but he obviously has the course memorized. Now and then the steering wheel in his hands goes into a violent seizure.

"Steering box!" he shouts, jerking the wheel left, then right with the vigor of a longshoreman slapping the face of a hysterical opera star. We float and drift across the crumbled asphalt like a stagecoach on ice. Scarlet hibiscus and morning glories wink out at us. The silhouettes of tiny, infinite birds flicker across the glass. The air heaves with the croak and shimmer of the endless

territorial conflict for union and death. I check back at Kate, who
is nestled in the corner, feet up (nice legs), eyes closed, riding
loosely and sedately, a thin contented smile on her lips. With this
single innocent glance I feel Mountain's mood cool, his mistrust
coagulate. I turn back quickly as if I've just been stretching my
neck. All at once before us the jungle opens and I'm staring down
at a shredded flap of peppermint-striped awning shading a
battered trailer that's attached to the side of a steep green gorge.
Mountain yanks the car over to the shoulder. The engine fumes
and pops. "Don't let it stall!" he shouts, with the slightest crimp of
brow, as if to say: Don't be messing with my girl either. Then he
jumps out and crashes deftly down the hill.

    I am alone now with Kate. If I am going to have a good look
at this woman it'll have to be while her man is not around. I try
to smell her. No way to distinguish her orchid-and-perfume bou-
quet from the jungle. She stares out the side window. I try to see
what she sees. I examine again her legs, and try to estimate the size
and shape of her breasts. The jawline is good, strong. Something
about the mussed hair and the uncovered neck stimulates me. I
am hornier than usual after several days of travel and three more
of Blue-Haven insomnia. I have never competed with Mountain
for women before and I am not about to start now. Just admiring.
Pretty fingers. I prefer a woman not overboard attractive. Like
many men I am intimidated by gross beauty. Nature in her effort
to restock the species sometimes overdoes it. I must admit that I
appreciate Mountain's taste in women. He doesn't pluck them from
the top branches but neither does he dig up the root varieties.

    Mountain is laboring back up the hill, grinning and bright-
eyed, skinny almost, an incompatible image with his wild hair
and that terribly seedy beard. He's a different man, I realize. Has
he grown up? I wonder. Has he discovered joy? Has he discovered *gold*? Has the wilderness (and all my notions of the purifying
force of nature) transformed him? And what role does the
luscious child in the backseat play in all this? And how long has
she been around? She must be just about overdue for return, but

then again, if they live among the "redlegs and the horseshoe crabs" maybe there aren't a lot of choices. If their lives are indeed as primitive as Mountain suggests, maybe they are more reliant on each other than the normal suburban couple nursed on birth control and situation comedy.

Mountain climbs into the car, out of breath, and tosses a white-wrapped package, cold and soft, into my lap. "Goat," he says, chunking the car into gear. The oil light flickers on.

"Seems small for a goat."

We pass a few shingle-roofed wooden shanties that don't seem inhabited, then a blue stucco apartment building with a corrugated roof. An old woman waves at us with a handkerchief from the open doorway.

"Lula!" shouts Mountain, waving out the window, and turns back to me. "Arthur lives there! He works at the Plantation." He turns, one eyebrow knitted, his forehead furrowed, his hair hanging in his face. "About the only work you can find on this island."

We are now following the sea, passing deserted coves full of warm blue and green rain. The road in some spots borders along sloppy marshes packed with clattering horseshoe crabs and groves of bowed coconut palms.

"What are redlegs?" I say.

"That's us," he says. "The poor whites."

"You got any papayas here?"

"Live right under a whole grove of 'em. Ripe in a month. We got a lime tree. Bay rum too. You just missed the mango season."

"How come nobody *knows* you, Mountain?" I say, narrowing my eyes at him. "If you've been here six months."

He shrugs. The steering wheel begins to shimmy and he wrestles it back into submission. "Oh, they all *know* me. They think I'm Sylvester Stallone."

Oh my God, I think, I've made the right choice after all. A warm, unpopulated island, a good friend, a place to stay, a perfect chance to start again. If I can't make it here, I have no excuses. Hefting the cool goat meat, I sniff its vague rankness. Kate seems to have dozed off. Against the purple foliage in the window behind her she looks with her succulent ears and tousled hair and thin eyebrows, like a beautiful young Taiwanese boy.

Mountain reaches over to rough my hair. "Nothing here!" he shouts. "Except the Mariner's Trove."

I'm trying to remember where I heard of the Mariner's Trove. "What's that?"

"Something I'm about to find," he says, striking the pose of a man awed by a great discovery.

The strip of road is now rolling. The tiny coves and bays flash past like a carousel of obscene vacation photographs. At any moment I expect a roller coaster to come screaming around the corner or a plastic boat full of laughing, phony pirates to sail past.

The swollen triangles of two sailboats in the distance uplift me for a moment. The road forks ahead. Mountain follows right. Something clacks and thumps away under us. I guess oil pump. Mountain glances up where the mirror should be. Kate opens her eyes to return my feeble smile. I try not to stare at her mole or the gem of saliva at the corner of her mouth. Mountain watches me, his lip faintly curled.

17.

"TURNER COVE," CRIES MOUNTAIN, HANGING A SUDDEN right and sloshing up a gravel driveway. He skids to a stop at the top under a canopy of green papaya trees where he yanks up the brake. "End of the line, folks."

I peer up through the bug-spattered windshield at a slumping, moldy, two-storied teal stucco building that looks like the mezzotint of a Louisiana sanitarium gone out of service long ago. Red and pink African daisies dangle listlessly through the wrought iron bars of the second floor balcony. Smoke begins to chug up through the rust hole in the floor. As we clamber out I try not to stare at Kate's legs. Faint wisps that smell of burnt wire curl from the cracks in the hood.

"This is where you live?" I hear myself saying.

Mountain sighs, hands on hips. "Godgiss, ain't it?"

No more than thirty feet behind us the sea slops and froths in the sclerotic volcanic bowl called Turner Cove. The insects chirrup, rattle, and croak. The waves slush in with a sound like the insistent whispering of the mad. A black hummingbird, shiny as a bullet, thunders around my head. I duck and it jets away. Something about the old tenement house and its mossy bungalows stimulate a languor deep in the marrow of my bones. "Crazy," I whisper. "Eerie."

"Looks like something straight out of an El Greco nightmare," Mountain agrees, tipping his head in admiration. "But we like to call it home."

Kate glides up ahead, palms out flat, eyes to the ground, as if balancing herself on an invisible wire. I note the carapace of a magnificent lobster nailed above a bungalow door. I'm growing accustomed to the litter that island people use to decorate their homes. My heart stalls for an instant as a familiar face with disapproving nostrils peers over the top of a pot of Easter lilies in the upper window of the main building. The heavy, ammoniac smell of frying pork mingled with the static of a baseball game on the radio floats out from one of the bungalows. A slim pale figure with striking blue eyes, a machete on his shoulder, emerges from the brush to the right and stops in his tracks, as if seeing two men steal the stereo out of his car.

"Hey Fish," calls Mountain. "This is Deadwood Donahoe. He's just in from the States. Good friend of mine. Gonna stay with us for a while."

Fish stares at me, offering not so much as a nod. I know the look already. Paradise is a place with me in it, buddy, not you. The blade drops from his shoulder and he lumbers away toward the road.

"Your neighbor?" I say.

"Next door."

"Charm school graduate?"

"His mother was Mary Poppins."

"Did she beat him with a spatula?"

"Should have, probably. He's a Deadhead, loves Jack Kerouac." He lines up the cove with his thumb and offers reflectively: "Possesses a curious Delaware solipsism."

"Ah, now it all comes clear. Bless my soul, but don't you look like a Jumbo Crusoe? What happened to Cal Tech?"

"Still there, I bet," he says, showing me his big teeth in an intimation of arch significance. Now in a somber FDR voice, finger raised: "Meanwhile, we will not violate the sacred cocktail hour. We have nothing to fee-ah but bee-ah itself. We live in this one up here."

I follow him, stopping abruptly at the sight of an enormous

colony of honeybees adhered to the eaves directly above the door. "You have a beehive," I say.

"You're a sharp-eyed lad," he says, as if it were the most natural thing in the world to have a beehive stuck to the top of your door. "But don't call me 'honey' in front of the boys."

"That is some beehive," I remark, regarding the sagging mud hut of a nest spinning and dripping with millions of swimming bees. "I don't believe I've ever seen one that big. It must have taken them years to build it."

"Mighty likely," he agrees, stroking the scrap on his chin and continuing to offer me a generous but hardly encouraging smile. "You ain't afraid of honeybees, Deadwood?"

"Not abnormally, no."

"Well then, come aboard, mate." His left hand waves at me in hypnotic assurance. "It'll be dark soon."

"Yes," I say, meat in my left hand, suitcase in my right, but wanting to scratch.

"Just act calm," he says, the grin of reassurance or shared secrecy or sadism or quite possibly a mixture of the three actually *widening* now.

"Calm," I repeat, thinking of Kate and her pretty legs gliding fearlessly under the hive. If she can do it, certainly I can. I take a deep breath and make a sudden plunge for the door, which instantly attracts several bees to my hair. In a panic I retreat down the stairs, swinging my head around and dropping my suitcase and the package of goat meat. Mountain gasps with delight. Not much entertainment on the island, but you can always invite people over and watch them run around with bees in their hair. His blue eyes are clouded with tears. "Now look," he instructs, a bubble of repressed hilarity still stuck in his throat. "You came up those stairs like a spastic go-go dancer. Just RELAX when you walk under." He continues to hold the door open for me, pushing air down with his palm, his eyes lit with the pleasure of my distress. "You know, ommmm."

I glance up once again at the main building, where the

familiar face of disapproval has disappeared. I close my eyes and limbo under. A bee grazes my forehead. I nearly bend the screen door slamming it after me.

Mountain roars and dabs at the corners of his eyes.

"Why don't you get *rid* of the son of a bitch?" I blurt indignantly.

"You just tell me when you're ready to do it," he says, still pleased as can be, "so I can move to the other side of the island."

I'm standing in a warm, dingy ground-floor kitchen with a cracked green-and-white checkered linoleum floor and the ubiquitous, dangling helices of sticky amber paper studded thickly with dead and dying flies. The ceiling is buckled and low like a hammock with orange Indochina-shaped water stains. The plaster is a drowsy aqua blue. A few pin streams of cockeyed sunlight filter weakly through the vine-congested window in the opposite wall. I glance back at the monstrous beehive. "Where's your fridge, Mountain?"

Mountain sets the Scotch on the table in a beam of sunlight. "What fridge?" he says.

"You don't have a fridge," I say, remarking on the sacred quality of the sunlit bottle.

"We don't have electricity," he says, as if I have left my good sense along with my scattered underwear at the San Juan airport. "Put the meat in the sink."

"Bees but no electricity," I mutter, complying. "How does the stove work?"

"Propane." He turns an imaginary dial. "We're gonna get a generator soon."

A bookcase filled with paperbacks and mostly empty liquor bottles stands in the corner next to the stove. Along with Mountain's five "traveling classics" are a few trashy bestsellers, Jackie Collins and Harold Robbins, undoubtedly Kate's collection since Mountain wouldn't touch a book like this unless there was no kindling. There is also a black leather-bound Bible, a slim paper volume entitled *Flora and Fauna of the Lesser Antilles*, and a *Chilton's*

Repair and Tune-Up Guide: Toyota. I admire the partial bottles of liquor, like metamorphosing jewels in the chambers of an absent-minded alchemist.

Two Gauguins are taped to the wall, *Anna the Javanese* and *Whence Do We Come? What Are We? Where Are We Going?* The blue paint on the walls is split like the thick tempera you see in old elementary-school paintings. The screen on the single window is bulged and ripped from the insistence of inexorable creepers. In the middle of the room are a round table covered with a plastic white tablecloth, two square, blue-glass ashtrays packed with cigarette butts, three coffee mugs, another bottle of nearly finished Johnny Walker, and the classified section of the *Miami Herald.* Here and there a giant roach rests on the wall like a brooch or a shiny brown spaceship, waving its feelers in the howdy-stranger mode. A few feet past the table, behind a moldy half-drawn plastic curtain, is a rough cement stall with a mossy toilet planted in the floor and a showerhead sticking out of the wall. More roaches wait inside. They go about six inches, including those feelers that wave about like batons.

"You have running water," I say in my most complimentary tone.

"All the modern conveniences."

"Where does it come from?" I raise my hand. "Don't tell me, plumbing."

"Cistern."

"Beg pardon?"

"You don't know what a cistern is?"

"Have I seen them hitchhiking from the convent?"

"Water tank," he says. "Rainwater." He makes descending motions with his fingers, as if we are two strangers who speak different languages. "Rainwater fall on roof, gutters drain into tank." He illustrates the concept of tank with the universal hand signs. "We've got an extra bedroom," he says, examining a lump of what appears to be molded garlic. *"Mi casa, su casa.* I Tarzan. You Jane."

"Don't call me that in front of the boys," I say, poking my

head into a small room furnished with bed and dresser, cracked blue walls arranged here and there with a jumbo roach and the fading scarlet burst of a squashed mosquito. A year-old Currier and Ives print of a snowstorm in January hangs crookedly from a bent nail.

Mountain pours me out a tall Scotch in a jelly glass, no cumbersome mixer. I admire the weight of its golden unction as it glides down my throat. Mountain lights a cigarette, smoking it with his whole hand over his face. "Don't believe you came, man," he says.

"Didn't come to be a burden, man," I say, my eyes flicking once to the bedroom door. "I'll be out on my own soon as I can."

Privately I wonder how I will make it here on this rough and sparsely inhabited island without selling out. I'll have to find my own place quick before I'm out of cash. But it won't have to be much. I've seen enough bamboo around, I could probably fashion myself a temporary hut. And I don't mind the barrenness of this east side. The scarcity of comforts and so-called experts will lead me from temptation.

"Don't worry about it, Deadwood," he says, twirling the knob of a radio on a shelf above the kitchen counter and crackling in the top-forty station from Ravissant. "Hell, you fixed us up in Solana Beach. Now it's my turn."

Catching a glimpse of Kate half-dressed in the bedroom, I wheel quickly back around, my voice dripping with congeniality. "So you went and punched old Refried Clyde, eh?"

Mountain kicks off his torn-up shoes, wiggles his feet into a pair of flip-flops, and reaches up to flick a roach off the ceiling. "Yeah, he was an anthropology major so I put a bone in his nose."

"And they expelled you?"

"Close enough," he says, taking a can of insecticide out of the bookcase and blasting the fallen roach. He giggles as it bucks in its foam casing of death, but I'm surprised to see it leap up and take off again, the poison evaporating from its impressive armor. Mountain giggles again, shaking the can. "Roach feed," he says.

"Was your dad pissed?"

"Coming here was his idea," he says, returning the can of "roach feed" to the shelf. "He thought it might settle me down. I tell you I'm building a boat?"

"No, sir, you did not," I say watching the recently spritzed roach now fanning its wings and doing a little jig around the room.

"Yup," he says. "You find something worth going down for, salvagers want forty percent, half your take. That's too high for equipment rental, man. Once I learn the trade from Saul, I'm going to start my own salvaging company. You'll be my vice president, Deadwood."

"Your treasurer, you mean."

"How about a little more of that hair oil, Johnny?" he says, refilling my jar. "You're a quicker drinker than I recall. That's the stuff for the troops."

"Shake Your Booty" by the Sunshine Band comes on the radio. I thought I might've been lucky to leave this one behind. Catchy as the song is, it makes me self-conscious about my booty, which I never seriously considered until well into the disco era. I light a smoke and set my booty into a wooden chair.

Kate drifts out from the bedroom in a long sheer gown cut low at the neckline. With her moody reticence, willowy frame, narrow shoulders, prominent collarbones, and short, limp center-parted hair, she reminds me of one of those sad flappers in a party at Gatsby's place reclined upon a couch saying, "I've been sitting here since I can remember." One of the irises in her copper-colored eyes is blood flecked. I reestimate her age, early thirties. I can see half of a plump white breast through the bodice of her gown. She smiles at me with a slow and sardonic indifference, shakes her hair, and lifts a flame to the end of a long menthol cigarette.

The instant Kate appears Mountain changes, as if cued by a hypnotist. I feel suddenly as if I'm not even in the room. "Tea, dear?" he says, fuzzy-eyed.

Kate gives a languid nod.

Mountain brews tea, that dumb simper hanging in his big jaws, dangling the bag with loving care and topping off with a healthy portion of Scotch.

"*Hot* tea?" I say.

"Hot things keep you cool," she says, smiling thinly and letting her eyelids laze, as if she were just barely able to make me out across a foggy chasm.

"I have to admit, that is one expression I've never understood."

"It's true," she says, blowing at the vortices of steam lifting from her cup.

"We have nothing for stew," says Mountain, still standing and looking, if anything, like a giant houseboy.

"We have Scotch," says Kate, pressing the back of her neck with two fingers. "And papaya. You can make that dish you made last week."

"Seems a waste of good Scotch," I offer.

Mountain holds up the Johnny Walker bottle. "Plenty more where that came from. Come outside for a minute, Deadwood, and help me get a papaya."

"I thought you said they wouldn't be ripe for a month."

"They won't," he says.

I follow him back out under the beehive, holding my breath, forcing my eyes to stay open. It is easier this time. The bees are slowing as the light diminishes in the sky. My, my, it is going to be dark tonight, darker than summer camp. How will I adjust to this? How will I develop the discipline and the instincts necessary to wean myself from the saturated fat of society? Mountain shakes out his leg suddenly, as if he's trying to roll a ball down his leg, and cracks a fart that sounds like a bedsheet being torn in half.

"Jesus," I say, "don't scare the animals. Did you come out here just to fart?"

He smiles like a big kid, his cheeks ruddy. "I want to tell you something, Deadwood," he says, poking me suddenly in the chest. "Don't think I don't see the way you're looking at her."

"How am I looking at her?" I reply innocently.

"Looking at her," he glowers, his fist swelling at his side.

"Well, I have to *look* at her. I mean, I'll walk around backwards if you like. Come on, son, now it's your turn to relax. I don't steal people's girlfriends."

"Parrot droppings," he says tipping his head at me. "You stole Tooley's girl."

"She was a special ed. major—listen, I recognize your dedication, and the minute I find another place to live I am gonorrhea, baby."

He seems ashamed of himself. He kicks the ground and digs at his nose with a fist. "I didn't mean it. What's wrong with me?"

"No biggie, big guy." I let the fluttering in my gut settle and then I try for one of my savvy, forgiving smiles. Mountain is the perfect companion, just don't intersect with his girl of the month, that's all. Too bad the bungalow isn't just a shade bigger. Through the grain of a screen door to the right I make out a Spartan room packed with dusk, one small, tightly made bed draped with a box of mosquito netting, a table, a chair, a sink.

"Who lives here?" I say.

"Your buddy, Fish," he says in a sullen tone.

"That his name?"

"That's what they call him." He swipes at a cloud of gnats in front of his face. "Fishes for a living, sells most of his catch to the Plantation. That's his boat canopy over there."

"Ah yes. And his lobster."

"Fourteen-pounder."

I'm not interested in Fish or his unfriendly brand of escapism or his fourteen-pound lobster. I am disappointed to learn that he is our common-wall neighbor. However, if the feeling is mutual, perhaps we can just ignore each other, as city people do. There is plenty of room on this island for us all.

"This is a colette," Mountain says, holding spear-fashion a long bamboo pole with a hunting knife lashed to the tip. He tests the knife-edge with his thumb, then begins to hack at a cluster of green fruit dangling from the nearest papaya tree. I note the same dour Bette Davis face in the upstairs window, but now it hovers long enough for me to identify. It is a Hooks face, a dead ringer for the woman who rented to me on the other side. Mountain ignores her. A papaya almost hits me on the head. Mountain scoops the downed fruit, hefts it, and hands it to me. "They're like potatoes when they're not ripe," he says. A gash in the skin bleeds in beads of viscid white. He pats me on the back of the head. Even gently, the weight of his hand is notable. "I didn't mean anything," he says.

"Don't worry about it, Johnny boy."

The face vanishes from the window.

18.

THE AROMA OF THE FRYING GOAT MEAT IS FETID AS A barnyard or the camel cage at the San Diego Zoo. Mountain peels the papaya like a big green eggplant, scoops out the caviar black seeds, and chops the green flesh, adding it on top of the meat. He pours the Scotch and follows with two glasses of cistern water, sealing the pot with a lid.

"Whale hail," he says. "I can't boil a turd."

"He cooks better than I do," says Kate. "I can't boil water."

Mountain lights himself a cigarette off the stove. He's smoking more than I recall. Of course, he was a semidisciplined football player when I knew him last. "Speaking of water," he says, puffing until the tip of his cigarette glows, "we boil everything out of the faucet. Keeps you from getting dysentery."

"Splendid," I say, reaching across the table for more Scotch. Outside, the critters chitter and buzz in a solid waterfall of old-fashioned bedlam. The waves whisk and mingle with the hush of a haunted and tireless breeze. The air is no thinner than Vaseline. The smoke from my cigarette dissipates without rising.

"Whose Gauguins?" I ask.

"Mine," says Kate, tilting her face up to expel a languorous stream of rippled blue smoke.

I nod approval.

Mountain shakes his head.

"Where did you get them?" I ask.

"Baltimore," she sighs, staring at *Anna the Javanese*. "The art museum there. That one's my favorite."

"Why is Gauguin great?" asks Mountain, frowning.

Kate puffs delicately from her long white cigarette. Her voice is small and sounds faintly Southern. "He lived on an island."

"I know why he's famous, dear," says Mountain, "but why is he *great*?"

"I don't know if he's great," she says. "I just like him."

"Technically he's poor," says Mountain, turning a chair around and straddling it with his arms hugging the back.

Kate flicks up a shoulder as if to discourage a fly.

"And he left his wife and family," I offer.

She taps her ash into one of the jammed, blue-glass trays. "A lot of people do *that*."

"And died of leprosy," I add.

"This was a leper colony once," Mountain says, perched backward in his chair and staring Bambi-like into the eyes of his beloved.

"What was?" I say.

"Poisson Rouge," he says.

"Only Merriwether," says Kate, in her small, indolent Southern drawl. "They closed it long ago."

"Fanny lives over at Merriwether," says Mountain with a smirk. "They still call it a colony."

"Who's Fanny?" I say.

"Friend of mine," says Kate, lifting a bare leg to smooth with her palm.

Whenever my head even turns in the *direction* of Kate, Mountain tenses, so I stand up to look out the window, which is nearly obscured by vegetation. I'm thinking of Fanny who lives in a leper colony and makes Mountain Moses smirk. The screen is torn and you can almost watch the creepers sliding in toward the stove. Mountain begins scratching his legs with a hairbrush. "We can go sit outside if you want," he says. "The bugs are fresher out on the veranda."

"No no," I say, holding up my glass. "Two trips under the beehive a night is plenty for me."

"Tell us the news from the States," says Kate.

"Cities in the dust," I say with grim satisfaction. "The Empire has fallen."

"I'm hip," says Mountain.

"Looks like we got out just in time," says Kate.

"We can start the world all over," I say.

"What would we want to do *that* for?" she says, padding across the murky room toward her pan of steaming water. "We'd just screw it up again."

"Amen," says Mountain, closing his eyes.

I return to my chair. "Who else lives here?"

"Fish, the charm school grad," says Mountain, puffing from his cigarette and clenching a blue eye against a curlicue of smoke. "You already had the pleasure."

"He's antitechnology," says Kate, unwrapping her tea bag.

I have a gulp from my jar. The Scotch tastes of fire and wood and every color of the rainbow except black. "How does he fish?"

"Has a boat," says Mountain, aiming at a mosquito on his forearm.

"A dugout canoe?"

"Fiberglass skiff," says Mountain, slapping the mosquito into oblivion and flicking away the corpse. "Six-horsepower engine. But he won't use a net."

"You can't live in a cave," says Kate, lowering her tea bag into her cup.

"Who lives in the room with the flower boxes?"

"Iba, Queen of Werewolves," says Mountain. "She'll be over tomorrow. She comes over every other day. Willie lives down at the end. His son plays for the Pittsburgh Pirates."

"Really? What's his last name?"

"What is it, Kate?"

"I don't know," she says, staring down into the steam winding up from the pan. "Nillie?"

"Nobody understands baseball around here," explains Mountain with a British pinch of his sparse mustache. "The only game they play is cricket, you know."

"If his son plays for the Pirates, why isn't he in Pittsburgh?"

"Good question, Deadwood."

"I'll talk to him," I say. "I speak baseball."

"He'll be the one with the Pirates ball cap."

"That would follow," I say, trying not to watch Kate pour her tea, though the crown of blue propane flames seems dangerously close to the hem of her gown. She does not seem affected. *Hot things keep you cool.*

"Who owns the face in the upstairs window?" I say.

Mountain crosses his arms across his massive chest and leans back. "That would be Alvina, the landlady. Alvina is a weenah. She'll come nosing over here in the morning. She's already seen you. She won't like you."

"She doesn't like anyone," adds Kate.

"You know, she looks exactly like Malveen, the lady who runs Gladys Hooks' Blue Haven Inn."

"They're sisters," says Kate blandly.

"There are five of them," says Mountain.

"Their grandparents were slaves," adds Kate. "Do you know about the slave revolution here?"

"No."

"It was 1833." She glides back across the room, dunking her tea bag. "Tell him, Mountain."

Mountain accepts her deferment with a scholarly fondle of an invisible bow tie. "Back in the year of our Lord 1832, the Dutch plantation owners of this island mistakenly purchased a tribe of African royalty," he recites in his New England accent. "Warrior princes and the like, and brought them here to work their cane fields. The warrior princes didn't take to sugah cane and twelve-hour days with no pay, so they escaped one by one back into the forest and within a year of the date of their capture, every white man, woman, and child on Poisson Rouge was dead." Mountain fishes his cigarette from the tray and covers his face in that inimitable Charles Boyer fashion. Kate regards him steadily, lifting the bag and letting it spin above her cup, as if this might be the first time she's heard the story.

"They made fish-skin drums and fashioned elegant weapons from the jungle," Mountain continues, tugging once more at the illusory tie. "Their revolt was executed with chilling and brutal effectiveness. They were accustomed to war and knew better than the Dutchmen the first rule of the jungle. They communicated everything by drum and the white folks never knew what hit them." His eyes sparkle with cruel satisfaction. He's even worked up a dimple on the left side.

My leg, asleep, tingles like a Fourth of July sparkler. Gradually I ease its deadweight out in front of me under the table. "You seem pleased," I say.

"They brought the wrong people home from the party, that's all."

"But what about the white *children?*"

"First rule of the jungle," he says, rattling a professorial finger at the air. "Kill or be killed."

Kate nods.

"I suppose," I say, thumping my heel against the tiles to get the blood circulating.

"Oh, you'll learn that one quick enough," he says, exhibiting teeth. The gap between his two front teeth is wider than I remember, making him seem a little narrower of skull and somehow a bit less balanced. "Don't make the mistake of thinking of Poisson Rouge as a vacation wonderland, especially this side of the island."

"The island still has the old network of secret roads," says Kate.

"Kind of like an Underground Railroad," says Mountain.

"I understand the slaves were not actually kidnapped," I say, "but sold to white merchants by other tribes who captured them."

"True enough," says Mountain.

"But when the Dutch pulled out," Kate drawls, sipping delicately from her cup, "the slaves got everything. And a lot of them got *rich*. The Hooks own about ten percent of the island."

"Alvina's the black sheep," says Mountain, putting his head down on his arms. "She's lived out here fifty years. She's rich but you'd never know it by looking at her."

"She has electricity," I say. "I saw a fan turning in her window."

"Generator," says Mountain. "We're going to get one here soon too."

"Oh, a fan would be nice," moans Kate, leaning back and locking her hands behind her head. I battle a sudden amorous weakness for her armpits. Mountain is glaring at me again. My eyes drop to the newspaper under my elbows. "They blow off the bugs," she says.

Almost on cue the mosquitoes begin to descend. It seems asinine that the screens on the windows should be loose. Mountain produces a can of OFF! and we fumigate ourselves. The repellent hangs in the quivering air that shrills in my ears from the dense population of courting and mating outside. I smoke consecutive cigarettes and drink my golden Scottish elixir, holding tight to the glass, wondering if the asthma will return. My bare arms and neck gleam with poison. The Scotch goat and papaya stew begins to bubble and heat the room. A gargantuan roach waddles stiffly across the floor.

"You can feed it if you want to," says Mountain, with a yawn. "Can's up on the shelf there."

I enjoy another modest sip of fire, wood, and rainbow. "You know they can live on cardboard."

"And tile grout," says Mountain, gleaming with poison, his hair clinging to the sides of his head and almost dripping on his shoulders from humidity. He scratches with a hairbrush at the place the mosquito drilled him.

"They fall out of the rafters," says Kate, rolling her eyes up.

"Try to get in the habit of sleeping with your mouth closed," advises Mountain.

"The place is full of rats too," says Kate, crossing her legs and flipping back her bangs. "Mountain keeps saying he's going to buy us a cat."

"We *have* a cat," says Mountain with a sheepish swing of his long-lashed eyes. "Somewhere around here."

I pour myself another drink. If I knew we were going to make stew with it I would've bought a second bottle at the duty-free shop. As the insect repellent wears off, the mosquitoes begin to land again. They are agile, tough, and relentless mosquitoes that show no fear of death. I murder them with relish, taking each of their feeding forays personally. I increase my Scotch intake, hoping the fumes from my liver will kill them. Kate raises her gown from her knees and her hair from her neck. The heat shimmers off her. The goat stew begins to burn. Mountain swears and turns it off. The jungle shrills and ping-pongs and huzzahs. The radio burbles and fades.

Someone outside begins to shout.

"Who's that?" I say, turning my head so quickly I almost pinch a nerve.

"Shhh," says Mountain, finger to his thick lips, his lids lowered. He seems suddenly relaxed, his body temperature dropped.

We're all bent forward now listening to the sound of sharply struck leaves, the crack of a branch, the slushy whack of a tree or one of the struts of Fish's boat canopy going down, and then what seem to be the words: "Cuh-toff your leg, white muddafuckah!"

"Legion," says Kate.

I stare at her, rubbing my neck, waiting for explanation.

"Lunatic," she says, lighting another cigarette and shaking out the match with one leisurely snap of the wrist.

Mountain draws himself up from the table with a sigh.

I envy his bearing and his cool familiarity with aggression on and off the football field, but it seems to me poor judgment to face a madman at this time of night, especially in shorts and sandals. I have a ridiculous urge to call the police. I follow him to the door and poke my head out. In the streaks of moonlight I make out a small, yellow-eyed, bowlegged figure who appears to be naked, the dull pirate gleam of a cutlass flickering about. This is the same fellow I saw arguing with the cricket player down below the church days before. Still fuming over that theological debate, I imagine. Mountain is talking in low tones, head slightly cocked, like a pitching coach to his ace starter. I can see by his broad, faintly moonlit back that he is stooped. I know that Mountain's night vision is excellent, and though I'm sure there are thousands of people who can beat him in a physical contest, I haven't met one yet. Nevertheless, these are extraordinary circumstances, confronting raw insanity in the darkness of the jungle. Mountain's changed—of course, everyone changes—but it isn't for the better. His fuse is shorter, his suspicion darker. He's smoking and drinking more. Look at where he lives, look at what he does at night. He can't be content here with visions of gold. What is salvaging anyway? It's poring over someone else's misfortune, someone else's trash. The island has worn his mind down, the decay of his mother has triggered some deep latent reaction, or he's absorbed some rare tropical parasite. The naked madman continues to rave, the pitch of his voice desperate with rage, that dull blade whipping across the stars.

I pass under the beehive once more and down the stairs into the screaming of the insects. "You all right, Mountain?"

"Fine," he says, turning round to give me an easy smile.

My ears are a roar of hot fear and my chest feels as if it's wrapped in rubber bands. "You need help?" I ask.

"I keel you, white boy," the madman says to me.

He is so bowlegged I think I could do a somersault between his legs without his noticing. "Me?" I say. "Why me? You don't even know me."

"I cuh-toff your leg," he says, jacking his knife back. "I keel you chuppie much."

"What's wrong with him, Mountain?" I ask. "You smokie too much dopie?"

"Get back in the house," Mountain orders gruffly, as if I am Auntie Em out to view the tornado after too many glasses of wine.

Brave from Scotch and always irked by a stranger who makes personal remarks about the end of my life, I return to the house for my French knife, my head crackling like the tide sucking back through the clinkers in Turner Cove.

Kate is watching a red wasp spin around the lip of the hurricane lamp. "Let Mountain handle him," she drawls.

"I've got to help him," I say, plunging into my room and digging around through my bags, inebriated in the darkness. By the time I find my French knife the angry voice is fading off toward the cove.

In another moment Mountain ducks through the door, grinning through the scrap of his beard, tossing his tangled locks back, his fierce blue eyes shining with drunken vigor. He doffs an imaginary top hat, shuffles his feet, and raises his arms. It's the gay tap dancer or Fred Astaire with a squirrel in his trunks, he doesn't explain.

"What was that all about?" I demand, experiencing relief and umbrage at the same time.

"That's Chollie Legion," he says, cupped hand extended as if the potty-mouthed infidel were standing like Tom Thumb in his palm.

"I know him already," I grumble. "What does he want?"

Mountain's voice strains with suppressed laughter. "He wants us to leave the island."

"Us?" I growl, growing more irritated. "Why?"

He studies me as if he were being tickled, but refuses to give in. "We fucked it up."

"We?" I snap, looking for my jelly glass, only to find it empty again. "Who's we?"

"The *white* people, Deadwood. The same ones who ruined *America*, remember?"

"Oh shit," I mutter, the neck of the bottle clanking against the rim of my glass as I pour generously. "What kind of Rastafarian claptrap is that?"

"Well, it's exactly your kind of claptrap," he says, still amused, but now turned back to peer out the door.

"Yeah, well, they got *jobs* don't they? I read in the encyclopedia most of these people were starving until tourism came here. They left their farms in droves when the hotel opened. Your wealthy Hooks sisters wouldn't have two nickels to rub together without white tourists."

He leans down, hands on knees, obviously pleased by the evening's sport. "Legion doesn't know that."

"Where does *he* live?"

"Necropolis," says Mountain.

"*Where?*"

"The graveyard," intones Kate, with a crafty smile, her arms folded like a fortune-teller, her eyes still fixed on the green rim of the hurricane lamp. The wasp has navigated to the other side of the room, where it bumps in sleepy rhythm against the top of the screen door.

I wonder if my hair is standing on end from all the tingles crowding up from my spinal cord. Mountain arches his brows and his forehead shifts into ridges. "Watch out for him," he says, pouring out another Scotch and lighting a fresh cigarette. "He walks the roads. He *will* try to cut you."

"How did you get rid of him?"

"You know." He strikes another action-photo pose, wild-eyed, mouth stretched into a daft grin, hands clutching the air. "I out-crazied him."

"How did you know he wouldn't hit you with that knife?"

Mountain flinches a shoulder. "You have to know how to talk to him."

"What if I run into him? How do I talk to him?"

"Tell him about Jesus."

"Jesus."

"Yeah, he's scared to death of Jesus Christ."

19.

I AM DRUNK AND I DO NOT WANT TO GO TO BED, BUT THE radio has lost its signal and Kate and Mountain are making love audibly in the next room, so I toss off the lees of my Scotch, stab out my noxious cigarette, fog myself all over once again with the pine-scented OFF! (which smells about as pine-scented as any other brand of petroleum), and turn in.

It is hotter than I imagined it would be in paradise, so I sleep in shorts on top of the sheets. Exhausted, I tumble immediately into a dream where I am running along a road lined with oil derricks. I stop at a bar full of lepers. Then I'm in a dark, strange church with my mother. The smell is horrible. I wake up at the first gray light of dawn with a headache like Abe Lincoln's ax in my forehead. My room has a tattered screen door with a first-rate view of the beehive, the papaya grove, the dilapidating Toyota, and a few misty shreds of the silvery cove beyond. The waves shuffle in, you know they'll outlast mankind. A routine scratch of the hip leads both my hands to suddenly begin patting the rest of my body. I lift my head cautiously. Even in the early gray light, I can see that my trunk and limbs are ravaged. I look like a smallpox victim. The mosquitoes are still landing and drilling.

Ferociously scratching, I leap up and stagger across the dim room, hoping I still might be asleep and that when I wake up I will be back in America with sirens howling, smog coagulating on the windows, a live shoot out on KTLA, and sociopathic teen-agers from broken homes scrawling Krylon profanities across my door. A pair of shiny, humpbacked roaches, their antennae long enough to pick up TV signals, caper by like newlyweds across the tiles into a hole in the floorboard. I make a cup of tea. The Scotch is gone so I pour gin without fear. The burnt goat dish on the stove, yet unsampled, has begun to ferment.

Mountain and Kate are not up yet. I fear that they might still be making love until I note that one of them is snoring. I sit down at the table, smoke a cigarette, and listen to the babel and hiss of love from the Pliocene epoch, the clack and clatter of a billion chitin-armored contraptions with sawtooth legs and sandpaper wings, whose sole function in nature is to make a racket. Isn't there ever a respite? Can't someone simply call a two-minute moratorium on mating, consumption, and death? Wouldn't Greenland be nice about this time of year? I itch so badly I ache. I am 116 percent itch. I scratch my ribs, my stomach, my shoulders, my swollen ankles. My face and the soles of my feet have bites. The needle-nosed thieves have bitten me even through my underwear.

Mountain's specially-designated-for-scratching hairbrush turns itching into flaming and then back into itching fiercer than the original itching, so I set it aside. Aspirin or analgesic creams are not to be found. Gin is the only remedy about, and a swift ounce-and-a-half convinces me that another swift ounce-and-a-half is just what the doctor would order. I have one more quick ounce. There is a reason for gin. God bless it, farkle farkle, the very component of sufferable British tropical hegemony. I calculate the number of cases of Seagram's Extra Dry I can buy with the money I have left.

I need a shower but one glance at the roach-infested stall with the mossy toilet and a battalion more of these breeding bloodsuckers convinces me to have a swim out in the cove instead. I unpack some clothes and pour another gin. The sun is up now, glorious and undefeatable. I kill six mosquitoes. I am getting good at it. They take off backward most of the time. They don't seem to care if they die anymore than bubbles seem to care if they pop.

A shadow lurking outside prickles the hair on the back of

my neck. It is that bandy-legged lunatic from the night before taking seriously those ill-advised things I said to him under the influence of John Barleycorn—no, thank God, it is Alvina, the landlady, coming over to dislike me, as if I haven't enough problems with my popularity. I grind out my cigarette and rise from the table, grabbing my mug along the way. "Hello hello," I greet ginsomely, moving toward the door. "Good morning, how are you?"

Alvina is dressed in a threadbare, peach-colored bathrobe, a pair of rusty pruning shears protruding from the pocket. She wears terry slippers, wrinkled blue stockings to the knees, and the expression of a toad drowned in vinegar. Her legs are trembling, vein-roped rails. She stands in a cheerless hunch, ignoring the batting, drooping bees all around her, her eyes like bruises, her sheen of kinky blue hair spread out across her shoulders like the flaps on the habit of a flying nun.

"How you got tee wott?" she demands accusingly, without introduction.

"Me?" I say, pretending to understand. "I'm Edgar Donahoe, Mountain's friend. I just arrived last night. I hope to be working soon at the hotel. I'm a cook." I take a gulp from my gin, exhausted already from kissing up. I know there is no chance of making a good impression on her. I am ashamed of the room, with its roaches and liquor bottles and Himalayan Range of cigarette smoke and me standing here in the middle of it all looking like something sculpted out of raw hamburger.

She continues to blast me with the unintelligible. I answer questions I understand parts of, fabricate many aspects of my biography, and nod at the rest. I hit her with a few "Yes, ma'ams," which seem to soften her slightly. My bare feet, as I observe them from my great hungover distance, are marvelously swollen repositories of itchy mosquito poison.

"Now, dot Mountain, he doan pay de rent on tink he con cross *me*." she lows, shaking her finger at me.

"I'll only be staying a few days," I say.

Her mouth unpuckers and the lips flutter out in a bitter old hoot of a laugh. Does she know I am lying? Why would anyone in his right mind want to stay any longer than a few days in a rattrap like this? I'll be out of this dive in two weeks flat, you old apple-headed grouch, and living off the fat of the land. In the meantime I'd like Mountain to make an appearance and straighten out this business. He and Kate snore away, however, with more enthusiasm it seems than a few minutes before, lustily sucking the sand flies into their nostrils.

I try to think of something I can appease the old sourpuss with. I represent a culture that has been swindling native populations with trinkets for centuries. But do I have something that would sway her? A paring knife? Airline peanuts? A package of wintergreen chewing gum? Aha! Of course. The universal language.

"How much is the rent?"

All communication problems instantly melt away. She fixes me with a dubious but rejuvenated eye. "One-twenty," she says, without trace of an accent.

I lift my hand like the confident magician, disappear into my room, return a moment later with six twenties, snap them off and hand them through, careful not to admit any of my honey-loving friends. "Okay?"

She snatches up the bills, mumbling, counting, snorting, and peering up at me at intervals with incredulity or aggravated hemorrhoids, who can tell? The bees tumble all around her. She pushes out her lips, speechless.

"A great honor to meet you, ma'am," I say, running my fingers down my pebbled ribs. "And my best wishes for your appointment to the Supreme Court."

She wanders off, counting the money with her thumbs and murmuring to herself.

Across the way, a tall, shiny, blue-black young woman with cheekbones like a starving fashion model bounces out her front door. My heart soars. She wears a knee-length green organdy dress with a pinafore and low-heeled, rose-colored velvet shoes.

Her hair is a tumbling Gone-With-the-Wind job, with a yellow ribbon anchored at the top.

"Hello," she sings.

"Morning," I reply.

"You are de new one, friend of Mountain?"

"Yes, how did you know?"

"I saw you dribe up loss night," she trills, her chin burrowing at the sky.

"Oh."

"I am Iba," she proclaims, standing tall. "Is Kay-tup?"

I scratch for a minute. "Ah, no, not yet."

"Dey drinkin' all night agin?"

"I'm afraid so. I tried to warn them."

"Oh, ha ha."

Iba is the picture of the girl in my garden dream, so black and long-legged lovely and light on her feet. She tips a water can over a flower box full of purple peonies. The adjacent box is packed with tiny pink and white blooms.

"You have herbs," I say.

"Yes," she says. "Thyme dis, dat rosemary. Chibes."

"I'm a cook," I say.

"Dot right? I'm tinkin' a day right. You cook at de hotel?" she says.

"No."

"Attuh cook at de hotel." She smiles at me, watering her peonies and herbs, and tells me all about Attuh and how I should blimmy-tam and towly down-waddah, all the while regarding me with her bright, musical innocence and the sophistication that comes from the knowledge that I have fallen in love with her in 4.6 seconds, a notion probably no more novel to her than the honey in the heads of the bees stumbling around the top of the door.

"I might be combin' by dis evenin'," she says.

"Oh. That would be wonderful."

"If dey not drinkin' awready."

Well, not much likelihood of that, I reflect sadly. Nevertheless,

I hold out hope and encourage her with my dwindled, bloodsucked charm. I am glad to be standing behind the nebulous realm of the screen door, with the hundreds of bees spinning down and roping all about like a veil. She can make anything she likes out my middle-of-the-road image. I am tall enough anyway.

"I'm olla bock inside," she calls, waving with a fresh smile and twirl of green dress. The black legs flash, sending a charge through me that obliterates for the moment all traces of suffering.

I grit my teeth and wave. "Yes, very much," I reply.

Now I float a bit. The quickly drugged idiot. The slaphappy moth on the pheromone wind. There is fruit on the tree after all. Black children, happy, brown broad-shouldered children playing with the chickens by the sea of eternal laze and felicity. I finish my tea, resisting the urge to scratch. I resist the urge for another tea too, put on my shoes, and saunter out into the bright morning.

20.

THE SKY IS AS GAWDY BLUE AS THE BURSTING CRYSTALS of gin in my headache. I survey the papaya grove. Fried papaya for breakfast, and then you stroll out to the cove and catch a fish. The ravishing native girl stops by in the evening. Eventually she gives you her confidence. Time ceases to be relevant. Suddenly I know why I came.

Flocks of crane flies shift in and out of the sunlight. A swarm of swifts swoops and turns away among the trees. At the fringe of the jungle I lean in for a peek inside. In broad daylight it is dark as a tomb in there. Why does it so vehemently forbid me? With that bamboo bayonet called a colette I try to chop down a papaya. Alvina scowls at me from her window. Papaya later maybe, I think, ambling amiably down the gravel drive to the road, a long strip of baked and gleaming asphalt with no traffic on it. A thoroughfare any taxpaying, Volvo-owning milk dud would be proud of. Who pays for this road with no traffic on it that does nothing but pass one empty cove after the next? The wind stirs and everything speaks. Clouds like speckled animal cookies race by.

I stare out into the ruffled, parti-colored sea. The sky is blue until you look at the water: then the sky seems purple. The rocky shore is hard, rust-colored volcano spewage, rough footing. Mountain talked last night about collecting whelk from the cove for another of his marvelous stews. I don't know what whelk are. Maybe they are gentle creatures with German accents that emit soap bubbles. I remove my shoes, peel off my shirt, set my glasses carefully on top of my shoes, and tootsie-foot over the hardened cauliflower shore to stick a toe in. The water is warm as tea. I crouch down and slide gently in.

The cove is as crazily blue with me in it as it was from a distance. I float on my back for a while and stare up into the fuzzy purple sky. I find myself oddly uninspired. A car whizzes past out on the road and I want to chase after it, find out who is inside, make them give up their secrets. I swim out about forty feet, dive and touch bottom, then return to shore. This is Eden, I think, hands on hips. The genuine article. No doubt about it. Nothing could possibly be more enchanting or naturally honest or pristine. Why am I not changed?

From up the road north I discern a figure approaching. My glasses are still laid carefully on the tops of my shoes. I arrived with a vague hope that once removed from the artificial strictures of society, my vision would be restored to its native clarity. The figure draws nearer. I stand perplexed on the rocks for a moment, a ball of kazooing gnats like an exploded atomic diagram hovering around my head, my shoes four feet away, the steam whirling off my shoulders. All at once I make out the long knife and the pronounced bowed legs.

With gin-powered acceleration I dive behind the rocks and splash clumsily back into the cove, bumping my knee, heart slapping my ribs. Shhh, you fool. Quietly I wait with just my head poked above the surface, like a myopic turtle.

As Legion nears I prepare to submerge. He is a silent, swiveling, barefoot walker, a Scotsman who's lost his kilt, the eyes on his pivoting head slashes of yellow neon. Tangled dreadlocks tickle his shoulders like black ropes of tar. Shreds of beard dangle from his jowls and chin. The shining machete suspended somehow in the gird of his loincloth slaps rhythmically against the bulging muscles of his thigh. He wears a necklace around his black throat, curved bits of gleaming ivory, shark teeth, or human finger bones. His bearing is diabolical. He looks straight over at me just at the moment I duck under. I open my eyes underwater to see a school of tiny electric blue fish investigating my ravaged hands. When I pop back up again he is moving up the road, mumbling something, singing perhaps. The melody sounds so eerily like "The Banana Boat Song."

21.

MOUNTAIN SHUFFLES INTO THE KITCHEN YAWNING IN
his briefs about ten that morning, his deep and hairless chest
glittering with gold medallions.

I have finished seven teas with gin by now and I am in a
volubly optimistic mood. I raise my mug. "Morning to ye, cap'm."

Mountain studies me with one eye lazed shut. "Yer drunk,"
he says.

"You fucked my wife," I reply. "You owe me a *buck.*"

"You said a quarter. How long you been up?"

"I don't remember."

"Oh god," he says, holding the top of his head. "Feels like I
slept under a buffalo stampede." He rumples his disordered
hair and snaps the elastic on his shorts. His eyes are much lighter
than when I saw him last, and the loss of about twenty pounds
has only served to sharpen the facets of his big-cat muscularity.
"What time you go to bed?" he asks.

"I think about five."

He nods, smacks his dry lips, and begins to assemble the
equipment necessary for the decoction of tea. Straddle-legging a
chair, he commences to scratch his legs with the hairbrush. I feel
a sudden flood of affection for him. I hope that Kate sleeps on for
a while so I can talk to the old Mountain. "How'd you sleep last
night?" he asks.

"Like the bride of Dracula," I reply, holding out my arms.

"Looks like they got you pretty good," he admits, twirling a pinkie into his ear. "What kind of repellent you use, Worcester-shire sauce?"

"I used the OFF! Maybe if I drank it—"

"Don't worry. You get kind of immune after a while."

"After you run out of blood?"

He begins to scrub the top of his thigh with the brush, one eye lowered like a dog kicking fleas off its ear. "You didn't bring a chessboard, did you?"

"Didn't think of it," I say. "You could make one, eh?"

"No one to play with anyway," he says, disappearing under the table to scratch his feet. The mosquitoes particularly like the tender inside portions around the ankles. The bites stack on top of each other in delicate puffy layers, like fine French pastry—first come, first served.

"I ain't exactly Copacabana," I say, leaning down to talk to him under the table.

"Capablanca."

"Him. But I'll play you."

"Mebbe so."

"Alvina was over this morning," I say.

His head reappears. "I heard. When she comes around, don't answer the door."

I sip from my tea. Gin smells like summer in Southern California after the junipers have been trimmed. "I paid the rent."

"Much obliged," he says. "You're a lesbian and a scholar."

"The least I could do. What does Iba do?"

"Seamstress," he says, jumping up suddenly to grab the can of roach feed.

"She live alone?"

"Spinster as you can get," he says shaking the can, blasting a black shape in the corner, and returning to his chair.

"Sorry," I say. "Forgot to feed them last night."

"Don't sweat it. I gave them some extra."

"I never had a black girl before," I say.

"Forget about *Iba*," he says. "You might as well try to fuck the cat."

"What's wrong with Iba?"

"She's *Catholic*."

"So are *you*."

"I'm lapsed. Anyway, I'm going to hell." He frowns before taking a sip from his mug. "My mom died, I tell you?"

"No."

"Yeah, happened pretty quick. Or maybe not." He looks down. "You know, I always thought it would be better when she was gone." He closes his eyes. His long lashes give him a forlorn aspect, even when he isn't. "My dad and I went out and got drunk after the funeral. I said, man, I don't want a life like that, work drink die. My old man too. Hell." He folds his arms, flattening the biceps. His eyes shine. "She started fucking around on my dad when I was twelve. I'd give anything to catch the bastard who did it and plant him. Broke my dad's heart. But I'm going to bring him back a chest full of Brazilian gold. He worked his whole life at Ryan. Never had a day of fun in his life."

"I'm sorry," I say.

Bent nose aimed at the ceiling, he stares up through his eyebrows in a way that reminds me of a saint in a devotional painting expressing private doubt about his Maker. "'Bout a year ago, like a week before Iba was going to be married," he says, "her fiancé ran off with some white girl from Connecticut. The white girls are always running off with the natives here." He lifts his mug, as if for a toast. "Where is that cat anyway? Mongoose probably got her. A little more hair oil, Johnny?"

"Just a splash there, Johnny. How do you pour two bottles at once?"

"Went to barber's school." He tips out more than a splash into our glasses. "Have you heard her singing 'Abraham in My Bosom' through the wall?"

"So that's what it is."

"She goes to church about nine times a day and has a cross

the size of Eric Clapton on her living room wall. She's a West Indian Catholic." He turns his hand back and forth. "You know, African Voodoo Catholicism."

"How does that work?"

His eyelids droop. "One cup of Nicene Creed," he says in a Bela Lugosi accent, "one cup of mixed nuts."

"Was that before or after the white girl from Connecticut?"

"Catholics are born, son, not made." He yawns again and rubs his eyes with his fists. "Damn, I'm not used to getting up this early."

"She said she was coming over tonight."

"Yeah, well somebody has to keep track of the werewolves." He squints and frowns at his mug again before taking a pursed-lipped sip. "She's a sweetheart of a stray soul. Pardon my alliteration. She's gonna sew you a pair of pants."

"Werewolf pants?"

"No. Hippie pants. Don't think it's an invitation. She just sews people pants. You know, a welcome-to-the-island kind of thing."

"How does she know what size I wear?"

"Hippie pants," he says, slapping the back of his neck. "One size fits all. You'll see. You get breakfast?"

"Too bad I can't eat mosquitoes."

"Kate works at the bakery in town," he says, removing a fruitcake tin from the cupboard. "She gets day-old for free. Actually it's more like week-old. Marmalade?"

"Please."

"We don't have any butter," he says. "It's a butter-free island. No milk either," he adds, "unless you want to chase around a goat."

"No cows," I say. "No country Western music."

"Except at the hotel."

"The Rockefeller Plantation."

"That's right," he says, sliding the jar of marmalade across. "You're picking it all up. More tea?"

"One more for luck, Johnny. Jesus, it's not even noon and I'm already half in the bag. Well, strength in numbness, as they say."

"I hate breakfast," Mountain says, returning to his chair and tousling his hair. "I say, why not just start the day with lunch?"

I spread marmalade and take a bite of the day-old. Bread, marmalade, tea, and gin, this is all I need. That and maybe Iba...

Mountain inspects his bookcase containing the paperback classics, shameless best sellers, Bible, *Fauna Handbook*, *Chilton's* manual, and the wider array of nearly empty liquor bottles. "We're out of booze, Johnny," he says as if announcing a funeral.

"How did that happen, Johnny?"

"How much money you got?"

"'Bout fifty bucks."

"Good," he says, shaking the can of roach feed and blasting the huddled shape in the corner once more. "Now if you stop paying the rent maybe we can make it to the end of the week. Saul don't pay regular. That's the salvaging biz. He still owes me two hundred. What do you want to do this morning?"

"What time does the mini golfcourse open?"

"We'll go look at my boat," he says, disappearing into the bedroom and returning a moment later shaking a speargun at me like Che Guevara. "And we'll shoot us some dinner."

22.

MOUNTAIN AND I BANG OUT THE SCREEN DOOR DRESSED alike in shorts, tennis shoes, and full hangovers. Relaxed from tea, I say good morning to the bees, who revolve around their nest, I fancy, like souls around the face of God. Mountain squats in the gravel, trying to determine what fell off his Toyota the day before. Mumbling all the while about Alabama, he tugs on coat hangers, taps dried lumps of gum, and presses strips of buckled duct tape. The Bud can for a muffler is still intact. Over the years the Corolla has lost most of its frills, wheel covers, chrome strips, panels, mirrors, gas cap: it is hard to pinpoint the exact departure date of any of them. The average car has so many parts you don't really need.

We have to push the car to get it started. Willie Nillie is perched on his roadside bench under the shade of his Pittsburgh Pirates cap. He waves. Mountain honks. The car stalls, and we both jump out to push it again.

"Excellent way to keep in shape," I observe, out of breath.

"The Flintstone Weight Loss Program," Mountain agrees.

Soon we are wobbling and sputtering down the way. Between backfires and steering-wheel seizures, Mountain explains the roads: The one that goes round the island is called the Round Island Road. The one that crosses the island is called the Cross Island Road. When the natives pronounce them, they sound like "Roan-eye-lan Row" and "Cross-eye-lan Row." "They're actually the same row," he says. "Built by the Romans—I mean the Rockefellers. If you drive long enough you will always end up where you started."

"Heavy," I say.

"M.C. Escher."

I look about and try to see myself blended harmoniously into the wilderness. No pictures that aren't preposterous come into my head. Now that I'm practically out of money my transition will have to be more abrupt than I like. "You ever try to go primitive, Mountain?"

"You mean doggy style?" he says.

"No, I mean live without technology. Like my buddy Fish, except without fiberglass and The Grateful Dead."

"Oh yeah," he drawls. The Toyota goes into a fit. Mountain clenches the cigarette in his teeth and grabs the wheel, jerking it viciously left, then right, as if he's breaking a chicken's neck. "There's a couple of abandoned artist huts over on Glitter Bay there," he says. "Glitter Bay's a gold beach, not real gold, of course. I lived up at Scudder's place for a couple of weeks when I first came here. Decent cabin up there." He puffs twice from his cigarette before tossing it out the window. "Public land."

"Public land? Can I see it?"

"Not much to see," he says, grinding the shifter around, trying to get second gear. "It's right up here."

The Toyota chugs up a rutted incline that leads to a clearing in the middle of which sits a narrow, yellow-painted shack—two doorways, no actual doors, and four glassless windows. Mountain parks by the cistern, leaving the engine running.

"Place was in a little better shape when I stayed here," he says, leading me up the stairs. "Foundation's still pretty good." He bats a set of metal-tube wind chimes hanging from the eaves. The cement porch is embedded with seashells. Mountain has to duck to enter. The shack has two rooms, one with a wrecked couch and a crumpled, green plaid blanket stuck together with tar. The other has a weathered rocking chair posted in the door, the rusted frame of a bed, and a battered dresser. There isn't anything resembling a bathroom or kitchen. Vines have invaded and anchored themselves to every conceivable post. A badminton set is scattered across the floor. I right an overturned Folgers coffee can full of screws, washers, bearings, and marbles.

"Got a still out back," says Mountain.

An odor like sewage and rotting plums lifts to my nostrils. "Ever use it?"

"What do you need a still for when you can buy a bottle of rum for a buck?" He lights a cigarette, tosses the match out the window, and descends the stairs. He walks in a mincing step, with one arm hanging lower than the other, his body rolling slightly, like John Wayne in *The Quiet Man*. "Here's the cistern. Can't live without one on this island. No natural water, springs or creeks, except the waterfall in the graveyard and forget it."

"Why?"

"Chollie Legion."

I peek into a concrete sepulchre half-full of brackish green water and wriggling mosquito larvae. "Needs a gallon of bleach," says Mountain, leaning against the tank, his arm laid up along the edge. "You've got to watch these old cisterns. People hide stuff in 'em."

"Like what?"

His eyebrows climb to their height. "Treasure, me hearty," he says, scratching inside his shirt. "There's piles of gold scattered round these parts and I aim to find me a passel of it."

I study the view. Along the western border of the clearing stands a bank of bay rum trees. Beyond that is a view of Telescope Bay, a white rim of sand and its arsenical, magical blue sea. "What are the odds?" I say.

"Better here than most places," he says, eyes scanning the horizon. "This here archipelago we're in, French Hook, is built up considerable with reef. In the previous century there was abundant pirate activity. Over here," he says, pointing north, "marauders used to lure ships onto the reef with lanterns and then plunder 'em. There's whole fleets wrecked out there, even a Nazi sub."

"A Nazi sub?"

"Oh yeah, it's a real underwater museum down there, Dead-wood—prison ships, frigates, schooners, airplanes, yachts—most of it worthless." He leans down, one blue eye squeezed in a Popeye squinch. "You never heard of the Mariner's Trove?"

"Arrr, twice now, to be sure."

He covers his mouth with his hand and takes a thoughtful drag from his Marlboro. "My father's friend, Gene Ratel, very smart guy, passed the bar right out of high school, told me about it. He's in a home, falling apart, lost his leg, sits in a wheelchair smoking his Marlboro 100s all day. He says he knows for a fact that the Mariner's Trove is on the east side. He knew the man, Rupert Knapp, a client, who hid it and was killed shortly afterward by unscrupulous types who never got the information they sought. Very credible story, Deadwood, because Saul Schwartz, the man I work for, of sound business acumen, is looking for the very same fortune. Har har. Except he's looking on the wrong side and thinks it's a shipwreck." He taps his ash with authority. "It ain't a wreck. It's terrestrial, buried or hid."

"Hmm," I say.

"You help me find it, Johnny, I'll split fifty-fifty with you. A man don't need more than a chestful of gold."

"Avast there, me lardhopper," I croak with one eye clamped. "I don't know a thing about treasure. My idea coming here was to live a simple life, Johnny."

"Shiver me sides," he says, poking his tongue into his cheek. "The noble savage."

"Something like that."

He drills a finger at me. "And what would you do all day if you lived up here?"

"Just live in peace, man. Sleep, fish, read."

"And kill mosquitoes," he says. "Hell, you'd be bored or drove crazy in a week. You're a city boy."

"How long did *you* live here, city boy?"

"Long enough to know it was for the birdies," he says, flapping his hands.

"Why'd you leave?"

"Too much work. Man, carrying supplies up this hill? Taking a crap in the jungle every morning while the bugs buzz around your ass? Digging holes all day while the gnats drill your eardrums? Trying to find something to eat? Being alone all the time? 'Bout turned myself into a rum cake. You gotta be built for it." He points back up at the shack. "Like Scudder was."

"Who was Scudder?"

"He built this place, they say. He was a sailor, got tired of that life. I think his son died. Anyway, he had some money and he built this house about twenty years ago. Didn't care much for people. Lived here a long time before he disappeared one day. Some say he went back into the bush. I've been back there a bunch of times, though, and never seen him. Legion's the only one crazy enough to live back there."

"*Mariner's* Trove?" I say. "Maybe Scudder's your man."

"Don't think I haven't looked," he says, flicking his butt off into the brush. "That's why I lived here. But old Saul himself says it's a dead end. No one that ever knew Scudder saw him with gold. I dug about seven thousand holes anyway. Turned this place into an ant farm. Maybe somebody got here before me, but I doubt it."

The gentle, protective coating of gin has begun to erode, revealing the treacherous, volcanic hangover beneath. "What would I need to live up here, Mountain?"

"Depends," he says, tugging on an earlobe. "On what you want. Glass on the windows? Doors that open and close? Electricity? You want to cook? You like scorpions? You like ghosts? It'd be better if you just waited. I'll finish my boat, we'll get some diving equipment. I already got ten virgin wrecks mapped. One of 'em's bound to have bounty aboard. I'll need a partner."

"Mebbe," I say, feeling suddenly discouraged. Try as I might,

I just don't give a whit about sunken gold. I'd rather run around naked, brown, and free.

"Well, what do you want to do now?" he says, yanking open the car door. "Do you want to see the Nazi sub, the cannibal picnic grounds, the old sugar mill, or my boat?"

A yellow-headed hummingbird blurs out in front of me and just as quickly darts away. "I vote boat."

"Okay," he says, pleased by the choice. "Let's mosey."

23.

MOUNTAIN SWINGS OFF THE ROAD AND PLUNGES DOWN
a trail fringed with aloe, manzanita, and lavender pea vines.
Bamboo cane slaps against the windshield—then all at once we
are spinning and bogging down the pink and white sands of
Perception Bay, a curved mile of desert beach and numbing, limpid, vitriolic, sea, cinnamon bay trees, slender guava, goobla
plum, and coconut palms rustling poetically in the breeze.

Mountain has to drive fast to keep from getting stuck. He
crouches over the wheel, shouting like an Apache warrior.
The sand flies out from our tires like speckled pink snow. Through
the corroded hole in the floor I watch it tumble under us in
rippled purity. When we hit hardpack, Mountain wrenches down
the wheel and jerks up the brake and we both jump out in case
anything catches on fire. When the smoke clears, it appears that
the Toyota is sinking. Mountain seems unconcerned.

The shoal beneath us is mottled with kelp and jeweled with
the deep flicker of tropical fauna. The sky is mauve above the
pale, silver-blue bay. The air smells of brine and jasmine and tar.
We make our way across the sand toward a set of framed timbers
sitting on a cement pad. Under the keel sits a weathered, red
wooden sea chest stenciled with the letters H M S *Victoria*. "Here
she is," says Mountain. "Just a little workboat to fiddle around in
the reefs."

"You're calling your boat the H M S *Victoria*?" I say.

"No," he says. "I salvaged that. My boat is *Colleen*. Named it after my mom. Dan Cordova's helping me build it. You met him?"

"Dan? Not yet."

"He's already built four." He pinches the bridge of his bent nose and shows me the split in his front teeth. I'm suddenly envious of him. Homemade and content, he's found his own way.

The bushes behind us rustle and I turn to see a chubby young blonde girl, naked and brown as a Brazil nut, smiling at us. She looks down bashfully and brushes sand from her navel. Her dark legs are also sugared with sand. Her eyes are as pale as sunlight. Around her neck is a string of lilac-colored orchids.

"Mountain?"

Mountain, arm raised, dimples rippling on his deltoids, is pointing out at the bay and saying: "There's a ship wrecked out there about two hundred yards. Thirty-two-gun British frigate."

"The H M S *Victoria*."

"Right. Most of the cannons are still intact. I got a brass sextant and a silver tea caddy off it. Not bad for a free dive."

The girl ducks behind a bush, flashing her white rump like a deer, and then begins to peek at me from behind a stunted palm tree. "What's a tea caddy?" I ask absently.

"It's a thing they put tea in. Why are you whispering?"

"I don't want to scare off the wildlife."

"What are you talking about?" he says, arm dropping to his side.

"The girl," I whisper. "Do you see her?"

"Are you—where? Oh her," he says, shielding his eyes. "That's Judy Van Schorr. She runs wild all over the island."

"Where are her parents?"

He turns up his palms.

"How old is she?"

"I don't know," he says, growing solemn. He swipes at his nose. "Best to stay away from her, though."

"Why?"

"You wouldn't believe me if I told you."

"Try me."

"There's a host of tales about her, the favorite one being that she's a lost soul from the days of the revolution."

"A ghost, you're saying."

"Along those lines."

I'm checking his face for tics or other signs of repressed skylarking. He's apparently serious, hand on the back of his neck. I clap my own neck. "What say you to this ungainly rumor, Doctor Livesey?"

He scratches his chin. "I'm a man who reckons by his lights and not the wisp, as you may know, Jim. And if a number don't have a square, by gum, then it's a zero." Perplexed as I've ever seen him, he lifts a hill of sand with his foot and lets the grains sift through his toes. "She did come up to the cabin a couple of times and give me the shivers, though."

"What'd she do?"

"Well, she's naked at midnight staring into my windows with those white eyes of hers and jabbering about some infernal molasses vats."

"She seems fairly well fleshed out for a ghost."

He screws up an eye. "Do you know of the snake-god voo-doo cults of Western Africa?"

"Wait, don't tell me, she's a *zombie*."

Mountain wears a look that suggests nausea or indigestion. "That's the legend."

I have to laugh. "She moves around fairly well for someone with no brain waves," I observe. "Of course, so too have many of our great leaders."

"Yes," he says, flexing his jaw muscles, his mind elsewhere, perhaps on the young spook jabbering at him through the glass-less windows of Scudder's old abandoned cabin. In the meantime, the subject of our bizarre conversation has slipped back into the foliage.

"Tea caddy, huh?" I say, returning my attention reluctantly to antiques. This plump, smiling, nude cadaver with orchids around her neck must be some sort of complicated riddle or fancy confusion that will be illuminated later by someone with a less-mathematical bent. "What's a hundred-year-old British tea caddy worth?"

"Saul gave me seventy for it," he says, fondling the point of his beard. "Could've got maybe four or five hundred in the States. They say there was gold coin aboard. Somebody got there before me, but there's more down there, plenty more." His expression seems troubled now as he calculates the imperceptible distance between himself and "the gold out there." He turns to me suddenly. "You know what one *bar* of gold bull is worth, man?"

I glance around for Judy again. She seemed a friendly spirit for such a dire portrait. "You know what a gold *curse* is?" I counter.

He waves me back.

"I'm serious. Gold ruins everyone, Johnny: Spaniards, Incas, Egyptians, Romans, lost Dutchmen, the drones who count it and guard it. Remember Fred C. Dobbs babbling alone in the desert? The glory of Israel would've never been lost had the Ark of the Covenant been made of wood instead of gold and jewels. What did the Philistines want with a couple of stone tablets?"

He scratches his head patiently. "Those old gold myths are about greed, man, not gold. Fred C. Dobbs was *greedy*."

"Mebbe," I say, watching a flock of large, blue-footed birds coast overhead.

"Boobies," Mountain says, squinting up at them. "Blue-footed boobies."

"Those are some big boobies."

"Used to be white flamingos out here," he says, picking up a rock and flicking it out into the water. It skips twice and then sinks. "But they got hunted out. A delicacy." He turns a fist and admires the sinewy bulge of his arm. "Same thing happened to the iguanas."

"People ate iguanas?"

He nods. "The tail. Roasted."

"Roasted to extinction."

"People will eat anything."

"Except cockroaches," I say.

"I ate one once," he says. "Fell into my pan while I was cooking some fish."

"How was it?"

"Crunchy."

"Your car is sinking."

He scratches at his stomach, then digs around in his pocket and comes out with a ball of lint that he examines and dissects for a few seconds before saying, "Hilton plans a hotel here."

"Where?"

"Right here, man," he says, pointing at the ground. "Perception Bay. The safest harbor on the east side, the only place to anchor a boat in hurricane season." The leaves on the plum trees rattle suddenly in the breeze.

"Maybe they'll change their minds."

"Not likely," he says, with a sad gaze at the horizon. "Everything's gonna be like California here soon. Pizza Huts and when the stoplight turns green some asshole honking his horn." He drops his head as if he's finished a prayer. His hair hangs down in his eyes, a young, blue-eyed martyr.

Two boats hover on the horizon, sails flapping. The eight-inch waves shush in silkily at intervals of eight to ten seconds. The sky is hot and deep as a dream. I am conscious of my heart squashing sidelong, the gin evaporating from my consciousness, and time careening rapidly.

"Cheer up, Johnny," I say, glancing around again for my mysterious sand pixie. "We're all going to die anyway."

He smiles deliberately, the balls of muscle on his cheeks pushing his eyes up into lofty slants of artificial cheer. His big biceps flicker. He points a toe and looks absently down the length of his nearly hairless leg.

"What's in the sea chest?" I say, scratching my calf where I've already raked it raw.

"Few tools, rain gear," he says, lifting the lid on the old wooden trunk. "Dan helped me rivet it to the pad for hurricane season."

"When they build the Hilton you can rent it out to tourists, charge them ten bucks to see the naked dead chick."

"Let's take a swim," he says, producing fins and masks. "We'll get us a fish. Don't worry about sharks. Most of them are harmless. If something gets too close just punch it in the nose."

"I'll emit a cloud of urine."

"Spit on your mask. It'll keep it from fogging."

"Thanks, Johnny."

I strap on my snorkel and stumble into the ocean, tripping on my fins. I have never snorkeled before. Be careful not to cut your legs on that reef! My mask and then my nose fill suddenly and I think I might drown. The saltier the water the more buoyant you supposedly become, but I feel about as buoyant as a boiled egg. I suddenly empathize with pelicans. The seawater will be a salve for all my mosquito bites, I think. Mountain frolics around me, adroit for such a large human being, but there isn't much he isn't good at.

I've been comfortable in the water all of my life but these rubber and plastic attachments and my unwilling distance from the innocent joy of nature bemuse me, as if by being a member of a military industrial complex and a one-time Vega-owner with big rubber feet, I am barred forever from the grace of Eden. The fish rip and flame in a million varieties below my fins: black-and-white fish, X-ray fish, bright blue parrot fish with Oliver Hardy grins, diamond-spotted jewel fish, blue-green angelfish with orange fins, triggerfish with luminous blue stripes, damsel, butterfly, cardinal, and clown fish. Mountain shows me how to use the speargun and I give chase through tattered reef walls reminiscent of the crumbling ramparts of sunken castles, the tall herds of silent creatures tipping and disappearing before me, the surreal hulk of the foundered British frigate floating hazily in the distance. It is weird down here, a dark, confounding Salvador Dali

blue, everything magnified half again and distorted by the mask.
A barracuda, lean and green as a snake, jaws gaping with long,
needle-sharp teeth, flies up into my mask and just as I prepare to
punch it in the snout, it darts away. My heart beats sharply in
quick pulses to the tips of my fingers and toes. I glance around for
other ruffians of the sea. A fat pink snapper wiggles by and I fire
an arrow at him but miss by a foot. My pink target flicks and jinks
away, propelled like a cartoon.

Mountain finally nails a six-pound grouper and swings the
writhing fish aloft on the steel arrow. We slosh back into shore
and plop down on the beach, our glassy-eyed, speckled brown
dinner twitching between us. I am mesmerized by sun and color,
blood loss and gin. The air is the same temperature as the water
as the sand. Crumbs of pink quartz, like confectionary bits you
might give to your second-grade sweetheart on Valentine's Day,
glimmer in the coarse white sand. The small waves shimmer up
the shore. The sky is so blue it makes my heart ache.

I scratch at a cluster of bites on my neck for a while. "As
soon as I get some money together," I say, "I'll move out."

"Forget what I said," Mountain says, his dark hair dripping on
his shoulders. With the big sad eyes, those sensual lips, the coiled
dark hair, he looks very Italian today. He tips his head and knocks
his ear with the heel of his hand. "We're not using that room.
Where would you go anyway? It's too expensive to live in town."

"I'll move into Scudder's place."

He waves at the air. "At least wait till you have enough to
buy a *door*. The goats and the jackasses used to come up the hill
when I was gone, eat all my food, and crap all over the floor.
Anyway, that part of the jungle is pretty well haunted."

"Zombies going door to door?" I say, amused.

"Live up there for a few nights. You'll see."

He's still serious. I don't ever quite know what the story is
with Mountain. I let the waves whoosh in, three, four. The sun
drifts behind a cloud and like the explanation of Rayleigh scatter-
ing or the myth of the sky, everything seems suddenly drab.

"How long you been with Kate?" I venture.

"Couple months," he says, lifting a shoulder at the precise moment the fish between us gives a twitch.

I lean back on my elbows. The sun shows again. "That's a long time for you."

He shrugs.

"How old is she anyway?"

"Thirty-two."

"What did she do back in Baltimore?"

"Social worker. She was married for a while." He drops back on a forearm, pinches up a measure of sand, and watches it trickle down. "None of it worked out."

"How long she been here?"

He sniffles, then rubs vigorously at his nose. "Bout a year, I think."

I watch him closely while I scratch my hip. "How'd you guys meet?"

"They show movies in town on Saturday nights. Sat next to each other one night. We were both looking for a place to live. One thing kind of led to another."

The fish flops between us. Mountain's hooked, I see, and it isn't the usual three-week variety. It must be her age. It must be an extension of his mother complex, now irresolvable by death. I'm familiar with the textbook pattern of the psychically damaged child reliving events and even inventing scenes to somehow resolve the past. I guess by the ease with which she moved in with Mountain and by watching her the night before—"what we do every night," as she termed it—that Kate is as alcoholic and pro-miscuous as Mountain, and that he must protect her at all costs, as he would his own mother, to keep her from meeting the same fate. I recall his wish to "catch the bastard and plant him," which I understand he might translate into any figure showing interest in Kate, i.e. me. The last thing in the *world* I want to do is get tangled up in this kooky oedipal psycho-triangle, so the quicker I can get out and on my own, the better.

"I need a job," I say. "Your boy Schwartz hiring?"

Mountain shakes his head. "It's strictly commission. You might not make any money for a month. Only reason I'm doing it is to learn the trade. Best thing is to go with me. I'll teach you how to skin-dive." His eyes sweep the forest behind us and then he glances once at the sun. "But don't worry about that now. You just got here."

"But I'm broke."

"First requisite to great reward," he says, getting to his feet. "Come on, let's get this fish in a pan before it stinks. Then we'll go into town and get us some liquor."

24.

THAT NIGHT, WHILE I'M IN THE MIDDLE OF THE STORY about the customs people in San Juan throwing my underwear all over the baggage conveyor, Iba knocks on the door. I've forgotten she said she'd drop by and I'm aware I've drunk too much to make a good impression. Dishes are stacked on the counter. The taint of burnt grouper fillet still clings to the bowed and water-stained ceiling. The room is dim, as those who drink a great deal often prefer. The single candle flame flips about, throwing Rorschach shadows across the walls.

"Come in out of the bees!" bellows Mountain.

For a moment Iba's face hovers tentatively in the doorway. She is dressed in a short bombazine nurse's uniform and black church pumps, her hair wrapped in a shiny bun, her expression a tight register of nerves. I can sense her need for society overpowering her fear of habitual drinkers. Kate, who can imitate the native idiom to a T—stress, pitch, and tone—jabbers a welcome. Mountain does a pretty fair Jamaican accent himself.

"Sit down, chile," he says.

"Drink, Iba?" I say, trying to sound as thin-tongued as possible.

"No tank you," she says, perching at the edge of a chair and hugging her arms.

I have a glance at her gleaming legs and finish the story about my underwear.

"You're lucky you didn't lose anything valuable," says Kate.

"I didn't have anything valuable, except my knife."

"They stole all my jewelry," says Kate.

"I lost a camera," says Mountain, "and a hundred bucks in the casino in five minutes. They cheat. I almost threw over a table." Iba listens with horror as we lean our faces into the candle burning in the center of the table and recount our corrupted passages to her innocent home.

"Have you been to Puerto Rico, Iba?" I ask.

"My brudduh live in Bridgetown," she says, touching her bun.

"Bridgetown?" I ask.

"Barbados," says Kate, scooting back her chair with a grating honk against the linoleum.

Iba's brother is a customs agent, whom she stayed with for two weeks once, the great adventure of her life. We also learn more than I would ever care to know about the churches there and Claudette Colbert's house and where the Empress Josephine, Napoleon's wife, got a cannonball in the stomach. Barbados as I calculate it is about 150 miles north.

"Have you been to Florida then, Iba?" I say, fondling my jar of Scotch and then reluctantly replacing it in its watery ring.

"No," she says, with a wave of the hand. "Barbados is de fardest away I been."

"You've never been to the United *States*?" I say.

"No," she shakes her head tightly.

"Maybe we can take her back to San Diego," I say to Mountain.

"Or Baltimore," says Kate.

"I never heard of doze," Iba says, recrossing her arms.

"My grandmother lives in New York," I say.

Her eyes light. "I would like to go dare," she says.

"What would you do in New York?" Mountain says.

"I would watch television all day," she announces with a proud lift of the chin.

We all laugh but she's serious. "You could watch television anywhere," Kate says.

"Not here," she says.

"The old girl's right," says Mountain.

My neck is sore from trying not to look at Kate. She has a way of glancing at me smoky and sidelong from under her lashes that not only defies Mountain's wishes, but seems designed to aggravate him. Every night that we sit together drinking and conversing, I fit another piece into her psychological profile: the bald way she exhibits her breasts and legs, her Southern affectations, her unwillingness to discuss her past (except vague references of distaste for America). Coquettish, dissolute, withdrawn, a bit worn out and cynical, she seems like the type of person to stake claim to a tropical island. The expatriates on the whole here are a rather miserable lot. When I asked why she came to Poisson Rouge, she answered one word, my word: Paradise. She seems selfish, but I imagine there was a time when she was more giving (her marriage and her social career, for example) and it earned her nothing but snubs. America is no place for an altruist, don't I know it. Except for her stick-out ears, mussed black hair, and devotion to cocktail hour, she shares little in common with Mountain. She is really much more like me.

Iba leaves early after listening, almost disdainfully, I would say (doesn't she understand how difficult this transition is for me, that I *must* drink to cope?), as I try to fill Kate in on *General Hospital*—I happened to see it once or twice, Luke and Laura were getting back together—and then I am sitting alone at the table with the radio going *ffffffff* and Mountain and Kate whooping and hollering in a mating frenzy in the next room. I turn in still thinking of Iba. I have always thought of Americans as being like anyone else in the world, interchangeable, but it isn't true. Our level of competition, standard of living, complexity of existence, love of technology, and violent, compressed history set us apart. Iba's lonely, it's obvious. It must crush her, for I don't believe she's built for it. Her beauty will become another profligacy of nature if she doesn't learn how to get back on her feet soon. I fancy I can hear her undressing through the walls. I must learn to speak the idiom and then I will take her on a picnic and seduce her in a coconut grove. I sleep under double sheets that night while the roaches cool their bodies against the sea breeze floating through the screens.

25.

I WAKE UP THE NEXT MORNING IN POISSON ROUGE, wearing a tight, three-cornered headache. I finally get up the momentum to close the lid on the toilet and climb into the crude cement stall for a shower. The jumbo roaches hanging on the walls wave their feelers good morning to me. I think the cold water will feel good but it only feels *cold*. I hop lively, glancing sidelong at the roaches, which are apparently receiving signals through their antennae. The water is so cold I almost sprain my back. I lather up quickly out of a glass bottle of brown castile soap plastered with extravagant, old-fashioned claims such as "Live forever honestly with curly hair," shave clumsily in a distorted, blue-frosted mirror hung from the neck of the showerhead, and hop out ASAP.

The room must be seventy-five degrees, but I am actually cold for a few minutes. There are no towels about—only a stack of old newspapers that serve as a bath mat—so I sit dripping at the table for half an hour, studying *Flora and Fauna of the Lesser Antilles* and waiting for Mountain and Kate to get up before I realize they are gone. The car is not in the driveway. Imagine sleeping through the starting of that rattletrap. I must have slept for a change. It is so difficult to relax while you are the main course.

In the flora book I read about the machineel tree, whose bark has an acid that can dissolve skin. Goats standing under machineel trees in the rain have been observed to lose their coats. The Caribs used the poison from the bark to dip arrows and kill

Europeans. I mark this page and close the book. Then I put on a shirt, light a smoke, and wonder what I will do. I have nothing really to do. Laundry, maybe, but I'm not up for washing it in the sink and then hanging it on a line where it will never dry. Mountain has promised to drive me to the Laundromat on the other side of the island. Expensive, and all your clothes end up yellow, but at least they have D-R-Y-E-R-S.

Leaning back in my chair, I conjure up images of scrambled eggs and bacon and a piping mug of fresh coffee. I rummage through the cupboards. The "day-old" in the fruitcake tin is gone. There is literally nothing to eat. I decide I'll catch a fish, clean and fry it. I spent many days as a youth upon the lake. Just out the door the seas are chock-full with gratis delicacies. I find a spool of four-pound test on the top of the bookcase, along with several rust-powdered hooks. No pole, but a man who lives by his wits in the wild cannot be burdened by the unavailability of a specific tool. No bait either. What will I use for bait? Maybe the fishing can wait. Even with the right equipment, I was never much of a fisherman.

I feel like having a drink, but it is a crime to spend the day indoors crocked in the tropics in the Pepsi-Cola vibrancy of my youth. Even in the States I hardly ever drank in the mornings. So, I walk outside. The bug-eyed, loose-jowled old man whom Kate calls Willie Nillie sits on his bench by the road in his Pittsburgh Pirates cap. He waves. I stroll down and introduce myself. "I'm Edgar Donahoe."

"I'm Willie," he says in a scraped voice, like Scatman Crothers.

"Your son plays for the Pirates."

He smiles. "Dot right."

"What's his name?"

"He Willie too."

Willie? I think. There is only one Willie on the Pirates roster as I recall and it's the great Willie Stargell.

"He play last night?" I ask eagerly, taking a seat next to him.

"Went one for tree wid a walk." He smiles mistily and studies the backs of his large weatherworn hands. "No RBI."

I pat him on the back. The people on this island probably don't even know who Willie Stargell is. Maybe that's a good thing. Willie seems at peace with it. I have never known anyone who even knew anyone who was a Major League ballplayer, much less a shoo-in for the Hall of Fame. "You must be proud."

He has these smiling, rheumy eyes that answer for him. We chat for a while about the lowly Padres. San Diego is an embarrassing sports town—it's really a place where people go to "enjoy the weather" (i.e. turn off their brains)—but I miss sitting in those plastic bleachers above left field in San Diego Stadium and drinking sneaked-in beer from a two-gallon thermos with my excellent friend Pat Fillmore, who left one day without a word and returned to Montana. It feels good to talk baseball, but Willie's not much interested in the Padres, as it should be with any honest fan, and I don't want to wear out my welcome.

"I've heard of a gold beach, Willie," I say. "Do you know it?"

"Glitter Bay?" he suggests, one eyebrow poised.

"That's the one."

He points north. "No gold dare, dough."

We laugh.

"I think I'll go south today, Willie. Maybe I'll find diamonds."

"Try Diamond Bay," he says.

We laugh again. I don't know if such a place exists. I turn up the road south. It seems unfamiliar to me once again, forbidden. I think of Kipling:

Something hidden. Go and find it.
Go and look behind the Ranges—
Something lost behind the Ranges.
Lost and waiting for you. Go!

Up the rise and over the hill I go. A squirrel cuckoo peers down critically at me from a locust tree. I pass under a steeple of cool bamboo and out in the watery distance I descry the profile of the unfriendly Fish—a lean and dark brown figure, like a Daumier drawing of Don Quixote—standing in his slow-moving skiff. I try not to dislike him. He may be a hypocrite and a misanthrope who listens to spongy electric folk music, but in many ways he stands for the same things I do. I don't need any more enemies than I already have.

A shack patched together from tin and different-colored boards comes up on the right. A pink-legged chicken scratches in the yard. Pant legs kick alternately from a clothesline in the breeze, like a man running in place. Along the side of the shanty sits a wide Buick washed with rust. Everything about the place is neat and trim, though there is no demonstration of the concept called paint, which is probably a hundred dollars a gallon. A sign nailed to a tree out by the road reads: Goats Will Be Shot.

Behind me the Bowlegged One has appeared, trudging insanely under the sun. He doesn't see me yet, I don't think. I spy a trail off to the left, which I know will bring me out again to the sea, and duck in quickly. I wait for him to pass. He spits evil, incoherent oaths. His yellow eyes, I note, are mismatched, as I have often seen in photographs of the wickedest and most disturbed criminals. I hold my breath in wonder. As soon as he disappears over a rise I turn and scurry away down the trail.

The flora here is oddly reminiscent of Southern California, waist-high manzanita, yellow-plumed bitter aloe, and even a few startling flourishes of the flat-lobed prickly pear. Down into a long prairie of white sand that glitters like broken glass, I arrive upon a motorcycle leaning against its kickstand. The water beyond is a frosted oriental blue gleaming with golden sandbars. Down close to where the thin and almost transparent waves fall up the shore is a Navaho blanket with a female figure sitting on it, undressed, my zombie teenybopper. No, she's too tall, with a thinner neck and dark hair.

Though the beach would be public, I feel suddenly like an intruder. I am about to turn silently and sneak away when another naked female emerges from the sea. Nymphs of Atlantis!

She has a spangled yellow fish with blue eyes, caught and wriggling in the bottom of a long net. Her attention is on the fish. She seems pleased with her catch. She is superbly shaped—long legs, high, clean haunches and breasts. My vision of paradise reblooms. She looks up at me suddenly and stops, the tide sucking around her knees, the fish struggling in the bottom of its nylon prison. The seated woman turns and studies me with a dark squint. It is Kate. When she recognizes me she smiles and waves me over.

I walk along stiffening, my neck tight, wondering what I will say.

The golden fisherwoman, who has the most delicate and downy of muffs, like a plump young apricot, has freed her yellow, blue-eyed fish and is rapidly putting on clothes.

Kate remains blithely and unselfconsciously naked. "Hey Edgar," she says. "Take off your clothes!"

"Can't," I say. "I'm a Seventh-Day Adventist."

Kate's small mouth glistens as she roars with appreciation. This is the first time I have been with her away from Mountain and the difference in her personality is notable. Her smile is warm. Her copper eyes glow in the sun. Her short, dark, wet hair is combed straight back in the fashion of early Lloyd Bridges. Her white breasts fall steeply and then suddenly jut upward giving me a thrill similar to an amusement-park ride. And speaking of muffs—well, not that I'm *staring*—but let's just say she looks just spanking today—better than I could've ever hoped—and her lack of inhibition is a relief.

"Didn't know you were down here," I say.

"This is Fanny Trouet," says Kate, indicating with a gesture that I do my best to follow to its end.

"Fanny," I say with a courteous nod as she continues to scramble into her clothes. Fanny has clear, mescaline-green eyes: a straight, elegant nose: heavy, laterally compressed lips that are shaped like the O in *Orgasm*: and gold hair plastered in a wet cap against her head. I want to say, "Don't get dressed on my account," but manners and an inherent diffidence around nude strangers get the best of me.

"Fanny is from France," says Kate, turning her pretty foot and then leaning forward suddenly to grab a bottle of lotion. I try to concentrate on the folds of her stomach, though her wonderful breasts gently swinging and lusciously formed seem to be in the way.

"How do you do?" says Fanny.

Am I bowing? I hope that I'm not bowing. No, really it's more of an adaptive posture. I glance helplessly up the beach.

"I joze come from Dominica," Fanny explains with a certain recuperative and perfectly understandable hauteur, buttoning her blouse and tilting her head at me like a cockatoo.

"Is that a French island?" I say.

"At one tam it was," she says, rubbing her hair vigorously with a towel and then attacking it with a comb. "Lak all of zeeze." She gestures at the sea. "Zee culture eez steel French."

"It's very lovely, I imagine."

"Oh, very, very lovely," she replies, her nose wrinkled.

I point at her fishing net. "You threw your fish back."

"I can't bear to keep zem. You can't keep zeeze ones anyway." She squints compassionately.

"Is that your motorcycle up the beach, by any chance?" I ask.

"Oh, yes ... "

"Fanny lives over on Merriwether Cove," says Kate, shaking her bottle of lotion.

"The old leper colony?" I say.

Kate seated below me is everything a man could ask for, but it's all there, isn't it—no mystery—and I find myself now more earnestly drawn to the woman in clothes. I wonder all about Fanny, her Frenchness, her goldness, her trim blonde apricot—I mean her compassion. I wonder if she is single. Perhaps sex fantasies about an eligible female would be a healthy change of pace. She tips her head at me suddenly. "You are zee kook?"

"I have kooked—I mean cooked, yes."

"You wheel show me zee secret of a buttermilk beeskits?"

"The what?"

"Biscuits," says Kate, stretching her shoulders back.

"Man always come out so flat," says Fanny.

"I can't picture you with flat biscuits," I say. "Probably the baking powder."

"Ah don't theenk so," she says. "We have a fresh from Ravissant."

"Are they flaky at all?"

"No, I would say not."

"Where do you get your buttermilk?"

"We have a goats."

The bottle of suntan lotion clenched in her teeth, Kate rolls her eyes up at me. A strand of saliva glistens as she pulls the bottle away from her lips. She shakes the bottle and squirts a puddle of coconut-smelling lotion into her palm and creams it into her thighs. Then she shakes the bottle again and spurts the white fluid all over her brown shoulders and the tops of her breasts. I swing my attention to the sea. Though it is all the same ocean, obeying the same chromatic and electromagnetic laws, every cove has a different complexion. This one is stained with basalt and glowing with fire coral. Wouldn't it be perfect if Fanny needed a roommate? We could get a place in town, split the rent, and never leave the bed except to make biscuits. She could teach me how to French kiss. I wonder suddenly who the "we" is in "we have a goats."

"Are you going out to sweem?" says Fanny, breaking my reverie.

"No, actually I was looking for a place called Diamond Bay? Willie was telling me about it."

The women exchange looks. "There eez no place like zat."

"Ah, Willie was joshing me then."

"Willie Nillie?" says Kate.

"You know, I think he is actually Willie Stargell's *father*. He said his son was named Willie too."

The women stare at me. They don't know Willie Stargell either. Kate's breasts are brown bombs poised to blast me out of the sand. You can see why certain civilizations with loose dress codes never really get off the ground.

"Is Mountain working on his boat today?" I ask.

"Every day," she drawls. "We'll all be living in a mansion soon."

"I may as well go out and help him then, if I can remember how to get there. Why didn't you wake me this morning?"

"You were snoring so sweetly," says Kate, chin down on her shoulder. "And I hate to disturb the mosquitoes while they're feeding."

"How long are you here for?" asks Fanny.

"I don't know," I say, assuming the position of a famous explorer, hands on hips, one knee bent, chin raised. "Actually, I thought I might try to make a go of it here."

I'm already familiar with the disappointment that registers in her eyes. "I'd better get going," I say, glancing once more down at Kate, who leans back on her arms and squeezes her eyes sultrily. "Too bad you can't stay," she says.

"Next time."

"I'll see you back at the ranch," she says.

26.

AT THE SOUND OF KNOCKING I ROLL CRUSTILY FROM BED.
A few too many teas this morning sent me off to an early nap a
while back. My socked feet hit the floor. Thank God I am dressed.
After only a few nights on Vampire Island I sleep fully clothed—
like a businessman without a home—to give the mosquitoes,
which drill through any gauge of cotton, sheet, or underwear, the
minimum satisfaction. I hobble to the door. I have been dreaming I am in hell and it is hard to distinguish the waking state. Iba
stands on the other side of the screen, gorgeous and ascetic,
a half-moon smile on her beautiful black face, her collarbones
calling to me, a bundle of bright fabric rolled under her arm.

"Oh hi, Iba, come in."

My stately neighbor ducks in gracefully under the swarm
of bees. She wears a blue chiffon leisure suit with a black
macramé sash, the waist drawn tightly in. Her hair is cornrowed
with aqua beads and the lids of her knifelike eyes are streaks of
Cleopatra green. She smells ripely of woman, witch hazel, French
crullers, and fried cheese balls.

I swipe at the sleep in my eyes and smooth back my hair.
The sink is full of the same dishes that were here last time she
dropped in. "Taking a nap," I explain. "Up a little late last night."

Iba looks around with concern. Does she secretly want
me? I wonder. Despite her distrust of me, I think there's a good
chance of something happening between us. I just wish she'd
quit catching me at the wrong time. Her eyes flick to the door.

Solemnly she unfurls her bundle and holds it up for examination. "I made you deeze," she says.

"Pants?" I say. "For me?"

"Yes. Try dem on."

I hold my new purple-and-orange striped trousers up to admire. Not since the first Beatle prototypes hit the streets when I was in junior high have I seen a color scheme like this. "Wait right here."

In the privacy of my room, I shuck off my Levi's and pull the baggy island breeches over my mosquito-suckled legs. *Now* I look like a pimp. No member of The Grateful Dead or even the jesters of the court of Louis XVI would have the balls to be caught out in public in these pants. I don't know where she found the material. A Der Wienerschnitzel flag may have washed ashore. The pants make me look like a twit. But they are comfortable in a Barnum and Bailey sort of way and I want to please her. Tightening the drawstring, I stroll back out. "Perfect fit," I say, hands raised and giving a turn.

She tips her head critically. I can see she would perhaps give a tug at the inseam, but no touching. I know that rule already, especially the inseam. "You like dem?" she says.

"Very much. Thank you."

Chin elevated, she surveys the room. I feel the silence rushing in. Religion would be her topic. For me the challenge of a devout Catholic girl is a bit like cracking the three-minute mile, but I am a good sport and the journey to bliss is always uphill. I imagine her in bed, the sounds of the springs under us, the roused expression on her face, the position of those hands, the tilt of her chin. Lord, I'm a comin'!

"Shall we sit outside?" I suggest.

Alvina spies on us from her second-floor window as Iba and I take our places in the redwood chairs on the gravel terrace that overlooks Turner Cove, which I have learned recently was named after a buccaneer who killed a garrison of British soldiers. Tell me why the murderers of history—the Bluebeards and Billy the Kids and Charles Mansons—are remembered over the men and women who toiled and lived honestly all their lives. Maybe I'm in hell after all.

Behind us is a blue stucco garage, where Alvina has been storing junk for fifty years. I prop my feet on the stone retaining wall that serves as a fortification against high seas and also cradles a low hedge of black wattle and a bed of blue aloe and barrel cactus. Yellow allamandas grow out of the black wattle straight up the guava trees. A family of athletic lizards wearing red ascots comes out on the flat rocks in the sun to do pushups for us.

Iba treats me to the melody of her idiom. Quickly we fall into one of those embarrassing silences that happen when you have been talking ten minutes with a person and not understood a word she's said. Baseball statistics begin running through my head. Across the road stands a locust tree, two blue doves sitting inside. Good omens, I imagine, until Legion, the Horseshoe-Legged One, shining with perspiration, strolls into view. My heart slams against my chest. He stops and turns his gaze on me, his deranged eyes clouded with blood.

Iba is not impressed. She snorts contemptuously. "Step you feet down dat road, duppy," she scolds, shaking her finger at him. "A dead man doan have no business roun here."

Legion offers a relaxed smile and waves at the flies dancing around his head. The blade of his usually polished machete is dull as if with rust or blood, perhaps it is only the tree shadows. Leaves adhere to every part of his body, whether by design or circumstance I don't know.

"You hear me now," calls Iba, now whipping that finger of approbation above her head. "We doan tek de devil's children here."

Legion smiles at her with the tolerant, cocksure misunder-standing of a juvenile delinquent. He is stoned, I reckon, good and plenty. A finger floats up from his side and wavers on us in a funky, undulant voodoo, then both hands rise and jiggle at the heavens. His body shivers, his bloodshot eyes roll back in his head.

Then he turns all at once with a wolfish guffaw and strides away up the road.

"Yo spells ain't no good against de Lord of heaven," she shouts after him, her face clenched in a fearsome scowl.

"You know him?" I ask eagerly.

"Don't everybody?" she replies, arching her brows, her dark eyes glinting with righteousness. "Dey ought to trow him in jail and bury de key."

"There's no law against being crazy, is there?"

"What about one for *killin'* a man?" she counters, her left eye shriveling.

"Killin' a man?" I repeat, feeling my head wobble on my neck. "Is that what you said? Where?"

"Over on St. Vincent, a year or so back." She brushes a fallen leaf from her thigh.

"Who'd he kill?"

"I don't know de man *per*sonally," she replies, turning her head on her lovely neck and wetting her lips with her tongue. "A touris of some type. He doan like de white man, doan like de touris. De troot of it." She nods the slow and woeful affirmative. "He doan like no one."

I make a mental note to corroborate the murder rumor with Kate or Mountain. You'd think they would've mentioned it. Funny that she's calling him dead. Quite the raft of zombism over on this east side. I decide that this must just be colorful island metaphor. "He seems to come around a great deal," I say.

"I don't see im much. He stay outta my pat. I tell him about de Lord Jesus." She nods at me hard. "He been followin' you, dough."

"Has he?"

"Yes, he wait across de road dare, sit in dat tree." She indicates the locust tree where the two good-luck doves reside. "Follow you roun' like a ghos'. You don't see 'im?"

"Well, once or twice, yes. I thought it was a coincidence."

"Coincidence, my black foot." I look down at her foot.

"Sump'm about you," she continues, squinting at me. "He know de black art too. His mama was a witch."

"What?" I say, my head wobbling again cartoonlike on its stalk. "Witch?"

"Das right." I know that look on her face. I've seen it already when she's finished a story and you've laughed or she's given you triumphant herbal advice or a pair of handmade pants.

"Why would he care about me?"

She shrugs. "He toll you once awready he intend to kill you. He might be dead, but dat don't mean he lie too."

I chew on the quick of an index finger. "What do you mean 'dead'?"

"Dead to me," she says with a toss of the head. "Killin' an scarin' people. Walkin' dem roads all night. Rollin' around in is tombs. Humph."

"What should I do, Iba, to get rid of him?"

"Start goin' to church, I'd say." She glances piously at the clouds.

"Church is eleven miles. Besides, I'm not Catholic. I mean, I admire Christianity in principle, don't get me wrong."

"Well, you can't *run* away from trouble," she says, shaking her head slowly, "'cause there ain't no place dat far. Maybe you need a *garde corps*."

"What's a *garde corps*?"

"It's a charm dat ward off evil," she replies crossly, dangling an imaginary pendulum. "To protec you when yo back is turned from de Lord."

"Where do I get one?"

"Cinnamon Jim. He lib in de village at de top of de hill." She might be indicating heaven with her large beautiful hand. "Chollie know de black art. Jim know more. He an obeah man."

Obeah and voodoo are both imported fetishistic forms of witchcraft from Africa, I'm vaguely aware, but I don't appreciate the difference. "What's in a *garde corps*?" I ask, noting that Legion has slipped back into the jungle. He's quite adept at vanishing and appearing, yes, quite uncanny. Mountain says he spends most of his days in the backwoods keeping clear all the old slave trails built in the days of the 1833 revolt. And Iba says his mama was a witch?

Iba shrugs and fondles a green bead in her hair. "Dried chicken blood, a wari bean, seben bone of a rattlesnake tail…"

"Parakeet livers?"

"No, but a gris-gris powder."

"What's a gris-gris powder?"

"From a gris-gris bird."

"How much is a *garde corps*?"

"Depen'," she says, turning her hand on an outstretched arm. "Maybe two, tree hundred dollah."

"I could buy a pistol for that much. That's what Americans use to ward off evil, you know."

"Or," she says, opening her extended hand as if balancing a tray of freshly hatched sunbeams, "you could get a big stick and knock him upside his head."

A motorcycle zips past with a barely dressed woman aboard leaned into the wind, her gold hair flying in the breeze.

"Fanny," says Iba mildly. "She lib wid de women in Merri-wedder."

"Yes," I answer absently. "The old leper colony."

"Lesbian," she corrects, lifting that long finger again, seemingly about to set it into whipping motion.

"Leper."

"Les-bi-an." Her teeth flash as she enunciates.

"Beg pardon?"

"Dot right," she says with a forceful nod, another triumph over the Ignorant Tourist.

"Fanny's a lesbian?" I say, rubbing my head, which has begun to ache.

"All de women dare at Merriwedder," says Iba, fingers slipped into her waistband as she bends suddenly to examine the gravel. "Abomination of God."

I stare at her exquisite neck, her small edible ear. I'd like to count the beads in her hair. A lesbian colony. I'm flummoxed and dashed. That ridiculous bathroom ditty pops into my head: "The French, they are a funny race, they fight with their feet and they fuck with their face ... "

She lifts her chin knowingly. "When you scratch your palm like dat, mean you about to take a long trip."

"I just took one."

"Anudder one, den."

Now in the distance comes the refreshing clatter, misfire, and clunk of the Toyota. I stand up relieved in my purple-and-orange striped hippie trousers as the car sputters up the driveway, banging and popping, its struts wobbling frightfully, the molding on the right-hand side flapping, the hood bouncing against its coat-hanger restraint. Mountain is hunkered massively behind the wheel. The Corolla diesels before shuddering off in a belch of maroon exhaust that for a moment envelops the entire car. Mountain climbs out and slams the door, waving at the smoke. The other door slams and in a moment I can see Kate. I can tell they've been arguing. Kate has a bag in her arms—chocolate bars, I hope.

Iba smiles with relief. "Hello, Kate," she says.

Mountain bears his tooth gap at me. He's wearing a T-shirt about to burst at the shoulders and chest. He waves an imaginary bandanna through the air, as if he were stoned out of his mind at a Grateful Dead concert.

"Shut up," I say.

"You all getting acquainted?" he asks, reaching into the backseat through the window.

"The roller rink was closed."

"Look at what ran out in front of us," he says, whipping up a dead mongoose by its back legs.

"Jesus," says Kate, with a duck and turn of the head. "Don't swing it around like that."

"They're quicker than snakes," says Mountain with a chuckle, giving the pelt a thump, "but not cars. Not bad suppah either."

"How do you cook a mongoose?" I ask, glancing over at Iba, who is licking her chops.

Mountain lifts the mongoose in the air, admiring its meaty hips and canceled ratty scowl. "Boil it in rum and bay leaves."

"I'm so hungry I could eat a weasel," I say. "I'll go sharpen my skinnin' knife, Dan'l. Join the redlegs for Christmas mongoose dinner, Iba?"

"I have potatoes," she says, her eyes wide as a child's. "And onion."

You never know what might please a woman: perhaps roadkill is the key to her heart. "Bring some thyme," I add.

She dashes off to her bungalow.

"Don't forget the Vouvray!" I shout after her.

"Nice pants," says Mountain, tonguing his cheek.

"Yeah, well, you can have the prize inside."

"Mountain has a pair too," says Kate, moving up the steps in her usual floating gait but still keeping a wary eye on the dead rodent, which Mountain keeps giving little shakes, as if to reanimate it. "He wears them all the time."

"Comfy, ain't they?" says Mountain with a chuckle.

I clear my throat. "Iba was telling me that Merriwether is a lesbian colony."

"That's the word for it," says Mountain.

"From leper to lesbian," I say. "That's quite the colonial leap."

"Well, if you think about it," Mountain says, "they only had to change a few letters on the sign."

We're standing at the door now. "We just saw Arthur," says Kate. "And he's invited us all down for lemonade on Monday. He's anxious to meet you."

"He can probably get you a job at the hotel," adds Mountain.

"Lemonade?" I say. "With what?"

"Sugar probably. He doesn't drink."

Iba, plucking thyme leaves behind us, turns and smiles sweetly. She seems content to be with us, as little sense as we make, as full of quills and ironies and secret deprecations and television as we are, the urbanites sick of themselves and their cleverness, trying to start the world all over somehow.

We move back inside. Mountain throws the mongoose into the sink. I hope that my pants do not attract bees or other poisonous insects. They are certainly bright enough to attract birds and prostitutes. I know I have not made a good impression once again on Legion, a killer? What have I done pissing off a murderer who knows the black arts and has no job? Since Iba will stay with us for a while I decide to drink moderately and leave my pants on. Even a plain fool who knows nothing about sewing can tell that these pants have been made with loving care.

I wonder why she lives out here so far away from everything, all alone. So what if she lost the love of her life. Who hasn't?

27.

IT ALARMS ME WHEN I LOOK OUT MY SCREEN DOOR THE next morning and see Legion sitting comfy in the crotch of the locust tree across the road, his yellow-eyed head bobbing along indolently as if he were listening to Stevie Wonder. What Iba said was apparently true. A witchcraft lunatic who lives in a grave-yard and kills tourists has assigned himself to me. I see him smile suddenly and I bolt into the kitchen, where Kate is painting her fingernails at the table. The room smells of sweat, propane, rum-boiled mongoose, and the acrid banana scent of the phenol in the polish. Kate is wearing a green-and-gold bikini and straw sandals. Her toenails shine with fresh, metal-mango polish and her dark hair hangs in wet strands in front of her eyes.

"Where's Mountain?" I ask.

"Off to work," she says, bent to her task. "You know, the Bloody Mariner's Trove."

I pull up a chair and pour a jigger of Scotch into a used coffee cup. If I were Gauguin I would've done this one: *Woman in Bikini Painting Fingernails*.

"Sleep well?" she asks.

I study her wide-set, copper-colored eyes and small, bunched, roseate mouth with its partially discolored tooth. She has a cat's snout, sleek but short. Her hair is split at center and curls under her chin, giving her face a nearly round appearance. I'm ashamed for devaluing her attractiveness before I knew her. I'd like to make it up to her by volunteering to hand-wash her bikini in the sink and blow dry it before Mountain gets home. "Like a sunken ship," I answer suavely.

"Kind of a relief when he's gone, isn't it?" she says, her top lip curling back, halfsnarl, halfsmile. Her voice when Mountain is not around turns sultry, a horny telephone operator at three a.m.

"Well," I say, fumbling with a matchbook.

"I mean, you won't get any neck injuries," she says, still having fun with me. The brush swirls around in the bottle and she wipes the excess along the ridge of its narrow neck. "Rather flattering to be possessed by a jealous man. But it's more natural for people to look at each other when they speak, don't you think?"

"I'll get a pair of blinders next time I'm in town."

She laughs.

"I'll be moving out soon," I add, feeling my hair, which seems to have been styled by dynamite. I realize I'm in need of a haircut, or at least a comb. I hadn't really thought I'd need a comb here.

"Don't do it on account of me," she says, carefully dipping her bristles into the bottle. "It's hell getting a decent rental on this island. Anyway." She flips her hair back and studies me for a moment. "Hasn't Mountain told you I'm leaving him?"

I have a gulp of Scotch that burns a crack in my lip. "No, he didn't mention it."

She's still smiling faintly and somewhat dangerously, or perhaps mockingly, which I counter by fantasizing her wearing nothing but fishnet stockings and an inner tube. I can hear the creaking of valves as my heart pumps along sideways. "Who's the lucky guy?"

She crosses her wrists loosely and lays her chin on the back of her hands, batting her lashes. "I don't know yet. Maybe you."

"Godfrey," I say, shaken. "Don't talk like that."

She tosses her head back and laughs.

"You want to see me with my head through the plaster?" I ask.

She holds up ten fingers like a Phoenician queen and moves her head slowly left to right. "I only wanted to see what you would say."

I scratch my raw and bumpy forearm, then work for a while on my raw and bumpy knee. "So you're not leaving him?"

"Not in the immediate future."

"You do like him, though?"

"Of course. What girl wouldn't? Besides, I'm drawn to heavy-drinking dreamer types." She licks her lips. "They satisfy my motherly instincts."

I take a sip from my empty cup. "You know, when I knew him in college he was more levelheaded. He was planning on Cal Tech. I think his mother's death unbalanced him."

She squints at me. "What did you study in college anyway?"

"I was a psych major."

"Thought so," she says, blowing a lock of hair out of her face. "So was I before I switched to sociology."

"I switched to beer."

"I put more stock in beer than I do the social sciences."

"Psychology is not that bad," I say, propping a cigarette in my face but unable to find a match. "It just lacks imagination, that's all. Everything interesting about humans is empirically denied. Which is why most psychologists are such gloomy people."

"Yes, social workers are worse."

"Is it all right if I smoke? I don't want to start your nails on fire."

She snickers and lifts her eyes, that mocking look that I haven't been able to decipher yet: it's either vague appreciation or a veil of toleration.

"You want a splash?" I say.

"Splash of what?" she says, turning a lacquered pinkie in the sunlight. "A swim?"

"No," I say. "A Scotch."

"I'd rather swim." That look again, but now a genuine smile, my first from her. I feel flattered.

As I tip the bottle to fill her cup, dry cigarette hanging from my lip, I'm aware of staring at her mouth and teeth and having no thought processes, except for little snapshots of her naked on the beach with suntan lotion on her tits. I am aware of wanting to follow her as if I were the neighborhood dog. What's gotten into me? Snap out of it, old boy. I glance to the screen door.

"Expecting someone?" she says, crossing her legs and spangling me with her twenty glowing nails.

"No." I sip from my mug, which smells of stale tea. "But Legion is out there sitting in a tree across the road."

She leans forward with a sharp intake of breath. "Is he?"

"Iba said he's waiting for me. She said he follows me."

"Oh dear. You shouldn't have made him mad. Chollie is bad news." She screws the cap back on her polish.

"Where does he come from?"

Kate squints up at the ceiling, waving her freshly painted hands through the air. "His father was white, I believe. A sea captain, I'm thinking. He was out of the picture very early, you know a sea captain."

"And his mother was a *witch*?"

"Yes," she whispers, eyebrows raised. "She lived in the back-woods and stirred her cauldron all day. Crazy voodoo priestess. Died when he was eight or so. Iba knows the whole story."

"Chollie *is* a son of a witch," I whisper, scratching my shoulder.

"Yeah," she says, tugging absently at her bikini top. "And he's a funny looking boy, an orphan, and he was ostracized from the beginning, and they don't have conscripted education here, so he fell through the cracks." She stares at me, eyes narrowed. "I'm sure you're familiar with the type."

"Yes, back home he would be on medication at the dog track."

She nods and flips the hair from her neck with the crooks of her thumbs. "Except here there is only the wild outdoors."

"And his mother taught him a few spells," I offer.

"I expect," she says in that breathy drawl. "And he's no slouch with that machete either. I've watched him clearing the old slave trails."

I bury my mosquito-ravaged head in my hands. "What have I *done*? I can't go back *home*."

"Don't panic," she says with sudden sympathy. "Mountain will take care of him for you, won't he?"

"Don't be ridiculous," I say, recovering. "He's done nothing but follow me and make a threat. He obviously has a drug problem." I pour myself another Scotch.

"Would you like to go see Cinnamon Jim Joyeux?"

"The voodoo man?"

"Obeah." She blows on her nails, lifting up that pernicious and intoxicating scent of phenol. "The guy has a great reputation. Charms and potions, you know. An office visit is only ten bucks." She smiles and fans her fingers through the air. "What the hell. It's worth a try. Fire with fire. A trip to town would be nice anyway. I've got nothing else to do today."

I'm in no swoon over voodoo but I would like to spend a little more time with Kate. Lord knows I can't even look at her while Mountain is around, and not being able to look at a nice-looking woman is rather like not being able to breathe. And if Chollie Legion knows the black arts, then maybe a $10 trip to the witch doctor (and even a magic trinket from the gift shop) is a rational investment. When in Rome, as they say.

"Do you think we can get back before Mountain?" I ask.

"Don't worry about that," she says with a wave.

"How we going to get into town?"

"Hitchhike," she says, putting out her thumb.

"It's Sunday. It'll take hours to get a ride."

"I can get a ride in ten minutes," she says, glancing into her cleavage. "Let me shed this bikini." I'm shocked as the bikini top falls from her body before she's made the bedroom door. She turns to smile and wink. "Don't you think it'll be pretty easy to get a ride?"

28.

THE LOCUST TREE THAT CONTAINED CHOLLIE IS NOW unoccupied. I stare through its scaly branches pendent with pods and look up and down the road. "Maybe you imagined him," says Kate.

"Possible."

We stroll together up the empty road amid the grinding of flies and the shriek of the cicadas. Out in the cove a few thick-kneed plover are wading in the shallows for brunch. Kate has decorated her delectable form with surah hot pants and a pink halter that gapes, disproportionately revealing her hitchhiking secrets. She walks slightly ahead of me. I don't know if this is because she is a born leader, we are following island custom, or she just wants me to enjoy the view.

We step aside at the sound of a motorcycle approaching. Fanny goes whizzing past, raising a hand without lifting her head.

Kate waves back. We watch Fanny rise up a hill, then bank left and disappear into the forest. Kate says, "Mountain tells me you were in a rock band together."

"Betty Estrogen and the Marching Hormones. It was a gin band with tennis rackets. We only did songs by transgressionist French poets."

She wiggles her behind. "*O saisons, o chateaux!*" she says, looking back at me. "I did a paper once on Rimbaud, but that's all I remember."

"We were mainly Verlaine," I say, as I continue to admire her thin legs and narrow shoulders, her ripped-off bikini top still vibrating across my *corpus callosum* and the atrial valves of my heart. "We were primarily interested in poets who shot their boyfriends. Fanny doesn't like me, does she?"

"Well, if you're thinking about *converting* her you might want to dunk your head in a bucket of ice water. How's your Creole coming along?"

"I'm a dolt."

"You'll get over it," she says, shaking her drying hair, although nothing ever completely dries on this island. "In the third world they just accent every syllable differently. Apart-MENT, instead of a-PART-ment. Your ear gets used to it after a while."

"Where is Cinnamon Jim from?" I ask.

"Grande-Terre, Guadeloupe," she says, skipping once and then hopping twice, as if negotiating an invisible hopscotch square.

"That's French?"

"Most islands around here are," she says, passing through a ray of sunlight and lifting her hands as a leering, blank-eyed silver rodent lumbers across the road in front of us.

"Sure are a lot of mongoose," I remark.

"Yes," she says, stopping with hands on hips as if waiting for mongoose number two to pass. "They're a nuisance. They brought them here to eat the snakes. Now the snakes are all gone and they eat the songbirds and the chickens."

"And nothing eats the mongoose."

"Nothing except us," she says with a disdainful swat at the air. "Of course, I've never been a huge admirer of animals boiled in *rum*."

"So Chollie's father was white?"

"Yes. Wait a minute. I got a rock in my sandal." She hops and digs for a minute, her breasts bouncing. "Bob Marley's father was white too, did you know that?"

"No."

"They tried to assassinate him a couple of years ago." The source of her discomfort dislodged, she pries her sandal back on and we resume walking, her breasts still bouncing in my brain. "Imagine, a *musician*."

"Well, art is a tough game."

"Especially when you mix in race and religion." She balls her fist. "Powder keg."

At the junction, there is a sheer chunk of gneiss against which people hitching rides west can lean while they wait. On Sundays it's hard to get a ride because there isn't much traffic except for churchgoers, and that would've been earlier. Kate and I lean against the speckled, soapy volcanic boulder. She smiles at me. The sun strains down on us through the canopy in long seeps and dusty trickles of amber vapor. Golden-orb spiders rock in their giant water-beaded nets. Thrushes and black macaws and yellow-breasted chaffinches dart and scold from every limb. Something rustles above, and a shower of mist falls upon us, the fresh spill of leaf dew or a tree lizard finding relief.

"Do you know about the walking dead, Edgar?" she asks, shaking the sparkles from her hair.

I sniff my sparkles. I don't know what lizard whiz smells like, but the droplets seem innocuous enough. "I used to see them downtown in their business suits."

"No, I'm talking about the real walking dead. This is lemon-grass here," she says, stooping to pluck a blade, her breasts shifting and almost freeing from their restraint. Even though I've met them already I would like to say howdy again.

I cross my arms. "You're talking about zombies."

"They call them jumbies here." She reclines upon the boulder, chewing like a handsome hillbilly chick on her sprig of lemongrass, dewdrops clinging her arms and hair. "Most of the natives believe in them."

"Do *you* believe in them?"

She chews for a while, wrinkling her forehead. "It's very strange to say, but I do. There are spirits here, call them what you like. After you live here a while, you'll see what I mean, especially when you're out on the roads alone at night."

"I've already met the chubby blonde one. Judy, I believe they call her."

"I've never seen her," she says. "She comes only to young men, they say."

A shiver in my bladder tingles down my left leg. "Tell me about the jumbies."

"Oh, let's see." She knuckles her chin, wetting her lips with the tip of her tongue. "This is the list according to Iba. They walk backwards. They hate the color red. Let's see, they come out of a mirror at night if you don't turn it, face to the wall before going to bed." She bends to scratch her ankle, permitting me the full profile of a chocolate-tipped breast. "And they don't like alcohol."

"I should be safe then," I say, my ears beating hotly. "Why do they walk backwards?"

"I suppose it has to do with the contrary nature of their being."

"Yes," I say. "From death to animation, like the funeral of Walt Disney. How do you, pardon the expression, 'kill' a jumbie?"

"Oh, you don't want to *kill* them," she says, pressing palms to thighs. "Is that a car? I thought I heard a car."

"I didn't hear a car."

She lifts her head, her nostrils dilated, listening for the car. "Anyway, the jumbies, they're in purgatory, you see. The duppies are the ones you want to kill."

"What are duppies?"

"They're evil ghosts," she says, lips whitening as she pulls them back against her teeth. "They live in the roots of the silk cotton trees. They're creatures from hell. You can summon them to your bidding by throwing coins and a glass of rum on a gravestone."

"I heard Iba call Legion a duppy."

She lifts a cautious shoulder. "Maybe so. You know, Iba—I love her—but she's very superstitious. And Mountain eggs her on, so you never know if *he's* serious. Personally I think Chollie's just your average schizophrenic in need of medical attention. Cinnamon Jim will be able to tell you, though. He knows just about everything and everyone on this island."

"You're telling me the voodoo guy—"

"Obeah."

"Whatever. You're telling me this guy who sells charms and potions will be able to give me rational answers."

"We're not talking about rational *questions*, Edgar," she says, throwing her head, and the way she's just pronounced my name, as if we've known each other a long time and get together every Saturday for bourbon and big-band music, makes me feel as though we really *do*. I hope a car doesn't come. We can just sit here and talk about the weather if she likes, and when the sun goes down we'll slip into the jungle, build a fire, catch a mongoose, find a lagoon, build a tree house, suck on some lemongrass, and never return.

"Anyway," she's saying, "if you want to kill Legion you won't need a petition. He's nothing but trouble wherever he goes. I know it's not his fault but the fact remains, he's a threat to innocent people. The jumbies on the other hand can actually help you."

"Oh?"

She nods and then leans into me, whether accidentally or not I don't know, and brushes her arm against mine. "That's how they're freed from purgatory."

"Oh," I say, savoring her electricity. "The moral dead."

"And the sexual afterlife," she adds with a wink.

"The *what*?"

A native in a faded red Volkswagen Beetle putters alongside us and leans down with a grin. He looks dressed for church. I've never seen him before but he smiles at Kate over his Windsor knot as if he's just died and she's the angel at the gates. I sit in back and listen to them talk. Kate is one of those whose personality changes with her audience. Now she chatters like Iba and her fingernails shine like oil.

29.

IT'S NOON BY THE TIME THE NATIVE IN THE BEETLE
drops us next to the Chase Manhattan Bank under construction.
Kate and I walk toward the plaza. "I'm famished," she says,
having nodded or said *hello* to at least three people I've never
seen before. "Let's go get a Reuben at Pete's."

"What about Cinnamon Jim?"

"Later," she says, as if she's forgotten the reason we came.

"If we don't get home before cocktail hour," I remind her,
"our gooses will be cooked."

"Geese," she corrects. "Anyway, we can't visit Cinnamon Jim
until evening."

"Why?"

Palm on her lower back, she shoves out a hip. "Because
obeah works best at night."

"Why didn't you tell me this before?" I ask, scratching my
head.

"It slipped my mind."

"What about Mountain?"

"Do you want to see Cinnamon Jim or not?" she asks crossly,
then takes my hand: "Let's go get a sandwich. You don't want me
to die of starvation."

We sit at a table for two on the deck of the Swiss-Family-
Robinson theme restaurant called Pete's that overlooks the
entire town and most of the bay. I catch a glimpse of Chollie glaring up at me from behind a mahogany tree, then he's gone. The

waiter arrives. Kate orders a mimosa. I decide to stay with straight Scotch.

"You're like two different people," I remark, as the waiter brings the drinks. "With and Without Mountain."

She removes the orange twist from the edge of her glass and sucks on the flesh. "Well, it's obvious why, isn't it?"

"Do you know everyone in town?"

"Why?" she asks, turning her head to look at me from profile. "Are you jealous too?"

"Of course not. Well, not with *you*."

Elbows planted on the tablecloth, she leans down as if to examine some secret hidden in my eyes. "Mountain tells me you're an old surf bum."

"That was long ago, when you could still get to the beach."

"Well, here you are again," she says, gesturing at the bay below, to indicate my reunion with the virgin sea , I suppose. "What's funny?" she says, raising her eyes.

"No surf on this island."

"What about hurricane season?" she asks.

"I make a rule about not riding waves over people's houses."

"Well, what do I know?" she says, fluttering her lashes and laying the curl of orange peel neatly next to her drink. "I'm just a little old landlubber from Baltimore."

"Anyway," I add, having another blast of liquor and straining my neck to see if that isn't Chollie Legion now directly below us, waving his knife around, "I'm done with my water realm."

"Your what?" she says, tilting her head at me in a gesture of graceful condescension and tipping out a bit of lovely white breast, which I shamelessly absorb.

"Realms," I say. "We all pass through them. Water, Fire, Art, God."

"Yes, go on. Waiter!"

"You know how kids are fascinated with puddles and water holes and swimming pools?" I explain. "And then one day they wake up and they're interested instead in soccer or algebra or girls.

And then later it's chess, the stock market, and politics. And then one day it's pills, enemas, and last will and testament. Everyone moves through different realms at different times for different reasons. Anyway, I'm done with my water realm."

" "I see," she says, balancing her chin on her index finger with a provocative smile that lifts that chocolate-chip mole. "So what's the next realm then? Booze?"

She's caught me licking at my glass. I smile humbly and clear my throat, about to expand on my great wilderness project through which I will discover and rebuild my essential self and therefore my tainted haywire consciousness and poor relationship with nature and nature's God, but it all sounds rather silly at the moment, and I think I went over this half-blasted a night or two before, so instead I say, touching the top of my head, "Enough about me. Tell me something about yourself."

The waiter arrives with sandwiches and fresh drinks.

"Lemme think," she says, turning her head to stare down into the bay. "I divorced my husband, I quit my job, and I don't have any money. I must be in my Going-to-Hell realm."

"You never know when your luck might change," I offer.

She sniffs, her eyes filling with resentment or shame, and rubs the back of her neck. Upper lip curling, she says: "Since I was twelve my father's told me I'd never be good for anything but sucking cock."

"Your father said that?" I say, almost spilling my drink.

"Yes," she says, her expression now something of a sordid challenge, her lips parted and wet.

"He must have been a tower of inspiration."

She unfolds her napkin and lays it across her lap. "You got the tower part right."

Now I've got it, the last piece to the puzzle. Sexually abused from an early age, perhaps an incestuous relationship, she found "love" by sleeping with various, usually older men (father figures). Later she sought to right her ruined childhood by getting a social degree and helping the disadvantaged, but discovered that she had no effect. Now getting older, she revolts and abandons her cloisters for a return to the sensual life. The pattern of behavior was set early. What a disastrous combination she and Mountain make, each looking to recover an opposite and irrevocably failed parental figure.

"You're not afraid of Mountain?" I ask, watching the steam rise from her sandwich.

"No," she says, looking down at the table, her hand now kneading the flesh of her shoulder. "I'm just tired of being possessed. I gave up everything and came all the way here to live a peaceful life and nothing's changed. I can't even laugh at one of your jokes."

I take a bite of my Reuben, a tough little varmint with Swiss cheese aged on the premises. "Leave him then."

"Easy for you to say." She forks up her dill pickle wedge, sniffs at it, returns it to her plate. "Where would I go? You wouldn't be interested in moving into town, would you? I don't make enough money at the bakery to live on this side alone."

"Funny that you would so casually entertain my death by strangulation," I say, sinking my teeth into my sandwich again. "Since we just met."

"Just thought I'd ask," she says. "It would be nice to have a conversation with someone without worrying about getting slapped."

"Has he hurt you?"

"Not *yet*," she says, scowling. "I thought he was going to hit me one night when one of my old boyfriends came by just to say hello. He knows I'd move out on him in a second, though," she continues, peering up at me apologetically. "But I don't think he'd hurt me. Do you?"

I have another bite of my sandwich. "He's a good friend, a Marianas trench of sensitivity, but I haven't known him that long. Everyone's got a dark side, you know, and I can't tell you much about his."

A troubled look crosses her face and she nibbles at her sandwich. "Oh, these aren't very good, are they?"

"What else are they going to do with all the mongoose—excuse me, mon*geese*—running around the island?"

"They should boil them at least." She picks up her napkin, stares at it, and covers it again with a spoon. "The way he talks. He's so knowledgeable about things. For a while there, I thought he was really going to find that Mariner's Trove or one of those other lost treasures he's always yakking about and we'd be rich. But Mountain's just one more big dreamer. Poisson Rouge is full of them."

"Me too," I concede, raising my hand.

"No." She shakes her head firmly. "You're different. You didn't just come here to lie in the sun and find a bag of doubloons, I can tell. All that stuff you were talking about the other night, when you were drunk, about mastering your consciousness."

"Oh Jesus," I say, rubbing my head. "I talk when I drink."

"It was fun, though," she says, cocking her head at me brightly. "I've never heard anyone compare their consciousness to the control board of an alien spaceship on the wrong planet."

"I did a lot of acid as a teenager."

She laughs, tipping back her head and showing the undersides of her teeth, which are in good shape, I estimate, for a woman in her early thirties. I feel ashamed of myself for admiring her tongue. A loose woman, divorced, from an abused background, discarded, dropped out, lost her way, one discolored front tooth—she's exactly the sort of girl I usually end up with.

She taps the corners of her eyes with a napkin. "Well, it sounded like you really meant what you were talking about anyway. Even if you're a dreamer, Edgar, at least you're believable."

"You just don't know me very well, that's all."

"Well, I hope to," she says, touching my hand. "Shall we go have a few drinks at Harry's? I want to show you one of my favorite secluded beaches too. And if you want, we can go to the cannibal picnic grounds."

"Oh no," I say. "No cannibalism on the first date, I'm firm on that."

She smiles in a distant way.

By the time Kate and I are climbing the hill to the top of the village, where the famous sorcerer lives, I've got a good Scottish buzz on and I've forgotten what a rotten little island this is. Remnants of a sinking sun spread along the horizon like clouds of rising grenadine in a Shirley Temple. A game of cricket is in progress on the Queen's Park Cricket Grounds below.

"How are we going to get home?" I ask.

"We'll have to stay in town," she says, smoothing the fabric on her silk hot pants. "I've got some friends up in Dutch Corner, the Sissons. They work for Standard Oil. They've got an extra room."

"What will we tell Mountain?"

"We'll tell him we went to town and got stuck," she says simply. "He can't expect us to walk home in the middle of the night through the jungle with all those duppies and jumbies running around."

I scratch my head for a minute. Mountain is home by now, checking the rooms, sharpening my knives, and testing the spring on his speargun. If he could only understand that I want nothing more than to help, and all Kate has done is go out of her way to practically save my *life*.

"We'd better hurry up," she says, picking up the pace, still leading me by a step or two, and I haven't tired of the view. "We don't want Cinnamon to run out of juju. Do you know he has 107 children?"

"Doesn't sound like he'll run out of juju anytime soon."

"I'm not supposed to tell, but Iba is one of them."

"Is she?"

Kate nods. "Don't say anything to her. She doesn't want anyone to know."

"Daughter of a juju man," I reflect. "Does he take care of her?"

"In his way."

"Where's her mother?"

"Barbados."

"She seems awfully isolated for having 106 brothers and sisters."

"She doesn't know most of them. I think she's ashamed and at the same time proud of her father," says Kate. "Cinnamon Jim's about as famous as a man gets around these islands. But he's not exactly the pride of the diocese."

30.

CINNAMON JIM JOYEUX LIVES IN A REDBRICK, TWO-STORIED house that, with its stone portico, pagoda, and tessellated balcony, looks like a Chinese restaurant. His is the most prominent residence in the village and affords the widest view, with the Caribbean on all four sides. His consulting rooms around back reside in a neglected-looking wooden hut in a grove of monkey-tail trees full of squabbling brown ravens of the speckled variety.

"I'll wait for you," says Kate with a good luck touch that makes me want to say, *Screw it, let's just spend the ten bucks on a room at Gladys Hooks'*. "Just remember to tell him I sent you. He likes me."

"OK."

"Don't be nervous."

"What if he wants to trephine my skull?"

"If he hurts you, you just give 'ol Kate a shout," she says, pressing the flesh on my bottom lip with her index finger. "She'll be waiting for you outside, and she has a pink sucker for you if you're a good boy."

Hectored and bemused, I nod and slip into line. The air rings with crickets and the boiling racket of speckled brown ravens. The woman in front of me has the lower part of her head wrapped in bandages, and she holds in her left hand a small iron pot of smoldering camphor. I think with some satisfaction of Legion sitting in a tree and waiting for me while I stand in line for magic against him.

The line moves along briskly as in a well-organized amusement park, and soon I am inside the hut, which is lit murkily with candles. Dusk has fallen outside, perfect timing. Yellow muslin drapes the single south window. The walls of the room are decorated with motley odds and ends that make it similar in appearance to the homemade altar of a Catholic church. Among the icons and references to Christ are a crucifix framed in a horseshoe, a moth-eaten banana bird with a rosary around its neck, old cigarette cards, and a torn French leprosy poster. On a nearby table are colored bottles containing crickets and large moths and scraps of paper. I don't recognize a theme unless it is Excommunicated Catholic Has a Garage Sale.

I stand reluctantly before the old man, who sits smoking behind a desk cluttered with diplomas, long seashells mottled like birds' eggs, a bottle of Epsom salts, a mortar and pestle, a shiny black calabash bowl, and a Cuban marimula small enough to play with your thumbs. He has a weathered catcher's-mitt face and I think at first by the narrowness of the eyes and the way he seems not to see me that he might be blind. He wears a long, silver-lamé robe, a Paul Revere hat and a chinchilla stole. I estimate that he is seventy years old. I don't know how to address him. Dr. Cinnamon? I feel myself bowing slightly, hoping he does not stick pins in me or read me a passage from L. Ron Hubbard. I especially hope that he will not charge me more than ten bucks.

"Kate Hunger sent me," I say by way of introduction.

He nods in a grimace of restraint, elbows planted on the desktop, fingers laced.

"It wasn't exactly my idea," I add.

With thumb and forefinger he begins to caress his chin, nodding all the while, shifting his weight and lighting a fresh cigarette, French and unfiltered, with the stump of the old. He taps the ash into the shiny calabash bowl. "Have a seat, my young friend," he says, pressing the button on a stopwatch. "For the friends of Kate Hunger," he says, "the first consultation is free. You got ten minutes."

I face him from a green wicker chair, still warm from the rump of the previously afflicted. "You don't have an accent," I remark.

"*Papa moin Français, maman moin Africaine,*" he says, left hand floating out philosophically. "I went to school in Montreal. What is the nature of your problem?"

"Chollie Legion is stalking me," I say. "Do you know him?"

"Oh, quite," he replies, with some savor, as he licks each corner of his mouth and his pale eyes seem to glow. "Impossible to live here and be unacquainted with Chollie Legion."

"I believe that he has evil intentions."

"Distinctly possible."

"The first day I met him he promised he would kill me," I explain, massaging my knee. "Now he sits in a tree outside my house and waits. My neighbor, Iba, says he follows me wherever I go. She says he's a duppy, a ghost."

He nods along, as if waiting for me to get to the point.

"Both Iba and Kate thought you could help me."

Cinnamon puffs on his cigarette and shakes his head. "Where are you from?" he asks.

"San Diego."

"Why are you here?"

"I thought I would simplify my life."

He presses the tips of his fingers together and his eyes continue to glow like two suburban swimming pools lit at night. "And how have you found it so far?"

"More difficult than ever."

He nods along more slowly now as if I have given the correct answer. "Tell me why you think he is following you."

"I can't say exactly," I admit. "I may have angered him on our first encounter. I suspect that he has attached some symbolic significance to me, since I am white and I represent the expanding Western technological forces that threaten his way of life."

"I think you may have hit it on the button," he says, blowing a stream of smoke across one of the candle flames and adjusting his chinchilla stole. "Certain forms and colors are mutually hostile in nature, yes? Do you know the saying 'East is East and West is West, and never the twain shall meet'?"

"Samuel Clemens, isn't it?"

"It's always difficult far from home," he says, tipping his head sympathetically.

"Yes."

"And I'm afraid that I won't be able to help you."

"What? But you seem to understand."

"Oh yes," he says. "Quite."

"I was under the impression you helped people."

"Whenever I can," he says, "but only for those who take me seriously. You don't believe in obeah." He shakes his head. "Faith is 90 percent of the ball game, baby."

"Well, what if I said I *did* believe."

He continues to shake his head. "It doesn't work like that."

"I'd still be interested in what you have to say. I came all this way."

He tugs at his sleeves. "I've got impotence cures for fifteen, ulcer for twelve-fifty. Love potion thirty-five. *Maladie Garçon*, fifty. Mental illness is also fifty this week. Job promotion, two hundred. But Chollie Legion … " He shakes his head heavily and lights another tube of French tobacco. "You couldn't afford it. You might as well ask me to take on the devil himself. Have you tried one of these?" he says, rummaging through the drawers of his desk and producing a King James edition of the Bible, which he slaps on the desk.

"Got one."

"Carry it with you," he says, finger in the air. "Hold it up to him." He thumps the cover. "But you've got to *believe*, man. Faith, like I said. Besides, it's free. I got this one in a hotel room in Guadeloupe."

I feel suddenly tired. I peel off my spectacles and wipe at the oily dampness at the bridge of my nose.

Cinnamon Jim puts away the book. "Maybe sometime you

could do us all a big favor and give him a good swift kick in the chest. Maybe he falls backward off a cliff a few hundred feet. They'd probably name a holiday after you."

I look up sharply at him.

He clicks the button on the watch. "Time's up. If you ever need a love philter or a little something for depressions, give me a ring. You know where I am. Cinnamon Jim never closes." He rises to shake my hand. "Good luck to you, young man," he says. "And give my regards to the lovely Kate Hunger."

31.

MOUNTAIN IS HUNCHED AT THE TABLE, HIS BACK UP LIKE a Doberman pinscher and his eyes narrowed blue mirrors of fury, a glass full of Scotch clamped in his right hand, when Kate and I return the next morning from our overnight (I almost said the word *affair*) excursion. "Where've you two been?" he growls.

"No salvaging today, dear?" Kate replies breezily, strolling into the bedroom to change.

Moses scowls. I plop down in a chair. "Nothing happened, man," I say, with affected casualness, tipping myself a dribble from the bottle. "We just went into town and got stuck. Kate introduced me to Cinnamon Jim. Have you met him?"

Moses stares at me like a rhino about to charge, coils of hair fallen into his eyes.

"Chollie Legion is *stalking* me, man. Do you believe that? And the old mojo-meister won't help me."

He slams his drink down, spilling Scotch on a month-old section of the *Miami Herald*, the one with the page-five story I've read a dozen times about the fourteen-year-old boy who floated all the way from Cuba to the Dry Tortugas on a picnic cooler.

"Nothing *happened*, man," I repeat with a grin that I'm sure would nauseate me if there were a mirror at hand. "We got stuck."

He gulps from his glass, staring all the while at a point about one inch to the right of the top of my head.

Kate strolls out of the bedroom, buttoning her blouse. "Don't forget we have a lemonade party tonight, boys," she says.

Mountain rises deliberately, a meager smile playing in his masonry lips. "I found an oil pump for the Toyota," he says, crossing the room to remove the Chilton manual from the bookcase. "Want to help me put it in?"

"Love to," I say, clapping my hands.

IN THE TIME SINCE I STEPPED OFF THE FERRY, THE TOTAL sum of my experience on Poisson Rouge is drinking, listening to the radio, being thwarted sexually, fouling the mood of an implacable Mountain, listening to the jungle and the rats in the cupboards, and waiting like a child on Christmas morn for Kate's tits to fall out of her blouse.

All right, I've seen a *witch* doctor, I'm being hunted by a misguided environmentalist qua zombie, no, make that duppie, and apparently the island is infested with werewolves and the inconsolable spirits of the departed. Also I've learned how to install an oil pump. But this is not exactly text ripped from a travel brochure. It's not why I fled to paradise.

So it's refreshing to dress up in the great majority sober, put a part in my hair, and drive slowly through the heavy tropical evening to a lemonade soiree down the road. I remember one sober night when we were in college, no money for booze, Mountain unable to hustle any Bud, that he and his Christian roommate and I played board games. It may have been the most pleasant night of my short academic career.

"Car sounds pretty smooth," I say, admiring my greasy hands and split knuckle.

Mountain glances off silently to the east. The whole time we worked on the car he didn't say three words outside of "hand me the wrench."

The sun is heading down as we park in the gravel next to Arthur's 1971 Chevrolet Nova, which, despite the proximity of perennial salt spray, is in pretty fair shape.

Arthur lives in a room behind the small beer bar called the Santa Breeze, its doors open, one man sitting thoughtfully on a stool, hand in his hair. We knock on Arthur's peeling red door. Arthur greets us in a stiff, pistachio-green striped suit with Boeing 707 lapels and pomaded hair. "Come in, come in," he says, bowing and smiling and sweeping us with his left hand into his groovy bachelor's pad with green shag carpeting and plaid bean-bag chairs and the slick-looking wet bar of a teetotaler. Arthur is a young, thickly built black man with big gums in a large sleepy head. He is from the British Island of St. Kitts and has a bit of a Welsh accent, which makes him doubly hard to understand. Mountain falls into a beanbag chair, hair dangling, his blue eyes darting about under the ledge of his brow, his big feet sticking up like a clown's. The lemonade klatch is not exactly his milieu. Nor mine. Kate, fashionably remote, a comely center-part in her hair, and gold gleams on the lobes of her ears, perches herself at the wet bar and crosses her pretty legs.

Arthur pours not lemonade, but limeade, from a pitcher. There are no lemons (or bananas or grapes or oranges) on this island that I'm aware of. "So how are you, Kottie?" he says to Kate, as if they are friends from elementary school. He wonders how her job at the bakery is going. He wonders about all her friends. We would call this fawning if he were not so genteel. He's obviously known her longer than Mountain. Kate answers mildly, sulkily, monosyllabically, with single's-bar smiles she knows will give him pleasure.

Just as Mountain's glare seems about to ignite, Arthur turns and begins to converse with him about his boat. Arthur is so attentive with the quick smile and the squinted eyes he might be memorizing everything you say.

I tour the room, annoyed at my inaction. All the subjects that absorb *me*—living off the land, returning to the wilderness, and mastering my consciousness—I have not made one credible gesture toward. Kate accuses Mountain of being a hopeless dreamer, but at least he is building a boat. At least he is learning the salvaging business. If his dreams flop he will be left with practical knowledge, and a boat. When I flop I'll be right back where I started, flirting with someone else's girl.

Arthur has a record player and a three-speed table fan. He has tight screens and a sliding glass door. He has a refrigerator. I have to examine all these items, touch them cautiously like one of the apes in the prologue to *2001: A Space Odyssey*.

"So how are you liking de islan so far, Edgar?" asks Arthur, crossing the room to refill my glass.

I answer with a shrug, unwilling to violate the rule of courtesy. "Things can only get better."

"It's borin', ain't it?" he says.

"Not the exact word I would choose."

"He needs a woman," says Kate with another of her enigmatic smiles.

Arthur nods heartily. Kate does seem to know. I wonder what will I do alone in the jungle without a woman. I will have to bring one with me. Kate. No, don't be a fool. Iba is the natural choice, once I win her confidence and demonstrate to her my woodsy competence.

"What else is there in the world but love and Hunger?" Kate is saying.

Arthur laughs agitatedly. "What a name for a girl dat is, Hunger," he says, with one slightly anxious glance to Mountain, who turns up the watts on his glower.

"It's Germanic," continues Kate, undeterred. "When my grandparents came to the United States it was Hunger*bottom*, but they shortened and Americanized it. I still feel like a Hunger-bottom most of the time."

Arthur blinks, vexed by her cheek. With a hankie he wipes the jiggling beads of perspiration from his brow. I don't know if he's nervous, horny, or poorly equipped for the humidity. Maybe the trifecta. Me too.

"Yes, well, all my ancestors from Scotland were Em*bar*-*r*assed," I say with a brogue, trying to maintain levity as jealousy simmers to the top of the pot, "and I still feel Em*bar*rassed."

Mountain only scowls, a monument of reproach.

Armpits itching, I plunge in: "Hot tonight."

"Well, it's always *hot*," drawls Kate, flapping aside the entrance to her blouse.

Very difficult to steer away from sexual metaphor, I think, hungering for the white curve of that bosom. Impossible. "Oh look, is that a raindrop?"

A tidal wave of silence.

"Do you play cricket, Arthur?" I ask desperately, my voice clamoring up an octave.

"Oh yes." He rises, enlivened, and makes another tour with his pitcher.

"You'll have to teach me the rules," I say.

"Laws," he says. "I'll teach you."

"I've tried to learn. It still escapes me."

"It's easy," he says, sitting down on the edge of the chair across from me. "You have two sides, one out and one in. Each man dat's in go out, and when he's out he come in and de next man go in until he's out. When dey all out, de side dat's out come in and de side dat's been in go out and try to get doze comin' in, out. Sometimes you get men still in and not out." He checks me. I'm nodding out of good manners.

"When a man go out to go in," he continues," de men who are out try to get him out, and when he's out, he go in and de next man in go out—"

I hold up my hand. "Maybe we can watch a game sometime."

"Ah right," he says, smiling and mopping his forehead with the hankie.

Mountain declines more limeade. I have never seen him looking so morose. I wonder suddenly if he's worried about losing his girl. Then again, cricket laws may have exhausted him. Perhaps a drop or two of spirit in these handicapped gin rickeys would help. We'll get him home straight away since the belly of this soiree began to turn up the minute we entered the room.

Arthur tells us he is thinking about joining the Catholic church so he can meet women. We all laugh.

I think about joining the Catholic church myself. Something about the tropics and being around Kate all the time has honed my desire to a wicked edge. I need guidance, I need discipline, structure. I need an eager young woman easing down her brassiere. Mountain stirs and a shadow crosses Kate's face.

"So yer tinkin' about workin' at de hotel, Edgar," says Arthur.

"Yes," I say. "I didn't expect to need work so soon. But Scotch and groceries have finished off my bankroll in short order." I smile, the good sport.

Arthur nods with his great, heavy-headed understanding. "When can you start?"

"Sooner better."

He snaps his fingers, startling me.

"Let's go," says Mountain.

32.

EARLY FRIDAY AFTERNOON, MOUNTAIN STILL BROODING, the three of us drive together cross-island and up the long hill to the Rockefeller Plantation. The guard, upon seeing our Corolla, is reluctant to let us in. Mountain and Kate wait for me in the car. I move with the confidence of the breadwinner through the chilled halls of gilt and fluted columns and piano music and tranquil, sun-stained guests dressed in sneakers and gold who regard me as if I am a faint breeze from a dumpster. This will only be temporary, I tell myself. Soon I'll find a decent spot in the woods somewhere, erect a rudimentary domicile, buy a few basic supplies, make my permanent move to independence, and thus solve a thousand problems in one fell swoop.

I find the chef's office, a glass booth in the center of the kitchen, and stick my head in. "I'm Edgar Donahoe. Arthur sent me."

"Ah, right." The chef seems frazzled. His eyes are darkly pouched. He's wearing one of those terrible paper hats, tall as one of the columns in the Lincoln Memorial. "Come in," he says, gesturing amiably. "Take a chair. I'm a little disorganized at the moment." He lights a cigarette and props his elbow on the arm of his chair. "So Arthur tells me you're looking for work."

"Yes, that's right," I answer, taking a seat.

"Arthur says you're a good cook. He says everyone is a good cook." He takes a drag from his cigarette and shuffles some papers. "Arthur is a great one to have on your side. Where have you worked before?"

I yank at my collar, already feeling stifled in clothes. Language seems unnecessary too. The honking and squeaking we make, the riddles we create with our abstractions, are the curse of every modern denizen of civilization and his bulwark to happiness. One is born with pure consciousness and perception, which deteriorate through the gradual accumulation of honking and squeaking. Replacing real perception with mouth sounds, the world becomes parsed, divided, and artificial, parsing, dividing, and making artificial the very nature of our consciousness and thus happiness in the process. Once a man returns to the peace and purity of his origin, however, so too does the purity of his consciousness, and thence does he recover his soul.

The chef stares at me, watery-eyed, slightly humpbacked in his baggy white suit, that ridiculous column of sweat-stained paper tilted on his head, his chin beginning to wattle. He's expecting me to say that I have no experience cooking, but I stun him with a five-star hotel.

"Broadmoor, really?" he says, showing a mess of yellow teeth that seem to spell Massachusetts. "Where?"

"Tavern kitchen."

He pecks at his cigarette and sets it to rest in the ashtray. He is one of these kinds of smokers, I can tell by the many long-ashed butts lying in the tray, who lights them and leaves them. "I was *Chef des Jeux* there in '68. Ferran still there?"

I lean back in my chair, folding my hands, and wish I hadn't left my cigarettes back in the car. "He was when I was."

"Now there's an old-fashioned son of a bitch for you." He shakes his head and taps at his hat, unintentionally set it straight. "You know, he grew up in a time when corporal punishment in the kitchen was the norm."

"Yes, he would get quite obsessive over the smallest things," I say, crossing my legs and feeling kinship with this overworked man who is undoubtedly younger than he looks. I feel sorry for him and wish I could explain to him my theories of happiness and pure consciousness. "When I worked there people said you'd get fired for serving a brown omelet, but I never saw it, did you?"

"No," he says, shaking his head, savoring the memory. "But he was a terror. I remember once he came at Giovanni, one of our cooks upstairs, with a hot pan, for not deglazing the *shallots*."

"I was down in the Tavern," I say. "Except for the omelets, he mostly left us alone."

The chef adjusts himself in his chair. He seems to be glad to have found me. "Cooks are always hard to come by in this part of the woods." He fishes up the wrong cigarette and returns it with a grimace. "In the States you usually settle for an alcoholic drifter or a guy just out of jail. Here it's different: They fall into two categories. Stateside desperadoes who don't stay, or natives, who may or may not blossom into culinary geniuses but who in the beginning generally don't know a béchamel from a box of brown sugar. What are you doing here?"

I show him my palms. "Paradise?"

"You drink?"

"Beg pardon?"

"I'd give my left lung to be in San Diego." He blows up his cheeks. "*That's* paradise. Libraries? Water pressure? Sober medical care? Mexican food? A month without rain? Why'd you leave?"

"Sick of it."

"You're daft," he says.

"Why?"

A hand slides into his jacket and he begins to scratch with his thumb the green T-shirt underneath. "How long you been here?"

"Couple weeks."

"This is just a big rock covered with bird shit." He puckers his blond eyebrows at me.

"Well, I'm here now," I offer.

"Fair enough. Anyway, the thing to remember is that we cater to the rich, who are not searching for Eden, but prefer good service, blended rum drinks, and dishes with butter and cream." He finds the live cigarette at last, puffs it suspiciously, grinds it into a heap of butts in the ashtray, and then tips the still-smoldering dish into the trash can. We both watch the can smoke. Fire is something neither of us is concerned about. The relative humidity here is the ultimate sprinkler system. "You've got a nice résumé," he says, "but I can't put you anywhere except breakfast. The cooks here work their way up. Some of these boys have been here twenty years. I'll move you into a better spot when you've been here a while." I think he might add, "If you stay," but he seems content with my future.

"I'm not picky about the shift," I say.

"You've got a car, right? I see here you live on the east side."

"Yes, we have a car. Fresh oil pump and everything."

"Be careful about driving after dark," he says. "All kinds of stuff out on that Cross Island Road. And you can't see it." He stares at me but it's clear his thoughts are elsewhere. "I ran smack into a guy one night. Came round a corner, stepped right out in front of me. Had a face like a rotten peach, the blankest eyes. He must've been drunk." He shakes his head. "I didn't have time to stop. He flipped up on my hood, cracked my windshield. I stopped and got out, but couldn't find him." He scratches under his paper hat. "That scared me more than hitting him. Never did find him."

"Was he walking backwards?"

He whips his head around at me. "What?"

"Never mind."

"I don't drive anymore at night." He stands and sighs, tips his hat back to wipe the sweat from his forehead. "Nothing much on the east side anyway. Gotta say I'm glad I don't live out there. Nice and quiet, though, huh?"

"Cheap too."

"Got a point there," he says. "That's another reason a lot of my cooks leave. Can't afford to live on this side. Anyway, we send all our new employees up to Turquoise Bay. Have you been up there?"

"No."

"It's very posh. Beautiful view. You'll work with Stanley Robinson, one of the real gentlemen of the island. Wonderful cricket player. There he is over there by the stockpots, do you see him? The lithe fellow with the mild expression. Well, you'll meet him tomorrow. Let me give you a quick tour of the place. Then we'll issue you a uniform. You won't have any trouble keeping it laundered and ironed?"

"Shouldn't, no."

He shows the mess of yellow teeth. "Splendid. Personal appearance is very important here. Can you start tomorrow?"

33.

AT 4:55 A.M. MY ALARM GOES OFF. I ROLL OUT OF BED, pull on my white cooking jacket and checkered nylon pants (a uniform designed for a hot, steamy kitchen so it's more suited for the tropics than you might think), tie my shoes, and shuffle through the darkness into the kitchen. Bleary-eyed, Mountain strolls out a few minutes later, wearing a brown wino shirt with all the buttons missing, his favorite ripped boat shoes, and short pink terry cloth shorts that he may have borrowed from Kate. I'd make fun of him, but I don't want to give him an excuse to deck me. Despite their bulkiness, his hairless legs are still knobby at the knees. I watch him carefully. Quiet as ever, he gives me the feeling that I don't exist in the room. I've been waiting for him to backhand me across the mouth, but I've given him nothing to justify it, not so much as a glance in the direction of his girl. Gradually I've come to suspect that he lives on the east side not because there is the greater likelihood of finding treasure here, but so that he can keep Kate in the greatest possible isolation.

"Look, babe," I say, with a defeated sigh. "As soon as I have the cash, I'm moving out. You can stop fretting."

"Lemme trim the fog here," he says, rumpling the mop on his head and grinning at me with pure, old-fashioned Mountain charm. "Cup of grog for ye, Johnny?"

"One then, Big John," I concede. "Don't want to be blasted on my first day."

"We'll have you to work by six," he says, "sober as the pope."

Mountain, making a show of friendliness, is good this morning for three action-photo poses: gorilla surprised by its wristwatch, Julia Child with Alzheimers (one cup of sugar, one cup of sugar, one cup of sugar), and William Shakespeare with his greatcoat caught in a hay baler. Though not terribly funny, I appreciate the effort, and we have a good laugh.

By 5:30, we have the old Toyota with its Bud can for a muffler wobbling and winding through the floral gloom, occasionally splashing through a pothole. I watch from the window as the forest flashes past. It feels more like an overland journey in a covered wagon than a twelve-mile car commute to work. As the first sunlight seeps through the canopy it occurs to me that someone has been running alongside us, his feathered head appearing incongruously now and again through the vegetation.

"Mountain, is that *Legion?*"

"Where?" He leans down, his eyes swinging back and forth beneath his brow.

"Running alongside us." I point. "No, there he is to larboard, captain, your side. How did he do that?"

Mountain crouches, squinting, hands gripped at ten and two o'clock on the wheel.

"Watch the road," I say.

"I don't see anything," he says, head swinging, a confetti of vermilion jungle blossoms flittering all around, and a collared forest falcon, wings motionless, coasting low enough across the road in front of us to get grilled á la Toyota.

A whiff of smoke lifts up through the hole in the floor as Mountain bends into a turn. "There he is again!" I shout.

The steering wheel seizes. Mountain yanks it to submission. "Could be," he says, whipping his hair out of his eyes. "Like I said, he knows every old slave road and tunnel on the island."

"Why is he wearing feathers?" I cry.

"What's he got, *wings?*"

"No, he's wearing a headdress of some type."

Mountain downshifts, his jaw muscles writhe. "He's fruit loops."

"Paranoid schizophrenic," I mutter. "Delusions of grandeur, textbook case."

I see Chollie's head pop up again and he grins at me.

"Does he do this to EVERYONE?" I shout, freeing my collar from the inhibition of its two top buttons.

"He's never done it to *me*," Mountain says, jabbing his naked chest through the brown wino shirt with the ball of his thumb. "Apparently you're special."

"He certainly can run like the wind on those bulldog legs," I remark. "Amazing he doesn't trip on a vine or something and collide face-first into a tree. I wonder why someone doesn't shoot him and put him out of his misery."

"They only do that in the States," says Mountain, taking his right hand off the wheel for a moment to scratch his leg. "Here, it's more common to be poisoned or found at the bottom of a cliff."

"He can't be a killer, Mountain, can he?" I hear myself whining. "He's wasting his energy proving some trivial tribal point. He's the curator of an old race wound that will never heal."

"Well, I know he's *cut* people."

"Who?"

"I don't know 'em, but he'll cut you, trust me."

The car sets about to coughing, then stalls, and Mountain and I have to get out and push again. The steam from the asphalt pools all around us waistdeep, which is good because now I don't have to see Mountain's ridiculous pink shorts. Anguished insects attempt to shatter our tympanic membranes. I swing my head about, looking for Legion.

Once we're at the top of the island we can coast, and if the car stalls again Mountain can bump-start it without us having to get out. Chollie cannot keep pace with us now unless he knows how to fly, the possibility of which I cannot yet rule out. We sail past the island junkyard called the Valley of Miracles. Glancing up where the rearview mirror should be, Mountain says, out of the blue: "You can fuck her if you want."

"Fuck who?" I answer warily, my heart giving a jump.

"Kate." He's staring straight ahead now, his lips welded together. "I'll sleep in your room tonight."

"Wait a minute, Mountain." I twiddle my collar buttons.

"Why not?" he says.

"I am not a swinger, OK?"

"Look, she likes you. You like her." He turns his hand over like a teacher explaining the simplicity of algebra. "Just pretend she's a special ed. major."

"Yes, but she's yours."

"Do us all a favor," he says, turning his gaze on me at last, eyes imploring, lips twisted, "and take her so we can be friends again."

I consider the offer, rather like a hungry man imagining a New York strip medium-rare and butter running out of his baked potato. But the proposition is rife with flaws. What kind of happy triangle does Mountain think we can make? A rivalry would develop and we'd break apart quicker than The Strawberry Alarm Clock. I'd end up buried somewhere in one of Mountain's treasure holes. "I'm not going to sleep with her, Mountain, all right?"

"Give me one reason," he says.

The road in front of us is bathed in sunlight. A porcupine waddles into the bush. Mountain's eyes are preternaturally bright and his jaw muscles flex against his seedy beard.

"I appreciate your generosity," I say. "But I think it would cause bad feelings. I'm going to move out with my first check. *Then* we can all be friends again."

We roll out of the forest down into sunlight. Below is the immaculate cricket field. A mangy, green-eyed dog lopes alongside us for a while. At the gate of the resort Mountain averts his eyes. His hands are tight on the wheel and his left foot in its ripped white boat shoe pumps the clutch with a nervous squeaking. The Toyota sputters and hacks like an old smoker. The new oil pump hasn't made much of a difference in its overall performance, though I suppose we have extended the life of the car by a month or two.

"I'm sorry I came," I say. "If I'd have known it was going to be like this, I would've gone somewhere else."

"No, forget everything I said," he says, reaching up to bang the roof liner with the back of his hand. "I don't know what the hell is wrong with me. I'll see you at 2:30."

34.

AT 6:00 A.M. I HELP LOAD A VAN WITH PASTRIES, A BUCKET of whipped eggs, and a tub of iced kingfish, and we drive up to the club on the pinnacle overlooking Turquoise Bay. The waiters in white duck trousers and loose, brown floral shirts are all black except for one who seems vaguely familiar, beautiful eyes, light-haired. This is the first time in my life I've been attracted to a man. After a few minutes, I realize it's Fanny. She smiles at me vaguely, offers her palms in a what-are-we-going-to-do gesture, then turns off and hurries away.

By seven o'clock, the orders are pouring in. I have neither the talent nor the speed to keep up with a dozen breakfast waiters, so I'm on the flattop with the flapjacks, cottage fries, canned corned beef hash, the kingfish, ham, and French toast. Slim, sleepy-eyed Stanley, who is no more than a boy, is nevertheless a warm soul. He's also the best egg-man I've ever seen. He flips eggs in a pan so quickly you don't see them turn. He can flip four pans at once. He does three-minute eggs in two and beats the waiters every time. I can't get the temperature on the griddle right, and burn the flapjacks, then it's too cold and they stick. Stanley, in the middle of his own pandemonium, walks over to line the flames up right. All the while he maintains a constant banter of good-natured insult with the waitstaff. "Pick it up, you no-good, shifty bums," he says, banging the steel counter with his poaching net. "If you was a real man you'd be cookin' like Edgar and me."

He winks at me. "Dey just started hiring waitresses," he mutters off the side of his hand.

"How long she been here?" I say.

"Couple weeks," he says, yanking down the oven door, whipping out a set of shirred eggs, and spinning the dish up into the window. "Hot plate!" he shouts. "De men don't like it much, women in de kitchen." He fishes up a pair of poached and tips them into a bowl.

Fanny, even if she's been here two weeks and represents the progress of all womankind on this microcosm of a still basically feudal island where the men resent a woman in the kitchen, can't seem to get an order straight. It doesn't help that she's being harassed, though she must understand her role as trailblazer. Neither can it be helpful in a male-dominated kitchen on a predominantly Catholic island that she lives in a lesbian colony. She continues to deliver food to the wrong table and drops several plates in her consternation. Stanley rides her genially, but he has to cook three of her orders over again. "Come on, man," he chides her. "You givin' the white boys a bad name." He winks at me again.

I try to encourage Fanny and I finish her orders promptly. If I am somehow understanding, offering the sophisticated Stateside perspective, she will come visit me for rum punch in my new bamboo hut. Certainly we have more in common now than ever, and our mutual vision of paradise, its seductive facade hovering in the dining room windows, couldn't be farther away.

At lunch I sit alone at a picnic table under a sun-flooded canopy, feeling like a colonial child on his first day in public school in Nigeria. I look around for Fanny, my only chance at a sympathetic dining companion. On my tray is a breaded veal cutlet, fruit salad, glass of tomato juice, and a powdered dinner roll. I've also poured myself a cup of coffee, a toothsome treat, something you won't find on the east side. I shouldn't really mind being alone. After all, it's the very cornerstone of my goal. I watch the gardeners, their hair tied in flowing white bandannas, manicure the vast hotel lawns. I wish I were hungry, but I feel rather dyspeptic instead, nerves on the first day.

About a hundred feet away, where the shaved lawns stop and the woodland tangle resumes, that strange little Van Schorr girl with the orchids around her neck is leaning out of the greenery, crooking her finger at me. I look all around, pointing at myself. She nods. I set my napkin aside. She smiles as I cross the lawn. She has the weirdest eyes, the deepest lips. She beckons at me like a mermaid in an underwater dream. Behind her the jungle seems gaslit, the tree trunks slimy, the leaves opalescent. Far above, ice clouds like scattered phantoms are strung motionless across the vault of the sky.

Smiling welcome, left hand on the small of her back, my snub-nosed beckoner has strewn her blonde hair with comely blue gems. The irises of her eyes are so light that they're almost white. Funny how Dutch she looks, like a girl straight out of a Vermeer. She has tender peaks for breasts, like mountains on a milk-chocolate map of Kansas. I note a coarse scar, still suppurating, that completely encircles her neck. "Hey buddy," she says, as natural as can be.

"Hello there," I reply.

"Lose something?" she asks.

"Eh?"

"Why are you looking down?"

I swing up my gaze.

"What are you doing?" she demands.

"Having lunch. You?"

"I'm bored," she says, flicking her hair from her shoulder and making the blue gems tremble.

That raw scar on her throat makes it difficult for me to swallow. "Put on some clothes, can you?" I say, with a glance back across the lawn at my co-workers. "All those people back there are watching us."

"I don't have any," she says with a cunning smile. "Do you think I care what they think? I was here before they were."

"Well, a towel then. Just humor me. I'm old-fashioned, you see."

"You're so much like Hendrik Hooft," she says, pressing her palms together and tipping her head in fondness. "He was an older boy too, an alderman. We used to run back behind the molasses vats and get sticky."

"What are you talking about?"

"Do you know that Doors song, 'the men don't know what the little girls understand'?"

"Do you know that Maurice Chevalier song 'Thank Heaven for Little Girls'?"

She crosses her arms with a pout. "I am *not* a little girl."

"Where are your parents?"

"Come with me," she says, gesturing, turning. "I'll show you."

Tempted, I recall Mountain's warning. "I have to work."

Her eyes widen with censure, the pale eyebrows fix in a rigid arch. "This is no place to be," she says, as if someone has just opened a wrapper of Limburger under her nose. "This is where it *happened*."

Now the gems in her hair are moving. They also have little feet. I remark that they are not gems but tiny blue toads clinging as if to a cool and damp surface, their transparent eyelids skimming at me, their glistening sides alternately ballooning. Someone has slipped a Mickey into my tomato juice, I decide, or Mr. Walker needs a vacation.

"I need to go back," I say, grinding my heels into the grass. "I only have half an hour. It's my first day."

"This is a horrible place," she says, wide-eyed. The tiny blue toads quirp in seeming agreement.

"I know that," I say, "but I can't live without money."

"Yes you can." Her arm sweeps back, her hand turns palm-up. "I'll show you."

"Gotta go," I say, wheeling round.

"I'll see you again," she calls.

As I return across the grass I see that everyone is watching me, including Fanny, who sits next to one of the frontdesk clerks, a woman who looks like Sigourney Weaver. A seagull poised above my tray is about to steal my dinner roll. I clap my hands and shout. Startled, the gull thumps its wings, sending my napkin sailing, and flaps away. How much more fascinating can this new white boy in our midst be, the expressions all around seem to say. Nude pubescents beckon him from the forest, grossly disturbed infidels shadow him, and he won't even give a damn seagull a dinner roll. My face and ears burning with embarrassment, I toss my cutlet in the air, remembering how, to the delight of the tourists, gulls used to snatch fish out of the air down along the wharf at the San Diego harbor but my veal only plops unceremoniously in the grass.

35.

A HORRIBLE PLACE PERHAPS, AN ANACHRONISM, AN oppressive colonial regime, the Rock Resort is still a nice place to get away from squalor, vermin, lethargy, jealousy, lust, frustration, vice, and the Vacuum of the Voluptuous Triangle from which I need to extricate myself before it turns homicidal. Here at the Plantation we also have DAIRY PRODUCTS, AIR-CONDITIONING, PASTRIES, and AVOCADOS. I can actually eat *breakfast*. I can actually sit down in a chair and see what I'm doing. The vines do not wrap themselves around my ankles while mosquitoes empty the plasma from my capillaries. The roaches do not topple out of the rafters into my mouth. The windows are not covered by the sneering mouthparts of relentless vegetation. I am not hunted here or stared at from the trees like some rare breed in a cage. Every morning I sneak into the walk-in refrigerator for a moment just to enjoy the fragrance of raw bacon, lemons, grapefruit, and ripe strawberries.

Also at the hotel we have WOMEN. You might accuse me of optimism, but there is a pretty black girl in the dish room who smiles at me. She is the sort of girl you could watch all day, one pleasing curve meeting another endlessly and those striking feline eyes, that strong neck, the deep strength of clear, primal health, those sculptured nostrils, that wide, genuine, knee-weakening smile. She must be nineteen. I'm not sure how to make an overture. I hope one day to talk with her at the end of the shift as we stroll out the doors to our free lives, but she always seems to vanish.

I won't get a paycheck for almost a month, so in respect to the voluptuous triangle, I'll just have to hunker down a bit, keep my eyes askance, and mind my own business. In the meantime, I've decided to grow a beard, first because it's almost impossible to shave with a rusty razor blade shaped like a Ruffles potato chip, second because I hope my vaguely Christlike aspect will help to discourage Legion, who has begun to follow me around in his feathered headdresses and leaf motifs as if I were the new messiah, and (third, and foremost) because I hope it will change my luck with women. So far I'm a complete strikeout with all native girls, who regard me as a representative of historical oppression, the brutal master, rapist conquistador, megalomaniacal spice-crazed explorer importing syphilis and firecrackers to the New World, and so on. And even if I am not a slaver, an invader, a plantation owner, a greasy real-estate tycoon, or a Republican senator from Alabama, I am distantly related to them through Europe. And the tourist girls, my suburban sisters, sick of the whiny, impuissant, and equivocal U.S. male, and constructing their own ideology of oppression, where again I'm assigned the role of the heavy (despite my whiny impuissance and historical predilection for dressing like a fairy), have mostly returned alone after the family vacation to get themselves a bolt of virile African seed.

The beard, however, does seem to attract Kate. I've put out catnip and caught the wrong pussy. "Oh, you're so *handsome*," she loves to say in front of Mountain at our coveted cocktail hour. It's obvious what's she's doing. Witness how the humans entertained themselves before television. Soon, I imagine, I will be fertilizing a palm tree.

One night gathered around the table drinking Johnny Walker Red, the station floating between a Yankee game and Casey Kasem out of San Juan, Puerto Rico, Kate is a little drunker than usual and shucks off her blouse. "It's too goddamn hot for clothes," she announces, giving her sharp breasts a shimmy. Speechless, I stare at the beads of candlelit sweat jeweled upon her sternum. Mountain, shifting his weight, seems to be recalling an old joke about hydrochloric acid. The drink in his hand looks like a grenade.

I mumble and escape outside for fresh air and a whiz by the cistern. I hear the screen door whack shut behind me, and then the crackle of approaching footsteps. A powerful hand grabs my arm.

"What is it, Mountain?" I demand, irritated to be accosted midstream.

"What do you think you're doing?" he snarls.

"Writing my name in the snow?"

"Why don't you fuck her?" he rumbles, still gripping my arm. "I told you already."

I wrench free from his grasp, zip up, and turn to face him. The bridge of his nose is wrinkled, his teeth bared, like a rabid animal. "I didn't tell her to whip off her shirt."

He glares at me, teeming with occult spirits, the sinews and veins squiggling out on his arms and neck. "You didn't answer my question," he growls through locked teeth, his blue eyes blazing, the hair hanging down into his face. He's mad as a cat. I wish I *recognized* him.

"No," I reply with all the dignity I can muster. "Because it's a ludicrous question."

"She laughs at all your jokes," he spits, right fist balled at his side. "She called me Edgar the other day when I was fucking her." His chin jerks up and he glances toward our bungalow. "Every time you walk through the door her tits fall out of her blouse."

"Look, man," I say slowly, feeling about blindly for a way to neutralize him. "All I want is peace until I get my paycheck, then I'm moving out, O K?"

"I see the way you look at her," he snarls. "And I see the way she looks at you."

I'm not afraid of Mountain, not the Mountain that I knew a year ago anyway, but neither do I want him to punch me in the nose and give me a lesson on the constellations. "Put yourself in my position, Mountain," I explain, moving the air in front of me with succinct carving motions. "You come to visit me, you've got nowhere else to stay, and I force you to sleep with my girlfriend."

He blinks, tipping his head, as if this peppering of reason might make him sneeze.

"We've never competed for women," I continue, "because we're good friends and because that's exactly how friendships are destroyed." (The real reason we don't compete for women is that when Mountain is around they don't generally even see me.) "Think of Grace Slick and the Jefferson Airplane. Do you understand what I'm saying to you, Johnny?" His savage eyes seem to be shifting between chagrin and distrust. "I have not and I am not going to fuck your girl, OK? I'm quite capable of getting my own dates. Matter of fact, I have several lined up at the Plantation." I might add that I'm not attracted to older women, but why push it?

Mountain seems relieved despite his inclination to disbelieve me.

I reach up to pat him on his big shoulder. His head drops, his untidy hair falling over his eyes. "Let's go back inside now and behave like adults," I say. "I swear to God I'm moving out the minute I have the cash. I don't care what you say."

36.

IBA HAS LITTLE TO DO, AND APPARENTLY LESS PLACES TO go. She attends church on Sunday mornings, sometimes Saturdays. People drop off piecework and items that need mending. A cousin (or is it a brother?) who lives in town delivers weekly groceries. She listens to religious radio and recites passages from her Bible ("Where your treasure is, dat where your heart be too."). She has no beau, no dates that I have ever seen. Her social life seems confined to Sunday meetings and whatever gossip she might exchange with her neighbors as she tips her watering can.

With her mother gone, father a local pagan celebrity, and fiancé run off with a white girl, I don't blame her for visiting us almost nightly. I'm barely interested in her gossip and old wives' tales, but she knows I want her thin-night-black body. She avoids me, sitting whenever possible on the other side of the table. All my attempts to set her at ease only seem to compound her angst. At last I refer back to social psych, remembering that people are not generally motivated by "niceness." They are generally motivated by fear and desire. I hate using social psych principles, but I didn't make up the rules. Iba, like most women, probably wants a man who doesn't care about her so she can exercise her power to attract and socialize him (see romance formula), and so I do her the favor of ignoring her.

Almost instantly she responds with longer and more frequent visits. As I pile on the disinterest, she begins to bring me herbal remedies and comic-strip Scripture pamphlets. One night, the first since she delivered the hippie trousers, she even visits while Mountain and Kate are out.

I pretend to be tired, even though I know I'll be up flaming the mosquitoes off the walls with a Bic lighter until at least midnight. I yawn. She flutters her lashes at me and sits across the table. I fold my hands in my lap and wait for her to speak first. The obligatory sheen of perspiration often gives its tropical wearer an oily or labored cast, but in Iba's case it becomes her, as does the candle flame playing over the recesses of her high cheekbones and graceful neck.

"You have lamb tonight," she says, leaning in as if confiding a secret. "I smell it cookin'."

"Yes," I say, refusing to submit to natural laws of attraction. "Kate knows the butcher. He killed the lamb last night."

"De meat is always sweetis' on de bone," she says, with a lowering of lashes and a pout of plump lip, which I'll take over lamb any day. "Dat's why men like slim women."

I laugh, of course, and have a drink. I feel so reckless when I don't have a chance. But if I am patient with her, I might be able to lure her out of her shell. I know now the majority of her key emotional secrets. What she needs is someone to restore her confidence. Despite her remoteness, my persistently moronic hormones insist there's still a good chance of something happening between us. The white women come to the island for the black men, which leaves the white men and the native girls twiddling their thumbs. So why shouldn't we have our own dance?

"Let's steal the fisherman's boat, Iba," I say, almost making the mistake of touching her hand, the fingers of which play with the tufts of a burnt towel we've been using lately for a pot holder. "And row until we come to New York City."

"Oh no," she says with a tortured but somehow delighted smile, even if it seems to say: *Back to this crap again, eh Donahoe?*

"Tell me about your old man," I say, lighting myself a cigarette. "The one who left you."

She blanches, shakes her head. The candlelight jumps and

everything shifts for a moment. She's half in the darkness, one eye drilling into me as if I have changed into someone else.

"He wasn't worth it if he left you," I announce, getting up to turn on the radio. I like news if I can find it. The top forty is a strain. There is no news to be found so I turn the volume down on "Sail On" by the Commodores. "He did you a favor."

She's upset now, lips compressed, head turning rigidly on her neck. I'm not helping.

"I've had about twelve girls leave me," I say, trying to console her. "Most of the time love is a poke in the eye. Most of the time love has nothing to do with love at all."

Now her eyes are misting. I love her suddenly for her naked innocence and that arched and adamant pride. If she were in the States she would be reading self-help books and glamour magazines and learning the fine art of masturbation and blaming everything on someone else. But here she'll be alone with only God for consolation, and I know I'm being a prick with this psychological approach. I'm not good at manipulating people. Or check that, I'm good at it, but I don't enjoy it. I don't want the fruits of "deceitful pursuit". Which may be the real reason I'm running off soon to live in the wilderness: I can't accept the predatory reality of human relationships. I want love that doesn't hurt, the unabased ideal, and these simply don't exist, except alone, in the mind, withdrawn from human society.

I'm afraid now that Iba may cry. Her shoulders have begun to tremble. How can I salvage this? What does she love? Oh yes, *stories* of course, tall tales and tittle-tattle. "Iba, tell me a duppy story."

A wild but contented look comes into her eyes, and she begins to recite one as if in a trance, about a man walking down the road who meets a duppy, whose "teet are like fire." He asks the duppy for a light. The duppy "gash his teet at him," and the man runs away. Down the road a few minutes later he runs into the same duppy, whom he doesn't recognize. "I met a man jus now, ask im for a light," he complains to the duppy, "an he gash his teet at me.' The duppy grins his teeth again and asks, 'Teet like dese?'"

Iba laughs. I replace an urge to kiss her with a gulp of Scotch. One day like the bodhisattvas I'm going to give up my lousy self for someone else. Then at least one person in the world will be happy.

Uncertainty flickers in her eyes. Here is the point at which the plunderer leaps through the hole in her fence and saws down her apple tree. Instead I say: "I need to go to bed, Iba, because I have to get up in a few hours and cook for the masses. But if you need anything, I'll be up for a while killing mosquitoes, so just knock on the wall. And when you're ready to steal the fisherman's boat, let me know. You know, someone told me recently I'm about to go on a long trip."

37.

IN MY FOURTH WEEK OF EMPLOYMENT, THE CHEF, CON-
fident in my Stateside experience, leads me to the meat saw.
I've learned to appreciate this flummoxed middle-aged man. He's
fair, he pays attention, and he works hard. He doesn't try to be
hip around the mostly younger, mostly black help. I like his sense
of humor and he's read a few books too. What I don't understand
is how people surrender their lives to toil. Here he is in the
middle of a vacation wonderland resigned to the inevitability of
bleeding ulcers and emphysema until they bury him among the
willow trees. "Ever use one of these before?"

"Once or twice," I lie, not wanting to miss an opportunity to
advance to the dinner shift, where I won't have to get up at four
every morning and I can catch a ride to and from the resort with
Arthur.

"There are no guards," he says sternly, cupping the front of
his paper hat as if it were about to fall off. As I've said, I loathe
these hats. They're like wearing giant toilet-paper tubes and every
time you walk under a door they get knocked off. "So you've got
to pay attention. Thrushie always cuts the crab legs for the Sunday
buffet, but he's sick today, so you're the one." He flips on the
saw, selects a frozen crab leg from one of four crates sitting on the
floor, and zings it thrice through the blade, dropping the three
clean joint-cuts into a plastic bucket to the right.

"Like that. Let's see you do it. Right. Yes, very good," he says.

"Just put the buckets in the walk-in. Now don't fall asleep. The blade hypnotizes you sometimes. OK?"

I'd like to finish these legs in two hours, make a good impression. At first I am sweating across my lower back and the flesh above my lip. Think of what that blade with no guard will do to you if you slip. Eventually I get the rhythm. I finish three cases of crab legs in an hour. The blade blurs. The same crab legs over and over, the same three joint-cuts over and over: *zing zing zing*.

I get to daydreaming about the seduction of Iba: I steal Fish's skiff for an afternoon and lure her into a cruise. Not far away is an uninhabited cay, where someone has tried to live before and abandoned a small hut and cistern. I imagine empty rum bottles with messages in them and a pineapple tree with a heart carved into the bark. Iba is elegant and prim, chin elevated to match the prow—until the boat founders. Then I must save her. We are desperately gripping one another in wet clothes, struggling for our lives. Finally we drag ourselves up on the shore, panting and exhausted and grateful to be alive, wrecked on a desert island with only each other, and all the buttons have come undone on her blouse.

I run the legs through the whirring blade of the saw, a smile on my face, zing zing zing. Then I run my thumb through the whirring blade of the saw, *zing zing* BUZZZ. Blood slaps warmly against my face. Iba's form disappears from the sand. I clutch my hand to my stomach. Someone reaches over and shuts off the machine. The blood pitter-patters onto the red ceramic tiles. The chef jumps from the chair in his glass-enclosed office. Hall, a long-nosed steward with button black eyes, passing with a great cart of China, his face drained of color, hands me a linen napkin.

"You all right, man?" he shouts through my jangled fog of pain. "You all right?"

I cover the wound without looking at it. I can sense spectators gathering, though I refuse to look at their faces. I feel the thumb hanging. I think to myself: *I have lost my thumb*.

In another moment I am sitting in Hall's gold Volkswagen

Beetle, tearing down the hill for town. Hall is from Jacksonville by way of Brookings, South Dakota. He still has the faint semi-Southern drawl of the urban Floridian. In profile he is mostly nose. I ask him feebly for a cigarette and smoke it greedily with my bloody, napkin-wrapped hand in my lap. You may smoke a million cigarettes in your life, but you will never remember any more than nine or ten. This is one. It is a wonderful cigarette, friend and companion. My reflection is spattered green flab in the side mirror, the eyes ringed with doom. My heart throbs in dark, veiny splotches at the bottoms of my eyes. I feel hot and woozy and hollow as a worm. I am more worried at the thought of losing the thumb than I am at the loss of blood, which is considerable.

Hall drives tensely and a tad wildly on the turns, making me think of those unlucky patients who crash in ambulances on the way to the hospital. "That ain't nothing," he says, trying to comfort me. "Butcher last year was boning out a steamship? Slipped and gutted himself." He gives a hara-kiri pantomime with one hand on the steering wheel, his button eyes glittering. "All the way to the hilt."

"Is he all right?" I ask.

"No, hell no. He ain't all right. Went back to the States. Got peritonitis. Almost killed him."

"You have no future as a motivational speaker, you understand that."

Hall swats the air, then looks up just in time to swerve and miss a dog sniffing at carrion in the middle of the road. "You're gonna be all right, man. That ain't nothing," he chides, glaring in his rearview. "What the hell were you doing anyway?"

There is a small clinic down behind the post office in the town square. I haven't noticed it before. There are no patients in the lobby. The nurse behind the desk shoots up out of her chair, more at the pallor of my face, I think, than the sight of the blood-soaked napkin.

"We called ahead," says Hall.

She gestures me into the back room.

In a few minutes a white doctor about fifty years of age strides into the room, fists jammed into his smock. He has a rubbery, vein-spidered, hawk-nosed face. His stiff, lacquer-blond toupée is shaped in an annoyingly straight geisha-girl line across the forehead. The nametag on his smock reads DR. TOBACKOO. I glance up to the wall and see a diploma from the University of Virginia.

"Let's have a look at that, son," he says, the smell of alcohol stronger on his breath than in the bottles marked ISOPROPYL. I hadn't expected Christiaan Barnard, but it isn't even noon yet. Obediently, I open the red napkin.

He nods without commitment. "You've got good red blood," he says. "You're a healthy young man."

I glance down and nearly faint, not so much at the sight of blood but at the gaping exposition of my personal and innermost precious meat with the thumb bone like a too-thin chess piece with a nick out of it.

The nurse bustles in. She is fleshy lipped with an overbite, wears white stockings, and is haunchy enough to make you forget for a few moments your careless self-amputations. Dr. Tobackoo drags some equipment out of a glass case. He moves to a drawer and with trembling hands tries to thread an upholstery needle. After a few botched attempts the nurse finally threads it for him. The room begins to turn. The nurse is swabbing my wound. I bite down on my lip.

"Open your hand," he orders. "No, like this."

The blood streams down flat and red as a West Texas river. I feel prickly and stabbed with remorse. I feel childlike and stuck in time. I am still wearing my cotton French hat and my beard itches and I'm suddenly angry at all the crabs that ever walked along the bottom of the sea.

"How did it happen?" the doctor asks.

"Meat saw."

"Looks like it saw you first."

Oh, he's Dr. Tobackoo from the University of Vaudeville.

"This isn't much," he says, laving me with his liquorish breath. "Relax."

I feel the catgut drawing and snagging through the flaps of my hide. He cinches, loops back under, cinches. I watch him sew me up like a Christmas turkey. God, Doc, did you ever dream it would end like this when you were a young comedian at the University of Vaudeville? The stitching hands tremble: the sutures are crooked, but he ties them down for the most part in parallel rows and the bleeding slows, then beads, and then finally comes to a stop.

"One dozen even," he announces as if he were buying eggs from the market. "I wish I had a dollar for every stitch I put in a cook." He swipes at the perspiration on his forehead with the back of his hand. "Why don't they put guards on those saws?"

"You can't French a lamb chop."

"Don't French it then."

The nurse wraps the thumb in a mile of gauze. She holds my hand for a minute and looks me softly in the eyes.

Dr. Tobackoo scribbles into a clipboard. "That's the end of that," he says. "You cooks up there keep the old doc busy." He sounds offended. I am glad that I didn't catch him three or four hours later.

"How much do I owe you?"

"The Rockefellers will cover it," he says, checking over his shoulder. "Louise has a little paperwork for you. Are you right-handed?"

"I am."

"Well, that's a good break, isn't it?" He wipes again at his brow. I'm tempted to invite him for a drink. I don't know what the Hippocratic oath says about having one with your patient after surgery. Anyway, he seems like the type who might prefer his alone.

"When can I go back to work?"

"That's up to you," he says. "But I'd give it a week at least. Come back Thursday and we'll have a look at it."

"Thursday morning all right?"

"You'll need to change that dressing daily," he says, moving to the sink to wash his hands. "Apothecary's got bandages and the like, but if you want anything for pain, you'll have to go to Ravissant to pick it up. Antibiotics too. I've got some penicillin but it's not good for much."

"I'll be all right," I say, climbing off the table. "Thursday morning then."

38.

I CAN CATCH THE SCHOOL BUS EAST, BUT I DON'T FEEL like going home right away. I keep seeing the black vibrating saw blade, the crab leg, the thumb. Kate gets off at four from the bakery. It's only eleven now. I wander light-headed around town, the sailboats hovering out on the bay, Legion standing devotedly behind a tree, peeking out at me, then moving out to follow as I walk away. Several people have said that, because of the church, he doesn't like to come into town, but he seems to make an exception for me.

I turn into Harry's, where I know he will not follow. He's afraid of alcohol, I imagine. I wonder what he thinks about the color red. It is cool and dim inside Harry's, no big afternoon crowd, only a pair of codgers in Disney T-shirts against the wall and two middle-aged black men sipping Maltos at the bar. Harry's is my apothecary. He has painkillers and antiseptics. Antibiotics too. The blue parrot sitting above the door preens under its wing and cackles at some private toucan joke. Corny vibraphone music oozes from the stereo. I take a stool. Through the bamboo-framed window I watch the ferry land and I remember my first day here, vaguely, as if many years have gone by. Legion waddles past the glass, turns his gaze on me, gives a bark and a rattle of his saber at the bewildered passengers, and then disappears into the shadows of the plaza.

My barman is George, who never smiles. "Gin and tonic," I tell him. He glances once at the bulb of gauze on my thumb and mixes me a drink without any questions. I sip and watch Harry's ghost TV in the tiki-green light. As far as I know, it is the only TV on the island. There is no point in having a television if you can't get a signal. But people watch it anyway. Now and then shadows appear, the ghost of a baseball game, a Doris Day movie, or Mussolini stepping onto the train platform to greet Hitler, make it what you please.

I order a second drink and while waiting for another glimpse of Legion, I see Cinnamon Jim glide through the entrance dressed in a white linen suit. Around his waist is a royal-yellow sarong, on his gray-eyed mummy head a red fez, and on his feet a pair of yellow Converse All Stars. A tiny monkey in a bellhop outfit sits on his shoulder, long tail curling around the juju man's hat.

"Ah, here you are," he says, striding down and taking the stool next to mine, as if he expected to find me here. He smells of dust, licorice root, headcheese, and marzipan. He's sweatless, the only human on the isle who doesn't perspire. "What are you up to?" he asks.

I turn my drink on its coaster and admire the concaves in my ice cubes. "Just staring out the Ferry Land Window."

"Heard you took a nasty cut."

"News travels fast," I reply, regarding the thick gauze already pink from suture leakage.

Gesturing at the primate on his shoulder, he says, "Permit me to introduce my companion, Oscar Wilde, the only monkey on the isle."

I extend a hand. The monkey chatters at me, showing his sharp yellow teeth, then grabs my ear.

Cinnamon claps his hands. The monkey leaps in the air to land on Jim's other shoulder. "I apologize," says Cinnamon. "Some of these old patients can be such pests." He laughs, lifting all the wrinkles on his face. Outside the window two native kids swat a hoop with a stick right into the bay and then laugh as it disappears. "You've a spot of blood on your forehead there," says Jim. "Oscar, give your new friend a swab."

In a darting move the monkey dips a cocktail napkin into my drink and begins to dab at my forehead.

"How's the pain?" asks Cinnamon, lighting one of his French cigarettes.

"Tolerable," I say, closely observing the monkey, who tips his head back and forth and, apparently satisfied, flits back to his human perch.

Cinnamon reaches up to massage Oscar's back. "You're aware of the number of first-rate indigenous herbs available for pain?"

"I'll stick with the gin, thanks. Can I buy you one?"

"I'm the one buying." His eyes swirl with a slow glitter.

Smiling George the barman is standing dourly above us.

"The usual, George," says Cinnamon, patting his monkey on the back, "and another of whatever the gentleman from San Diego is having."

I fish up my lime wedge and crush the juice into my drink. "What's the usual?"

"Absinthe."

"Absinthe?"

"Would you like one? It's French, not bad."

"I'll give it a try. Let me pay."

"Don't be insulting. Give him two sugar cubes." He holds up two fingers and scoots in his stool. "I regret my inhospitality at our last meeting, my boy."

"Rabbit crap. You were on the button. I can't ask help from something I don't believe in."

He smiles, spreading the web of seams across his face. "Exclusivity should never be the oath of the healer. Vain is the word of the philosopher who does not heal any suffering of man, eh?"

George sets down two cloudy, green drinks. Cinnamon nods and holds his aloft. We touch glasses. The absinthe is bitter despite the extra sugar and I note a hint of fennel or anise. It seems to have an immediate effect. The Ferry Land Window quavers and despite the possibility of Legion I feel a suggestion of peace.

"Overrated stuff," says Jim, smacking his lips. "But it does the trick."

"Eats your brains, though, doesn't it?" I ask, having another sip. "Wormwood?"

"Hardly," he says, rustling his sarong. He pours a mound of sunflower seeds on the bar and Oscar Wilde leaps down to have at them. "Unless you want it to."

"I was all ready to have a hallucinogenic experience."

Cinnamon chuckles and wipes his lips with a cocktail napkin. His eyes in that plundered face are as pale as the oceans of the world on a Ptolemaic map. The monkey, now sitting on the bar, contentedly cracks and consumes the sunflower seeds.

Chollie appears in the window again, drawn up, chest expanded, as if ready for a confrontation.

Cinnamon shakes his head as if a bull pigeon has appeared instead of the most sinister soul on Poisson Rouge Isle. He puffs from his cigarette. "When you came to me first I thought you might have been exaggerating," he says, finger laid up along his temple. "But I've watched him from my window and I see he's your veritable shadow."

"Yes," I admit, "he's quite attached. I'm afraid if I ever left the island for more than a day I'd have to kennel him."

Cinnamon opens his hand and a tiny, black onyx Christ falls from a chain, catching the light and flashing as it turns. Chollie's eyes lock for a moment on the glittering, pinioned icon and he backpedals, mouth agape.

Cinnamon's pale eyes glimmer with pleasure. "I've considered your problem and found the solution within my grasp. Take it," he says.

"Oh, I couldn't."

"Spirit is spirit, old boy. Don't fear the sublime."

The monkey, with a sunflower seed suspended in his grasp, gazes at me with such intensity I wonder if he really wasn't some more intelligent form very recently. *Always pay the obeah man*, I think. "You kidding?" I say. "I always get two in my gin and tonics."

Jim extinguishes his cigarette. "You Stateside chaps are all about the multiplication table of the soul. Take your port in a storm. Consider Pascal's gamble. It won't matter to Chollie if you believe or not. *Honi soit qui mal ye pense.* Evil be to him who evil thinks of it."

Standing in the window, Chollie is still transfixed by the gleams of the onyx figure and has let several tourists pass without growling at them. Cinnamon lets the little Jesus dangle before me and I'm not sure if I'm tingling from absinthe or abracadabra. "The world is the mind," he says. "Wear it."

I toss back my absinthe. My mind feels rinsed. As I slide the necklace over my head, Chollie turns and stalks stiffly away, the great knife bouncing comically against his muscular thigh. The pain in my thumb is entirely gone.

"Jesus," I say. "Thanks. Let me buy this next round."

He glances at his watch. "Sold to the boy with the Salvation Army necklace."

Blinking from the change in light, Dr. Tobackoo strolls through the door, looks about, and motions nonchalantly at George, who delivers a double-olive martini without asking. I wave at the doc. He doesn't seem to recognize me until he notices the lump of gauze on my thumb and then the man with the monkey sitting next to me. Tobackoo seems to tense, then he waves and smiles, holding up his drink as if it is midnight at Times Square. I toast him on that one, the miniature Christ gleaming on my chest.

39.

FOR FIVE DAYS I'M HOMEBOUND NURSING A BUTCHERED thumb, trying to sleep under the shifting acres of relentless, kamikaze vampires, listening to baseball games, pouring out Seagram's Extra Dry, flinching at the sight of Mountain as he passes to and fro from his salvaging job and the work on his boat, and reliving the hideous half-second horror of the grinding meat saw. The rhythmic, muttering breakers whoosh up the clumpy, igneous shore. Mountain has lately become scarce. He says he wants to finish *Colleen* before monsoon season, but I believe he wants to try and force me and Kate together. She likes to bait him, parading around as if our crumbling aqua bungalow were a Caribbean nudist colony and studying me with sultry airs (as I try to ignore her) and laughing at everything I say. I'm broke. I'm stuck. I've got the redleg blues. All I can do is laugh and persevere. I wear my black onyx Christ and memorize passages from the Bible, stacking up my talismans against the great day of fate.

Except for my travel alarm, all the clocks in the house have stopped for lack of batteries. It's 4:10, 2:22, and 10:16, depending on where you look. We've run out of Off! too, which is all right since my blood has been converted 100 percent to the fluid that circulates in the veins of the anopheles. All forays now by the mosquito are official acts of cannibalism.

The night before I am supposed to have my stitches removed Kate appears in the bedroom door, barefoot in a Tyrolean peasant dress and topless, hair fallen over her eyes.

"Hi, Edgar," she whispers, her cat's face lit with mischief.

"Go back to bed," I whisper at her sharply. "Don't wake the giant."

The Herb Alpert song "Rise" is on the radio and Kate sways to the beat, arching her back to scratch between her shoulder blades. I admire her neck, her shoulders, the slatternly bend of her body. "Don't worry, he's dead to the world. He drank a fifth of Scotch. I love your new charm," she whispers, scratching her haunch. "I didn't know that Christ was *black*."

"He was a Semite, not a brewer's servant."

"I can't sleep," she pouts, leaning into the jamb, lifting her skirt like a curtain coming up, revealing those thin shapely legs gleaming with perspiration. "I've got an itch. It's so hot."

Put on some clothes, I want to say, but I only smile, as if she were my drowsy little sister getting up for a glass of water.

"What are you doing?" she asks, her hair mussed, I imagine, from unfulfilled desire.

"Writing a letter home," I say. "Go back to bed, will you? You're not the one who'll pay if he wakes up."

She smiles and rubs her back against the doorjamb. "How's Mom and Pop and the old picket fence?"

"No idea. I haven't gotten any mail yet."

"General delivery sometimes takes months. Oh, I've got an itch," she says, reaching back and accentuating the already jaunty line of her breast. "How's your thumb?"

I taste my drink and flex my thumb, which still burns stiffly, as if the doctor sewed a jalapeño pepper inside. I've been changing the dressings twice a day and drinking extra gin to ward off infection. "OK," I tell her. "I'll be testing plum puddings any day."

"Like Little Jack Horny," she says brightly.

"Horner."

"I like my version better."

"I'm licking my lips only because they're dry."

She toes the linoleum. "Did you see Iba today?"

"Yes. She brought a fiddlewood poultice that gave me a rash."

"How goes the courtship?"

I set my pen down and pick up the Seagram's Extra Dry.

"I'm playing hard to get."

She smiles at me, coiling a lock of hair around her finger. "She won't sleep with you, Edgar, you know that."

"She's a woman," I reply firmly. "She must have desires."

"She's a prude," Kate says, looking down her nose at me. "Like you."

"Me?" I blubber.

She laughs, throwing back her head. "You're a *Victorian*."

"Well then," I sniff. "Two prudes in a pod, as they say. The Victorians were notoriously lascivious, you know." I gulp directly from the bottle, which opens that familiar gilded invitation to the Paradise of Alcohol and its glorious wild orchards of unimpeachable art and philosophy.

"There are plenty of women on this island," she says, raising her peasant dress another notch. "You're just not looking in the right place."

My loins begin to rustle in their dungeon. "Go to bed."

"Mountain wants me to give you a ride in the morning," she says, combing her fingers back through her hair with both hands, a gesture that lifts her nipples to attention.

"Ride?" I say, still wondering if I am a prude. How can I be a prude? I've been as sexually irresponsible as anyone I know. It's only my abysmal success rate that gives me any appearance of being upright.

"To get your stitches out."

"Oh." A mosquito lands on the table and I crouch, frozen, reaching meticulously for a rolled-up newspaper. On my second day of leave from the hotel I tried to patch the holes in the screens with a needle and thread but it was like trying to mend clouds or mayonnaise in a film by Kurosawa and I gave up. I squash the mosquito with a muffled cry of victory. The furry brown vermin have become my sworn enemies. They whine all night in my ears, whine and dine. They crouch on the walls, waiting for me to fall asleep. They fly in single file through the holes in the screens, waving, honking party horns, and snapping off mock salutes as they pass. I don't care if they reproduce at a rate of one-billion-per-second-squared. I have become obsessed with the personal destruction of every last one. "When did he tell you that?"

"Just before he passed out. He said he wants to work on his boat in the morning."

I think of fucking her right on the table, knocking the coffee mugs and the *Boston Globe* and the ashtrays to the floor, startling the roaches, startling the moon, stealing the giant's gold and scrambling back down the beanstalk.

"Don't you ever sleep?" she asks.

"Not much," I say, gazing into the bottle in my hand. "Too much like giving blood downtown."

Mountain groans in his sleep.

"Better get back to bed," she says, winking at me and giving her skirt a saucy flip. "I'll see you in the Monet."

Good idea, now that the table can be held up without any legs.

40.

KATE DRIVES WORDLESSLY, SPLUTTERING UP THE SIDE of the bosky volcano. She does not manage well the potholes, the turns, or the epileptic steering wheel, which she treats more as a personal affront than a soluble mechanical problem. When the car vibrates off into a frenzy she gasps, loses her grip, then begins to swerve about the road swearing instead of simply seizing the wheel and giving it a jerk. This dark, early, pumpkin-smelling morning she wears a short, low-necked aqua shirt that's basically a tortilla, inside of which her breasts jostle around tantalizingly with the motion of the car. Most of her legs are showing. It's a little early for this, but Kate, a misplaced exhibitionist, obviously needs the attention, so as we clamor and jiggle through the dark pulsating forest, I give it to her—attention I mean. I find juggling bosoms and bare legs a more pleasant form of stimulation than the coffee I would enjoy in the morning if we had any.

"You ever been to old Doc Tobackoo?" I shout to her.

"I got a prescription from him once for a yeast infection," she says, with a half smile and a roll of the eyes.

"I warned you about that bakery position."

She laughs and flicks me a hungry glance. "He probably doesn't remember me," she says. "He was *gassed*, Edgar."

"You must have caught him late in the morning."

"I don't remember what time it was. Would you scratch my shoulder?"

"What, here?"

"Lower," she says. "No, down a bit, down a bit, go *down*, that's it."

"That isn't your shoulder."

"That feels good."

"Yes, it does," I mutter absently, my hand practically down her blouse. As many times as I've seen her naked, this is the first time I've actually touched her. Maybe we should just get this over with, pull off into the jungle and go cannibal. My testicles are beginning to ache, and this Corolla has reclining fu—I mean bucket seats. A mongoose dashes out in front of us. Kate swerves, dodging him. Tree limbs slap our windshield. I settle back into my corner, vexed by the symbolism of the weasel.

Kate hunches close to the windshield as the old Toyota clatters through the quivering hullabaloo. Soon splashes of dawn begin flickering over. The steering wheel, shuddering, is poised for conniption. I glance left and right for the crazy head feathers of my adversary. I touch the onyx Jesus at my breast for consolation. I'm trying to believe, I'm really trying, but it's hard to concentrate watching the easy rhythm of Kate's breasts.

"Tell me about Baltimore!" I shout to her.

"You ever *been* to Baltimore?" she says, turning a scornful glance on me.

A blue-throated hummingbird appears for a moment at my window. "You ever think about going back?"

A wry smile lifts the chocolate-chip mole. "Never."

"No friends, family, memories?"

"Plenty," she says.

"You didn't like social work?"

She downshifts and I stare to the left down an overgrown dirt road that bends out of sight through the transpiration of two towering calabash trees. "I grew up in a safe middle-class neighborhood," she says. "I couldn't get used to people being treated like animals."

"How long were you married?"

"Three years," she says, with a distant look. "Let's not talk about Baltimore anymore."

Sheets of mist twist and billow all about as if the forest thickets are draped in cheesecloth. "What do you want to talk about?" I ask, sniffing at the heavy odor of the jungle and other proximal blooming delights.

"Does Mountain always force his girlfriends on you?"

"Never. I don't know what's gotten into him. It's my fault."

"*Your* fault?" She turns the scorn on me again.

"Yes. I should have got my own place the first day. Fear of losing his woman, that's his great weakness. I knew that before I came. It's a mother complex."

"Oh, don't give me that *mother* shit, Edgar," she scoffs, tapping on the brake and thus revealing even more of the long lines of her legs. "Pretty boys, they're all alike. My husband was a pretty boy. He cheated on me for three years. The minute I had an affair he filed for divorce."

"I don't think Mountain sees himself as a pretty boy."

"Pretty boy, football hero, big man on campus, they're all the same," she says, reaching out the window to peel and flick away a wet leaf from the windshield. "If they don't get their way, they throw a fit."

The car begins to make a hissing sound.

"You know what I say about men, Edgar?" she continues, pulling herself forward suddenly.

"No, what?"

"Fuck 'em."

"I've always said the same thing about women, all night with vegetable oil."

Kate turns to me with an approving smile. "Christ," she says, "I think we're going to be *late*."

There is enough light now that I am looking for places where we might pull over and do the bunny hug in the jungle. The steady and eccentric thrum of the engine and the smell of frangipani and the perfume on her armpits combine to amplify my arousal. Moral tests should not be this *long*. Suddenly the steering wheel goes into a fit.

"Grab it, will you!" she shouts.

"Grab *what*?"

"The *steering* wheel. I can't—"

My instinct is to plunge my hands down her blouse but what good are two handfuls of mammary gland when you are crashed upside down in the bushes with anteaters sniffing at your ankles?

"Let off on the gas!" I yell, jerking the wheel back and forth.

Instead she stomps on the brakes. Something explodes under the hood and a hot fog spews the windshield. We skid on the turn, hop through a pothole, thump over something that feels like a dog or a corpse, and crash softly into the brush, the spiky shadows of leaves spreading darkly over us. Kate strikes the steering wheel with her fists, her chest heaving. "I *hate* this car," she says. "What the hell *was* that?"

"An orgasm?"

She throws me a my-god-don't-you-ever-stop-joking glance. "Are we screwed, Edgar? Is it the radiator?"

"We may be screwed," I say. "But I'm fairly sure it's not the radiator."

"What is it?"

"Heater coil, I think."

"Didn't know it *had* a heater."

"Kind of like your air conditioner going out at the north pole."

Kate climbs out, her tortilla shirt disarranged. She yanks up the hood and sticks her head in, her rump poised high in the air. At least she is wearing panties, of a simple white cotton variety, though they are crammed to accentuate the gorgeous portions of her curvilinear tenderloin. Images of us burning ourselves on the manifold as we copulate like baboons swamp my every thought. "Oh Jesus," she says, throwing the hood down. "This fucker will never run again."

The hood swings open again. "We can push it out and try to bump-start it," I say, looking around. "Where are we anyway?"

She swipes her palms down her hips, tugs at the shoulder

of her shirt so that it doesn't cover her chest so completely, and squints into the brush. "It's the old graveyard."

"What graveyard?"

"Necropolis," she says. "Chollie's house."

My heart thumps and stalls. I stroll down the road for a quick peek. I have heard much about this ancestral burial ground, but we have always sped by too fast in our smoking Corolla to get a decent look. The sun is gaining in the sky. Kate and I stand at the arched gate of the ancient churchyard with its carefully spaced gingerbread and black willow trees shrouded with Spanish moss. A few zebra butterflies flit about the majestic old headstones, which are wrapped in jumbi-bread vines and infested with wild bumblebee orchids. I tug on my black Jesus. My neck chills with African superstitions.

"Well, they picked the right *spot*," I say.

"It was Dutch," she says. "They don't bury people in here anymore. Most of the white people who were murdered in the 1833 revolt are buried here."

"One hundred percent creepy," I say. "Even the smell."

"The orchids smell like rotting flesh," Kate agrees. She smooths her hands repeatedly down her hips. "Ever fuck in a graveyard, Edgar?"

My zeppelinesque testicles swing about to face her. "What me, no, you?"

She shrugs with that faint, confidential smile that says two, maybe three graveyards, who's counting? Her gaze drops. The brown tips of her breasts nudge high against her sheer wrap like the noses of eager coondog pups. I'll be late for my appointment with Tobackoo, I think, bending to take her mouth. The birds titter at us like teenaged nuns. Kate meets me hungrily, yanking at my fly buttons, and we fall in a fever into the brambles.

Kate has it, now I know why Mountain is hooked. It's the boyish flatness of her stomach, the kiwi down of her *mons pubis*, the high-button profile of her rocklike nipples, the zesty aroma of her sassafras ass. All that sweat and musk floating up from her body, the forbidden and long-suspended thrill of new flesh, and the scattered, delftish sky above send me into a humping frenzy like a mad hare. The black chalcedony Savior on the chain around my neck swings back and forth, knocking against my chin.

The lanes between the stones are fairly worn, as from foot traffic, (does Legion maintain this ancient yard of his antithesis?), and we rake over the bones of the long-departed Dutch, Kate's panties clutched like victory in my bandaged left hand.

I'm aware of someone watching us, but there is no privacy on this island with a million eyes, and the thought of danger and voyeurism only doubles my pleasure. I scoot Kate's winking fanny as she grabs me, desperately moaning and yipping from an occasional collected quill, until till we bump with a shuttering climax into a tombstone marked ERIK VAN SCHORR 1792–1833. Off in the shade I see the veil of a tiny waterfall misting a shady patch of carefully tended marijuana plants. The sun breaks through the canopy and angles down on us in a scatter of pencil-thin shafts.

"Well, to answer your question," I say. "Yes. But only once."

Kate smiles weakly. "You sure know how to drive a girl home."

"Oh," I say, looking all around. "This old cemetery must be *Victorian*."

She stares at the swinging onyx Christ.

"I should've taken it off," I apologize.

"It's all right," she says, her head twisting about. "What happened to my panties? Have you seen them?"

I peer into the brush at the mist of the waterfall. Now the rational hangover, the postcoital letdown, the sudden rush of remorse, complete with pictures like matinee cutouts of a betrayed Mountain. Just a few minutes ago I thought we might take another row through the cemetery and maybe even clip a few sticky buds from Legion's reefer oasis on the way out. But in the shadows by the waterfall I catch a restless flash of steel and the wink of demonic yellow eye. Son of a witch.

"We'd better get going, Kate," I say. "It's already seven martinis after ten."

41.

THAT NIGHT AT DINNER, MORTIFIED BY GUILT, I CAN'T meet Mountain's eyes. I'm certain he knows. I'm certain he can read it in my face or smell it on my conscience. I've sowed his girl in Satan's graveyard, broken my vow, spread my hypocrisy thinner than mayonnaise on a mission sandwich. Forgive me, old friend, I want to say. I've never let you down before. That convulsive exhibition of lust in the graveyard was a fluke. You should not have left me alone with her two hundred times, or suggested that hard Germanic word with the *f* in front of it. The bee cannot be expected to resist the sticky open blossom indefinitely.

But it will not happen again.

Wordlessly, Mountain cuts his fish, lifts his jelly glass of Scotch, and stares off obliquely at the wall, the muscles in his cheeks bunched, his shovel jaw shoved stubbornly outward, his eyes shining with mayhem. Kate is heavy with chatter about art and books, topics that Mountain would normally have a bundle of opinions on. "You know I wouldn't have even cared about *Lady Chatterley's Lover*, except my mother hid it from me so naturally I had to read it. I was twelve years old. Have you read that book, Edgar?"

I make an excuse to turn in early with the sports section of the *Miami Herald*, which I've been reading in lieu of fresh print for two weeks, but I like looking at the baseball standings. Pittsburgh looks a cinch for the National League pennant, every day they're ahead by seven games, wonderful news for my friend down the road. An argument wells: Kate's sharp reproof, "So what am I supposed to do? Get up at daybreak and make you hash browns?"

"You could at least clean the house," he bellows. "You only work two days a week."

"Well, at least I make *money*."

"I made eighty-six bucks today. What'd you do, get a tan on your ass?"

"I cleaned your goddamn fish, didn't I? You didn't even catch it. And Edgar cooked it."

"Edgar, Edgar, Edgar. Is that all you ever say?"

"I'll say what I like. It's my mouth."

"*Fuck* your mouth," he says.

"No, fuck *your* mouth," she replies.

Now they are getting to the heart of the matter. I hear the screen door slam. "Come back here, bitch!" The door slams again. I hope he doesn't hurt her. I think of taking her away, stealing her into my wilderness dream, then I remember the promise that I made and the reason that I came.

42.

SHAMBLING, SHUDDERING, AND SLIDING THROUGH THE
predawn pandemonium one morning, Mountain almost has
the Toyota to the top of the grade when a thump and scatter under
the hood sends us careening into a bizarre seizure, like an
elephant with acute gastritis. Mountain shuts off the engine and
lets the Corolla coast to a stop with a funny last hiccup under a
horseradish tree. We climb out into the benighted forest. Mountain, wearing a straw hat with a tightly scrolled brim, a tight
yellow T-shirt, and a pair of Iba's madcap clown pants, lights a
match. A cochineal bandanna is tied around his throat. He lifts
the hood, peers in, strikes another match, and shakes his head.

"What is it?" I say.

"Dunno," he says. "Can't see."

"Bad?"

"Not good." He waves his hand through a pall of blue smoke,
the motion reminiscent of last rites. The match flickers out.

"Oil pump?" I say.

"No. Block maybe. Smells like it. If it's the block it's
finished."

"Last Tango in Paradise," I sigh, looking around "How many
more lives does it have?"

He shakes his head and slams down the hood. I light another match. The plastic digital clock adhered to the dash blinks
5:50. I was already late for work. Now I'll be late for lunch. I

wonder how much longer before the chef lets me go, and then what will I do for money?

"You gonna walk back home?" I ask apprehensively. "We're not halfway yet."

He shrugs without meeting my eyes. "No," he says. "I want to talk to Saul anyway. He still owes me money."

Even though I have kept my word to myself not to touch Kate again, we seem to do it with our eyes. In the shower she hands me the soap. I see her lingering in the darkness of my doorway at 2:00 a.m., or undressing in the bedroom so I can watch her from the table. She gives me winks, pats, and secret (and often public) gifts of the bared breast. I wish I could stop leaning toward the drowsy scent of her body and longing for her bonbons. I'd even like to give Mountain some advice: laugh with her, stop being so possessive and gloomy, fuck her in the wide outdoors under the brazen gaze of the dearly departed. But give Mountain advice? Tell someone losing his girl to be *funny*? I know he can't help himself. And I know he wouldn't do this to me.

And the shakier and more confused and miserable he gets the better Kate seems to like it. Mountain can't understand that she despises being possessed. But does she comprehend Mountain's potential for violence? She's seen him fight. She knows he's fearless, but she also believes she is somehow protected by his sickly egotistical fixation, which she mistakes for love and devotion.

The way before Mountain and me is a sylvan tunnel of shag and foggy silhouettes, and I stay close to Mountain, whose night vision is much sharper than mine. We have about seven miles to cover. Even if Mountain is inconsolable, I'm glad he's decided to come along, especially now that I note with a glance backward that Legion is following us. "Action photo!" I cry, freezing in the middle of the road in a senile crouch.

"What is it?" says Mountain, barely interested.

"Old Chinese man with string bean up his ass."

"Funny," he says.

"Chollie's behind us," I mutter.

"What's new?" he says, not even bothering to glance back.

I'd like to mention the marijuana patch and the waterfall but I don't want to open any insights into how I might know.

"Might be able to find something in the junkyard," I offer.

"The car is finished," he says flatly, gliding silently ahead, as if he were talking to himself. I fall into a bleak silence. Dawn begins to creep over the canopy. The asphalt feels like velour or taffy under my feet. The wind rustles but never touches. The creatures fill the forest with seventy-seven layers of madhouse babble. The sunlight blossoms on some of the turns, dappling the pavement in gold blotches I want to peel up and put in my pocket. Soon butterflies are dancing through paper-thin curtains of sunlight. The birds and the bugs shrill like the last high-pitched, atonal chord in a modern symphony for the tragic demise of a Japanese compact. I look back and Legion is gone.

"How am I going to get to work from now on?" I ask, straining for the sound of an automobile. I want to see Fanny ride up on her motorcycle. I persist in thinking that machines will save us.

A hermit crab scuttles out in front of Mountain and he crushes it with his heel. "School bus," he says.

"What time?"

"About five. You'll be early to work."

"How novel. Do I have to pay?"

"No, just stand there by the big rock at the junction."

"How about you?"

"I'll be all right."

"How's the salvaging?"

"Saul's looking in the wrong place for the Mariner's Trove," he says, "but that's all right by me. It's his money."

"If he'd pay you."

"He will." His bicep swells as he clenches a fist. "One way or another."

We pass the Dutch graveyard with its large movement of vagrant shadows and lambent flicker of butterflies and I think of that outrageous romp with Kate. The sound of the waterfall is more like drips hitting a bog and I imagine Legion lounging in its mist and toking on his ganja like a modern Pan. Mountain hardly gives the old burial ground a look.

"Jesus," I say, in a genial tone that almost scores a ten on the Gomer Pyle scale. "I'm going to be at least an hour late. I might as well not even go to *work*. And isn't *that* the definition of paradise?"

"Is it?"

"Remember, Adam and Eve were banished to a life of labor after they broke their covenant with God?"

"How could I forget?" he says, again moving ahead without me.

I chew the inside of my cheek. He's right of course. I've unwittingly picked an infidelity metaphor. Perhaps I should tell him now, confess and clear the air. I did his girl once, and I'd like to do her again, but since I'll be off soon to my tranquil sunlight in native colors, I reconsider: why not just let it pass?

Behind us a green Land Rover gleams stealthily around the bend. Mountain and I move to the side of the road. The Rover glides up next to us. The window slides down. I see amber dashboard lights and smell Freon and leather. I haven't seen this vehicle before. The driver, a man of forty or fifty years with a dignified haircut and a camouflage uniform, sticks his head out, a scrap of green cigar slotted into his jaw. "Boys," he drawls. "That your Toyota back there?"

"Yussir," I say.

"You run out of gas?"

"No," I say. "Ran out of luck. Looks like the block cracked."

He nods and smiles. "Too bad," he says. He's got good strong teeth and a tan like Barry Manilow. "Looks like I've come at the right time," he says. I notice that he seems to be appreciating Mountain, who still behaves as if he were alone out on the road.

"How do you mean?" I ask.

He extends a hand. "I'm Sergeant Valparaiso," he says. "Ex-USMC, explosives expert. We're training our own force over on St. Lucia. Had three AWOLs last week. These black boys don't want to fight. You boys want to join up with me? Free meals, weapons training, adventure, excitement, women, and spoils."

"Who are you fighting?" I say.

"We go where the money is. This week it's Argentina."

One of Mountain's eyebrows lifts. Despite his rash mood, he can't resist the mercenary line, especially that word *spoils*, which I can see he translates to *gold*.

"Can you give us a ride into town?" I ask. "Argentina is a bit ambitious today. I'm late for work."

"Where you work?"

"Rockefeller Plantation."

"Hop in," he says. "I'm headed that way. Don't mind the ammunition."

"How much you pay?" asks Mountain, slamming the door and staring down into a wooden crate full of loose grenades.

"Depends," says Sergeant Valparaiso, switching the cigar to the other side of his face and studying Mountain in his mirror. "That's where we had the area of disagreement yesterday. They didn't believe me about the gold in Angola or the museum figurines in Cyprus. Isn't always the same. Here, let me give you my card."

I feel, despite the madness of this *Mission: Impossible* caricature, that he is part of a grand scheme to protect me. Thanks to Valparaiso I am no more than ten minutes late to work. The chef shakes his head at me as I clock in. I note that my uniform is badly wrinkled. I think about becoming a mercenary for paradise. First thing, though, I should probably buy an iron.

43.

FROM ALVINA'S PLACE, IT'S A MILE-AND-A-HALF WALK
past Arthur's and the Santa Breeze to the junction where I catch
the school bus, an open coach with a scalloped, red-and-white
striped canvas roof, the kind of rig you would expect to see at
a zoo or a Homes-of-the-Hollywood-Stars tour. The black driver,
hunched over his wheel, nods gloomily as I board. The children,
all black, their moist faces etched in the pale silver of predawn, are
dressed in sharp parochial uniforms. No one is thrilled to see
me. The only available seats are in the Selma, Alabama, section
in the back, which suits me fine. We roar up into the opulent
forest, stopping now and again to pick up a child. Dozens of people
must live in the interior, though I don't know who they are or what
they do.

The bus lurches left and right, hums on the hills. The wheel,
like a helm in the driver's lap, slips easily through his hands as
he leans into turns he knows by heart. The sun begins to strain
through in dusty, slanted pillars all around. We pass our old
disabled Toyota, a red-throated lizard shamelessly doing pushups on the hood.

A storm of pink butterflies appears in the crooked spindles
of sun and we hit them broadside and it's like blasting through
autumn leaves on Mars. A mile or so down the other side, my
heart begins to race as I peek into the dank shadows of Necropolis and spy Legion crawling with some effort, on account of his
short legs, out of the largest central mausoleum. Naked as a troll,

his hair stands straight up like the bride of Frankenstein. What amazes me most is that he sees me and *waves*, and even more incredibly, I *wave back*. I sense the suspended gasps of my fellow passengers and I know the children must think that if I am not wicked I'd better be crazy. I wonder if the driver will ever pick me up again.

The bus thunders down the hill past the Esso station and drops me off at the johnnycake stand. Everywhere in the world there is someone with a cauldron of hot fat willing to fry you some scrap of flour for a buck. I hurry up the Round Island Road to the hotel and clock in ten minutes early.

All day as I turn my flapjacks and then later break flats of eggs into eight-quart *Bain Marie* pans, layer bacon on sheet pans, slice Pullman loaves for French toast, and peel last night's baked potatoes for home fries in the morning, I wonder about Legion crawling out of that mausoleum. There is nothing useful you can say about a man who sleeps among the dead, yet he must be credited for courage and originality. I avoid admiring him and concentrate instead on his early threats to murder and dismember me.

Gradually, my thoughts turn to Kate and her body, and what a well-made body, especially those cordlike prehensile sinews that extend from her inner thighs, and her steep, sharp breasts that just seem to shout, "Family reunion!" I push her out of my mind and begin to worry about more pragmatic subjects, such as life without a car. How will we get to town for food and booze? We don't have the cash for another auto, much less the steep fee to have it ferried over. Maybe this is a sign—maybe it is time that I finally address the whole reason I came to Poisson Rouge in the first place.

When I get off at 2:30, I take a seat at the top of the concrete steps below the church. A dozen hopefuls sit with me. Fanny whizzes by on her motorcycle, head down, oblivious to her surroundings. I resist the urge to stand and shout at her. In the next hour a few cars pull up and people climb inside. Soon there are eight hopefuls, then six, then four, and then I am alone. No one offers me a ride. I hate being white.

The sun is heading down. I glance down at my lucky onyx Jesus and light cigarette number six. It is now 5:00 p.m. Four more hopefuls join me on the stairs. Finally, an old man in a faded blue Chevy pickup scrapes up along the curb. The four recent arrivals smile in recognition and clamber on down. In an obsequious lunge I follow them, straggling up to the driver's window. "You going to the east side?" I ask.

"Yeah," he drawls, "but we ain't takin' *you*."

Poor me. I schlep back up the stairs. I hate my fingers and shoes and the glasses on the bridge of my white nose. I loathe my niceness, my inaction, my bogus "Christianity in Principle," my souvenir voodoo necklace, and my *National Geographic* daydreams. For a while I sit with head in hands, hoping someone will feel as sorry for me as I do. This is usually a long wait. I let the sun sink another foot. I think of getting drunk. If I had any money I'd spend it on a room at Gladys Hooks'.

Suddenly sports clichés begin to ticker across my brain: *They could've thrown in the towel, but they've battled back.* I rise from the steps with a rush of indignant pride. Who needs that old coot in his piece-of-shit truck? Remember why we came here, men. We've already wasted half a lifetime blubbering over technology. If I'd walked home from the hotel the minute I clocked out, I'd be home now safe with gin and a fading ballgame on the radio, slapping my arms and waiting for Kate to come out of the bedroom half-dressed.

I stride up the Cross Island Road and into the gaping maw of the jungle, the dense anarchy of the winged things, and the carnival scent of lemongrass, Christmas rose, mawby bark, black horehound, allspice, and jasmine. A deformed licorice tree drips its papery blossoms. The parrots and jacamars upbraid me for being out so late. A tarantula bumbles shyly off the shoulder to take refuge in the boll of a fallen mahogany. The pale vanilla orchids seem to float by themselves in midair. Far below, the dark heartache sea mutters in against the cliffs. I move briskly, swinging my arms, my steps as light as Danny Kaye. I cover the first mile in ten minutes. I say to myself in the gravity of my innocence, *This isn't so bad*.

But there is no dusk in the Caribbean Sea. Along the equator the sun rises and sets with little variation—six to six—and there is nothing to hold the light in the sky. The witch moths, which appear only at night, make their first alarming display. I pick up the pace, reproving myself for wasting precious light.

Daylight crumbles rapidly all around. At some points the jungle is arched, as in a great Gothic hall: at other turns it is rather more like entering the mouth of an underwater cave. The widening shadows shift and run. A bright, laughing, blue-and-yellow macaw flaps off like an apparition into the gloom. A few wild swine crash and snort along the ravine below. Up ahead I see a man and his dog, walking stiffly toward me, no, away from me. I blink twice. They are gone.

Now comes the well-timed drone of an approaching automobile. I step to the side of the road and turn to let the driver know I am not begging for a ride, but it would be nice anyway since in about six minutes I will not be able to see my hand in front of my face. A green Jeep materializes and flies by. The inhabitants, Frank of cricket fame, a breakfast cook at the hotel, and his newly arrived exflower girl from the hotel—now devoted sex slave—wave as they pass. I watch them turn out of sight, dusk splintering in their wake, night roaring in through the cracks.

I stand stunned for a moment, the index finger of my left hand fanatically exploring the disfigured tissue on the ham of my thumb. Didn't they understand? Is their erotic union more important than my *life*? I curse them in a curdled whisper as the last glow clinging to the branches withers away.

I have been warned by many not to be out on the roads after dark, but the all-encompassing night is beyond comprehension. Sky, tree, and road instantly become one indistinguishable mass. Fixed in my tracks, immersed in the absolute void, I think of turning back. But it is just as incalculably and impenetrably black behind me. I turn twice, careful to keep my bearings. I lift my foot as if from a bottomless pit.

I must keep moving. I must get home. If I'm stuck in the middle of this babbling abyss for long, I'll lose my mind. The din of the jungle increases, as if to mock my impotence. Gnats whine in my ears and I stumble along with hands out like a zombie or Helen Keller getting out of the shower. I must be careful to follow the road, because some places simply drop straight off the mountain, no fences, no nothing, just your scream thinning away to a cold echo, the scrabble of bones being picked over by frigate birds. Then there is the deadly machineel tree, with sap like Drano and leaves that will burn out my eyeballs. I picture my face dripping down onto my shoes. To prevent myself from having a nervous breakdown I clutch my elbows, close my eyes, clasp my little Jesus against my chest, and promise myself that any second God will make the canopy open. Moonlight will pour munificently down. Stars will break effulgently. The miraculous gift of vision will be restored.

And not far away is the old Toyota. When I find it I will crawl inside, roll up whatever windows are left, lock the doors, and take refuge until dawn. There will be something in the glove compartment—flashlight, flare. I will turn on the headlights! Perhaps it will start and I will drive away! God bless machinery! God bless electricity!

Inch by inch I feel my way along the road like a snail, my toes grabbing like fingers at the asphalt. I am tempted to crawl. I try to laugh at my helplessness but it only feels like crying. Voices like children singing plague-rhymes start up from the left. Then the unmistakable pounding of drums. The slippery sweat of terror begins to drip down my ribs and arms. A headless figure in a splattered, phosphorescent dress tiptoes backward across the road in front of me, oddly reminding me of Judy, the lollipop girl with the toads in her hair.

Remembering an Arab proverb about singing when danger

approaches, I belt out a few shaky bars of "The Stars and Stripes Forever." Astoundingly, the jungle falls quiet.

"Hello?" I venture.

Heckling and vague whispering. The rolling of the slave drums resumes. *Go back home, boy, before you die.*

I wipe my sticky face with the sleeve of my cook's jacket. Legion is behind me now, I'm certain of it. I can feel his breathing inside the rhythm of my own. He is the author of this madness. These are his rum and coin incantations, his dead Dutch buddies, the slaughtered and lynched, the scapegoats of race. He tips his head at me and smiles at my inadaptable ignorance. His knife is raised. This is my punishment, for being weak, for being white.

Fire, I think, in a sudden revelation, gulping the shrill black air and fumbling in my pocket for matches. Thank God I'm a smoker! The booklet is damp. Desperately I scratch the paper matches against the damp flint. The disintegrating bits of sulfur scatter in feeble, incandescent crumbs. Finally a match head catches, spurting in the dark. I hold up the flame, illuminating the gruesome blue forest. The road curls up into murky, woven obscurity, at the top of which stands a wasted man in a stained fedora and riding boots twirling a bullwhip above his head.

I drop the match, heart banging in my ears. Jesus and angels help me! Something stings me on the neck. A grinding sound starts in the distance. A plane? Ghouls grinding human bones? Werewolves filing their teeth before the moon rises? No, a car! Salvation. I turn to listen, hand clamped on the back of my neck. It seems to approach from miles away. By the reedy clutter of the engine I decide it must be of ancient make. I hope it is not that goddamn blue truck. I stand immobile, tongue dry as chalk, the sting on my neck beginning to swell, the gnats whining in my ears. Heedlessly I burn one match after the next, scorching back the darkness. My armpits stink like a frightened zookeeper.

Weeks seem to pass before a Model T finally swings around the corner, lighting everything chaotically: the ghastly blue ugliness and lurid, concupiscent jewelry of the forest. I stand dumbly, thinking that naturally the Model T will slow and that my adversary and his entourage, enlightened, will flee. The headlights slice around and fall like two suns in my eyes. I step dazed out into the road. There is a dent in the passenger door. The jalopy slows, lurches, and swerves out toward me. Jumping aside to keep from getting hit, I catch a glimpse of two rotten faces grinning behind the glass.

"You BASTARDS!" I shout after them, shaking my fist. Then flowing up into the red glow of fleeting taillights comes the calmly trudging and maniacal image of Chollie Legion, feathered and painted as the devil, the machete glittering behind him. He gashes his teeth at me, teet like fire. Chollie doesn't *live* in a graveyard, I realize. He *rises* from one.

Madly I turn and flee straight off into the brush, fronds and saw grass whipping my face, two corrosive splotches of blue cooked onto my retinas. Crouched, breath suspended, heart cottonhammering in my ears, I clutch my little talisman and pray. Red-eyed varmints with wings like wooden propellers begin to clack around my head. A centipede crawls up my pant leg. The skin on the inside of my mouth has shrunk to plaster. Something hums past my ear and smashes inches away into the brush. Whimpering and cringing, I scuttle on hands and knees, collide into a tree trunk and black out. I dream six-legged on white cardboard that I am stuck through the belly with a pin. When I wake I am sitting alone at the edge of a cliff, glasses upside down on my face, blood trickling from my ear. The moon is out, lighting the ghastly sea below. I feel at my throat. My black onyx Christ is gone.

44.

I WILL NEITHER REPEAT THE SCENE WITH THE OLD MAN who refused me a ride nor will I enter that witches' Sabbath of Chollie's design on the road after dark, so each morning I catch the school bus in and each afternoon after work I set out immediately from the hotel and with arrogant discipline walk the twelve miles cross-isle home. If I don't dawdle I can beat the sun by an hour. I've taken to bringing my ten-inch French knife, freshly honed on the hotel's three-way stone and jammed between the long sleeves of my cook's jacket, which I tie in a sash around my waist. My hair is long, my beard full, my eyes packed with crazy glitter.

Today, striding down the hill from the Plantation, just waiting for someone to say something to me, I run into Kate, who wears a black dress with spaghetti straps and espadrilles.

"Thought I might find you here," she says, tipping her head with a coy smile. Her center-parted hair is damp and curls flapper-fashion under her chin.

"Don't you look like a birthday cake?" I say, forgetting my manners.

"And don't you look *savage*?" she replies, with a wink and a gleam of thigh.

"Tired of being intimidated," I mutter, grabbing at my knife handle and swinging my head about. "Tired of being the lily-ass white boy."

She takes an appraising step back, hands on hips. "If you were wearing leaves and feathers you'd look exactly like Chollie."

"What are you saying?"

"It's true," she says, touching her lips. "Look at you, shirtless, long-haired, wild-eyed, knife on your side, an environmental renegade walking miles and miles through the jungle *mumbling* to yourself."

"I suppose sometimes it's necessary to mumble," I sniff, unable to keep my eyes from her legs. "Every culture has a healthy respect for insanity. Remember how Mountain handled him the first night? He said he 'out-crazied' him. Well, I'll out-crazy him too."

"One night alone in the woods has really made an impression on you," she says, widening her eyes at me. "If you want, we can go back up to Jim's and get you another Jesus."

"I don't need anymore gimcrackery."

"Can I buy you a drink then, wild man?"

"You know damn well if Mountain sees us together there'll be a double murder."

"Mountain sailed to Pain Fermente with Saul this morning," she says in her sultriest of coos, toeing the ground. "They've found the Englishman's booty at last and we're all going to be millionaires. He won't be back for at least a day."

"A day?" I say.

"Cat's away," she says, lowering her chin onto a raised shoulder.

I realize this is a move toward darkness in every sense of the word, but I haven't had a drop of fun in weeks, and someone should keep an eye on this delectably leggy child while her boyfriend is away and all those goblins are running around loose.

So Kate and I have a drink at Harry's, followed slowly by two more, as time oozes down in a libidinous honey, and my shoulders relax and then it's too late to travel, so we decide to stay over with her two Standard Oil friends, the Sissons, from Canada, whom we lodged with platonically the night I visited Cinnamon Jim. Tonight, however, Plato, vexed with desire, has hitchhiked to the cathouses of Pompeii. Kate keeps crossing her legs and smiling and she's altogether a steaming pink tart, and after a decent chardonnay ferried all the way from San Juan, Puerto Rico (I can barely taste it), we find an excuse to retire early. The Sissons chuckle, as if at the folly of love.

The second time with Kate is better than the first. A bed gives us a stationary platform for fervid acrobatics (as one spring insists: *er-kee, er-kee*). Kate understands the fine points of physical resistance and bangs me on the rump with her heel. At one point my back is so arched I fear a cramp. I want to say: "I love you, I love you, I love you," the same way a thirsty dog would lap water from a steel bowl. The sweat drips from my arched neck between her cool and hardened breasts. There is some quality about Kate—perhaps it is only her insouciance and the chiseled lines of her body—that gives me a monolithic and cross-eyed stamina. I lunge into her like a beggar at a mission door. The full moon wiffles through the slats in the blinds. I harvest her blossom, the pollen sticking to my legs, and then I am at once atwitter and aglow, moaning and blinking (action photo!) like a man stumbling from a cave into light. "Oh God," I groan, falling aside, arm over my head.

"He *wants* you to screw me," she consoles in a tuneful croon in my ear. "And so do I."

The next day I'm like another person on another island. I don't feel angry, left out, troubled, or dissatisfied. I'm content as the village idiot. Indeed, as I review my situation I must be the village idiot. Traveling around with Kate is like being with an influential politician. Everywhere we go she snaps her fingers and a door opens, a check is signed, a car appears, always a salivating male with acute macula lutea and a hormonal simper on his face. Granted there is a difference between a drab male hitchhiker and a woman standing on the side of the road in a black miniskirt and espadrilles, but there are whole DAYS when a man can't get a ride on this accursed rock. She seems to know every soul on the island. And I wonder with a sensation like an ulcer forming in my duodenum how many of them she has slept with.

After fried okra, corn fritters, bull-foot soup, and a couple of Bloody Marys at Harry's, Kate and I head out and of course instantly catch a ride east with Jeff, a civil engineer with the National Geographical Society who drives a World War II jeep, painted red. He's here on temporary assignment only. I was under the impression that in his official capacity he was not allowed to pick up riders—he's passed me a dozen times on the road—but here he is now pulled over and smiling gallantly at Kate's legs as we climb into the back. "How ARE you, Kate?" he asks.

"Good, Jeff," she says. "Do you know Edgar Donahoe?"

His expression says that he's also seen weasels overturning trash cans, but he nods and offers a dry, "How's it going?"

"We're headed to the east side," says Kate.

"I'm only going halfway," he says, nearly spraining his eye muscles accounting for her legs.

"No one goes halfway with me, Jeff," she chides with her mocking eyes and throaty laugh.

His lips seem numb as he smiles. "All the way then," he concedes. "Alvina's place?"

"That's the one, Jeff," she says.

He pushes into gear and starts away, one eye fixed on the rearview mirror.

Kate and I sit in the open back of the jeep clutching the roll bar as Jeff winds up into the jungle. The wind tosses Kate's hair and she uses her elbows to keep her skirt from flying up, not that there would be objections from any aboard.

"You're beautiful this morning!" I shout, making Jeff scowl.

"And you're *fun*, Edgar," she calls to me through cupped hands over the roar of the wind. "Isn't it wonderful being *free!*"

Jeff leans sharply into a turn and I have to grab the edge to keep from toppling out onto the road. I see him grimacing into the mirror. Foiled again.

We pass our old Toyota, which after only nineteen days is already tipped midair in the arms of flailing, steel-eating creepers. The love bush, which grows in orange parasitic nests like spilled Franco-American spaghetti, has infested the interior and burst out the remaining windows and poured down the doors like some horrible science-fiction accident. A tambourine vine braiding up the antenna mast terminates in a large yellow blossom that quivers like a plateful of Tweety Bird feathers. Cracked block, some would say. Seized pistons, others would offer. It is not a car anymore, but a powder blue Toyota terrarium.

When we arrive back at Alvina's place it's almost four in the afternoon. There's no sign of Mountain, though I have the strangest feeling he's been here, that he's skulking nearby.

"You want a drink?" Kate asks.

"Yeah," I say, rubbing my forehead and looking carefully about. "My Marys have worn off."

"Here's a Scottish Mary," she says, pouring out Scotch in coffee mugs.

"Mary, Queen of Scotch," I say, up for a toast.

"Do you think I'm a queen?" she says, giving a turn. She knows just how to flick that dress up. I repress a groan with a gulp of whisky, almost hot from the temperature of the room.

"No, I think you're a witch. The wicked witch of the West Indies."

"Wasn't she the good one?"

"Very good," I say.

"Edgar, I want to take you up to my special place in the sugar mill. Have you been to the sugar mill?"

"Not yet."

"They have two-hour blow jobs up there."

"Do I need a coupon?"

She throws her wrists over my shoulders and pecks at my bottom lip. "I'll go get a blanket. Should I change?"

"Kate?"

"What?" She's breathing up into my face, flapping her lashes at me. It's much more powerful voodoo than that Montreal mumbo jumbo they have up on the hill in the village.

"What are we going to tell Mountain when he finds out?"

"Finds out *what*?" she groans.

I glance to the door. The sunlight is melting down the front stoop and the bees have begun to slow. "That, you know, we're playing Columbus discovers America."

"Come on, it was his *idea*. I didn't tell him to be the King of Spain, did you? Besides, he thinks the world of you."

"Not anymore, he doesn't."

"If he asks, we'll tell him the truth, that we went to the sugar mill to get some sugar. Now stop being such a prude." She slaps me across the backside. "We'll be back before dark."

45.

KATE AND I STROLL SOUTH UP THE ROAD. I EXPECT TO see Mountain coming the other way any minute, wild and bearded with sore feet and a machete or a pistol in his hand, so I'm grateful when Kate takes my arm suddenly and pulls me off into the bush.

"Where are we going?" I ask, ducking among the fronds.

"This is the shortcut," she says.

"Are you sure?" I say, glancing left and right into foreboding blotches of the type of inchoate darkness that seems to breed evil spirits.

"It's one of the old slave trails. It's a lot quicker this way. Don't be afraid. It'll clear out in a minute. Legion clears all these old paths." She swats at a golden jonquil and scatters its tube-shaped blossoms. "He's like a nutty little park ranger."

The trail does open up after a few dozen yards, though head-room is a bit low for my taste. I crouch and follow the wonderful, wagging black miniskirt and wonder how form is created, how it is maintained, and why it must continually decay. Consider the remarkable creatures of the forest—the orange-footed parakeet, the stripe-headed Great Kiskadee, the pearl-eyed blue caiman— but no animal or colored feather rivals the splendor of Kate, her slim neck, her dimpled shoulders, her gracefully furrowed back. As we move toward the interior the hooting and screeching of birds and their prey become more insistent, and the passage before us dims.

"Imagine being torn from your home," says Kate, tugging on my hand and brushing away the fragrant yellow jonquil petals from her shoulder. "Watching your family separated, murdered, and sold. Imagine being crammed into a diseased ship's hold for weeks. Imagine being lucky enough to land here." She looks about as if she might be seeing the island of Poisson Rouge for the first time. "In the beginning it might not have not felt that much different from home."

"Except for the great fields of cane, barrels of rum, wood houses, boats, cheese, muskets, pianos, Bibles, and the strange, pale people who brought them here."

"After they killed them all," she says, looking up, "it must have been a kind of weird heaven."

"Yes," I say, clinging to her fingers and inhaling the scent of her flesh mingled in with the jonquil blossoms and the wild mustard and Chinese sacred lily of the forest. "Like those fantasies you had as a kid, being the last one left on earth with a whole truckload of Heineken."

Off to the right the trail drops away to a gully of exposed tree roots that form a pattern like the orange-dyed cross section of a human brain. "But then those ships appeared on the horizon again," she says wistfully, slowing now, releasing my hand, then stopping to turn.

"I know," I reply. "And that's the story of how rock and roll was born."

She slaps me across the shoulder.

Off to the left I spy a rare, blue-crested Mot Mot in a cage of hogplum limbs peering out at us shyly, its long tennis-racket tail twitching left or right with each little charming hoot it makes. "Home is a funny thing, isn't it?" I say. "We spend all our efforts trying to leave it, and then we can never get back."

She hushes me sharply, her finger rising as the green shadows flow over us, and scarlet tanagers, greenlets, and black-bellied wrens squawk and zing in excited trajectories overhead.

"What is it?" I ask, crouching.

"Someone's here," she whispers, her head swiveling.

"He's following us," I say.

We both crouch, wide-eyed as Adam and Eve on the Day of Knowledge.

A wild pig dashes across the path in front of us, and then just as quickly with a roll of white eye crashes back into the brush.

I stand and wipe the sweat from my brow. "I've never been so relieved to see a pig."

She slugs me again. I reach for her cool hand, but she's off. I give chase.

About half a mile in we come over a rise, where Kate stops and points breathlessly down into a glen to a ghostly complex of stone ruins and decaying buttresses wrapped with black medusa climbers and masses of wild, parasitical pink orchids. An old, rotting windmill stands by, hopelessly engulfed in strangler figs. There are tulip and tannia trees, umbrella, ebony, fiddlewood, tan tan, and painkiller trees. A flywheel, once powered by steam, is now bearded with moss. Three or four huge iron cauldrons digest in the arms of the jumbi-bread vines. Turquoise dragon-flies hover in the currents like jeweled biplanes.

"Here it is," says Kate. "Beautiful, isn't it? Eerie, like another world."

"Yes," I agree, sneaking glances at her body. "The world of failed industrialism, failed agriculture, and failed revolution. Did you ever bring Mountain here?"

"Oh sure," she says, rustling and shimmering the pleats on her skirt, her chest rising and falling. "But he wants to run around in the caves all day looking for treasure." She points up toward the top caves. "Once he found a gold coin with all the dates worn off. Oh, and an old rum bottle. Treasure." She waves her hand around as if to expunge it all. "I'm tired of waiting to live."

"Well said."

"Did you know that the people who built this place used molasses instead of cement for the mortar?"

"When they make molasses," I say, glancing up at the

tattered blue holes in the canopy, "I wonder what they do with the rest of the mole."

"Poor moles. What's holy moly anyway?"

"Moly is that magic herb they gave Odysseus to break the spell put on him by Herpes, the god of cunnilingus and conveyor of the dead to Sears. It's just more voodoo."

"Greek voodoo," she says.

We make our way down the trail. I say, "The travel agent told me they still make rum here, but he'd obviously been drinking from his desk drawer."

"You see the caves up on the ridge?" she says. "We'll have to climb. I'll show you my favorite one. I call it 'Love Cave.' It has a view of the sea."

A flock of bats explodes from a portal and we both crouch as they come cackling and squeaking through the thickets at us to clatter palpably over our heads. I estimate their number at somewhere near a hundred thousand. "I hate bats," I say, straightening with caution.

"They eat mosquitoes."

"Did I mention that I admire bats?"

Kate begins to ascend the rock face. We follow a long diagonal gash, which seems to have been formed by water runoff. At the top of the escarpment is a honeycomb of caves, more caves than I can count, gaping and moping at us like the eyes and mouths of dim-witted ogres. Many of the caves appear to be homes to bats or birds. I stay behind Kate, studying her rump carefully as she guides herself along the cliff. I'm impressed by her leg muscles and her scaling ability in flimsy sandals. "So Mountain found a doubloon here?" I say.

"Yeah, he thinks there's a whole bag or chest here. But who would hide doubloons with all the faces and dates worn off?"

"Still, if they're gold, they're worth something."

"That's what he says. This one's mine," she says, offering me a hand. "Come into my Love Cave."

Even if I'm not the first, stepping up into the shallow, high-walled, and well-lit Love Cave with its partial view of the cove beyond, I still feel like a pioneer. Though these caves were formed by rapidly cooled magma, the rocky, sun-speckled floor is carpeted with sand. Kate throws down the blanket at the entrance and takes a seat. "Please pass the Scotch," she says. "Isn't it perfectly crude up here?"

I light a smoke and fall in next to her, natural as can be. "Do I get to write my name on the wall?"

Kate's knee touches mine. She sips from the Scotch as if it were a life-giving force. "Funny how you meet people, isn't it?" she says, handing me the bottle.

"Life is a four-letter word for surprise," I agree.

Kate hugs her knees and she lays her head on top of them. "I'm happy here, Edgar," she says.

"I'm glad," I say, taking a blast. "It's very difficult to be happy."

"In the city, you don't even know you're unhappy, because you have everything, or you think you do, but it's just a box to live in, and a toaster, and sadness."

"And a traffic jam."

Her lips bunch. "And a job that doesn't mean anything."

"Why do you think I'm here?"

"I got so sick of going to the movies," she says, sinking her teeth gently into a kneecap. "Watching other people live. That's all my friends wanted to do was go to the movies, watch someone else live." She sighs and turns to me with a smile. "Sometimes I fantasize that my old friends are watching me on the screen now, you know?"

"My whole life I pretended I was on camera," I say. "I drove a television through my childhood. I've traveled all over the world and seen countless men die, but I can't do anything useful like build a house or weld or ride a horse."

"You can make biscuits," she says helpfully, gazing up at me through her brows and taking a slug from the bowels of Scotland.

"I mean *important* things."

"What do you want to do?" she asks, giving me the bottle. I take a belt. "I want to live primitively in the jungle."

"Oh Jesus."

"I'm serious. I know it sounds like I'm just running away from my problems but I want to get my head straight. In the city, with everyone trampled under the beast of 'progress,' it'll never happen."

"What about Chollie who wants to cut off your leg?"

"Chollie is exactly my point. He despises industrial values and Hilton Hotels as much as I do. Once I quit working at the Plantation and return to the wilderness I know he'll leave me alone. It's the answer to everything, don't you see?"

She cradles her knees and sighs. "Don't go hippie on me, Edgar."

"Well, it's what I want to do." I have another slug from the bottle and return it to her. "I'm not chasing a bunch of lemmings in tie-dyed T-shirts. I've got my own ideas, my own plan. I'm my own man."

Kate tips back the bottle, lets the liquid jolt up in a bubble, swallows, and squints at me tight-lipped. In a hoarse voice she says, "But I don't want you to leave."

I stare at her chocolate-chip mole, her discolored tooth, her sweet-melted-copper eyes. "Yes, but if I don't leave, Mountain will kill me. You remember the first rule of the jungle?"

"You're taking Mountain over *me*?" she says with a sulky, wet protrusion of her bottom lip.

"I wish I'd met you first," I say, hanging my head.

She stares at me, her face moving imperceptibly toward mine, her teeth glazed, her legs out straight now, the line of her clean panties visible. We kiss for a long time. The speckles of sun on the sandy floor lengthen and fade. I try not to think of Mountain, who is probably waiting at home for me in the kitchen with a baseball bat.

46.

KATE HUNGER'S GOTTEN UNDER MY SKIN, TATTOOED HER estrogen on my limbic system. She gives off that hormone that produces within me monumental, even suicidal stupidity. I understand now why Mountain is so tangled and enravished. I think of her compulsively, the muscles of her thighs, the cartilage on her ears, the bristle on her armpits, the liquor of her voice, her brown-nippled tits spilling into my eyes, the way she drinks me— like a summer harlot from a garden hose. In my mind I seek an honorable solution. Did Mountain ever steal my girl? Did he ever *once* mock my pathetic notions of self-reliance as I have his treasure and salvaging dreams? So what if he's obsessively jealous? I knew that coming in. I wonder who's been the friend all along and who's been the rat.

And now it's been a full week since I've seen him. Kate, unconcerned, says he's still off on the wild-gold chase with Saul Schwartz on Pain Fermente, but I get this feeling in my stomach that he's lurking, watching us, waiting for some final piece of evidence before he swoops down to justice. My fear is that he's transferred all his feelings about his mother entirely into Kate, which makes me the bastard responsible for debasing her.

What's more crazy is that Kate and I continue to sleep together, not in caves, secluded beaches, or cannibal picnic grounds, but in the very bed that Mountain calls his own. Even when I insist that I sleep alone in my own room, she slips back into my bed late and we have it out, like a collision of moose in heat, me listening all the while for the sound of footsteps on the gravel drive.

Tomorrow, Friday, is my day off. I've decided to move out and I won't ever talk to Kate again. It's absurd to pursue her. I am achieving nothing through this but a slide into turpitude. It's trapped me worse than poverty. I must break free. Because I'm broke I have only two options, craven, compromised retreat to a cheaper, more commercial island and a conventional life, or the raw and dangerous self-sovereignty of Scudder's abandoned cabin.

It must be 4:00 p.m. I'm almost halfway home on my daily walk from the Plantation. Behind me the brush begins to rustle and flap. I turn and stop for a moment. My hair falls in my eyes. I clear my French knife from the sleeves of my cook's jacket and thumb the edge. It's disconcerting to think that not only do I look and behave like my adversary, but I share his goals. Yet save for the mythical Scudder, he's the only one on the island who is remotely self-reliant, who denies the slothful neurosis of machine-dependency. And he grows his own pot.

So I don't understand why he isn't more sympathetic. He's misinterpreted my position. He assumes that I represent Mickey Mouse and Standard Oil. But look at me, Chollie, I'm broke and trapped and I've made all the wrong moves. I'm mystified as to why I have to be the scapegoat when there are so many more deserving candidates. Is it because I'm nice? Is it because if you pick on me you know there will be no consequences, as it was my entire childhood? Is it because I do not exploit fear and desire? Well, those days are over now. I'll die before I play the chump again. This is the jungle and there is one simple rule. If you don't believe it, give me a try. I don't care how good he is with that knife. I am angrier. I am *righteous*. He will swing that heavy blade at my head once and I will duck under him and flick out his spleen. Or if there is a hunt, I will outwit him. He will end up hanging over the sea by his heels from a banyan tree or lying skewered on a bed of bamboo spikes at the bottom of a pit.

He hasn't read "The Most Dangerous Game." Is all I've learned in Western Society *entirely* useless?

I cannot for another day tolerate the idea of him following me home again, so I fool him at the junction and go straight. In fifteen minutes I'm climbing the steep grade to Scudder's old cabin. The jungle seems to whisper a welcome. I should've had Mountain just leave me here the first day. Everything I need is here, fruit on the trees, fish in the seas, stars in the sky, freedom freedom, amen and why else did I come? OK, the house needs a little work. The cistern needs to be flushed. I realize that many people have failed here, but I don't need a car, badminton, scientology, newspapers, or poker on Friday nights.

I calculate an hour and a half of good light before sundown. A wild jackass crashing off down the hill startles me for a second. Then my heart soars with the sudden realization that I will succeed here. I can *do* it. I will garden and fish. I will live with primitive fire and books. Whatever I don't have I can work or trade for. I'll put in my two-week notice at work *tomorrow*. The last check will buy me supplies. I will tell no one. By the time Mountain finds out, Kate will be gone and he will have forgiven, forgotten. Intoxicated by a long-absent optimism, I leap off the porch so high that I nearly sprain my ankle.

I feel so good about my decision that I decide to take a swim. I live on a tropical island thirty feet from the warm, jade-colored sea and I haven't even touched saltwater in six weeks. I'm pale as a specter. I spend more hours working and commuting than I ever did in the city. Preposterous. My life is worry and Calvinism and puerile, misdirected desire. It is time to shed the craven old snares and live the life I came to find. I'll be a man finally, and I'll do it on my own terms.

Across the road and through a brake of buttonwood trees, the coarse white sand of Telescope Bay greets me with its glittering, silicate flecks of black and gold. Mangrove trees grow straight up out of the limpid blue water. The fronds of a date palm rustle. A whiff of clam and lilac and kelp mixes euphorically with the drug smell of my dream. Wrapped in a trance, I stroll down the flat white beach to the water's edge. The tiny combers hush in, whispering the mother comfort of peace.

Here, Telescope Bay, is where I will fish. Lobster and conch lie at the bottom for the plucking, no need for a license, no limit, no competition. I'll pull on my shorts and dive. Fat, veiny-legged tourists will eagerly pay top prices for slow-moving and even immobile creatures that are simply strewn by nature in abundance across the seafloor.

I am so giddy I want to shout. A robin-breasted sailboat skims by a few hundred yards out and I wave with abandon. A few cormorants wheel overhead. My reveries are snapped suddenly by the sight of a lone figure doing the backstroke into shore. Confused for a moment, I think at first it might be an otter or a seal. To the north I spy a green beach towel and a radio. I think of turning and sneaking out. The Van Schorr girl, naked as the rain forest, stands and strides in, the foamy green sea rolling from her hips.

"Fancy meeting you here," she says, seawater streaming from her hair.

"Judy," I say, looking for toads.

She walks backward to her towel.

"Why do you walk like that?" I ask.

"Old habit, I guess," she says with a shrug and a twitch of the hip. "What are you doing here? You change your mind?"

I scratch at my ribs. "No, just on my way home from work."

"Still at the Plantation?" she says in a monotone, snapping the sand out of her towel.

"Afraid so. But not for much longer."

She dries her broad forehead and flat nose, then dabs each shoulder. "You look like a pirate," she says, staring at me with her washed-out eyes and now cuddling the towel and twirling a corner into each ear. "Are you looking for booty?"

"What? No. I'm on my way home."

"What's at home?" she asks, whipping strings of water beads from her hair.

"A candle, a bottle, and a tin of stale bread."

"You sound so much like Hendrik Hooft. He never liked it here either, except behind the molasses vats. How old are you anyway?"

"Twenty-one. You?"

"A hundred and fifty-eight." She laughs.

"You carry your years well."

"One-a-day Vitamins," she says, beginning to arrange her towel, snapping it again, shimmying the flesh on her thighs, oblivious to me.

"So where do *you* live?" I ask.

She runs the towel back and forth over the small of her back. The sand clings to her thick brown ankles, on one of which resides a rusting chain. Around the circumference of her neck that ghastly scar is like a necklace of thorns. "Hither and thither," she says. "Scudder's place tonight, I think. I like to play solitaire on the bed."

"Really? And where did you say your parents were?"

"Murdered," she says, snapping the towel out two-handed again, then kneeling and laying the billow neatly into the sand. "Long ago." She flips her hair off her shoulders, seats herself on the towel, and draws up her knees.

"Your father was Erik?"

"Yes, how did you know?"

"I bumped into his stone the other day."

"I barely remember it," she says, her head floating in a vague nod. "Anyway, I still see them now and then."

"Well, I'd better get running," I say.

"What's the hurry?" she asks, turning her gaze on me, her eyes as white as ice.

My heart does a little Watusi off to the left. "Not much daylight."

She turns her foot and studies the chipped, red-painted toenails. "What are you doing out here anyway?" she asks.

"Just looking over the, uh, Scudder place. Thinking about moving up there."

"The last guy who lived there was a reggae dork," she says, swiveling at the waist. "Jeemy Cleef and Peetah Tosh till I had to bust his stereo." She pushes a button, a tape begins to play Wendy O. and the Plasmatics, *Live at C B G B 's*. "I hate native music," she says. "I have to listen to it every night. You like punk?"

"Punk's all right."

"I bet you like disco."

"Not so much."

"What do you like?"

I tap my foot in the sand. "Oh, I'm pretty easy to please."

"I bet you are. Do you smoke?"

"Cigarettes."

"Can I get one from you?"

I pat my trouser pockets. "Just out. Sorry."

Chest shoved out, she flings her hair about and squints up at me. The sun balances itself at the top of the island. I have about fifty-eight minutes, pushing it. Judy bounces her heels in the sand.

"Anyway." I raise my hand, my voice climbing with it. "Nice to have met you."

"I didn't meet you yet. You always run off. What's your name?"

"I'm Edgar."

"I know," she says, smiling easily. "I saw you and Kate together up in the caves last week."

"You did?" I say, fumbling for a cigarette. "Yes, we were looking for treasure."

Her brow dimples and she shows me all her nubby white teeth, the white eyes burning like phosphor. "No, you weren't."

I have to scratch a match about seven times across the flint before I can get it to light.

"I thought you were out of cigarettes."

"You're too old to smoke, 158. You'll get emphysema."

"Really I'm only twelve," she says, raising her right leg to survey the drooping, rusty chain. "And Kate's married to Mountain."

"They are *not* married."

"What are they?"

"They're just—living together."

"Well, what are you doing with her then? He's going to kill you."

"Mountain is not going to kill me. He's my friend, O K?"

"Trust me, he's going to kill you," she replies with a furrow of the brow that would be cuter without the prophecy. "That's all anyone ever does on this island. Chop chop chop, every night. I can't wait till you move into Scudder's place. Do you like molasses?"

"I've got to go. The sun is going down."

She stands and flips her hair back and laughs, her broad mouth turning up at the corners. Her eyes spin with sparks.

"I'll walk you to the road if you like," I say.

"I'll be fine," she says, touching the wet scar on her neck as if it might still be sore.

"You aren't afraid of the jumbies?"

She laughs. "They don't bother *me*. Anyway," she says, kicking sand at me, "you'd better get home. Mountain is waiting."

47.

RETURNING HOME I'M AS NERVOUS AS DON KNOTTS, cran-
ing my neck all about, peeping into the cracks of forest, thinking
of that punk-loving, Dutch jumbie playing cards on that broken
mattress in the cabin of my dreams, of the book I read as a child,
Island of the Blonde Goblins. Edges of curved leaves scrape along
the asphalt in the breeze. Anyone who saw me talking with a naked
twelve-year-old must know now that I am sick, that I left the city
for a reason, that I cannot be trusted. The word is traveling this
moment like brushfire: he likes little *girls*. Oh, but if they only *knew*.
I whip out my knife and slash it through an overhanging branch.
Legion, my faithful stalker, is nowhere to be seen. Judy is one of
his entourage, I bet, unleashed when he can't find me. Or then
again, perhaps he's horrified by her too, still paralyzed, mesmerized, watching her through the ferns and listening with disbelief
to "Butcher Baby."

Is the sky darker today? Do the seasons really change here?
Can moral turpitude affect the jet stream? Are there a million
simultaneous worlds, each with its own independent moral com-
posite and hierarchal dispensation of justice? I cannot identify
the smell, but it takes me back to a rainy day in childhood (that
time that Doris and I played shipwreck and cannibal in the garage
when we were twelve), even if the sky is cloudless and bright
as the eyes of a TWA stewardess. The wind rattles the leaves in the
papaya trees as I crunch up the driveway. It appears that no one
is home. I wonder why Mountain is always gone. I would like to talk

to him again. I miss him as if he were two thousand miles away. I'm aggrieved by the power of sex and its ability to divide. When we were in college there was no force in the world that could rend us, never mind that he got most of his girls from the third floor.

When I open the door the room is dark. A match head flares. Mountain is sitting with his feet up on the kitchen table. He twists the flaming match between his fingers.

"What's up, Deadwood?" he says, reaching across the table to light a candle.

The wick deep in the wax makes a hollow splutter and hiss. "Not much, Johnny," I reply.

He shakes out the match and smiles, the candle flame cutting deep shadows of relief on his bearded Olympian face. His hair now falls in twirling columns past his shoulders. He's wearing the pink shorts again, and his favorite tattered Hawaiian shirt, unbuttoned as always. "Out a little late."

"Yes, Dad."

"Almost dark. Where were you?"

"I went out to the wax museum. It's half price on Thursday."

"Funny," he says, crossing his feet up on the table. I hate it when he's like this, calm as a hit man, enjoying the squirm of his victim, basking in my fidget the same way a TV judge would feed off the energy of a couple seeking a TV divorce.

"Actually I was out at Scudder's place," I say, picking up a section of the *Miami Herald* I may have read twenty times. Yes, this is the one about the heat wave in Greece, three dead. "What about you? Where've you been lately?"

"Here and there," he says, locking his fingers and stretching his elbows back behind his head. "What's out at Scudder's place?"

"Looking it over," I say, throwing the *Herald* and its Greek heat wave back down on the table. "I've decided to move out there."

"Why?"

"Three's a crowd, like I said."

His voice insinuates warmth. It's that looking-for-trouble tone that up to this point I've been lucky to have never been on the other end of. "I'm not in the way, am I?"

I laugh nervously. "Where's Kate?"

"She's not here."

Instantly I sense something amiss. I check the floor for bloodstains. The Gauguins are still there. "You're strange this evening, Mountain. Everything all right?"

"Fine," he says in a tone brimming with false cheer. "You want a brew? I picked up a sixer at Lula's."

"Sure."

"Let's go drink it outside. We need to talk."

"Yes, we do."

Out on the gravel terrace with its view of the cove through the guava trees, I wait for Mountain to speak. He doesn't. We're a foot apart in wooden chairs. We seem wooden ourselves. We should be holding cups of cigars out in front of a five-and-dime. The waves glide in over the shallows in tubes of glowing chromium green. Behind us Alvina's three top windows smolder with sallow light. This black castle of a volcano with its three lonesome east-side lights must be a ghostly sight to boats sailing past. When the clouds cover the moon it is so dark all I can see is Mountain's stern profile, the coal of his cigarette glowing against his thick lips.

"So," I venture, "how goes the boat?"

"Coming along," he says with a faint nod.

"And the Mariner's Trove?"

"Closer every day," he says.

"Good." I peck at my smoke. "What did you want to talk to me about?"

"I think you know," he says, coldly.

"The Dow Jones industrial?"

"No, Kate."

My heart flutters and my vocal cords all seem to constrict as I force sound over them. "What about her?"

"You're sleeping with her from now on. She's your girl. I'll move out soon as I find a place."

My beer all of a sudden tastes like rust. Two boats searching for safe harbor pass under a massive storm cloud that has just appeared to the east.

"Don't you think it's a good idea?" he asks, his gaze riveted out on the black velvet shine of the cove. "I mean, since you're fucking her anyway."

Stoically I nurse my beer.

"Why don't you say something?" he presses. "How dumb do you think I am? The whole fucking *island* knows. Even Father Edmond at the Catholic church."

Again I take the fifth, or I should say, not having a fifth, I gulp again from my rust-flavored beer.

"I don't care if you fuck her," he says, with a muscle-crammed and anguished grin. "Do you think I care?"

"If you don't care, then why won't you let it drop?"

"Because sluts are only good for one thing."

I throw my cigarette aside and set my can on the wooden armrest. Mountain watches me with a vicious smirk, as if he's finally found that bounder who bedded his mom. Still I don't believe he'll hit me. He has too much respect for me—I'm a smart guy with glasses who can recite Hobbes—and his code of virility prevents him from picking on someone clearly weaker. "I'll sleep in your bed tonight," he says.

"Homosexuality is no solution."

"Don't *joke* with me," he growls, yanking down at the air as if on an emergency stop cord in a train. "You sleep with her."

"Have I got a say in this?"

He startles me by standing abruptly and flinging his can into the brush. "I'm *giving* her to you."

"Who made you the island chieftain?"

Fists bulging, he rises over me like the shadow of a locomotive. "I ought to smash your face in," he snarls. "You fuck her behind my back and I'm the last one to find out about it."

"It isn't true—you're drunk, Mountain," I whine. "You don't know what you're saying."

"I know what I'm *saying*," he snaps. "You're a backstabbing bastard, and she's a fucking *whore*."

"Take it easy, man," I bleat, pressing myself back into my chair. "I'm out of here with my next check. I mean it this time. I'll never see her—"

I catch the mad flash of his teeth and eyes as the moon slips from under a cloud. Except for the veins standing out on his neck, his face is granite. His head turns. I think for a minute he will yank me throat-first out of my chair and break me like a doll, then I realize he is listening. The jungle has fallen silent. The temperature has plunged and the leaves are quivering on their limbs. In the distance comes a faint sizzling.

"Squall," he says.

"Let's go in," I say.

The moon flashes out. A blistering sheet of rain rips up the bay. I dive for cover under the eaves, the wind behind me flipping over my chair. Mountain sits calmly in the downpour, eyes closed, his hair flying back, a dead cigarette clamped between his lips. He seems to be smiling as the storm engulfs him.

In two minutes the squall is chattering west up through the forest and we're left with the fresh wreckage of the lee shore, tangled branches and salted rain. The insects slowly grind back up. The moon resumes its position in the sky. The asphalt below us glistens and begins to steam. Mountain, drenched and looking thin now with his rain-straightened hair, sparse beard, and exposed cheekbones, the hollowness accentuated in his eyes, rises slowly from his chair. "You sleep with her," he says, flicking his wet cigarette against the garage wall, turning on his heel, and crackling off through the gravel. "Or I'll break your neck."

I linger back, hands in pockets, gazing out at the scalloped, moon-flickered bay. The sky is remarkably black, scrubbed clean and freshened by violence. Hands trembling, I light a cigarette, blow smoke rings at the woozy blue stars, and think about walking into town. "What *she* wants," I mutter. "What about what *I* want? What about what *you* want, Mountain?"

Kate is waiting for me at the table wearing a pale lemon satin décolletage. She scratches a match and lifts it to her cigarette. The radio on the shelf is playing nostalgic rock from Puerto Rico, "Photograph" by Ringo Starr, which reminds me of a half-Indian girl I once knew in El Cajon and kick myself to this day for never sleeping with. Kate smiles at me.

"Where were you?" I ask.

"Over at Iba's. She's added a new teacup to her collection."

"Where's Mountain?"

"He's in your room," she says, bending a finger, eyes warm and misty above her cleavage.

I peek in and see him lying on my bed, pretending to sleep.

"Poor thing," she says. Her thin gown glows in the candlelight like the phosphorus in the waves along the cove.

"I have to sleep with you," I say. "Otherwise he's going to break my neck."

"Oh well," she says with a sigh. "I suppose it's the price we must pay."

48.

THE NEXT MORNING MY EYELIDS ARE SO HEAVY WITH
guilt I can barely lift them. I am a scoundrel, a rascal, a villain,
and a rake. Kate is gone. I roll out of bed, drag through the mosquito netting, and peek into my old bedroom. Mountain is
gone too. I hope for the best. If they've reunited then I'll just be a
cheap footnote, disgraced but forgiven. Yes, and maybe it will
snow three feet this afternoon. I shuffle groggily into the kitchen
and set a pan of water on the stove.

    Outside, a peculiar commotion of grunting and whacking
has begun. The bees seem suddenly disturbed. I peek out to
see Legion chopping coconuts on our stoop. His eyes shine with
blood, stoned again. His scaly feet look like the chunky clay
ashtrays I made in sixth-grade ceramics class. I can make out the
beetles that call the braided thatch of his hair home. The bees
swim agitatedly around his head. He pays them no mind. Neither
will I. I've tried and tried, but I can no longer pretend to understand him. My water is boiling. I pour a tea, take a chair at the table,
and listen to the wet thunk of Chollie's machete.

    A minute later Mountain drags Kate through the door.
Her lip is split, her eye swollen. She's out of breath. Adrenaline
floods my chest. I am suddenly inspired to protect her. She
retreats into the bedroom without looking at me.

    Mountain holds me in a spiteful glare, chest heaving. He's
shirtless, and wearing khaki cutoffs and shower sandals. His

shoulders are sunburned and the polio vaccination scar on his left shoulder is a puckered white ring.

I meet his stare, refusing to yield at the guilt sign. Nevertheless, I'm grateful for the sideshow of Chollie's eccentricity. "What's going on out there?" I demand.

"What?" says Mountain, showing me all his teeth, front gap like a door into hell.

"What's Legion doing out there?" I repeat.

"Chopping coconuts. What's it look like?"

"Yes, but why *here*?"

"He asked for you."

"For *me*? He said my *name*?"

"'The one who walks,' he said."

Legion raps his long knife on the door.

I'm astounded that Mountain, his expression gleeful with scorn, lets him in. Legion waddles up through the doorway to unload a dozen halved coconuts on the kitchen table. I get my first close look at his cutlass, a dense, two-foot, carbon-steel blade, brightly beveled and handsomely sharp, I know, by the way he was splitting those coconuts. The copper-riveted handle is grayish-yellow, teak maybe. It might be a ten-pound machete. Chollie smells of elephants and turnips and chamomile tea.

Mountain nods at the coconuts, and hauls up his shorts, which fit him two weeks ago. He's lost a few more pounds. "Drink, Leedge?"

"No," says Legion.

"You want fish?"

"No," says Legion.

"Arm-wrestle for a buck?"

Legion tips his head.

"Ah right," says Mountain, yanking on his chin hairs like an obese Mongolian emperor and letting his eyes roll side to side. "Well, take it easy then. Praise the Lord and thanks for the nuts."

Legion scratches his chest. Kate, topless, rips open the

bedroom door. "I'm leaving you, you bastard!" she screams. "And you can't *stop* me."

Mountain's blue eyes pop with an eager rage. "Get back in there," he says, pointing like God on an Italian fresco. "Don't you see we have a *guest*? Don't you have any goddamn *modesty*? What the hell is wrong with you?"

Legion, open-mouthed, whirls and bumps backward out the door. The sight of the naked woman has confounded him, it appears. I feel the first ray of empathy for him.

Kate slams the door. Mountain shouts: "Put some fucking clothes on!"

The door opens again. "You don't own me," she bellows at him. "I'm not your chattel. You're just a *boy*."

Mountain's chin trembles, his cheeks are crimson. "You're not leaving," he retorts, jabbing his sternum with his thumb. "I AM! You two can *have* the place."

"Don't be a fool," I mutter.

"What?" he says, turning on me with the wrinkled and enraged brow of a Neanderthal. "What did you call me?" I know this expression. I've seen it in a dozen working-class bars. It's not a question you answer unless you want your head tenderized.

"No, Mountain," I say in my most passive and defeated tone. "I'll go."

"Stay, Edgar," says Kate.

"You son of a bitch," says Mountain, lunging at me, his hairy face a detailed study in anguish and betrayal. Instinctively I swing the table full of coffee cups, liquor bottles, ashtrays, newspapers, and empty cans of OFF! into his knees. He howls. The coconuts fly in the air, and before they hit the floor, I'm out the door and headed down the gravel drive.

The screen door smacks shut behind me and I glance back to see Mountain lumbering deftly in grinning pursuit.

As a child I entertained myself nightly with ways of dying, imagining which animal would be the hardest to escape from. A black panther, for instance, can outrun or outclimb you, but once in the water you're safe. A timber wolf can outswim or outrun you, but it can't climb a tree. A bull might pierce your lung with its horn, but not if you can make the fence first. After much thought I decided a bear would be the worst thing to be chased by, since it can outrun, outswim, outjump, and outclimb you. And even if you have a gun you're only taking the risk of aggravating it further.

But Mountain, especially since I don't have a gun, is worse by a league than a bear. He can outrun, outswim, outclimb, and outjump me, he's smarter than I am, and he knows this island twenty times better than I do. And he's mad, and unlike an animal, knows no appeasement rituals or territorial boundaries. If it weren't too late to stop I would turn around and apologize.

I clatter down the drive, Mountain closing in on me like a *T. rex*, his shower sandals snapping against his heels. I have no choice other than to leap straight into Turner Cove. Base animal fear gives me the oomph to clear the shoals and I slap in chest-first and swim frantically until the water is deep. When I turn, treading water, Mountain is standing on the shore. My glasses, thank goodness, are still perched on my face.

Mountain shakes his fist. "I'll get you, Burt!" he shouts. "You can't stay in there all *night*."

"Damn it, Mountain," I call to him. "You *told* me to sleep with her."

"Not behind my back!" he screams, his biceps bulging, the muscles in his legs flexing. He's on the brink of jumping in after me. "I thought you were my *friend*."

Oh love and hate, those incestuous twins, how bawdily they swap their masks. I knew I should've moved into town the first time Kate showed me her tits and laughed at one of my jokes that wasn't funny. The day I cut my thumb, I should've taken my check, bought a bottle of absinthe, and moved back into the Blue Haven Inn.

"All right, buddy," I call to him. "It's been a long time since I've played any *boys'* games, but if that's the way you want it."

He kicks off his sandals and yanks up his shorts. I dive,

pocket my specs, and head for the sandy bottom, scooting along the scalloped shadows, lungs burning. I don't have the air to make the promontory, but when I gently pop up and look back, Mountain is nowhere to be seen. Diving again, I make the headland and then swim round to the next cove. Looking back: still no Mountain in sight. One more cove for good measure, I crawl up the shore, slide on my glasses, part the waxy evergreens, and slip into the jungle.

49.

MAYBE THE SUGAR MILL ISN'T THE SMARTEST PLACE TO run, but I don't know where else to go. I don't know these roads (there are hundreds of them and I am an ant in the maze), and I can't go back north to Scudder's place or Arthur's house, for example, because Mountain would likely anticipate me, and it's dusk already and beginning to drizzle. A raft of fog slides in and swallows up my ankles. My shoes are wet, squeaking with every step as I wade through the mist. The leaves drip and the rain clicks as I crouch down the vaguely familiar tunneled path. I hope this is the right one. I remember this cluster of bread-and-cheese trees, the sprinkle of golden jonquil, the smell of mustard and sacred Chinese lily. And I'm fairly certain that this was the hogplum tree that contained the rare glimpse of the blue-headed Mot Mot. And here is where the road veered and suddenly dropped off to a gulch of twisted roots like an exposed cranium.

All right, let's admit it: I never had the courage to fulfill my Arcadian fantasy, but now that I've been compelled—and in combination with beating Mountain in a physical contest for the first time in my life—I am *exhilarated*. I know I can't return to society, and good riddance, I say. I will teach all those naysayers a lesson. I will become like those kids in *Lord of the Flies*. No, bad example. I will become like Robinson Crusoe. No, all he wanted was to return to backgammon and sandwiches. I will become like Scudder, that's it, utterly self-reliant: reading by homemade candlelight, roasting a fish over a fire, mending my jacket with a needle made from bone, sitting in my cane chair quoting Whitman above the sullied realm and trying not to think about those promiscuous spring-break sylphs cavorting buck naked on the beach below.

Far away and invisible, the sea waves shuffle in. The sweet and decaying odor of mace and tree orchids filters down like a drug from the gods. From its perch a spectacled owl asks the question, what are you doing walking around down here in the drizzle at this time of night? I try to clean my glasses on my wet shirt but manage only to smear the lenses. I am relieved when the sugar mill, with its crumbling bastions and solitary silhouette of the rotting windmill, finally appears. A ragged cloud of squeaking bats veers toward me and I duck, grinning an awkward hello (eventually I'm going to have to befriend these furry mosquito-lovers) and hurrying down through the drippy ruins to scramble back up the weathered face of cliffs to the honeycomb of a hundred caves.

A deeper cave might be safer or warmer, but it also might be packed with vampires, and who knows what other predator or pirate may call it home, what sort of midden heap I might have to share, skeletons clutching rusty knives and muskets—so I climb aloft to a smaller aperture: it's little more than an arch. From the entrance I can almost touch the back wall. The sandy floor is dabbed with clamshells and fragmented footprints, but they seem old. Not an ideal shelter, far from it. In the daylight, however, I'll regroup and find better quarters. Tonight I don't ask for much more than the security of seclusion and the basic comfort of a roof.

The mouth of my cavern faces east so it's dark already. Staring down into the sugar-mill ruins I can see nothing but the crepuscular gleams of the liquid void. It's still drizzling, no help from the moon. I wish I had a cigarette. The evening shrill of the tropical birds seems to mock me. I wish I had a fire. Fear begins to nibble at my stomach. True freedom is a frightening prospect. Only a small percentage of American colonists voted to revolt against Britain for independence (and if they hadn't we'd still be speaking British). The rest swallowed subjugation and out-landish taxes like good little bourgeois dumplings. Think of the discontent most of us settle for just because we're afraid to lose. But I will fight and resolve to live unmolested. The best journeys always start out rough. When daylight comes, everything will be right once again.

Drawing my feet up, I begin to think longingly of Kate, her damp panties and common sense, and I hope she's all right. If I can keep Mountain occupied, it will allow her to escape, the thought of which only makes me feel more dejected and alone. Now it seems I've lost everything, love *and* friendship. Perhaps I will find solace in the hermit's life. Love of self eventually leads to love of God. I heard someone say that once. Well, what difference does it make now? I'm making my own rules, constructing my own pathetic, onanistic society. I reach down for the fine dream of me in my jungle cabin, with the Rousseaus on the wall and a lobster boiling in the pot, my two goats tethered out back, nibbling the zucchini. I will learn how to play the harmonica. I will finally read *War and Peace*.

All night I hear souls marching the trail below, crunching and whispering, familiar taunting voices, snickering, arguments, the pounding of drums, knives chopping, horrid, muffled cries. I strain my eyes but the black, blank night is solid as steel. I have no doubt, since my first real encounter with the sarcastic lunacy of dark spirits, that the jungle is possessed. At one point the goatlike scent of Legion floats up faintly to my nostrils. But the zany little bushman is the least of my worries. A madman and a sorcerer he undoubtedly is, but he brought me *coconuts*. He called me "the one who walks." I took enough psychology to know that people who intend to kill you do not bring coconuts or assign you respectful, Indian-sounding sobriquets.

Thirsty, I cup my hand out into the rain and sip from my palm. It feels as if it will be cold tonight, the first cold night. I have to shut out the prospect of the monsoon season, hurricanes and two months of unyielding rain. I curl up as tightly as I can.

In the morning I'll dry my clothes in the sand, drink from leaves, find a fruit tree. Eventually I'll build a lean-to, maybe a tree house, and learn how to spear fish and trap small game. I will make my own shoes out of sailcloth. Mountain will never find me. Reunited with nature, I will wake and join my dormant native spirit to contentment. No one will ever find me. No one will ever know.

I am not aware of nodding off, but Judy is suddenly with me. She holds her severed head under one arm, then fits it nicely back on like a diving helmet, blinks at me with her white eyes— a winged, purgatorial, netherland sibyl with lips like Twinkies— and says in flawless Dutch, which I somehow understand: "Let me save you so I can leave this murderous isle." I agree on the condition that she bring me some aged Vermont cheddar. Wings blur as she floats away with a smile. The dream is simple perfection, like a vision of the future in the reflections in a virgin's oiled fingernails. The dream feels like heaven after death. I wake up freezing to the sound of my name. The rain has stopped, with only occasional drips from the arch above, and the moon is burning through the tendrils of a cloud. The jungle is shrieking, chilling me with terror. I hear my name again, the syllables intoned like the mockery of menacing children: "Deeead-wood. Deeeead-wood," Mountain calls in a terrifying imitation of Elmer Fudd. "Wheah ah you, Deadwood?"

I stick my nose out of the cave and see Mountain in the darkness below holding a roaring, sizzling torch over his head. His hair is wet and coiled in serpentine masses upon his shoulders. He's got a muddled grin on his face, and his eyes under the primal ledge of his brow are two miniature versions of the torch. "Shhh," he says, finger pressed to his lips. "Be vewy, vewy quiet. We're hunting Donahoes, ha-ha-ha-ha-ha-ha … "

My breath grows stale from suspension. At last he moves away up the road, still calling my name (come out, come out, wherever you ah), absolutely at home in the sodden darkness of the haunted jungle.

50.

IN THE MORNING I AM COLD AND MY BACK ACHES FROM
sleeping against bare rock. I slide on my smeared, water-
stained glasses and peek down at the trail below. The parrots and
iridescent grackles zip back and forth between the trees in a
giddy caterwaul of trigonometric color. High up in the boughs the
mockingbirds twitter their infinite repertoire. My clothes are
as wet on my skin as the night before, when like an amphibian of
sin (longing for evolution of the soul) I crawled out of the
primordial sea. With a shiver, I climb back down the escarpment,
my ears pricked for danger, and head through the bush for the
sound of water.

It's a good quarter of a mile before I come upon a small
horseshoe-shaped beach with mahoe trees. The surf is a
mere ruffle. The water is thirty-three varieties of spellbinding
green. A long palm curves over my head and rustles like the
pom-pom of the cheerleader I never had. I strip off all my clothes
and spread them out in the sun, tipping my shoes for optimum
exposure. A gray harrier hawk circles above with a buzzing
cicada in its claws. After a quick dip (the water is warmer than
the air), I lie on the talcum-white sand in the sun. It feels so right
after seventy-five generations of scriveners and nearsighted
clerks to be back naked again with nature in the dangerous wild
with no guarantees and the thrilling obituary of complacency.

But I cannot remain supine very long with my pecker
pointed at the sky. Mountain understands my citification, my dim

instincts for the wilderness, and knows he can track me to one of three or four places. I'll have to push myself, pick up my game, and somehow beat him with my wits. It will be a while before I can relax again. Soon enough, though, he's going to forget Kate. He's not the sort to stay the course of romance or hold a grudge. He'll forgive me. And I'll make it up to him somehow. I'll recover for him a chest bursting with British guineas lying at the bottom of an uninhabited cove or the diamond necklace of a Hapsburg princess snagged in the skeletal jaws of a sunken killer whale. We'll make sure that his father receives the lion's share, and the Curse of the Lost and Fallen Mother will finally be broken.

When my clothes are sufficiently dry, or at least warm, I dress and return the way I came. As long as I follow these old slave routes, I won't get too lost (like the asphalt roads, I imagine they probably all meet up in the same place), but at the same time, I'll be vulnerable to discovery. Tourists do occasionally venture back here. Judy Van Schorr, the chubby jumbie child, likely knows these trails, as well as Mountain, and of course Legion. Before it gets dark I'll have to find someplace more original than the caves to lodge. I've seen a few crumbling lean-tos and rotting huts along the way, probably more remnants of the slave days, none of them habitable. My eyes are peeled for any advantage, some vaguely commodious relic with a roof that doesn't leak. Hundreds of modern young hermits, explorers, scavengers, and pioneers have ventured into these backwoods to make claims. There must be many serviceable structures available. Legion must know them all. Mountain, the treasure hunter, is probably acquainted with many of them as well.

In the early afternoon I squat against the base of a mango tree and take my fill of the orange fruit, whose fragrance is vaguely reminiscent of chloroform. Nevertheless, the flavor of food is indescribably pleasurable. Instantly I am connected to the divine meaning and gift of fruit. I drink from and wash my hands in a granite scoop of rainwater and gauge the sun. My eyes scan the hills. I'm getting used to this. It isn't so bad. I think of goldfish, dwarfed and genetically manipulated for thousands of years, but which return to their original form within two generations in the wild. Everything I need to know is already built inside me.

Venturing off the track for a moment to seek a safe place to rest, I find a flat rock amid a shady bower and sit. Instantly I begin to feel lonesome. I wish I had a smoke. I can't live for the rest of my life alone. I wish I could talk to Mountain. If he weren't after me, trying to kill me, we could have a couple of beers and laugh. I begin to think of raiding Legion's pot garden. And wouldn't a mausoleum drawer be the perfect jungle domicile, water and bugproof, if you weren't too picky about a roommate? I should not have stopped to rest. I think of Kate and absorb myself in the scent and image of her shape until I can almost hear her voice.

Edgar!

It is her voice! She's in the jungle, looking for me. She's calling my name. I stand up so quickly I crack my head on a branch. We'll live happily ever after in a tree like Tarzan and Jane!

Edgar!

No, it isn't Kate. I crouch and recede. Around the corner and through the leaves I see Judy, dressed in jeans and a New York Dolls T-shirt, her decapitation scar looking particularly raw today. "*Edgar!*" she calls, casting about her haunting white stare. "Where *are* you?"

I hunker back in my thicket. It's the first time I've ever seen her dressed. She seems out of place with clothes on. It's difficult to trust her this way. I think of the dream and my promise to let her save me, but my dreams have never been prophetic and what if this is a trick? What if Mountain has conscripted her to lure me out? They must know each other, if he spent two weeks living in Scudder's cabin. Perhaps Mountain is a zombie too! That's why he was so full of dismay the first time we discussed her. That would explain the dark and mysterious changes. Who can I trust now? Lord of Nations, I'm more alone in this B-movie tangle than I could ever have imagined. Judy drifts by with that cool, dead, lemony Band-Aid smell and moves away up the trail. "*Edgar?*"

I wait for her voice to fade. They're all looking for me, I bet. Pretty soon I'm going to have to swim to another island, perhaps that little cay I saw today that was so overgrown with trees no one would ever find me. Something above flashes at me, a *spyglass*, I think, in a fright. Squatted and peeking up through my water-spotted lenses from my unusual position slightly below the road, I study the strange gleam coming from the top of an overgrown hillock. It certainly must be glass. It seems I can also make out a vague rectangular form, something possibly built around the glass?

There is no trail to the gleam, and I regret having not gone back to Alvina's place to pick up a few items, especially my knife, while Mountain was madly traversing the island with his torch. With a knife I could halve coconuts, clear brush, clean fish, and defend myself against the insistent. It would be my first choice of tool, second a rifle, third a pack of smokes and a book of matches. But I don't have a knife or a rifle, etc., so I pull myself, vine by vine, feet slipping in the stony undergrowth, up the devious grade, until my square apparition has fleshed out to definitive form. It's a building of some kind, concealed by neglect, tilted and warped from weather and brush, but still intact. I grow excited. I see another window, and a patch of exposed planks. My feet find part of a set of stone stairs leading to the leaf-encased door.

Judy's faint voice lifts to my ears one last time. I shove at the door until it gives with complaint and I am inside a dank chamber ruined by plants, rats, and rain. The room is so thick with vegetation that at first I don't notice the skeleton enlaced and corkscrewed in vines sprawled in the chair before me.

"Begging your pardon," I say, my heart doing forward and backward somersaults, my hand still clenched to the handle behind me. "I should've knocked."

Quite all right, the rack of grizzled bones seems to reply, its clothes so shredded with decay they appear to be bandages. Haven't had a visitor in years.

The spongy floorboards, shot and split with creepers, creak under my weight.

"Who are you anyway?" I ask, taking a tentative step and picking up a book at my feet. Everything household appears to be on the floor, boxes, books, and shattered glass and bric-a-brac. The volume is some sort of navigational guide, nibbled and splotched with mold. I find a similar volume close by on astronomy. A Bible, in better shape, has an inscription on the frontispiece to the Morris L. Scudder family. A few pages have been torn from Leviticus.

"You're Scudder," I say.

The skeleton would make acknowledgement, I feel, if it were not so securely tethered by weeds. I bet he'd even play me a song from that ukulele in his lap if his strings weren't busted and if he didn't have that Bengal clockvine curling out of his nose.

"I've heard so much about you," I say, circumnavigating my host to tour the small room. Yellow tomatoes grow fat from the ceiling. Some of the vines have okra on them. The garden lost the war but still merrily sings its tune in Eden. This was probably a snug little shack, shelves packed with dry goods, salted fish and jerky hanging, tools all in their correct places, some kind of water-collection system, candles, lamps, fresh coffee, tobacco, whiskey, and tins of butterscotch candy. But the shelves have tipped and the foodstuffs have been plundered. The tobacco is dry as sand. Tattered garments hang from crumbling hooks. I find a box of useless matches. More of the dull books of the scientist. Some faded boxes of macaroni and cheese. A rusty can of Spaghetti-Os (but nothing to open it with). Hand-carved, unpainted wooden parrots, a hobby apparently. A lonely life ending anonymously tempers my aspirations. If you live a beautiful life and no one knows about it, did you ever really exist in the first place? (If a loner dies in the forest …) Maybe it would be better to have companionship and a compromised ideal, than a meaningless end in the Magnificent Alone.

The wind through a broken window hums in the neck of an overturned bottle. Whatever Scudder owned in the way of libation, except one heavy, half-potable bottle of cognac (praise the Lord), has spoiled or evaporated. And against the back wall is a straw-tick mattress that if beaten a few a times to scare out the mice and flipped over will serve a wayward guest for one night at least. Booze and a bed, what more can a homeless man ask for? If I can lie low here for a week or so, sneaking out only at the crack of dawn for fruit and a bath, everyone will finally assume I have left the island or died and they'll give up the search.

My ambition for a tight roof is shot. Even now, without rain, it drips. I'll just have to find a dry spot to sleep. I tell myself this will be no different than spending a night or two in a greenhouse. Through an okra-choked window I have a partial view of the trail below. It's getting dark already. I wonder what the relationship between Legion (who to keep these old slave routes clear must have passed this dwelling regularly) and Scudder was. Maybe Scudder died before Legion ever began his campaign. I wonder how old Legion is. He could be twenty, could be forty. Perched on the edge of the bed, I sip at the cognac. Scudder may have distilled this stuff himself from okra and yellow tomatoes, but despite its general inkiness, it does have a tropical punch and finally I have to lean back and smile. Oh, if they could only see me back home now.

Out of the wind and rain, it shouldn't be cold tonight. There are blankets in a basket at my feet. Not that I'm interested in rousing the scorpions that have built their nests inside, but it's nice to know they're there if I need them. And as far as mosquitoes go, I'll just have to resign myself to transfusion. Eventually they'll tire of Edgar medium rare. A few more gulps into the hooch, I stretch out on the mattress and listen to the creak of the foundation and the whirl and hoot of the wicked and wacky forest outside. I feel like I'm swinging in a great Peruvian hammock. With little to sustain me the past day except fear, flight, and damp cave-sleep, I find myself nodding off. No need to worry about invaders, I think groggily, not with that gruesome concierge at the door.

I fall into oceanic slumber. All the while I know I will wake in the dark without fire or water and it will be another long, difficult night, but I have made an improvement, and each night I will continue to make improvement, learning, accumulating tools, increasing perceptual, physical, and psychological health. I hear the voices below, the slash of stalks and leaves falling, the sun falling, and in my dreams I am looking from the point of view of the dead Scudder, his changeless world as he is crushed by the apathy of time—and then suddenly I start up from my bed and spy in the vaporous sphere of my semiconsciousness a hand protruding through the open front door.

I'm dreaming, of course. It cannot be. Yet the hand insists. Is there another Scudder? Have I entered into some tropical variation of "A Rose for Emily"? I grab my glasses from a ledge and shove them crookedly onto my face. The hand is now an arm.

"Hello?" I call over my hummingbird heart. "Who's there?"

"By thunder, *here* you are, Deadwood," says Mountain, throwing aside the door. He's got a machete in his right hand. "Bitch of a trail getting up here." He grins, brushing earth from his arm.

"How did you *find* me?" I ask, sitting up, incredulous.

"I tracked you," he says with the warmest of grins, staring up to admire the yellow tomatoes hanging from the ceiling. "I've seen this place. Never came up, though. Who's the skinny guy?" he asks, indicating my doorman-on-a-diet with the tip of his machete.

"Morris L. Scudder," I say.

"Scudder?" Mountain offers a low whistle.

"Found his name in a Bible," I say, touching my hair and feeling its electricity flowing like cold centipedes down my neck and legs.

"Well, he finally found his peace," says Mountain, dropping his chin for a moment, his greasy hair falling over his eyes. He's still wearing his cutoff khakis, but now he's back into the ripped boat shoes and that old red checkered shirt I saw him wearing the first day.

"I suppose we all do," I agree.

"Yes," he says, advancing with an expression of hearty

contentment, lunacy twinkling in his eyes. I so hate to see that look. "Some of us sooner than others," he adds.

"Don't kill me, Mountain," I squeak.

"Why not?" he asks, raising his brows. "You don't get to have *all* the fun."

"You're going to regret it," I say.

"No, I'm not," he says, sweeping aside a vine and then yanking down another as a piece of loosened ceiling falls upon us in a shower of moldy sticks. "I've got nothing. No girl. No gold. I don't even have a place to sleep."

"Neither do I!"

"No no no," he says, bringing the knife up like a hunter over a baby seal, his savage head wagging, his eyes giving off enough watts to light the room. "You're going to sleep *here* with your buddy, Scudder."

I grow faint. The room begins to turn. I'm going to die in paradise, by the hand of my own brother, just like Abel. My eyes sweep the ceiling, where abiding spirits reside, and I blurt suddenly from my blistered throat: "Sullie, Sullie. Remember margaritas at the Blue Bird? Remember that $120 exacta on Mountain Surfer and Betty's March? Remember listening to the Chi-Lites and smoking Kents at three a.m. in your dorm room? Remember God and Jesus and Father Calhoun?"

"Remember when you stole my fucking *girl*friend?" he counters. "Remember when you and Kate sat at the table for an hour while you thought I was asleep and made fun of my *boat*?" He chuckles so agreeably, the sound of a mountain spring or the miniature cataract of a pagan lunatic, but his pupils are still dilated with bloodlust. "And don't call me Sullie," he adds. "Only my ma called me that."

I never thought that my greatest weakness would spell my end. Doesn't the good book say the meek shall inherit? Aren't truly civilized people disinclined to bloodshed? I suppose the passive ones can survive and even flourish the entirety of their lives in city environments with teachers and police and the indoctrination and synthetic mayhem of TV to protect them. But in the jungle, now that I've been reduced to little more than an animal, the first rule has stepped to the fore and the inability to defend myself seems a crime. What a shame it is to die, twenty-one years old, gutless and misshapen, in the decrepit hut of a hermit at the hands of a boy who was too jealous ever to know love.

And when I'm gone what will *he* be? I wonder. Who will be his friend? Who will love him and forgive him, visit him in the penitentiary or the mental hospital and talk to him as if his dreams really matter? Oh, if he only understood this. If only he could see all that he was destroying.

The blade towers above me. Peace spreads across the film on his eyes, his tongue cocked out the side of his mouth. He's going to try and end me in one stroke, split me mercifully like the fatted calf. I mumble a short, dizzy apology to God.

Behind Mountain, just as in the first apparition, another arm reaches through the door. I know this chalky limb covered with leaves. It's been following me for months. Legion squeezes in through the door on silent bare feet. He is so thoroughly concealed in vegetation he might be a walking tree. He sizes up the situation instantly and moves across the floor with rapid stealth, machete raised. I'm speechless, my senses and allegiances scattered. Legion gives a little jump in the air and the knife rises to the top of his extended arms.

"Mountain!" I shriek suddenly, startling him. "Be*hind* you!"

But Mountain knows that trick, something behind him in a coffin cabin that hasn't been opened for years, right—yet his instincts, even bloodthirsty, are sound, and he whirls, just as the blade endeavors to part his skull. He shouts and throws out an awkward kick. Legion's blade hums once again for Mountain's head. Mountain ducks and in the same deft motion he lunges for the bushman's belly. Legion sidesteps the blow, leaps once again into the air, and knocks the machete out of Mountain's hand. Mountain catches his wrist, the two men tumble growling and spitting to the overgrown floor, and I take the opportunity to dash for the door. Even if I knew which side to take, I wouldn't know what to do.

It's all over for Legion, I think, stumbling down the hill, falling twice to my knees. Still I must try to find help. Why aren't there any police on this island? Why aren't there any phones? My feet hit the trail and I look back once. I can still hear the men growling and snarling like primates. I turn and scamper for the road. The earth tears under my feet, jagged shadows fly across my body, the world is tipping and reeling and sliced with green fruit birds and the roar of chaos and light German opera. Someone is already pursuing me. I can hear raspy, determined breath and the plunging of feet, the crash of underbrush. With all my momentum, I'm fixed on the asphalt road. I must make the road. It can't be more than a hundred yards away. The road is civilization. Philanthropists built it. My pursuer is closing ground. No chance to glance back. I think of diving left and boonywhomping off a cliff into the sea and swimming to the British Virgin Islands, where I'll become a bartender, mix tropical fruit drinks, eat runny cheese and raisin crumpets, and seduce rich women.

I've taken a wrong turn. Shrubbery slaps my face. I hear the grunt and puff of my pursuer. I am prepared to turn and quote from the Bible: "Then said Jesus unto Peter, Put up thy sword into the sheath: the cup which my Father hath given me, shall I not drink it?" Suddenly the jungle before me opens. A hundred feet below, the sea foams mutely against jagged pinnacles and spires of cooled lava. I grab for a tree branch. I do a glissade. A knife pokes me firmly in the back. I swear at the Lord above and go tripping into free space, ocean and eternity whispering gentle welcomes far below.

As I whistle through the air, plummeting at thirty-two-feet-per-second-squared (as Mountain would say it), the wind ripping at my clothes, stars wobbling in an amateur musical revue above my eyes, the inebriating, ethereal childhood memories of musty pup tents and dirty tennis shoes filling my nostrils, a powerful, cross-eyed nausea pressing into my brain stem, I know

I should be having some kind of vivid death revelation, some white-light judgment tunnel opening before me, or flashy recap of the myriad images of my small and contemptible life, or at the very least I should be trying to determine who forced me off this cliff so I can go back and haunt the son of a bitch for the rest of his life, but the whole experience of falling toward my certain destruction is really more like: AAAAAAHHHHH!

51.

I WAKE UP WRAPPED IN GAUZE IN A HOT LITTLE ROOM. Doc Tobackoo is standing over me, somber and smelling of cigarettes and an aftershave keenly reminiscent of green olives in gin.

"Tell me we're in heaven," I croak, raising my feeble head.

"If this is heaven," he replies drily, looking around, "it needs a little work."

"Where are we then?"

"My clinic."

"Your clinic?" I repeat, my mouth as dry as the Magna Carta, a headache like the bombing of Pearl Harbor pounding in my brainpan, the nerve roots in my various lacerations scalding. "What day is it?"

"Tuesday," he says, looking down at me in a way that makes me feel as if I'm arranged in a casket. "You've been out two days."

"What happened?" My tongue explores my mouth. I test the motion of various body parts, which seem to be intact despite an overall sensation of being flattened by a steamroller.

"You fell off a cliff," the doc says, stroking his chin. "Or were you pushed?"

"I was reenacting the events at Kitty Hawk."

"If you were meant to fly, Orville, God would've given you wings."

"You're a pip, Doc," I say, turning my head with a painful flash of orange. "Has Mountain been around?"

"Haven't seen him," he says, watching me closely, the geisha bangs on his blonde hairpiece glinting like the fresh plastic of a phony Christmas tree.

A lump of bandages that I recognize as my right hand bumps into my face. "Is my eye broken?" I ask suddenly.

"The orbit was shattered. The cheekbone as well. Don't sit up." He cups my shin reassuringly. "It'll be a while before you can move around on your own."

"Who found me?"

"Some girl in a New York Dolls T-shirt, but she vanished."

"Oh, that's Judy."

"Who?"

"Judy. She was born in 1821. I ran into her father's tombstone the other day."

Doc tips his head at me.

"Go up one night to Scudder's old place above Telescope Bay and see if you don't find a white-eyed girl playing solitaire on the bed. Better yet, catch her some night tiptoeing backwards across the Cross-Island Road with her head under her arm."

"I'm familiar with the story," he says, exuding a patience that says he understands I am delirious. "Perhaps then you've freed her from her tyranny of flesh. It's so hard for the dead to do us good turns when we keep running from them." He offers a meager, sinewy smile. "Whatever the case, your unlikely savior managed to flag down Jeff, the civil engineer from the National Geographical Society. We got a chopper down before the surge swept you out. You're a very lucky young man."

"Lucky, yes," I say, my lump of bandages bumbling around again to explore my face. My left arm is in a cast. My ribs are wrapped so tightly I can barely breathe. Three roaches scuttle down the rafters above my head, one slips and lands with a crack on its back on the tile floor. Without interest the doctor watches it waddle away. "What else is broken?" I ask.

He exhales with a labored effect. "The list would be shorter if I included what wasn't. Blood loss was considerable." The doctor takes a chair, clears his throat, and pats his trusty hair-piece. "The fact that you're still alive is a miracle."

"I don't remember the fall," I say, trying to wiggle my toes, wondering if I'm paralyzed and deciding finally that I must be drugged. "I only remember the ocean, the smell of summertime, and wetting my pants."

"You managed to hit trees some of the way down," he says, deadpan as the family butler, "and part of your fall was deadened by sea."

"A toast for the trees and the sea!" I cry. "Oh Jesus, remind me not to shout like that again."

The doc is strangely clear-eyed today. It occurs to me that he may have been working night and day to save my life and has only recently treated himself to a tightener. I take heart in the fact that I have assisted somehow in the rescue of his purpose. He presses the crystal of his watch to his ear. "I don't want you to mix the painkillers with the alcohol."

"Painkillers?" I say.

"Morphine sulfate. Pretty soon we'll start you on synthetics. Kate has the bottles and the instructions," he says.

"I must owe you a fortune," I say.

He cradles his chin. "Disasters are never cheap."

Kate appears in the door. Oh, it is fine to see her. I was certain she'd been harmed, or that she'd decided to leave. I try to smile but the muscles fail. Her gaze falls to the ground, her hands to her sides. The doctor stares into her cleavage and fond-les his blond toupée. I hear murmuring, the screen door closing, the rumbling of an engine, and then before I know it, I have tumbled back down the long tunnel to the blameless and blessed land called sleep.

52.

THREE DAYS LATER I AM MOVED UNDER HEAVY SEDATION back to the East End. Iba is the first volunteer to cross my threshold. She wears blue culottes over a silver leotard scooped inspiringly at the bosom, and her hair is pulled back in tails. Even if I'm fractured of bone and two quarts low, those dark legs and sharp breasts stir up my hibernating admiration.

"I brought you dis," she says, moving in tenuously and setting down a glass jar on my bed table. "Ointment from de willow bark."

"*Willow* bark." I lift my head. "So you read the July article in *The New England Journal of Medicine*?"

She tips her head and flaps her eyelids at me. "How you feelin'?"

"A little weak," I admit, trying to sit up. "My wounds are suppurating well, though. It only hurts when I breathe. Hand me that bottle."

"You busted up pretty good," she acknowledges, settling the vessel of Scotch into the fingers of my plastered arm and actually *touching my forehead*, a first.

"It's not as bad as it looks," I say, spilling Scotch into my shirt and smacking my lips. "Broke my arm, a few ribs, some fingers, kneecap, sprained my left ankle. A few minor kidney and lung contusions. No more than one or two hundred stitches total. I should've had you sew me up," I say. "Old Doc Tobackoo is a bit shaky with a needle." I raise the bottle in my left arm. "Forgive me if I don't salute."

Now she sits on the edge of the *bed*! Lawd, she is a tasty child, all those legs and innocent eyes and long lovely neck. *This is the secret, I realize suddenly, to tapping the fountain of feminine sympathy.* "Tell me something, Iba," I say, looking down at her leather sandals with the rosettes tooled on the toe straps and imagining her toes tickling my ears. "Did you hear who won the National League pennant?"

"I been hearin' you *moanin'* all night," she says, straightening my sheets and blotting my head with a damp cloth.

"I've been dreaming about you," I say, submitting with the gratitude of an old dog to her ministrations.

She tips her head at me, cloth suspended. "What you dreamin' about dat for?"

"Why haven't you been answering my taps?"

"What taps?"

I knock on the wall with my cast to demonstrate. "Don't you recognize the theme song from *A Man and a Woman*?"

She smiles mildly, maybe the first acknowledgment of a joke in our short and hysterically frustrating history. "I tot it was a rat."

"You haven't seen Mountain, have you?"

"Dat crazy man?" she says.

I get another cumbersome slosh of Johnny Walker. "Would you like to come back to the States with me, Iba?" I ask. "I'll get a job fixing radios. You can be a dance instructor. We'll open our own pharmacy."

She seems to consider this. All of her archness, her coolness, is gone. "Maybe if you wasn't *drinkin'* so much," she says, permitting me to study her elegant profile and sniff her heady fried-cheese-ball and witch-hazel scent.

"It's an old folk remedy for loneliness," I explain, taking another blast.

"It will make you sick," she says.

"Loneliness will make you sick too."

"Oh," she says.

Her body relaxes. She leans toward me. Her eyes are so sad. I could have her now if I wasn't so covered in stitches and plaster and gauze. I smile at her. She strokes my forehead. It's love high and beyond the union of gametes.

53.

THROUGH THE COMING BLUR OF NIGHTS AND DAYS I
slumber along the cool shores of Heroin Beach, waking only
intermittently for water, pills, or a cigarette, or to smile blearily
at the long face of Kate—God bless Kate. I love Kate. I think she
will stay forever and I dream that Mountain has fallen off a cliff
and she will be mine, but I know that none of this is true because
I have seen her kissing someone on the gravel drive. He is a dark
man, I think a native, perhaps that chap in the Beetle who picked
us up on my first day seeing Cinnamon Jim. Also I suspect
that Mountain's been here when Kate was out and I was asleep.
I've felt someone over me. I've heard matches scratching and
newspapers rustling, the whistle of the teapot when no one was
supposedly home. I've smelled Mountain's adrenaline lunacy
and his conflicted and bitter regret. I don't know if he's worried
that I might not live or that I might not die.

The mosquitoes graze lazily on my hide. I can hear Iba pray-
ing through the wall a few inches away. I try to identify the
passages. It strikes me that an attractive woman should be allowed
to mature and then falter morally before turning to the ironclad
guidance of Scripture. My room swelters like a Southern hotbox
where the warden sends you for complaining about the meat loaf.
Gold sparkles glued long ago to the ceiling flutter down from
time to time. If I squint I can make them into bubbles descending
in an old rerun of *The Lawrence Welk Show*, which only whets
within me a dull nostalgia for the corny music of my suburban

childhood and that fried chicken they used to have at the Jack in the Box. Some generous soul has set the radio bedside so that I can listen to the National League playoffs, and sometimes the announcer is shouting in my ear, sometimes the static is so strong it sounds like applause in a rainstorm. Last night in the sixth inning, before I lost transmission, Candaleria struck out the side. I have not missed a baseball playoff since I was eight years old.

Two weeks pass before I can get up to pee by myself. Old Doc T. has removed some of my stitches, but had to put in a fresh set here and there. I'll wear the cast another eight weeks and my right hand, which was crushed to a pulp in the fall, is still wrapped and bleeding. My walloped face droops on the left side, and I imagine I will always look like an ex-boxer who never won a fight. My ribs hurt the most. Kate, even though she's kissing someone else, stays on to watch me, helps change my bandages, supervises my drug regimen, flirts pitifully in an effort to buoy my spirits, and prepares meals that I force myself to be interested in. We both keep looking to the door, she in fear and hope and me in hope and fear, but Mountain doesn't show.

54.

THIS AFTERNOON CINNAMON JIM STRIDES THROUGH THE
door, a box fan in his arms. I get the feeling as always that he
has appeared out of some metaphysical vapor. I blink the sand and
grog from my eyes. He's wearing a black-and-white striped
Berber gown, shiny, white, pointed shoes, and a Milan weave rain
hat the kind Bing Crosby might've been photographed under on
a drippy day at the Del Mar racetrack.

"Greetings, my young friend," he says, a broad smile on
his pruny face, his hat tipped at a sporty angle. He hefts the fan.
"How are you faring?"

"Well, well, Mister Jim," I say, sitting up, happy to have a
visitor. "Come sit by the fire. Where's Oscar Wilde?"

"He stays in when it rains. I've brought something for you,"
he says, placing the fan on the dresser. "Payment for a case of
the clap," he explains, turning the switch. "It'll blow all the bugs
back to Amsterdam."

The paddles begin to turn and the mechanical breeze babb-
les over us like the laughter of orphans or a drink of cool water in
the desert. Gold flakes swirl about the room.

"How does it *work*?" I ask, staring into the blur of paddles.

"Batteries," he says. "You can get the double As at the apothecary."

"I'm speechless, Cinnamon."

"*Taisez-vous*," he says, pinching up his robe and taking a
seat in the sympathy chair. "I talked to Kate."

"How is she?" I ask, biting at the air.

He crosses his legs and watches for a moment as the miniature blizzard of gold flakes blow loose from the ceiling. "She says you're out here alone and refuse to come west like a sensible fellow."

"I'll be just fine here, Mr. Greeley." I take a short breath full of needles. "I appreciate your concern."

Glancing about the room, he says, "And where is your friend, the amiable giant?"

"Still working on his boat, I reckon." I kick the blanket off my feet. "When he finishes it we're going to sail away to find the Fountain of Youth."

"I saw him back in the jungle yesterday," he says, leaning down, elbows on knees. "Not far from the second Scudder cabin. Shovel in one hand and a bag of something that looked heavy in the other."

"What was he up to?" I ask, screwing up my good eye.

"By his look I'd say he's found something," Cinnamon says, his fair eyes widening with significance.

"Well, I haven't seen him since I went parachuting without my chute," I say. "Do I hear rain?"

"Yes," he says. "Two days of it now. The monsoons have begun."

"Already?" I say, tapping the ash from my cigarette. "Seems like we just took down the decorations."

"You haven't seen the east side when it rains," he says, lifting his water-beaded hat as if in homage to the elements. "That's why we want you to come west with us. There's no shelter here."

"Perception Bay."

"That's a mile off," he says, "And it's for *boats*. Anyway, if a hurricane hits this part of the island broadside, Perception Bay will do you no good. You know the song 'Wipeout'?"

"I'll be all right," I say, swiping my dirty cast through the air. "I can handle rain. I like rain."

"Kate said you'd be stubborn about it."

"What does she care?" I say, turning away from him.

"Don't mope, old boy. The women come, the women go."

Left-handed I find my trusty bottle of liquor and treat the cracks in my throat. "By any chance do you know who won the National League pennant?"

He turns his head, his hat still sparkling with drops. "The what?"

"Never mind."

"My ride is waiting," he says, standing. "The couch in the salon is yours if you change your mind."

"Thanks for the fan," I say. "But I'm going to stay. I didn't come here to be comfortable."

"You're going to get your wish, my boy." And with a nod and a tip of the hat he bids adieu.

The screen door slams with a pining, empty sound. I rise for tea and a sponge bath at the sink and to re-dress and disinfect my wounds. Outside, the leaves patter and hiss and I look out the door to see heavy fog and rain. Everyone is obsessed with the monsoons and battening down the hatches. Fanny is gone to Dominica for a witchcraft festival and her motorcycle is parked in Fish's canopy next to his boat, which is scraped and wrapped for winter. Fish himself is already locked away with The Grateful Dead and the complete works of Jack Kerouac, Founding Father of Antitechnology. The rain sifts down. I've always enjoyed extremes in weather, especially rain. I love the word *monsoon*. It sounds as if you could sauté one with onions and ham.

I put a pan of water on the stove and cut lengths of bandages. As I wait for my water to boil, I stare at the pale squares on the wall where the Gauguins once hung and I find myself yearning for those tense and treacherous nights with Kate. I think it was Louis L'Amour who said that adventure is nothing but a fancy name for trouble. With Kate it was worth the trouble. Kate, oh Kate. I look back to the door, which has fallen into shadow. On the radio, the latest number one love song for your pancakes by the Commodores segues into "Rapper's Delight," a song so immensely popular on this island that even I know the words, and I sing along absentmindedly: "I said a hip hop the hippie the hippie to the hip hip hop and you don't stop the rock it to the bang bang boogie…"

It's not easy rapping while I wrap my wounds. When the strips of cloth are tight, I soak them with rum, which is raw hell, but it almost guarantees the prevention of infection. Just to spite Tobackoo and his anal fixation on synergism, I take two Darvons and wash them back with a short glass of Johnny Walker. The sun fades from the stoop and I light a candle and then a cigarette with the same wooden match, sit for a while at the table, and spiral back nostalgically through time, recalling the blitheringly easy and carefree days of life in the USA. Up and down the freeway, in and out of the burger joints, ball game on Sunday, horny scientologist twice a week.

After a while I blow out the candle and climb back into bed. I turn the fan on high and blow the newspapers off the dresser, remembering that letdown feeling after the packages were all opened on Christmas morning, even when you got everything you asked for. A mosquito wobbles down for its customary leg of Edgar, but confusedly begins to flounder in the current. Several of her sisters botch similar assays. They are coming from everywhere now as the dinner bells chime, but they have no chance with their lacy wings against the electric hurricane. I close my eyes and listen with satisfaction to their tiny cries of confusion as they strain against the battery-powered current and are defeated time and time again.

55.

I MISS KATE MORE THAN ANYTHING, MORE THAN HOT water, more than cheeseburgers or ice cubes, more than Chinese food or tequila. It's been weeks since I've seen her. I wish she'd stop by just to say hello and tell me everything's O K, and maybe I could kiss her face once or scowl at her boyfriend, but I know she's busy with her new life. It's best for everyone that she's gone, even though it hurts to think that I was just another roll in the hay.

The flurry of concerned visitors has trickled to a stop. Cinnamon brought me a box of canned meat, a case of Johnny Walker, and a rabbit's foot. Fish brought me an underweight lobster. Judy walked in backward one afternoon, smoked one of my cigarettes, thanked me for falling off the cliff, and broke a bottle of Scotch before setting off for safer harbors, she said, with her father and mother. Arthur brought me a handshake, a grin, and my last check from the hotel. And though I have shelves full of herbal cures, in a few days Iba will be moving to the west side to stay with a cousin. Everyone is holing up. Everyone is leaving town.

But my body is healing well. And if I'm taking too many pills and mixing them with the booze it's only because I'm depressed about everyone leaving me, especially Mountain and Kate. A clearer mind would say I was in denial about Mountain, that I'm wasting healthy energy blocking him out of my mind, but I can't come to terms with a crime a hundred times as vile as mine. The thought of my old ex-wonderful friend wanting to murder me is unbearable. And what's all this about a shovel in one hand and a heavy bag in the other?

Sitting up in bed one afternoon half-delirious, sweating bandages wrapped around my ribs the only garment above my waist, my head a cloud from the Darvons and Percodans the doctor has prescribed and their marvelous, verboten, Slavic gestalt with alcohol, the roaches stumbling and scrabbling in the rafters, the waves whispering conspiratorially up the cove, I hear a voice above me somewhere saying: "You must call off the manhunt, Edgar."

I have barely the wherewithal to turn my head. The voice appears to be coming from the able-bodied wunderkind Doctor Tobackoo and his trusty blonde toupee. My mouth is too dry to reply. My brain crackles distantly like spent sea waves retreating through pebbled shores. My tongue is an aardvark. I must speak slowly to keep it from falling out of my mouth. I say: "Glummy glum gummm."

"You must call off the manhunt, Edgar," the voice reiterates.

"Me?" I say, unconvinced yet that I am not having a conversation with myself.

"You're the only one," insists the nebulous form of Tobackoo.

"Where did you come from?" I demand, at last pulling the old, spidery-veined M D into focus. "Haven't you got an aunt in Kansas to spend the monsoon season with?"

My devoted physician shakes his head. "You're still mixing the painkillers with the alcohol, I see."

I would answer him more distinctly if everything were not so wavery. My head feels like a mashed-potato sandwich. I reach down deep for a reply. The image of Old Doc Tobackoo shifts in a wooze. I am indeed mixing my daiquiris too rich. Physical pain is nothing compared to the confrontation of people you love who just up 'n leave you. It's like that picture I have of me standing on the toilet eating Crest toothpaste and my mother bustles into the room to tell me it's poisonous. Is this true? Did it really happen? I must call off the manhunt?

My tongue and eyelids are equally parched as I attempt to move them simultaneously. "Which manhunt?" I finally manage to ask.

"You're not aware that Chollie Legion is being tracked across this island like a common animal?"

"I've heard something to the effect," I admit thickly, trying to keep my eyes focused on the gauzy physician.

"Chollie Legion is innocent," he says. "You've got to tell these bloodthirsty mongrels that it wasn't him who drove you off that cliff."

I'm blinking now more smoothly at least and dealing now principally with the problem of a leather tongue. "Then who did?"

Tobackoo groans.

"How do I know?" I insist, getting my good hand under me securely. Now my forehead itches. I think maybe I will have my sweat glands surgically removed. "All I know is that someone chased me off a cliff and why wouldn't it have been Chollie Legion, who promised to kill me and hunted me dedicatedly for three straight *months*?"

His voice seems to boom. "You believe that Chollie Legion stepped into that shack to save your life and afterward gave chase to drive you to your *death*?"

I fall back into my sweat-stained pillow. It seems to me that the physician is making impatient gestures, largely with his thumbs. His voice is still ringing with condemnation. "Have you no qualms about the man who saved you from *dying*?"

"Where is he?" I offer weakly.

His lips are tight and his nose is wiggling rabbitlike. He shivers the bangs on his toupee. "I told him to leave the island for his own good."

"You *talked* to him?" I say, lifting my head.

"The town is in a frenzy," he roars. "They've even got federal parks people involved. The whole town's after Chollie, torches and flashlights. It's like an old Frankenstein movie. You're the only one who can stop them."

"Me? Diminished, poorly educated, inebriated, busted-ole-broke, unlucky, sweaty, unbathed, mosquito-ravaged, jilted *me,* going to call off a *man*hunt? Who am I, Efrem Zimbalist *Junior*? "

"Chollie Legion is *innocent,*" Tobackoo screams, his blood-shot eyes bulging.

"He's insane," I insist quietly. "He's killed people."

"Where did you hear *that*?"

"Everywhere." I indicate the ceiling and at least three walls. "My neighbor, the fellows at work. A hundred sources."

"You're repeating island *lore.*" His head is quivering as he speaks. "You ignore the ardor of these people to tell *stories.* Werewolves and walking trees. Your antics have given them fire. The fact is, he *admires* you. You're the only white person who walks, who refuses a car, who carries a knife and strives to live naturally. He's listened to a hundred of your quirky little mono-logues as you walked home from the hotel."

"He *admires* me?"

"Go figure," Tobackoo says with a shrug.

"He's been *stalking* me," I blurt. "He made threats. He-he-he lives in a *grave*yard."

"Call off the hunt, Edgar," he roars, his fingers grasping at the air like claws. "You can't have this on your hands. You can't have this on your conscience."

"Make up your mind."

"I'm going to stop prescribing the painkillers if you con-tinue to mix them with alcohol. Are you listening to me?"

"You're right," I say, snapping to. "Assemble the masses. Tell them to blow out their lanterns. I'll tell them immediately."

I feel myself flagging under the strong disapproval of my physician. I wake up, hours later, days? My painkillers are still on the dresser and I feel relief as one who has been reassured of an old friendship. I wash one back with a swig of syrupy, eight-year-old Scotch and think of my interview with Tobackoo and the revelation of Legion as an innocent man. I've known it all along. I must do something. I am the only one. I stagger up out of bed and into the kitchen, cup water from the spigot, and splash my face. I look longingly for Kate, the smell of her, her panties slung across a dining room chair, all gone forever. The batteries in the radio are weak, as are those in my box fan. I twirl the dial until I find a clear signal. Instead of telling me about the Pittsburgh Pirates, a crisp British voice informs me that a hurricane named Daisy has a dead bead on Poisson Rouge Isle.

56.

THROUGH THE SCREEN DOOR OF MY MAKESHIFT INFIR-
mary drifts a mélange of incompatible sounds: a clatter of
hooves, a clapping of thumb tambourines, a low Hindi wailing,
mariachi trumpets. And so I rise from my damp and rumpled
bed to look out but the fog is so dense I can't even see the bees. It
must be a fever-dream, a hallucination of the damned.
I make myself a tea with Scotch and tenderly change my shirt.
On the radio I hear a comforting bulletin: Daisy has weakened
and veered north. This queer fog must be its fallout. I step outside to the smell of toasted coconut, Iba taking a bath, and Fish
frying bacon as he listens to *Workingman's Dead* for the two
millionth time. I don't understand The Grateful Dead, although
they fit well against the backdrop of the approaching caravan.
Personally I would rather watch Iba take a bath.

The gravel makes a wet crunch as I shuffle down toward
the road. The mending bone-deep gashes on my shoulders, back,
legs, and ribs are shrinking and drying against their threads
like grins on shrunken heads. My left arm is still encased in plaster. My face is half-numb. I walk as if one leg were shorter than
the other. I want to massage the old scar on the ham of the thumb,
feel the rough, familiar knit of complete but damaged flesh.
Above the tinkling cacophony rises a chant whose words form thus
in my ears:

Donna the wibber
Donna the sea

Donna the waddah
Ah set me so free.

And it seems to make sense. I wonder if I have finally appre-
hended the opposite logic that rules this island, its intentional
disregard for primary Western values, excluding money and the
internal combustion engine. A procession of burros, a milk
wagon, and an Olds convertible glued with paper streamers and
holding two men in blonde wigs and skirts and two women
beating trash can lids, emerge from the fog. Children dance all
about. The pace of the ceremony is funereal but there is an unmistakable lilt of festivity in the air. Willie Stargell sits under the
eaves, fog sucking at his legs. Baseball season is over. I missed
the entire World Series for the first time in my life. But I can't bring
myself to the sacrilege of asking him who won. All I know for sure
about baseball is that six-foot-eight J.R. Richard of the Houston
Astros, most dominant starter since Sandy Koufax and key to the
defeat of the LA Dodgers, left a game in the third inning last
July complaining of a dead arm and later was found eating from
a bucket of Kentucky Fried Chicken in the locker room. I've read
this article seven or eight times, searching for meaning. I take the
place on the bench next to Willie and slap my knee. The fog laps
over us.

"What's this all about, Willie?"

"Dey foun Chollie," he answers somberly, his old lips trembling, his glaucous eyes filled with an indistinct fear.

"Chollie Legion?" I say with a gasp. "Where?"

He points vaguely, several times. "At de bottom of a cleef."

"When?"

"Loss night." He shakes his head.

I rub my head with my cast. "Where?"

"Wes side. Trunk Bay, I tink."

"Dead?"

"As can be," he gruffs with heavy nodding. "Tree weeks, dey
say."

"Dead three weeks? Suicide?"

He shrugs, licks his lips, and lets his eyes return to the passing parade.

I feel desperate. I hoped against hope that Legion had left the island. Mountain must've gotten him, I think. "Ding-dong, de Chollie gone," I whisper, wanting to disappear into the fog.

Scratching a crusty patch on his head, Willie says, "You know his fodder was dat man, Scudder."

"Scudder?" I say. "The hermit?"

Willie nods. "Mad all his life, dat boy, Chollie. Can't blame 'im. Lotta people say he was dead. Well, he dead now." His bottom lip protrudes and he stares down in the dirt. "I hope he foun his peace. If not, we'll be seen 'im on de roads again soon."

A shaft of sunlight breaks through, lighting Alvina standing roadside in a cloak of fog and her peach-colored robe, shaking her head. Her expression seems to say: Look at what you've caused. Willie Stargell waves gloomily as the parade passes. Dozens of children tumble joyfully in its wake. Without hesitating, I step into the procession myself. After all, right or wrong, it is my parade. I wish I had a trumpet or a drum. I flip my tea mug off into the brush and begin to chant.

> *Donna the wibber,*
> *Donna the sea,*
> *Donna the waddah,*
> *Ah set me so free ...*

Chanting feels good, doesn't it? It's like listening to gospel music after your girl has left you. Or it's like knowing you're going to pass on, but to a better place.

The parade and its chanting, half-witted caboose swing out past Frederick Bay and then up the grade of the Cross-Island Road, the jingle of bells, clock of hooves, and bang of can lids fading up ahead. We leave the fog in a clinging, cottony lagoon below. So Scudder was Legion's *father*? And I broke into his sacred *tomb*? Yet he must've understood. Did he really try to save my life? Did he truly *admire* me? And now he's dead. But how could I have known?

Funny, I thought I was surrounded by children, but they seem to have all dispersed. I am the sole trailer, the anonymous sacrifice. My intention is to follow the parade to its natural conclusion on the sand, with a roasted pig and rum and other oblivious mischief and moonlight mysteries of death. Even the parade has gone on without me. I call to it through the cup of my good right hand. No sign, no reply. A few warm drops of condensation splash down on my forehead. The jungle here and there is veiled in shreds of remnant mist. I think about leaping from a cliff again, that peaceful coasting through a salted breeze and then the end of competition, feeding, destruction, and desire. But who would miss me? And what if I survived again?

The way is deep with shadow and heavy with the smell of wild gardenias and painkiller trees. Here is the spreep of a flycatcher, there the flutter of a scissortail. I feel a surge of euphoria. I feel like making love and eating roasted pork. I have to stop for a moment and rest against a tree. The warm fog envelops me. I nod off and wake up some time later to the thunder of surf and the smell of moldering crickets and worms.

To the east an unholy darkness has descended like a vast swarm of ravenous locusts. The mingling black clouds move in quick, bizarre, introrse patterns, like smoke behind a sheet of clear ice. In my life I have never seen clouds behave this way. I am spellbound for a moment, as a child who has stumbled upon a portal to the underworld. The air chills all at once and the leaves begin to quake. All I can think is, *Better get home.* A distant howling lifts from the sea like a demon roused after a thousand-year slumber and before I can think another sensible thought my unsteady legs have begun to run on their own, the jungle nattering and scolding all around me like the mockery of crocodiles and aging cocktail waitresses.

I am shivering badly, teeth chattering, by the time I arrive at Alvina's. My neighbors are *gone*. Every last one is *gone*. E-V-A-C-

U-A-T-E-D. Fish's screen door bangs with flimsy insistence against the stucco wall. Trash whirls about. The papaya trees bend like young hula dancers in the howling offshore gusts. Above the cove the alarming sky is filled with tipping funnels that are headed my way.

A radio crackles in the room of Willie Stargell, Senior— once a baseball game, now an urgent, nasal BBC radio broadcast: "Hurricane Daisy continues to press down on the mid-Caribbean archipelago of French Hook with winds in excess of 260 kilometers per hour."

Isn't this the same bozo who assured me this morning that Daisy had weakened and veered *north*? Iba's door is open and I poke my head into her soapy woman-smell and ominous religious sovereignty and call her name with a silly, hopeful grin, though I know she's gone, safe now playing rummy with her cousin. My stomach flashes and chills with panic. Everyone sure left in a *hurry*. Even the bees have bugged out. Why didn't they come get me?

For a moment I am petrified by indecision. The air warms suddenly, in no way abetting my tremors. I yawn nervously and my ears pop as though I've just descended a thousand feet in a small plane. Except for the wind keening, the surf booming, and the distant moan of the approaching storm, the island is silent. No insect or animal shrieking. Which means that anything with a brain has stopped thinking about reproduction and predation for a moment and found cover. I couldn't be in a worse place, in an unprotected cove in a slovenly castle made of pulverized seashells.

Back in the hovel I try to tune in a radio station. An urgent voice pierces the static: "Daisy has virtually destroyed the island of Dominica and has now drawn its bead on the small group of islands which include Ravissant, Pain Fermente, and Poisson Rouge Isle. Residents are advised to evacuate at once."

I scamper outside. Fanny's motorcycle sits kicked over on its stand in Fish's boat canopy but I can't ride it with one hand. Town is too far anyway. My only chance is Perception Bay.

I gallop down the road, my arm in its cast swinging double-time. I estimate that Perception Bay is one mile and that through panic I can cover that distance in six minutes, as I did once in high school in gray cotton shorts, but I am older now, out of shape, broken and upholstered, dissolute, and I'm out of breath after three hundred yards. I curse tobacco and painkillers, vow to quit, and slow to a jog. The jungle begins to shiver and boil all around, the sky darkens yet. Drops of chilly, iron-tasting rain smack me in the face. The branches of the trees lash like spastic monsters in a dance contest. I can hear surf off to the left rumbling fiercely up the shore. I think I may have to find a hole somewhere, a ditch, a place to lie low and pray. A mongoose skitters across the road, flings me a harried glance, then flounders off. We're screwed, buddy, it seems to say. Why weren't we paying attention?

Perception Bay is abandoned too, as if Jesus came in the wake of that fog-ridden parade and hauled everyone up into the promise without me. I would expect to find boats here, since this is supposedly the only safe, foul-weather harbor on the east side, but there is only one boat, Mountain's salvage craft, *Colleen*, sitting nearly complete on its cement pad. A tarp, which snaps and flutters in the gale, has been thrown halfheartedly over the bow. I move in closer, the rain smacking my forehead. The waves are lifting now agitatedly, flailing with violent wisps of whipping foam, beating with more-rapid succession on the shore.

I am all at once overcome by an unmanageable wave of dread and despair. There is nowhere to turn. I have to crouch and clench my eyes against the drilling rain. The grisly visage of a murdered Chollie Legion appears. It was my fault. He tried to save me and I did nothing in reply. I visited his *father*. I was the first one in ten years to visit his father. He probably appreciated me for that. He *admired* me. I'll be with you all soon. If we're lucky the hurricane will destroy this island and no evidence of our folly will ever exist. Scudder will be forgotten, Chollie, Kate and her service to Maryland Social Services, me and Mountain and our feeble fantasies of adventure and escape. Man *vs.* Nature in the rematch of the century, but Nature always wins.

The tarp on the boat stands straight-out, fluttering and buzzing, the brush on the headland is as erect as the feathers on the neck of an angry cock. A gust of wind knocks me back into the sand. I look around futilely for cover. My eyes fall on the red sea chest, which is riveted to the cement pad. It would be pointless to climb into a poorly tethered and unfinished small boat. My only chance, really my last card, is this trunk. Crouching against the driving rain, I lift the lid. My heart stops. Inside, mixed in among the tools, are dozens of ancient gold coins.

I stare at the outrageously glittering coins. My mind tumbles down a convoluted chute. The lid of the trunk bangs shut. The rain comes in a horizontal curtain. I am drenched, my trousers glued by the wind to my legs. I stagger back through the sand and out to the road, the trees doubled over like weary sinners being flogged.

The rain strikes like cold nails. I lunge for fronds, vines, branches, anything to hold me up. My hand has begun to bleed and one of the deep cuts on my back feels as if it has opened. Rain runs pink down my shirt. It doesn't matter, I'm dead anyway, but I continue to struggle, marveling at the mindless instinct for survival. The leaves on the trees razz like tattered hankies. I am toppled twice, blinded by driving rain. For a while I crawl over the blacktop, three-legged like a human tricycle. At certain turns the jungle is thick enough to provide cover, though it is so dark now it may as well be night.

Turner Cove is lathered as whipped cream, the mounting waves push eight feet and slam up to skim the road. Above the cove the sky is black and spitting sheets of iced rain. *Home*, what an odd thing to call this hellhole. The great blue crumbling sanitarium seems to be overrun by ghosts, its window shutters shivering, its tattered screen doors slamming, the leaves spinning upward like a great ticker tape celebration of the end of the world. Iba's flower beds are two miniature waterfalls. The metal

PO E BA L L A N TI NE

roofs buckle and snap in the wind. Fanny's motorcycle lies on the ground under the collapsed boat canopy. Where to hide? I wonder. The *cistern*. No, I don't want to die outdoors. Hail batters my head. I hurry into our bungalow, pulling the screen door after me. I try the radio for news—nothing—look about, nowhere but the stall to hide. Even the roaches are gone. I grab a bottle from the bookcase, twist the cap off with my teeth. A figure appears etched in the doorway.

My heart leaps. Mountain throws the door aside and enters the room feral and drenched, his jaw muscles writhing. Rain hammers the metal roof. "Blazes!" he roars through his dripping beard. "What are *you* doing here? I thought you were dead!"

"Give me two minutes!" I yell, gulping savagely from the bottle. "What are *you* doing here?"

"Got caught out in it," he screams, shaking back his long hair, his eyes glowing. "I had to move the R E S T of it!"

Above us the roof begins to wobble violently. Water has risen up the steps and now flows in a muddy tide across the floor.

"The rest of W HAT? The Mariner's Trove?"

"Ay!" he cries, his eyes glaring, savage and exultant. "Cruzados, matey, a hundred stone at least."

"Where did you *find* it?"

"When me and Chollie were tumbling around at Scudder's one of the floorboards came up," he shouts, throwing up his arms. "Lo! The old skunk was a M I S E R. Had to kill your little friend. Sorry."

"So it was YO U who drove me off the cliff!" I shout.

He smiles and swings his head, arms behind his back as if he might be ice-skating across the lake. "So where's your girl, KAT E?"

I stump forward painfully, shaking my cast at him, and smash my bottle on the floor. I can see that he's utterly lost, that the gold has ruined his soul. My "good" hand, still bleeding, clenches the table, which seems to be rocking of its own power. "She left us both."

"Devil take her," he cries. "I've got what I came for." He looks up as the ceiling makes a gruesome sound. The cove roars as it continues to rise and flood up the gravel drive. A long crack in the north wall begins to spread.

Mountain shouts incoherently as the screen door swings loose and flutters on the shred of one hinge. A welcome mat flies past outside and splats into the wall, followed by a trash can and all its contents, including a sidelong sheet of green slime like the sneeze of the Jolly Green Giant. Mountain turns with a mild flicker of irritation on his brow. The roof lifts, trembles for a minute, then rips and tears away like the lid on a sardine can. Water and wind—mixed with beer cans, newspapers, and tree limbs—pour down. The cupboard doors explode. I cover my head with my arms, looking up just in time to see the wall to our left give way. Under its tide we go. The darkness of Egypt. A dream of pink prime rib, not too much fat. I am bleeding like freedom. I have a tremendous, skin-splitting erection. No more of this bullshit, I think. My tongue is the sand.

57.

HIGH ABOVE ME A LONE FAN SPINS SLOWLY, COOLING THE back of a brown house-lizard with a very large head. The room is spacious, with mullioned windows that permit sunlight to stripe the walls. I'm lying on a couch with a sheet across my legs. A Styx song, "Babe," is playing on a radio somewhere. I have a sharp pain in my temple and the taste of dirty cashews in my mouth. My head is wrapped in bandages that smell of iodine and my left arm is in a fresh cast.

I sit up quickly, my eyes rolling about. The high, sun-striped room is painted bright yellow in the fashion of a Moorish palace. All around are cabinets full of curiosities, stuffed birds, Byzantine angels, and crocheted fruits. On the floor is a Brussels carpet and on the walls photographs in gilt frames of Cinnamon Jim Joyeux at various functions, here shaking hands with Charles de Gaulle, there smiling out of a crowd of African natives holding up dead meerkats by their back legs. The room is furnished like a seaside lodging house, but the chairs are covered in yellow silk.

Iba is perched nearby, rubbing a rosary between her fingers and staring at me intently. She wears a white bathrobe and white cotton socks. She seems disheveled and distraught, her hair limp, her eyes tired.

"Where am I, Iba?"

"Cinnamon Jim's," she says in a lifeless tone. "I been prayin' for you two days."

"I'm still alive then."

"They ain't no prayin' in heaven," she says.

The tiny monkey named Oscar Wilde, now dressed in a gold suit and red fez, leaps down on my shoulder and leans his wrinkled face into mine. Cinnamon Jim must be nearby. I hear a footfall in the hall, the mixture of misplaced voices. I thump my cast on the arm of the couch and the monkey leaps straight up and must be hanging on a curtain or a picture frame, because I can no longer see him.

I taste a cut on my lip. I feel all around the damp turban on my head. I test the bend of my knees. "How did I *get* here?"

"Dey brought you by boat. De whole eas side is destroyed. Nutting left." Her head falls.

I look around quickly. "Where's Mountain?"

"Your friend dead," she says, speaking to the floor.

I glance up at the ceiling, where the little brown house-lizard makes a successful dart at a housefly. "It can't be."

"Cinnamon Jim say he runnin' roun de islan tok-tok in de middle of de hurricane packin' up his gold. Say money ain't de root of all evil, say *desire* for money de root of all evil."

I fall back into the couch, testing the cut on my lip and watching the lizard. "Is Kate all right?" I ask. "Willie Stargell?"

"Willie who?"

"Willie on the bench looking out at Turner Cove."

"Oh, dey all fine. Kate run off wit dat black surveyor," she says, looking up at me without emotion, the long fingers working their beads.

"What will you do now?" I ask.

"I don't know," she says, with a hopeless shrug. "Don't have a ting. Don't have a stitch. Nutting left."

I move my head slowly, looking around for the monkey. The lizard creeps along another inch, flicking its tongue. Far away down the sunlit hall, I see Cinnamon Jim shuffling toward us, the monkey in his gold suit and red fez riding on Jim's shoulder. Jim must be swamped with the needy, a hundred sons and daughters, cousins and grandchildren, frightened and displaced. He sees me and smiles, lifting a dark wrinkled hand, the sun glinting off the tassel of the monkey's fez. I think of my magnificent friend Mountain crumbling under the deadly sins that he seemed to understand so well.

"Come back with me to America, Iba."

She stares at me for a moment.

"America the Beautiful," I add.

She smiles and drops her eyes.

Down the hall I hear the echo of the obeah man's laugh.

Hawthorne Books & Literary Arts
Portland, Oregon

Current Titles

At Hawthorne Books, we're serious about literature. We suspected that good writers were being ignored and cast aside as a result of consolidation in the publishing industry, and in 2001 we decided to find these writers and give them a voice. We publish American literary fiction and narrative non-fiction, although we won't turn down a good international title if we find one. All of our books are published as affordable original trade paperbacks, but feature details not typically found even in casebound titles from bigger houses: acid-free papers; sewn bindings which will not crack; heavy, laminated covers with French flaps and built-in bookmarks. If you like to read, we think you'll enjoy our books. If you like to write—well, send us something. We're always looking.

Core: A Romance

Kassten Alonso

Fiction
208 pages
$12.95
ISBN 0-9716915-7-6

FINALIST, 2005 OREGON BOOK AWARD

THIS INTENSE AND COMPACT NOVEL crackles with obsession, betrayal, and madness. As the narrator becomes fixated on his best friend's girlfriend, his precarious hold on sanity rapidly deteriorates into delusion and violence. This story can be read as the classic myth of Hades and Persephone (Core) rewritten for a twenty-first century audience as well as a dark tale of unrequited love and loneliness.

Alonso skillfully uses language to imitate memory and psychosis, putting the reader squarely inside the narrator's head; deliberate misuse of standard punctuation blurs the distinction between the narrator's internal and external worlds. Alienation and Faulknerian grotesquerie permeate this landscape, where desire is borne in the bloom of a daffodil and sanity lies toppled like an applecart in the mud.

JUMP THROUGH THIS gothic stained glass window and you are in for some serious investigation of darkness and all of its deadly sins. But take heart, brave traveler, the adventure will prove thrilling. For you are in the beautiful hands of Kassten Alonso.　　**TOM SPANBAUER**
Author of *In the City of Shy Hunters*

KASSTEN ALONSO takes the reader on a wild ride inside the mind of a disturbed man as he descends into madness and violence. A beautifully written book. Impossible to put down.　　**JAMES FREY**
Author of *A Million Little Pieces*

KASSTEN ALONSO'S AMAZING Core will startle you. A fierce story that taught me to read it as I went deeper and deeper—it's as if this book is written in a rich, beautiful language I'd once known and somehow forgotten. I'm happy and terrified to have it back.　　**PETER ROCK**
Author of *Bewildered*

Decline of the Lawrence Welk Empire

Poe Ballantine

Fiction
376 pages
$15.95
ISBN 0-9766311-1-3

"IT'S IMPOSSIBLE NOT TO BE CHARMED by Edgar Donahoe [*Publishers Weekly*]," and he's back for another misadventure. Expelled from college for drunkenly bellowing expletives from a dorm window at 3:00 am, Edgar hitchhikes to Colorado and trains as a cook. A postcard arrives from his college buddy, Mountain Moses, inviting him to a Caribbean island. Once there, Edgar cooks at the local tourist resort and falls in love with Mountain's girl, Kate. He becomes embroiled in a love triangle and his troubles multiply as he is stalked by sinister island native Chollie Legion. Even Cinnamon Jim the medicine man is no help. Ultimately it takes a hurricane to blow Edgar out of this mess.

I'M DRUNK AS I WRITE THIS and I wish I would've never left San Diego. San Diego is PARADISE. Billings, Montana is a PIMPLE ON MY BUTT. Edgar, Edgar, I loved you, why did you run away to a desert island? And why didn't you take me with you? I would've fought by your side. I would've drank with you all night and waited tables at that hotel. Jesus, the booze there is cheap. When I called your parents they said you'd gone to New YORK. How was I going to reach you? And why didn't you mention me more than once in your new novel about love and betrayal in the jungle? I thought I was your best friend, Edgar. I feel so bad about Bev. Oh, Edgar, Edgar, please forgive me (and put me in your next book, OK?). **BIG PAT FILLMORE**

YOU'RE LUCKY YOU RAN OFF to that island, Edgar, you *pinche pendejo. Chingada*, I'm still pissed and if you ever show your face around here again I'll kick you in your *pajarito*. My husband is gay and it was your fault. I'd still like to know what you did to him. **CHULA LA RUE**

I'M FAT NOW, EDGAR. I'm a blimp. I married this navy guy, do you believe it, and we're living at my mom's house on Mt. Helix. I see you're still drinking too much. And then you fall off a cliff and I can't stop crying. I'm so unhappy. Adrian told me about Bev. It wasn't your fault. Why do we have to grow old? Why can't we have another chance? **NORMA PADGETT**

God Clobbers Us All

Poe Ballantine

Fiction
196 pages
$15.95
ISBN 0-9716915-4-1

SET AGAINST THE DILAPIDATED halls of a San Diego rest
home in the 1970s, *God Clobbers Us All* is the shimmering, hysterical, and melancholy story of eighteen-year-old surfer-boy
orderly Edgar Donahoe 's struggles with friendship, death, and
an ill-advised affair with the wife of a maladjusted war veteran.
All of Edgar's problems become mundane, however, when he and
his lesbian Blackfoot nurse's aide best friend, Pat Fillmore,
become responsible for the disappearance of their fellow worker
after an lsd party gone awry. *God Clobbers Us All* is guaranteed to
satisfy longtime Ballantine fans as well as convert those lucky
enough to be discovering his work for the first time.

A SURFER DUDE TRANSFORMS into someone captivatingly fragile, and
Ballantine's novel becomes something tender, vulnerable, even sweet without
that icky, cloying literary aftertaste. This vulnerability separates Ballantine's
work from his chosen peers. Calmer than Bukowski, less portentous than
Kerouac, more hopeful than West, Poe Ballantine may not be sitting at the table
of his mentors, but perhaps he deserves his own after all.

> **SETH TAYLOR**
> San Diego *Union-Tribune*

IT'S IMPOSSIBLE NOT TO BE CHARMED by the narrator of Poe Ballantine's
comic and sparklingly intelligent *God Clobbers Us All*.

> **PUBLISHER'S WEEKLY**

GOD CLOBBERS US ALL SUCCEED[S] on the strength of its characterization
and Ballantine's appreciation for the true-life denizens of the Lemon Acres
rest home. The gritty daily details of occupants of a home for the dying have a
stark vibrancy that cannot help but grab one's attention, and the off-hours
drug, surf, and screw obsessions of its young narrator, Edgar Donahoe, and his
coworkers have a genuine sheen that captivates almost as effectively.

> **THE ABSINTHE LITERARY REVIEW**

Things I Like About America

Poe Ballantine

Non-fiction
266 pages
$12.95
ISBN 0-9716915-1-7

THESE RISKY, PERSONAL ESSAYS are populated with odd jobs, eccentric characters, boarding houses, buses, and beer. Ballantine takes us along on his Greyhound journey through small-town America, exploring what it means to be human. Written with piercing intimacy and self-effacing humor, Ballantine's writings provide entertainment, social commentary, and completely compelling slices of life.

IN HIS SEARCH FOR THE REAL AMERICA, Poe Ballantine reminds me of the legendary musk deer, who wanders from valley to valley and hilltop to hilltop searching for the source of the intoxicating musk fragrance that actually comes from him. Along the way, he writes some of the best prose I've ever read.
SY SAFRANSKY
Editor, *The Sun*

BALLANTINE NEVER SHRINKS from taking us along for the drunken, drug-infested ride he braves in most of his travels. The payoff—and there is one—lies in his self-deprecating humor and acerbic social commentary, which he leaves us with before heading further up the dark highway.
THE INDY BOOKSHELF

POE BALLANTINE REMINDS US that in a country full of identical strip malls and chain restaurants, there's still room for adventure. He finds the humor in situations most would find unbearable and flourishes like a modern-day Kerouac. With his funny, honest prose, Ballantine explores the important questions about being an American: Do I have enough money to buy this bucket of KFC? Can I abide another sixteen-hour Greyhound bus trip? Did my crazy roommate steal my beer again? It's a book to cherish and pass on to friends.
MARK JUDE POIRIER
Author of *Unsung Heroes of American Industry* and *Goats*

Madison House

Peter Donahue

Fiction
528 pages
$16.95
ISBN 0-9766311-0-5

WINNER, 2005 LANGUM PRIZE
FOR HISTORICAL FICTION

PETER DONAHUE'S DEBUT NOVEL chronicles turn-of-the-century Seattle's explosive transformation from frontier outpost to major metropolis. Maddie Ingram, owner of Madison House, and her quirky and endearing boarders find their lives inextricably linked when the city decides to re-grade Denny Hill and the fate of Madison House hangs in the balance. Clyde Hunssler, Maddie's albino handyman and furtive love interest; James Colter, a muckraking black journalist who owns and publishes the Seattle *Sentry* newspaper; and Chiridah Simpson, an aspiring stage actress forced into prostitution and morphine addiction while working in the city's corrupt vaudeville theater, all call Madison House home. Had E.L. Doctorow and Charles Dickens met on the streets of Seattle, they couldn't have created a better book.

PETER DONAHUE SEEMS TO HAVE A MAP OF OLD SEATTLE in his head. No novel extant is nearly as thorough in its presentation of the early city, and all future attempts in its historical vein will be made in light of this book.

> **DAVID GUTERSON**
> Author of *Snow Falling on Cedars*
> and Our Lady of the Forest

MADISON HOUSE TREATS READERS to a boarding house full of fascinating and lovable characters as they create their own identities and contribute to early 20th century life in Seattle. Every page reflects Peter Donahue's meticulous and imaginative recreation of a lively and engaging moment in American history. I loved reading this novel and sharing in the pleasures and labors of the diverse and authentic inhabitants of a remarkable city.

> **SENA JETER NASLUND**
> Author of *Four Spirits* and *Ahab's Wife*

So Late, So Soon

D'Arcy Fallon

Memoir
224 pages
$15.95
ISBN 0-9716915-3-3

THIS MEMOIR OFFERS AN IRREVERENT, fly-on-the-wall view
of the Lighthouse Ranch, the Christian commune D'Arcy Fallon
called home for three years in the mid-1970s. At eighteen years old,
when life's questions overwhelmed her and reconciling her
family past with her future seemed impossible, she accidentally
came upon the Ranch during a hitchhike gone awry. Perched
on a windswept bluff in Loleta, a dozen miles from anywhere in
Northern California, this community of lost and found twenty-
somethings lured her in with promises of abounding love, spiritual
serenity, and a hardy, pioneer existence. What she didn't count
on was the fog.

I FOUND FALLON'S STORY FASCINATING, as will anyone who has ever
wondered about the role women play in fundamental religious sects. What would
draw an otherwise independent woman to a life of menial labor and subservi-
ence? Fallon's answer is this story, both an inside look at 70s commune life and
a funny, irreverent, poignant coming of age.

JUDY BLUNT
Author of *Breaking Clean*

PART ADVENTURE STORY, part cautionary tale, *So Late, So Soon* explores the
boundaries between selflessness and having no sense of self; between need-
ing and wanting; between the sacred and the profane. Sometimes heartbreaking,
often hilarious, Fallon's account of her young life in a California Christian commune engagingly illustrates the complexities of desire and the deeply-rooted
longing we all feel to be taken in, accepted, and loved. Shame, lust, compassion, and enlightenment—all find their place in Fallon's honest retelling of her
quest for community.

KIM BARNES
Author of *Finding Caruso*

Dastgah: Diary of a Headtrip

Mark Mordue

Memoir
316 pages
$15.95
ISBN 0-9716915-6-8

AUSTRALIAN JOURNALIST MARK MORDUE invites you on a journey that ranges from a Rolling Stones concert in Istanbul to talking with mullahs and junkies in Tehran, from a cricket match in Calcutta to an S&M bar in New York, and to many points in between, exploring countries most Americans never see as well as issues of world citizenship in the 21st century. Written in the tradition of literary journalism, *Dastgah* will take you to all kinds of places, across the world ... and inside yourself.

I JUST TOOK A TRIP AROUND THE WORLD in one go, first zigzagging my way through this incredible book, and finally, almost feverishly, making sure I hadn't missed out on a chapter along the way. I'm not sure what I'd call it now: A road movie of the mind, a diary, a love story, a new version of the subterranean homesick and wanderlust blues – anyway, it's a great ride. Paul Bowles and Kerouac are in the back, and Mark Mordue has taken over the wheel of that pickup truck from Bruce Chatwin, who's dozing in the passenger seat.

WIM WENDERS
Director of *Paris, Texas*; *Wings of Desire*;
and *The Buena Vista Social Club*

WIDE-AWAKE AND SENSUOUSLY LYRICAL, Mark Mordue's *Dastgah* gets in behind the shell of the familiar, reminding us that the world is vast and strange and that everything is—in case we've forgotten—happening for the first time.

SVEN BIRKERTS
Editor of *AGNI* and
author of *My Sky Blue Trades: Growing Up
Counter in a Contrary Time*

AN EXTRAORDINARY AND DAZZLING VOYAGE across continents and into the mind. Mordue's book is almost impossible to summarize — reportage, reflection and poetry are all conjured onto the page as he grapples with the state of the world and his place in it.

GILES MILTON
Author of *Nathaniel's Nutmeg: Or, the True
and Incredible Adventures of the Spice
Trader Who Changed the Course of History*

The Cantor's Daughter   Scott Nadelson

Fiction
280 pages
$15.95
ISBN 0-9766311-2-1

IN HIS FOLLOW-UP to the award-winning *Saving Stanley: The Brickman Stories,* Nadelson captures Jewish New Jersey suburbanites in moments of crucial transition, when they have the opportunity to connect with those closest to them or forever miss their chance for true intimacy. In "The Headhunter," two men develop an unlikely friendship when recruiter Len Siegel places Howard Rifkin in his ideal job. Len and Howard buy houses on the same street, but after twenty years their friendship comes to an abrupt and surprising end. In the title story, Noa Nechemia and her father have immigrated from Israel to Chatwin, New Jersey, following the death of her mother. In one moment of insight following a disastrous prom night, Noa discovers her ability to transcend grief and determine the direction of her own life. And in "Half a Day in Halifax" two people meet on a cruise ship where their shared lack of enthusiasm for their trip sparks the possibility of romance. Nadelson's stories are sympathetic, heart-breaking, and funny as they investigate the characters' fragile emotional bonds and the fears that often cause them to falter or fail.

THESE STORIES ARE RICH, involving, and multi-layered. They draw you in gradually, so that you become immersed in these characters and their lives almost without realizing it. An enticing collection.

DIANA ABU-JABER
Author of *The Language of Baklava* & *Crescent*

NADELSON, A TIRELESS INVESTIGATOR of the missed opportunity, works in clear prose that possesses a tremolo just below the surface. His narratives about contemporary American Jews are absorbing and satisfying, laying bare all manner of human imperfections and sweet, sad compensatory behaviors.

STACEY LEVINE
Author of *My Horse and Other Stories* and *Dra—*

Saving Stanley: The Brickman Stories

Scott Nadelson

Fiction

220 pages

$15.95

ISBN 0-9716915-2-5

WINNER, 2004 OREGON BOOK AWARD
WINNER, 2005 GCLA NEW WRITER'S AWARD

SCOTT NADELSON'S INTERRELATED STORIES are graceful, vivid narratives that bring into sudden focus the spirit and the stubborn resilience of the Brickmans, a Jewish family of four living in suburban New Jersey. The central character, Daniel Brickman, forges obstinately through his own plots and desires as he strug-gles to balance his sense of identity with his longing to gain acceptance from his family and peers. This fierce collection provides an unblinking examination of family life and the human instinct for attachment.

THESE EXTREMELY WELL-WRITTEN and elegantly wrought stories are rigorous, nuanced explorations of emotional and cultural limbo-states. *Saving Stanley* is a substantial, serious, and intelligent contribution to contemporary Jewish American writing. **DAVID SHIELDS**
Author of *Enough About You: Adventures in Autobiography* and *A Handbook for Drowning*

SCOTT NADELSON PLAYFULLY INTRODUCES US to a fascinating family of characters with sharp and entertaining psychological observations in grace-fully beautiful language, remini-scent of young Updike. I wish I could write such sentences. There is a lot of eros and humor here – a perfectly enjoyable book.
JOSIP NOVAKOVICH
Author of *April Fool's Day: A Novel*

THERE'S A CERTAIN THRILL in reading a young writer coming into his own. The nuances of style, the interplay of theme and narrative, the keen and sympathetic eye for character—all rendered new by a fresh voice and talent. Scott Nadelson's stories are bracing, lively, humorous, honest. A splendid debut.
EHUD HAVAZELET
Author of *Like Never Before* and *What Is It Then Between Us*

The Greening of Ben Brown

Michael Strelow

Fiction
272 pages
$15.95
ISBN 0-9716915-8-4

FINALIST, 2005 OREGON BOOK AWARD

MICHAEL STRELOW WEAVES THE STORY of a town and its mysteries in this debut novel. Ben Brown becomes a citizen of East Leven, Oregon, after he recovers from an electrocution that has not left him dead but has turned him green. He befriends 22 year-old Andrew James and together they unearth a chemical spill cover-up that forces the town to confront its demons and its citizens to choose sides. Strelow's lyrical prose and his talent for storytelling come together in this poetic and important first work that looks at how a town and the natural environment are inextricably linked. *The Greening of Ben Brown* will find itself in good company on the shelves between *Winesburg, Ohio* and *To Kill A Mockingbird*; readers of both will have a new story to cherish.

MICHAEL STRELOW HAS GIVEN northwest readers an amazing fable for our time and place featuring Ben Brown, a utility lineman who transforms into the Green Man following an industrial accident. Eco-Hero and prophet, the Green Man heads a cast of wonderful and zany characters who fixate over sundry items from filberts to hubcaps. A timely raid on a company producing heavy metals galvanizes Strelow's mythical East Leven as much as the Boston Tea Party rallied Boston. Fascinating, humorous and wise, *The Greening of Ben Brown* deserves its place on bookshelves along with other Northwest classics.

CRAIG LESLEY
Author of *Storm Riders*

STRELOW RESONATES as both poet and storyteller. In creating inhabitants of a town, its central figure and a strong sense of place, he lays on description lavishly, almost breathlessly ... The author lovingly invokes a particular brand of Pacific Northwest magic realism, a blend of fable, social realism, wry wisdom and irreverence that brings to mind Ken Kesey, Tom Robbins and the best elements of a low-key mystery.

HOLLY JOHNSON
The Oregonian

Soldiers in Hiding

Richard Wiley

Fiction
194 pages
$14.95
ISBN 0-9766311-3-X

WINNER, 1987 PEN/FAULKNER AWARD

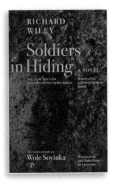

TEDDY MAKI WAS a Japanese-American jazz muscian from Los Angeles trapped in Tokyo with his band mate and friend, Jimmy Yakamoto, both of whom are drafted into the Japanese army after the bombing of Pearl Harbor. Thirty years later Maki is a big star on Japanese TV and wrestling with the guilt over Jimmy's death that he's been carrying since World War II.

This edition of *Soldiers in Hiding* includes both an introduction by Nobel Prize Winner Wole Soyinka, and a new preface from the author. *Commodore Perry's Minstrel Show*, the prequel to *Soldiers in Hiding*, is due out from the University of Texas 2007.

A rich and ingenious novel that succeeds brilliantly.
THE NEW YORK TIMES

Extraordinary... a feat of the imagination rendered with surprising skill... you'll remember this book for a long time.   **CHICAGO SUN TIMES**

Intelligent and interesting... daring and entirely convincing.
THE WASHINGTON POST

A mature novel... the spirit of Graham Greene is here.
KIRKUS REVIEWS

Wonderful... Original... Terrific... Haunting... Reading *Soldiers in Hiding* is like watching a man on a high wire.   **LOS ANGELES TIMES**

A work of exceptional power and imagination.
PUBLISHERS WEEKLY

Admirable, smooth, dispassionate... for an American to write from a Japanese standpoint, regardless of how long he has studied their culture, is an act of extreme literary bravery.   **CHRISTIAN SCIENCE MONITOR**

September II: West Coast Writers Approach Ground Zero

Edited by Jeff Meyers

Essays, Poetry, Fiction
266 pages
$16.95
ISBN 0-9716915-0-9

THE MYRIAD REPERCUSSIONS and varied and often contradictory responses to the acts of terrorism perpetrated on September 11, 2001 have inspired thirty-four West Coast writers to come together in their attempts to make meaning from chaos. By virtue of history and geography, the West Coast has developed a community different from that of the East, but ultimately shared experiences bridge the distinctions in provocative and heartening ways. Jeff Meyers anthologizes the voices of American writers as history unfolds and the country braces, mourns, and rebuilds.

Contributors include: Diana Abu-Jaber, T. C. Boyle, Michael Byers, Tom Clark, Joshua Clover, Peter Coyote, John Daniel, Harlan Ellison, Lawrence Ferlinghetti, Amy Gerstler, Lawrence Grobel, Ehud Havazelet, Ken Kesey, Maxine Hong Kingston, Stacey Levine, Tom Spanbauer, Primus St. John, Sallie Tisdale, Alice Walker, and many others.

Baudrillard and his ilk make one grateful for Harlan Ellison, the science-fiction novelist, who tells a story in *September 11: West Coast Writers Approach Ground Zero*.
THE NEW YORK TIMES

A remarkable anthology. **THE LOS ANGELES TIMES**

Physical distance doesn't mean emotional or intellectual remove: in Seattle poet Meyers's anthology of diverse voices, 34 writers from the left coast weigh in on September 11 in poems, meditations, personal essays and polemics. New and vociferous patriots beware: many of the contributors share criticism as strong as their grief. **PUBLISHERS WEEKLY**

[*September 11: West Coast Writers Approach Ground Zero*] deserves attention. This book has some highly thoughtful contributions that should be read with care on both coasts, and even in between.
THE SAN FRANCISCO CHRONICLE